HAUNTING ADELINE

H.D. CARLTON

Haunting Adeline Copyright © 2021 by H. D. Carlton

Cover Designer: TRCDesigns By Cat

ISBN: 9781957635002

Second Edition: August 2021

To Amanda and May
Zade and I will forever be yours.

PLAYLIST

Hish- Evil

So Below- Sway

Boy Epic- Dirty Mind

Croosh- Lost

Vi- Victim

The Weeknd- Pretty

The Weeknd- Loft Music

Something Better- The Broken View

Play with Fire- Sam Tinnesz (feat. Yacht Money)

IMPORTANT NOTE

This book ends on a cliffhanger. The contents are very dark with triggering situations, such as non/dub con between the main characters, graphic violence, human trafficking, child slave trade, stalking, child trafficking, child sacrifice, mentions of child death, kidnapping, near-death situations, and explicit sexual situations. There are also particular kinks such as gun play, somnophilia, bondage, breath play, and degradation.

This book was previously taken down due to the warning, but you can also find them in reviews, on my website, or feel free to message me directly.
Your mental health matters.

Cat got your tongue, little mouse?

Prologue

The windows of my house tremble from the power of thunder rolling across the skies. Lightning strikes in the distance, illuminating the night. In that small moment, the few seconds of blinding light showcases the man standing outside my window. Watching me. Always watching me.

I go through the motions, just like I always do. My heart skips a beat and then palpitates, my breathing turns shallow, and my hands grow clammy. It doesn't matter how many times I see him, he always pulls the same reaction out of me.

Fear.

And excitement.

I don't know why it excites me. Something must be wrong with me. It's not normal for liquid heat to course through my veins, leaving tingles burning in its wake. It's not common for my mind to start wondering about things I shouldn't.

Can he see me now? Wearing nothing but a thin tank top, my nipples poking through the material? Or the shorts I'm wearing that barely cover my ass? Does he like the view?

Of course he does.

That's why he watches me, isn't it? That's why he comes back every night, growing bolder with his leering while I silently challenge him. Hoping he'll come closer, so I have a reason to put a knife to his throat.

The truth is, I'm scared of him. Terrified, actually.

But the man standing outside my window makes me feel like I'm sitting in a dark room, a single light shining from the television where a horror flick plays on the screen. It's petrifying, and all I want to do is hide, but there's a distinct part of me that keeps me still, baring myself to the horror. That finds a small thrill out of it.

It's dark again, and the lightning strikes in areas further away.

My breathing continues to escalate. I can't see him, but he can see me.

Ripping my eyes away from the window, I turn to look behind me in the darkened house, paranoid that he's somehow found a way inside. No matter how deep the shadows go in Parsons Manor, the black and white checkered floor always seems visible.

I inherited this house from my grandparents. My great-grandparents had built the three-story Victorian home back in the early 1940s through blood, sweat, tears, and the lives of five construction workers.

Legend says—or rather Nana says—that the house caught fire and killed the construction workers during the building structure phase. I haven't been able to find any news articles on the unfortunate event, but the souls that haunt the Manor reek of despair.

Nana always told grandiose stories that wrung eye rolls from my parents. Mom never believed anything Nana said, but I think she just didn't *want* to.

Sometimes I hear footsteps at night. They could be from the ghosts of the workers who died in the tragic fire eighty years ago, or they could be from the shadow that stands outside my house.

Watching me.

Always watching me.

Chapter One
The Manipulator

Sometimes I have very dark thoughts about my mother—thoughts no sane daughter should ever have.

Sometimes, I'm not always sane.

"Addie, you're being ridiculous," Mom says through the speaker on my phone. I glare at it in response, refusing to argue with her. When I have nothing to say, she sighs loudly. I wrinkle my nose. It blows my mind that this woman always called Nana dramatic yet can't see her own flair for the dramatics.

"Just because your grandparents gave you the house doesn't mean you have to actually *live in it*. It's old and would be doing everyone in that city a favor if it were torn down."

I thump my head against the headrest, rolling my eyes upward and trying to find patience weaved into the stained roof of my car.

How did I manage to get ketchup up there?

"And just because *you* don't like it, doesn't mean I can't live in it," I retort dryly.

My mother is a bitch. Plain and simple. She's always had a chip on her shoulder, and for the life of me, I can't figure out why.

"You'll be living an hour from us! That will be incredibly inconvenient for you to come visit us, won't it?"

Oh, how will I ever survive?

Pretty sure my gynecologist is an hour away, too, but I still make an effort to see her once a year. And those visits are far more painful.

"Nope," I reply, popping the P. I'm over this conversation. My patience only lasts an entire sixty seconds talking to my mother. After that, I'm running on fumes and have no desire to put in any more effort to keep the conversation moving along.

If it's not one thing, it's the other. She always manages to find something to complain about. This time, it's my choice to live in the house my grandparents gave to me. I grew up in Parsons Manor, running alongside the ghosts in the halls and baking cookies with Nana. I have fond memories here—memories I refuse to let go of just because Mom didn't get along with Nana.

I never understood the tension between them, but as I got older and started to comprehend Mom's snarkiness and underhanded insults for what they were, it made sense.

Nana always had a positive, sunny outlook on life, viewing the world through rose-colored glasses. She was always smiling and humming, while Mom is cursed with a perpetual scowl on her face and looking at life like her glasses got smashed when she was plunged out of Nana's vagina. I don't know why her personality never developed past that of a porcupine—she was never raised to be a prickly bitch.

Growing up, my mom and dad had a house only a mile away from Parsons Manor. She could barely tolerate me, so I spent most of my childhood in this house. It wasn't until I left for college that Mom moved out of town an hour away. When I quit college, I moved in with her until I got back on my feet and my writing career took off.

And when it did, I decided to travel around the country, never really settling in one place.

Nana died about a year ago, gifting me the house in her will, but my grief hindered me from moving into Parsons Manor. Until now.

Mom sighs again through the phone. "I just wish you had more ambition in life, instead of staying in the town you grew up in, sweetie. Do something more with your life than waste away in that house like your grandmother did. I don't want you to become worthless like her."

A snarl overtakes my face, fury tearing throughout my chest. "Hey, Mom?"

"Yes?"

"Fuck off."

I hang up the phone, angrily smashing my finger into the screen until I hear the telltale chime that the call has ended.

How dare she speak of her own mother that way when she was nothing but loved and cherished? Nana certainly didn't treat her the way she treats me, that's for damn sure.

I rip a page from Mom's book and let loose a melodramatic sigh, turning to look out my side window. Said house stands tall, the tip of the black roof spearing through the gloomy clouds and looming over the vastly wooded area as if to say *you shall fear me.* Peering over my shoulder, the dense thicket of trees are no more inviting—their shadows crawling from the overgrowth with outstretched claws.

I shiver, delighting in the ominous feeling radiating from this small portion of the cliff. It looks exactly as it did from my childhood, and it gives me no less of a thrill to peer into the infinite blackness.

Parsons Manor is stationed on a cliffside overlooking the Bay with a mile long driveway stretching through a heavily wooded area. The congregation of trees separates this house from the rest of the world, making you feel like you're well and truly alone.

Sometimes, it feels like you're on an entirely different planet, ostracized from civilization. The whole area has a menacing, sorrowful aura.

And I fucking love it.

The house has begun to decay, but it can be fixed up to look like new again with a bit of TLC. Hundreds of vines crawl up all sides of the structure, climbing towards the gargoyles stationed on the roof on either side of the manor. The black siding is fading to a gray and starting to peel away, and the black paint around the windows is chipping like cheap nail polish. I'll have to hire someone to give the large front porch a facelift since it's starting to sag on one side.

The lawn is long overdue for a haircut, the blades of grass nearly as tall as me, and the three acres of clearing bursting with weeds. I bet plenty of snakes have settled in nicely since it's last been mowed.

Nana used to offset the manor's dark shade with blooms of colorful flowers during the spring season. Hyacinths, primroses, violas, and rhododendron.

And in autumn, sunflowers would be crawling up the sides of the house, the bright yellows and oranges in the petals a beautiful contrast against the black siding.

I can plant a garden around the front of the house again when the season calls for it. This time, I'll plant strawberries, lettuce, and herbs as well.

I'm deep in my musings when my eyes snag on movement from above. Curtains flutter in the lone window at the very top of the house.

The attic.

Last time I checked, there's no central air up there. Nothing should be able to move those curtains, but yet I don't doubt what I saw.

Coupled with the looming storm in the background, Parsons Manor looks like a scene out of a horror film. I suck my bottom lip between my teeth, unable to stop the smile from forming on my face.

I love that.

I can't explain why, but I do.

Fuck what my mother says. I'm living here. I'm a successful writer and have the freedom to live anywhere. So, what if I decide to live in a place that means a lot to me? That doesn't make me a lowlife for staying in my hometown. I travel enough with book tours and conferences; settling down in a house won't change that. I know what the fuck I want, and I don't give a shit what anyone else thinks about it.

Especially mommy dearest.

The clouds yawn, and rain spills from their mouths. I grab my purse and step out of my car, inhaling the scent of fresh rain. It turns from a light sprinkle to a torrential downpour in a matter of seconds. I bolt up the front porch steps, flinging drops of water off my arms and shaking my body out like a wet dog.

I love storms—I just don't like to be in them. I'd prefer to cuddle up under the blankets with a mug of tea and a book while listening to the rain fall.

I slide the key into the lock and turn it. But it's stuck, refusing to give me even a millimeter. I jimmy the key, wrestling with it until the mechanism finally turns and I'm able to unlock the door.

Guess I'm gonna have to fix that soon, too.

A chilling draft welcomes me as I open the door. I shiver from the mixture of freezing rain still wet on my skin and the cold, stale air. The interior of the house is cast in shadows. Dim light shines through the windows, gradually fading as the sun disappears behind gray storm clouds.

I feel as if I should start my story with "it was a dark stormy night..."

I look up and smile when I see the black ribbed ceiling, made up of hundreds of thin, long pieces of wood. A grand chandelier is hanging over my head, golden steel warped in an intricate design with crystals dangling from the tips. It's always been Nana's most prized possession.

The black and white checkered floors lead directly to the black grand staircase—large enough to fit a piano through sideways—and flow off into the living room. My boots squeak against the tiles as I venture further inside.

This floor is primarily an open concept, making it feel like the monstrosity of the home could swallow you whole.

The living area is to the left of the staircase. I purse my lips and look around, nostalgia hitting me straight in the gut. Dust coats every surface, and the smell of mothballs is overpowering, but it looks exactly how I last saw it, right before Nana died last year.

A large black stone fireplace is in the center of the living room on the far left wall, with red velvet couches squared around it. An ornate wooden coffee table sits in the middle, an empty vase atop the dark wood. Nana used to fill it with lilies, but now it only collects dust and bug carcasses.

The walls are covered in black paisley wallpaper, offset by heavy golden curtains.

One of my favorite parts is the large bay window at the front of the house, providing a beautiful view of the forest beyond Parsons Manor. Placed right in front of it is a red velvet rocking chair with a matching stool. Nana used to sit there and watch the rain, and she said her mother would always do the same.

The checkered tiling extends into the kitchen with beautiful black stained cabinets and marble countertops. A massive island sits in the middle with black barstools lining one side. Grandpa and I used to sit there and watch Nana cook, enjoying her humming to herself as she whipped up delicious meals.

Shaking away the memories, I rush over to a tall lamp by the rocking chair and flick on the light. I release a sigh of relief when a buttery soft glow emits from the bulb. A few days ago, I had called to get the utilities turned on in my name, but you can never be too sure when dealing with an old house.

Then I walk over to the thermostat, the number causing another shiver to wrack my body.

Sixty-two goddamn degrees.

I press my thumb into the up arrow and don't stop until the temperature is set to seventy-four. I don't mind cooler temperatures, but I'd prefer it if my nipples didn't cut through all of my clothing.

I turn back around and face a home that's both old and new—a home that's housed my heart since I could remember, even if my body left for a little while.

And then I smile, basking in the gothic glory of Parsons Manor. It's how my great-grandparents decorated the house, and the taste has passed down through the generations. Nana used to say that she liked it best when she was the brightest thing in the room. Despite that, she still had old people's taste.

I mean, really, why do those white throw pillows have a border of lace around them and a weird, embroidered bouquet of flowers in the middle? That's not cute. That's ugly.

I sigh.

"Well, Nana, I came back. Just like you wanted," I whisper to the dead air.

"Are you ready?" my personal assistant asks from beside me. I glance over at Marietta, noting how she's absently holding out the mic to me, her attention ensnared on the people still filtering into the small building. This local bookstore wasn't built for a large number of people, but somehow, they're making it work anyway.

Hordes of people are piling into the cramped space, converging in a uniform line, and waiting for the signing to start. My eyes rove over the crowd, silently counting in my head. I lose count after thirty.

"Yep," I say. I grab the mic, and after catching everyone's attention, the murmurs fade to silence. Dozens of eyeballs bore into me, creating a flush all the way to my cheeks. It makes my skin crawl, but I love my readers, so I power through it.

"Before we start, I just wanted to take a quick second to thank you all for coming. I appreciate each and every one of you, and I'm incredibly excited to meet you all. Everyone ready?!" I ask, forcing excitement into my tone.

It's not that I'm *not* excited, I just tend to get incredibly awkward during book signings. I'm not a natural when it comes to social interactions. I'm the type to stare dead into your face with a frozen smile after being asked a question while my brain processes the fact that I didn't even hear the question. It's usually because my heart is thumping too loud in my ears.

I settle down in my chair and ready my sharpie. Marietta runs off to handle other matters, shooting me a quick *good luck*. She's witnessed my mishaps with readers and has the tendency to get secondhand embarrassment with me. Guess it's one of the downfalls of representing a social pariah.

Come back, Marietta. It's so much more fun when I'm not the only one getting embarrassed.

The first reader approaches me, my book *The Wanderer*, in her hands with a beaming smile on her freckled face.

"Oh my god, it's so awesome to meet you!" she exclaims, nearly shoving the book in my face. Totally a *me* move.

I smile wide and gently take the book.

"It's awesome to meet you, too," I return. "And hey, Team Freckles," I tack on, waving my forefinger between her face and mine. She gives a bit of an awkward laugh, her fingers drifting over her cheeks. "What's your name?" I rush out, before we get stuck on a weird conversation about skin conditions.

Geez, Addie, what if she hates her freckles? Dumbass.

"Megan," she replies, and then spells the name out for me. My hand trembles as I carefully write out her name and a quick appreciation note. My signature is sloppy, but that pretty much represents the entirety of my existence.

I hand the book back and thank her with a genuine smile.

As the next reader approaches, pressure settles on my face. Someone is staring at me. But that's a fucking stupid thought because *everyone* is staring at me.

I try to ignore it, and give the next reader a big ass smile, but the feeling only intensifies until it feels like bees are buzzing beneath the surface of my skin while a torch is being held to my flesh. It's... it's unlike anything I've felt before. The hairs on the back of my neck rise, and I feel the apples of my cheeks heating to a bright red.

Half of my attention is on the book I'm signing and the gushing reader, while the other half is on the crowd. My eyes subtly sweep the expanse of the bookstore, attempting to scope out the source of my discomfort without making it obvious.

My gaze hooks on a lone person standing in the very back. A man. The crowd shrouds the majority of his body, only bits of his face peeking through the gaps between people's heads. But what I do see has my hand stilling, mid-write.

His eyes. One so dark and bottomless, it feels like staring into a well. And the other, an ice blue so light, it's nearly white, reminding me of a husky's eyes. A scar slashes straight down through the discolored eye, as if it didn't already demand attention.

When a throat clears, I jump, snatching my eyes away and looking back to the book. My sharpie has been resting in the same spot, creating a big black ink dot.

"Sorry," I mutter, finishing off my signature. I reach over and snag a bookmark, sign that too, and tuck it in the book as an apology.

The reader beams at me, mistake already forgotten, and scurries off with her book. When I look back to find the man, he's gone.

"Addie, you need to get laid."

In response, I wrap my lips around my straw and slurp my blueberry martini as deeply as my mouth will allow. Daya, my best friend, eyes me, entirely unimpressed and impatient based on the quirk of her brow.

I think I need a bigger mouth. More alcohol would fit in it.

I don't say this out loud because I can bet my left ass cheek that her follow-up response would be to use it for a bigger dick instead.

When I continue sucking on the straw, she reaches over and rips the plastic from my lips. I've reached the bottom of the glass a solid fifteen seconds ago and have just been sucking air through the straw. It's the most action my mouth has gotten in a year now.

"Whoa, personal space," I mumble, setting the glass down. I avoid Daya's eyes, searching the restaurant for the waitress so I can order another martini. The faster I have the straw in my mouth again, the sooner I can avoid this conversation some more.

"Don't deflect, bitch. You suck at it."

Our eyes meet, a beat passes, and we both burst into laughter.

"I suck at getting laid, too, apparently," I say after our laughing calms.

Daya gives me a droll look. "You've had plenty of opportunities. You just don't take them. You're a hot twenty-six-year-old woman with freckles, a great pair of tits, and an ass to die for. The men are out here waiting."

I shrug, deflecting again. Daya isn't exactly wrong—at least about having options. I'm just not interested in any of them. They all bore me. All I get is *what are you wearing* and *wanna come over, winky face* at one o'clock in the morning. I'm wearing the same sweatpants I've been wearing the past week, there's a mysterious stain on my crotch, and no, I don't want to fucking come over.

She flips out an expectant hand. "Give me your phone."

My eyes widen. "Fuck, no."

"Adeline Reilly. Give me. Your. Fucking. Phone."

"Or what?" I taunt.

14

"Or I will throw myself across the table, embarrass the absolute shit out of you, and get my way anyways."

My eyes finally catch on our waitress and I flag her down. Desperately. She rushes over, probably thinking I found a hair in my food, when really my best friend just has one up her ass right now.

I procrastinate a little bit longer, asking the waitress what drink she prefers. I'd look through the drink menu a second time if it weren't rude to keep her waiting when she has other tables. So alas, I pick a strawberry martini in favor of the green apple, and the waitress rushes off again.

Sigh.

I hand the phone over, slapping it in Daya's *still* outstretched hand extra firm because I hate her. She smiles triumphantly and starts typing away, the mischievous glimmer in her eye growing brighter. Her thumbs go into turbo speed, causing the golden rings wrapped around them to nearly blur.

Her sage green eyes are illuminated with a type of evilness you would only find in Satan's Bible. If I did a little digging, I'm sure I'd find her picture somewhere in there, too. A bombshell with dark brown skin, pin-straight black hair, and a gold hoop in her nose.

She's probably an evil succubus or something.

"Who are you texting?" I groan, nearly stomping my feet like a child. I refrain, but come close to allowing a little of my social anxiety to air out and do something crazy like throwing a temper tantrum in the middle of the restaurant. It probably doesn't help that I'm on my third martini and feeling a tad adventurous right about now.

She glances up, locks my phone, and hands it back a few seconds later. Immediately, I unlock it again and start searching through my messages. I groan aloud once more when I see she sexted Greyson. Not texted. *Sexted.*

"Come over tonight and lick my pussy. I've been craving your huge cock," I read aloud dryly. That's not even all of it. The rest goes into how horny I am and touch myself every night to the thought of him.

I growl and give her the filthiest look I can manage. My face would make a dumpster look like Mr. Clean's house.

"I wouldn't even say that!" I complain. "That doesn't even sound like me, you bitch."

Daya cackles, the teeny little gap between her front teeth on full display.

I really do hate her.

My phone pings. Daya is nearly bouncing in her seat while I'm contemplating googling *1000 Ways to Die*'s contact information so I can send them a new story.

"Read it," she demands, her grabby hands already reaching for my phone so she can see what he said. I jerk it out of her reach and pull up the message.

GREYSON: About time u came to your senses, baby. Be over at 8.

"I don't know if I've ever told you this, but I really fucking hate you," I grumble, giving her another scowl.

She smiles and slurps on her drink. "I love you too, baby girl."

"Fuck, Addie, I've missed you," Greyson breathes into my neck, humping me against the wall. My tailbone is going to be bruised in the morning. I roll my eyes when he slurps at my neck again, groaning when he rolls his dick into the apex of my thighs.

Deciding I needed to get over myself and blow off some steam, I didn't cancel on Greyson like I wanted to. Like I *want* to. I regret that decision.

Currently, he has me pinned against the wall in my creepy hallway. Old fashioned sconces line the blood red walls, with dozens of family pictures from generations in between. I feel like they're watching me, scorn and disappointment in their eyes as they witness their descendant about to get railed right in front of them.

Only a few of the lights work, and they just serve to illuminate the spiderwebs they're crawling with. The rest of the hallway is shadowed entirely, and I'm just waiting for the demon from The Grudge to come crawling out so I have an excuse to run.

I would definitely trip Greyson on the way out at this point, and not one inch of me is ashamed.

He murmurs some more dirty things into my ear while I inspect the sconce hanging above our heads. Greyson said in passing once that he's scared of spiders. I wonder if I can discreetly reach up, pluck a spider from its web, and put it down the back of Greyson's shirt.

That would light a fire under his ass to get out of here, *and* he'd probably be too embarrassed to talk to me again. Win, win.

Just when I actually go to do it, he rears back, panting from all the solo French kissing he's been doing with my throat. It's like he was waiting for my neck to lick him back or something.

His copper hair is mussed from my hands, and his pale skin is stained with a blush. The curse of being a redhead, I suppose.

Greyson has everything else going for him in the looks department. He's hot as sin, has a beautiful body and a killer smile. Too bad he can't fuck and is a complete and utter douchebag.

"Let's take this to the bedroom. I need to be inside of you now."

Internally, I cringe. Externally... I cringe. I try to play it off by jerking my shirt over my head. He has the attention span of a beagle. And just like I suspected, he's already forgotten about my little blunder and is staring intensely at my tits.

Daya was right about that, too. I *do* have great tits.

He reaches up to tear the bra from my body—I probably would've smacked him if he actually ripped it—but he freezes when loud banging interrupts us from the main floor.

The sound is so sudden, so violently loud that I gasp, my heart pounding in my chest. Our eyes meet in stunned silence. Someone is pounding on my front door, and they don't sound too nice.

"Are you expecting someone?" he asks, his hand dropping to his side, seemingly frustrated by the interruption.

"No," I breathe. I quickly tug my shirt back on—backwards—and rush down the creaky steps. Taking a moment to check outside the window next to the door, I see the front porch is vacant. My brow furrows. Letting the curtain fall, I stand in front of the door, the stillness of the night closing in on the manor.

Greyson walks up beside me and looks over at me with a confused expression.

"Uh, you gonna answer that?" he asks dumbly, pointing at the door as if I didn't know it was right in front of me. I almost thank him for the directions just to be an ass, but refrain. Something about that knock has my instincts blaring Code Red. The knock sounded aggressive. Angry. Like someone had pounded on the door with all their strength.

A real man would offer to open the door for me after hearing such a violent sound. Especially when we're surrounded by a mile of thick woods and a hundred-foot drop into the water.

But instead, Greyson stares at me expectantly. And a little like I'm stupid. Huffing, I unlock the door and whip it open.

Again, no one is there. I step out onto the porch, the rotting floorboards groaning beneath my weight. Cold wind stirs my cinnamon hair, the strands tickling my face and sending shivers racing across my skin. Goosebumps rise as I tuck my hair behind my ears and walk over to one end of the porch. Leaning over the rail, I look down the side of the house. No one.

No one on the other side of the house, either.

There could easily be someone watching me in the woods, but I have no way of knowing with it being so dark. Not unless I go out there and search myself.

And as much as I love horror films, I have no interest in starring in one.

Greyson joins me on the porch, his own eyes scanning the trees.

There's someone watching me. I can feel it. I'm as sure of it as I am about the existence of gravity.

Chills run down my spine, accompanied by a burst of adrenaline. It's the same feeling I get when I watch a scary movie. It begins with the beat of my heart, then a heavy weight settles deep in my stomach, eventually sinking to my core. I shift, not entirely comfortable with the feeling right now.

Huffing, I rush back into the house and up the steps. Greyson trails behind me. I don't notice he's in the middle of undressing as he walks down the hallway until he steps into my room after me. When I turn, he's stark naked.

"Seriously?" I bite out. What a fucking idiot. Someone just banged on my door like the wood personally put a splinter in their ass, and he's immediately ready to pick up where he left off. Slurping on my neck like one would slurp jello out of a container.

"What?" he asks incredulously, splaying his arms out to his sides.

"Did you not just hear what I heard? Someone was banging on my door, and it was kind of scary. I'm not in the mood to have sex right now."

What happened to chivalry? I would think a normal man would ask if I'm okay. Feel out how I'm feeling. Maybe try to make sure I'm nice and relaxed before sticking their dick inside me.

You know, read the fucking room.

"You serious?" he questions, anger sparking in his brown eyes. They're a shitty color, just like his shitty personality and even shittier stroke game. The dude gives fish a run for their money, the way he flops when he fucks. Might as well lay out naked in the fish market—he'd have a better chance of finding someone to take him home. That person is not going to be me.

"Yes, I'm serious," I say with exasperation.

"Goddammit, Addie," he snaps, angrily swiping up a sock and putting it on. He looks like an idiot—completely naked save for a single sock because the rest of his clothes are still thrown haphazardly in my hallway.

He storms out of my room, snatching up articles of clothing as he goes. When he gets about halfway down the long hallway, he stops and turns to me.

"You're such a bitch, Addie. All you do is give me blue balls and I'm sick of it. I'm done with you and this creepy fucking house," he seethes, pointing a finger at me.

"And you're an asshole. Get the fuck out of my house, Greyson." His eyes widen with shock first, and then narrow into thin slits, brimming with fury. He turns, cocks his arm back and sends his fist flying into the drywall.

A gasp is ripped from my throat when half of his arm disappears, my mouth parting in both shock and disbelief.

"Since I'm not getting yours, thought I'd create my own hole to get into tonight. Fix that, bitch," he spits. Still sporting only one sock and an arm full of clothes, he storms off.

"You dick!" I rage, stomping towards the large hole in my wall he just created.

The front door slams a minute later from below.

I hope the mysterious person is still out there. Let the asshole get murdered wearing a single sock.

April 4th, 1944

There's a strange man outside my window.

I don't know who he is or what he wants from me. But I think he knows me. He watches me through the windows when John's not home. He wears a top hat on his head, concealing his face from me. I've tried to approach him, but when I do, he runs away.

I haven't told John yet. I cannot fathom why, but something keeps me from opening my mouth and admitting that a man is watching me. John wouldn't handle it well. He'd go out with his shotgun and try to find him.

I must admit, I'm more afraid of what would happen to my visitor should my husband succeed.

I'm very afraid of this strange man.

But my God, am I also intrigued.

Chapter Two
The Shadow

The screams of pain bouncing around the cement walls are getting a tad annoying.

Sometimes it sucks being the hacker *and* the enforcer. I really fucking enjoy hurting people, but tonight, I have no goddamn patience for this whiny asshole.

And normally, I have the patience of a saint.

I know how to wait for what I want most. But when I'm trying to get some real answers and the dude's too busy shitting his pants and crying to give me a coherent response, I get a little testy.

"This knife is about to go halfway through your eyeball," I warn. "I'm not even going to show you any mercy and shove it all the way through to your brain."

"Fuck, man," he cries. "I told you that I just went to the warehouse a few times. I don't know anything about some fuckin' ritual."

"So, you're useless is what you're saying," I surmise, inching the blade towards his eye.

He squeezes them shut as if skin that's no thicker than a centimeter is going to prevent the knife from going through his eye.

Fucking laughable.

"No, no, no," he pleads. "I know someone there that might be able to give you more information."

Sweat drips down his nose, mixing with the blood on his face. His overgrown greasy blonde hair is matted to his forehead and the back of his neck. Guess it's not actually blonde anymore since most of it's painted red now.

I had already cut off one of his ears, along with ripping off ten of his fingernails, severed both Achilles heels, a couple of stab wounds in specific locations that won't allow the fucker to bleed out too quickly, and too many broken bones to count.

Dickhead won't be getting up and walking out of here, that's for damn sure.

"Less crying, more talking," I bark, scraping the tip of the knife against his still-closed eyelid.

He cringes away from the knife, tears bubbling out from beneath his lashes.

"H-his name is Fernando. He's one of the operation leaders in charge of sending out mules to help capture the girls. He-he's a big deal in the warehouse, b-basically runs the whole thing there."

"Fernando what?" I snap.

He sobs. "I don't know, man," he wails. "He just introduced himself as Fernando."

"Then what does he look like?" I grind out impatiently through gritted teeth.

He sniffles, snot leaking down his chapped lips.

"Mexican, bald, has a scar cutting across his hairline, and a beard. You can't miss the scar, it's pretty fucked looking."

I roll my neck, groaning as the muscles pop. It's been a long fucking day.

"Cool, thanks man," I say casually, as if I haven't been torturing him slowly for the past three hours.

His breathing calms, and he looks up at me through ugly brown eyes, hope radiating from them in spades.

I almost laugh.

"Y-you're letting me go?" he asks, staring up at me like a goddamn stray puppy dog.

"Sure," I chirp. "If you can get up and walk."

He looks down at his severed heels, knowing just as well as I do if he stands, his body will go pitching forward.

"Please, man," he blubbers. "Can you help me out here?"

I nod slowly. "Yeah. I think I can do that," I say, right before I swing my arm back and plunge the entirety of my knife through his pupil.

He dies instantly. Not even all the hope has vanished from his eyes yet. Or rather, his one eye.

"You're a child rapist," I say aloud, though he's no longer capable of hearing me. "Like I'd let you live," I finish on a laugh.

I slide my knife from the socket, the suction noise threatening to ruin any dinner plans I had in the next several hours. Which is annoying cause I'm hungry. While I do enjoy myself a good torture session, I'm definitely not a dickhead that gets off on the sounds that accompany it.

The gurgling, slurping, and other weird noises bodies make when enduring extreme pain and foreign objects being plunged into them is not a soundtrack I'd ever fall asleep to.

And now for the worst part—dismembering it into bits and pieces and disposing of them properly. I don't trust other people to do it for me, so I'm stuck with the tedious, messy job.

I sigh. What is that saying? If you want it done right, do it yourself?

Well, in this case—if you don't want to get caught and charged for murder, dispose of the body yourself.

It feels like ten o'clock at night, but it's only five P.M. As fucked as it is after dealing with human body parts, I'm in the mood for a mean ass burger.

My favorite burger joint is right off of 3rd Avenue, and not too far of a drive from my house. Parking is a bitch in Seattle, so I'm forced to park a few blocks away and walk there.

A storm is rolling in, and soon sheets of rain will be descending on our heads and shoulders like icepicks—typical Seattle weather.

I whistle an unnamed tune as I walk down the street, passing shops and an array of stores with people bustling in and out like a bunch of worker ants.

Ahead of me, there's a bookstore lit up, the warm glow shining onto the cold, wet pavement and inviting passersby into its warmth. As I near, I notice it's packed full of people.

I spare it a single glance before moving on. I don't care about fiction books—I only read the ones that are going to teach me something. Particularly about computer science and hacking.

By now, there's nothing those books can teach me anymore. I've mastered and then surpassed it.

As I'm turning my head to look at some other shit, my eyes get caught up on a board right outside the bookstore, a smiling face beaming back at me.

Without permission, my feet slow until they're glued to the cement sidewalk. Someone bumps into me from behind, their smaller stature barely knocking me forward, but it does manage to jolt me out of the weird trance I fell into anyway.

I turn to glare at the enraged guy behind me, their mouth opening and gearing up to cuss me out, yet the second he gets one look at my scarred face—he takes off into a half-walk, half-run. I'd laugh if I weren't so distracted.

Before me is a picture of an author that's hosting a book signing.

She's fucking incredible.

Long, wavy cinnamon hair brushed over dainty shoulders. Creamy, ivory skin with freckles dotting her nose and cheeks. Light and sporadic without overwhelming her innocent face.

Her eyes are what draw me in. Sultry, slanted eyes—the type that always look seductive without trying. They're nearly the same color as her hair. A brown so light, it's unusual. One look from this girl and any man would be on their knees.

Her lips are pouty and pink, stretched into a radiant smile with straight, white teeth.

I note the name below the picture.

Adeline Reilly.

A beautiful name fit for a goddess.

She doesn't have that plastic beauty you see lining the magazine rack. Though she could easily make it on one of those covers without photoshop and surgery, her features are natural.

I've seen a lot of beautiful women in my life. Fucked a lot, too.

But something about her captivates me. It feels like a hurricane is at my back, pushing me towards her and leaving no room for resistance. My feet are carrying me into the bookstore, my black boots soaking the welcome mat at the entrance.

The only lingering scent filling the air is one you attain from used books—though convoluted from the large group of people congesting the area. This small structure wasn't built to house more than the ten large bookshelves lining the left side of the room, the small checkout desk on the right side, and maybe thirty people. Now, there's a large table in the middle of the room where the author sits, and at least double the occupancy limit packed in the stuffy store.

It's too hot in here. Too crowded.

And one asshole beside me keeps picking his nose, his dirty hand touching all over the book he's holding. I glimpse *Reilly* on the cover.

Poor girl. Forced to sign a book that probably has boogers all over it.

I open my mouth, ready to tell the fucker to stop looking for treasure in his nostrils when it feels like heaven's gates open up.

In that second, the people in front of us seem to part at the perfect angle, providing me with a clear view. I only see her from the corner of my eye at first, but the small glimpse is enough to send my heart into a tailspin.

My head turns like one of those creepy bitches in an exorcist movie—slow, but instead of an evil smile, I'm sure I look like I just found out that there's evidence the earth is actually flat or some shit.

Because that's also fucking laughable.

Oxygen, words, coherent thoughts—all that shit escapes me when I get my first look at Adeline Reilly in the flesh.

Shit.

She's even more exquisite in person. The sight of her has my knees weakening and my pulse racing.

I don't know if God really exists. I don't know if mankind has ever walked on the moon. Nor do I know if parallel universes exist. But what I *do* know is that I just found the meaning of life sitting behind a table with an awkward smile on her face.

Taking a deep breath, I find a spot against the wall in the back. I don't want to get too close yet.

No.

I want to watch her for a while.

So I stay in the back, peeking through dozens of heads to get a good look at her. Thank god for my height because I'd probably barrel through everybody if I were short.

A tall, willowy woman hands my new obsession a microphone, and for a brief moment, the latter looks like she's ready to bolt. She stares at the mic as if the woman is handing over a severed head.

But the look is gone in seconds, barely there before she slides her mask in place. And then she snatches the microphone and brings it to her wobbly lips.

"Before we start…"

Fuck, her voice is pure smoke. The kind you really only hear in porn videos. I suck in my bottom lip, biting back a groan.

I lean against the wall and watch her, absolutely enthralled with the little creature before me.

Something inexplicably dark arises in my chest. It's black and evil and cruel. Dangerous, even.

All I want to do is break her. Shatter her into pieces. And then arrange those pieces to fit against my own. I don't care if they don't fit—I'll fucking *make* them.

And I know I'm about to do something bad. I know that I'm going to cross lines that I will never be able to come back from, but there's not an ounce of me that gives a fuck.

Because I'm obsessed.

I'm addicted.

And I will gladly cross every single line if it means making this girl mine. If it means *forcing* her to be mine.

My mind has already been made up, the decision fortifying like granite in my brain. At that moment, her wandering eyes slide right onto mine, clashing with a force that nearly sends my knees to the ground. Her eyes round in the corners ever-so-slightly, as if she's just as enraptured by me as I am by her.

And then the reader before her is pulling her attention away, and I know I need to leave now before I do something stupid like kidnap her in front of at least fifty witnesses.

No matter. She won't be able to escape me now.

I've just found myself a little mouse, and I won't stop until I've trapped her.

April 10th, 1944

My visitor is here, outside my window, watching me while I write. My hand is trembling, and I cannot tell if it's from fear or not. I couldn't explain this feeling if I tried. I've attempted to write down these feelings. Explain them. But no words seem to suffice.

I suppose the best way to describe it is thrilling.

I don't know what is wrong with me. But something is very wrong, needless to say.

When our eyes connect, my breath shortens. My blood catches fire. It feels as if an exposed wire is resting on my flesh.

It's a visceral reaction, and I fear I'm becoming addicted to it.

He's coming closer now. I keep meeting his eyes, getting distracted from my writing.

It's becoming common now. My distractions. John has begun to notice. He peppers me with questions, asking what's on my mind.

How do I tell the man I love that I'm thinking of another? How do I tell him I've begun to picture another when my husband kisses me? When he touches me?

My visitor is retreating, slipping off into the darkness.

I fear this man.

But yet, I am still far too intrigued.

Chapter Three
The Manipulator

This isn't how I imagined I'd spend my Friday night. Digging around in the walls of an old-ass house with god knows what kind of creatures trapped inside.

I'm just waiting for a rabid squirrel to jump up and latch onto my outstretched arm, driven mad with hunger and willing to eat anything due to so many years being trapped in the walls, nothing but bugs to keep it fed.

My arm is shoulder-deep in the goddamn hole Greyson created, a flashlight held tightly in my grip. There is just enough space to fit my arm and part of my head in at an odd angle to look around.

This is stupid. *I'm* stupid.

The second I heard the door hit Greyson's ass on the way out, I inspected the damage. It's not a massive hole, but what gave me pause was the rather large gap between the two walls. At least three or four feet of space. And why else would it be built this way if there wasn't a reason?

It feels like a magnet is pulling me towards it. And every time I try to pull away, a deep vibration travels through my bones. The tips of my fingers buzz with the need to reach out. To just look inside the fathomless void and find what is calling my name.

Now here I am, bent over and stuffing myself in a hole. Suppose if I couldn't get mine stuffed tonight, I might as well get my action this way.

The flashlight on my phone reveals wooden beams, thick cobwebs, dust, and bug carcasses on the inside of the wall. I turn the other direction and point the light down the other side. Nothing. The webs are too thick to see much, so I use my phone like a baton and start tearing down some of them.

I swear if I drop it, I'll be *pissed*. There will be no getting it back and I'll have to get a new one.

I wince from the feel of the hair-like webs brushing across my skin, imitating the sensation of bugs crawling on me. I turn back towards the left and shine the light one more time.

I bat down a couple more cobwebs, ready to just give up and ignore the siren call that got me into this dumbass situation in the first place.

There.

A little way down the hall is something glinting off the light. Just the barest hint, but it's enough for me to jump in excitement, knocking my head off the thick drywall and sending flakes tumbling down in my hair.

Ow.

Ignoring the dull throbbing in the back of my head, I rip my arm out and rush down the hallway, guesstimating the distance on where I saw the mysterious object.

Grabbing a picture frame, I unhook it from its nail and gently set it down. I do this several more times until I come across a picture of my great-grandmother sitting on a retro bike, a bundle of sunflowers sitting in the basket. She smiles wide, and even though the picture is black and white, I know she's wearing red lipstick. Nana said she'd put on her red lipstick before she'd put on the coffee.

I pull the picture from the wall and stifle a gasp when I see an army green safe in front of me. It's old, with a mere dial for the lock. Excitement burns in my lungs as my fingers drift over the dial.

I've discovered a treasure. And I suppose I have Greyson to thank for that. Though I'd like to think I would've taken these pictures down eventually for the sake of no longer having my ancestors look down on my extremely questionable decisions.

I'm staring at the safe as a cold breeze washes across my body, turning my blood into ice. The sudden freezing temperature has me turning around, my eyes sweeping the empty hallway.

My teeth chatter, and I think I even see my breath puff out of my mouth. And just as quickly as it came, it dissipates. Slowly, my body warms up to a normal temperature, but the chill down my spine lingers.

I'm unable to tear my eyes away from the empty space, waiting for something to happen but as the minutes tick by, I end up just standing there.

Focus, Addie.

Gently setting the picture down, I decide to brush off the weird chill and google how to break open a safe. After finding several forums that list a step-by-step process, I run off towards my grandfather's toolbox collecting dust in the garage.

The space was never used for cars, even when Nana owned the house. Instead, generations of junk collected here, consisting mainly of my grandfather's tools and some odds and ends from the house. I grab the tools I need, run back up the stairs, and proceed to force my way into the safe. The old thing is pretty shitty in terms of protection, but I suppose whoever hid this box here didn't actually expect anyone to find it. At least not in their lifetime.

Several failed attempts, bouts of frustrated groaning, and a smashed finger later, I finally crack the sucker open. Using my flashlight again, I find three brown leather-bound books inside. No money. No jewels. Nothing of value really—at least not monetary value.

I hadn't been hoping for those things honestly, but I'm still surprised to find none, considering that's what most people use safes for.

I reach in and grab the journals, reveling in the feel of the buttery soft leather under my fingertips. A smile breaks across my face as I trail my fingers over the inscription on the first book.

Genevieve Matilda Parsons.

My great-grandmother—Nana's mother. The very woman in the picture concealing the safe, notorious for her red lipstick and bright smile. Nana always said she went by the name Gigi.

A quick look at the other two books reveals the same name. Her diaries? They have to be.

Dazed, I walk to my bedroom, close the door behind me and settle down on my bed, legs crossed. A leather cord is wrapped around each book, holding them closed. The outside world fades as I grab the first journal, carefully unwrap the cord, and open the book.

It *is* a diary. Every page has an entry written in a feminine script. And at the bottom of each page is my great-grandmother's trademark lipstick kiss.

She died before I was born, but I grew up hearing countless stories about her. Nana said she inherited her wild personality and sharp tongue from her mother. I wonder if Nana ever knew about the diaries. If she's ever read them.

If Genevieve Parsons is as wild as Nana said she was, then I imagine these diaries have all sorts of stories to show me. Smiling, I open the other two books and confirm the date on the first page of each book to ensure I'm starting from the beginning.

And then I stay up all night reading, growing more disturbed by each entry.

A thump from below wakes me out of a restless sleep. It feels like being ripped from a deep, persistent fog that lingers in the recess of my brain.

Blinking my eyes open, I stare at my closed door, focusing on the faint outline until my brain catches up with what I heard. My heart is well ahead of me, the muscle beating inside my chest rapidly while the hairs on the back of my neck rise.

A cloud of unease rolls in the pit of my stomach, and it's not until several seconds later that I realize the sound I heard was the shutting of my front door.

Slowly, I sit up and slide out from under the covers. Adrenaline is coursing through my system now, and I'm wide awake.

Someone was just inside my house.

The sound could have been anything. It could have been the foundation settling. Or shit, even a couple of ghosts roughhousing. But just like when your gut is telling you something bad is going to happen—mine is telling me that someone was just in my fucking house.

Was it the person that pounded on my door? It has to be, right? It's too much of a coincidence to have a stranger deliberately trek over a mile to the manor just to bang on the door and leave. And now they're back.

If they ever left at all.

Shakily, I get up from my bed, a cold chill washing over me and puckering my skin into goosebumps. I shiver, nabbing my phone from the nightstand and pad lightly over to the door. Slowly, I open it, cringing at the loud creak that rings out.

I need the Tin Man to oil the hinges on my door just as much as I need the Lion's bravery. I'm shaking like a leaf, but I refuse to cower and let someone walk around my house freely.

Flipping the switch on, the few working lights flicker, illuminating the hallway just enough for my mind to play tricks on me and conjure shadow people residing just beyond the light. And as I slowly make my way towards the staircase, I feel eyes from the pictures lining the walls watching me as I pass by.

Watching me make yet another stupid mistake. As if they're saying *stupid girl, you're about to get murdered.*

Watch your back.

They're right behind you.

The last thought has me gasping and turning around, though I know no one is actually behind me. My stupid fucking brain is a little bit too imaginative.

A trait that works wonders for my career, but I don't fucking appreciate it in this very moment.

Forging on at a quicker pace, I make my way down the stairs. Immediately, I turn on the lights, wincing from the brightness that burns my retinas.

Better than the alternative.

I would die on the spot if I was searching around with a single beam of light and found someone lurking in my house that way. One second no one is there, and the next second *hello*, there's my murderer. No fucking thank you.

When I don't find anyone in the living room or kitchen, I whip around and turn the knob on my front door. It's still locked, which means that whoever left somehow managed to relock the door.

Or they never actually left.

Sucking in a sharp breath, I storm through the living room and into the kitchen, gunning straight for the knives.

But I catch a glimpse of something resting on the island out of my peripheral, freezing me in place. My eyes jump to the item, and a curse escapes my lips when I see a single red rose resting on the countertop.

I stare at the flower like it's a live tarantula, staring straight back at me and daring me to come closer. If I do, it'll surely eat me alive.

Letting out a shaky breath, I pluck the flower from the countertop and roll it in my fingers. The thorns have been severed from the stem, and I get the strange inclination that it was done purposely to save my fingers from being pricked.

But that notion is crazy. If someone is sneaking into my house at night and leaving me flowers, their intentions are the exact opposite of virtuous. They're trying to scare me.

Curling my fist, I crush the flower in the palm of my hand and throw it in the trash, and then I resume my original mission. I rip open the drawer, the silverware clanking loudly in the silence, and then slam it shut after selecting the largest knife. I'm too pissed to be quiet and sneaky.

Whoever is hiding in here will hear me coming from a mile away, but I don't care. I have no desire to hide.

I'm seething now.

I don't like someone thinking they can just break into my home while I'm sleeping upstairs. And I especially don't like someone making me feel vulnerable in my own house.

And then to have the audacity to leave me a flower like a fucking weirdo? They may have made that rose powerless by clipping its thorns, but I will gladly show them a rose is still fucking deadly when it's shoved down their throat.

I thoroughly check the main and second floor, but don't find anyone waiting for me. It isn't until I'm at the end of the hallway on the second floor, staring at the door that leads to the attic, that my search comes to a screeching halt.

I'm frozen to the spot. Every time I try to force my feet forward, berating myself for not searching every single room in the manor, I can't bring myself to move. Every single one of my instincts is screaming at me to not go near that door.

That I will find something terrifying if I do.

The attic was where Nana would often retreat, spending her days up there knitting while humming a tune, several fans blowing at her from every direction during the summertime. I swear I hear those tunes coming from the attic some days, but I can't ever bring myself to go up there and look.

A feat that I apparently won't overcome tonight, either. I don't have the courage to go up there. The adrenaline fumes are running out, and exhaustion is weighing heavily on my bones.

Sighing, I drag my feet back down to the kitchen to grab a glass of water. I chug it in three swallows before refilling and emptying it again.

I slump down on the barstool in front of the island, finally setting the knife down. A thin layer of sweat dampens my forehead, and when I lean over and rest it against the cold marble countertop, it sends chills throughout my body.

The person is gone, but my house isn't the only thing they intruded on tonight. They're in my head now—just like they fucking wanted.

"Someone broke into my house last night," I confess, my phone trapped between my ear and shoulder. The spoon clinks in the ceramic mug as I stir my coffee. I'm on my second cup, and it still feels like I have dumbbells for eyes, and my lids are in a losing weightlifting battle.

After the creep left last night, I couldn't fall back asleep, so I went through the entire house, confirming all the windows were locked.

Finding that they were unsettled me more. Every single door and window had been locked before and after they left. So how the fuck did they get in and out?

"Hold on, you said what? Someone *broke* into your *house?*" Daya shrieks.

"Yep," I say. "They left a red rose on my countertop."

Silence. Never thought I'd see the day Daya Pierson is speechless.

"That's not all that happened, though. Just the worst of it in the grand scheme of last night's fuckery, I suppose."

"What else happened?" she asks sharply.

"Well, Greyson is an asshole. He was in the middle of trying to locate a mysterious hole in my neck with his tongue when someone pounded on my front door. And I mean, like *hard*. We went and looked, and no one was there. I'm assuming it was my new friend that did it."

"Are you fucking serious?"

I go on to explain the rest. Greyson's douchery—I got hung up on complaining about that just a bit. Then his fist going into my wall and his dramatic exit. I don't mention the safe and the diaries I found, or what I read in them. I haven't processed it yet, or the irony in reading her sordid love story and then someone breaking into my house the same night.

"I'm coming over today," Daya declares when I finish.

"I have to clean out the house today to prepare for renovations," I counter, already exhausted from the thought of it.

"I'll help then. We'll day drink to keep it interesting."

A small smile forms on my face. Daya has always been a great friend to me.

She's been my best friend since middle school. We kept in contact after graduation, even after we both moved away to different colleges. Our lives only allowed us to see each other for holidays and an annual haunted fair the past several years.

I dropped out of college after a year and pursued my writing career, while Daya got a degree in Computer Science. Somehow, she wormed her way into some hacker group and is pretty much a vigilante for the people, exposing the government's secrets to the public.

She's the biggest conspiracy theorist I've ever met, but even I can admit that the shit she finds is disturbing and has too much evidence to be considered a theory anymore.

Regardless, both of our jobs allow us ample amounts of freedom in our day-to-day life. We're luckier than most.

"I really appreciate that. I'll see you soon," I say before hanging up.

I sigh and look over at the diaries sitting on the island in front of me. I haven't finished reading the first book yet, and I'm nervous about continuing. With every passing word, I want to reject Gigi.

Almost as much as I want to be her.

April 12th, 1944

He came back again. I dare say I would be disappointed if he didn't. John left for work, and Serafina went off to school. The minute the house emptied, I waited by the window. Not my proudest moment, I must admit.

This time, he walked into the house. I froze when he did. Terrified of what he would do, but also anticipating his next move.

When he revealed the entirety of his face to me, without shadows concealing his features, my breath caught.

He's beautiful. Piercing blue eyes. A strong jawline. And big. So, very big.

He approached me, still refusing to speak. He caressed my face with his fingers. So gently. He circled around me, letting his fingers drift across my skin.

I shivered beneath his touch and he smiled. His smile made my heart stop in my chest.

And then he left. Walked out without a word.

I almost pleaded for him to come back, but I stopped myself.

He'll be back.

Chapter Four
The Manipulator

"Your grandma was a *freak*," Daya announces before proceeding to hold up old, dusty lingerie. I balk, perturbed by the sight in front of me. My idiot friend is holding the sides of the lacy underwear and flapping her tongue provocatively. Or what's supposed to be provocative.

I'm far more disturbed than anything right about now.

"Please, stop."

She rolls her eyes to the back of her head dramatically, mimicking an orgasm, which ends up looking more like an exorcism to me.

"You're being entirely inappropriate right now. What if my Nana can see you?"

That sets her straight. The panties drop, and so does her expression.

"You think she's a ghost?" she asks, her wide eyes searching the house like an apparition of Nana is about to play peek-a-boo with her. I roll my eyes. Nana probably would if she could, too.

"Nana loved this house. I wouldn't be surprised if she stayed." I shrug my shoulders nonchalantly. "I've seen apparitions, and a lot of unexplainable shit happen."

"You really know how to sober a bitch up, you know that?" she complains, throwing the lingerie in the trash bin a tad aggressively. I smile, pleased by her assessment. Whatever gets her to stop waving my grandmother's crusty underwear in my face.

"I'll go make us another drink," I placate, heaving up a massive trash bag and hefting it over my shoulder. I'm not proud of the huff of breath that shoots from my lungs or the immediate sweat I break out into.

I really need to stop drinking and work out more.

I'll make it a new year's resolution. It's pretty much a given that I'll try for a week and give up, promising to try again next year. It happens every time.

"Make it extra strong. I'm going to need it now that I feel like there are demons watching me." I roll my eyes again.

"Just do a little striptease. That'll scare 'em away," I deadpan. A whoosh of air next to my ear sends my hair dancing, and a second later, a roll of duct tape hits the wall in front of me. I leave the room cackling, the sound of Daya's cursing following me out of the room.

She knows damn well that she's beautiful, which is why I tend to tease her about being the opposite. Someone's gotta humble the sexy bitch every once in a while. She'll get too big for this Earth if I don't.

I dump the trash bag by the front door and make my way into the kitchen. I grab pineapple juice from the fridge and turn towards the island to start making more drinks.

I draw short. My lungs constrict and ice flows into my veins, my blood flaking into ice chips.

On the island sits an empty whiskey glass with another single red rose next to it. Only a drop of my grandfather's whiskey remains.

The glass wasn't here before. Neither Daya nor I have left the second floor for the past hour, both waist-deep in old people things.

I circle the duo, as if they're a slumbering python and could snap and bite me at any moment.

My heart thunders in my ears as I tentatively reach out and grab the glass, inspecting it as if it's a Magic 8 Ball and going to reveal the person who drank out of it.

Clearly, no one is in this kitchen with me. I can see the front door from where I'm standing. Yet, my eyes comb through the entire expanse of the kitchen and living room, looking for the person who snuck into my house, grabbed a glass and a bottle of whiskey, and proceeded to have a drink. While my best friend and I were upstairs, none the wiser to the danger lurking below us.

I hadn't heard anyone come in. Not a single sound.

Angrily, I storm towards the front door and twist the handle. Locked. Just as it always fucking is. Needlessly, it seems, since a locked house isn't enough to keep a creep out.

"Where's my drink, bitch? I'm hearing whispers and shit," Daya calls loudly from the second floor.

"Coming!" I shout back, my voice breaking.

I walk back into the kitchen, still searching as if there's a wormhole to another universe and the weirdo is going to pop out at any moment.

There's an entryway on the right side of the kitchen that connects to the hallway on the other side of the stairwell. Darkness spills from the depths of that entrance. The person could be in that hallway, lurking just out of sight. Or hiding in one of the bedrooms even, waiting for me to pass by.

Another surge of adrenaline rushes through my bloodstream. I could be one of those dumb bitches you see in slasher flicks who go investigate that you want to yell and scream at for being stupid.

Do I really want to greet possible death that way? The stupid girl who couldn't just run out of the house or call for help? Or am I going to be intimidated by some asshole who thinks they can come into my home whenever they please? Drink my grandfather's whiskey. And leave evidence as if they couldn't care less if they're caught.

It makes me wonder—would they even bother hiding? They obviously have a way into the house undetected. What would be the point in hiding out in a bedroom or a dark hallway? They could easily sneak up on me at any point. Come and go as they wish.

That knowledge makes me viscerally angry, and equally helpless. What good would changing the locks do when they're not a hindrance in the first place?

Sucking in a deep breath, I decide to play the dumb bitch role. Grabbing a knife, I search through the entire house, keeping silent and my footsteps light. I don't want to freak Daya out right now if I don't need to.

When I find nothing, I make my way back into the kitchen, grab the rose, rip the petals from the stem, and drop them into the empty glass.

Part of me almost hopes they come back so that they can see my little masterpiece.

"Not gonna lie, I'm scared for you," Daya admits, lingering in front of the door. She spent the entirety of the day cleaning out the house with me. I rented a dumpster, and we loaded the sucker up until neither of us could lift our arms.

Ten hours and several trips to Goodwill later, we finished cleaning out the manor. My grandparents were never hoarders, but it's easy to accumulate trinkets and items you think you'll need but never do.

After Nana died, my mom went through the entire house and either sold or donated most of the things in here. Otherwise, it could've taken weeks, if not months.

"Don't be, I'll be fine," I say.

It took me the better part of the day, but after downing a few more mixed drinks, I got up enough courage to tell Daya about the whiskey glass. It would be wrong to hide that someone came into my house while she was in it. It wouldn't be fair not to give her the option to leave.

She freaked, of course, and then spent the rest of the day trying to convince me to stay at her place. I won't budge. I'm tired of people attempting to run me out of this house. First my parents, namely my mother, and now some sick fucker who gets off on being a creep.

I'm scared, but I'm also stupid.

So, I'm not leaving.

Honestly, I was surprised Daya stuck it out in the manor. Her eyes were shifty, and she probably said the phrase *what was that noise?* a few thousand times.

But we haven't had an incident since.

Now she lingers at my door, refusing to leave me here alone.

"Let me stay with you," she says again for the millionth time.

"No. I'm not putting you in danger."

She snaps her fingers at me, anger flashing in her green eyes. "See, that right there. That's a fucking problem. If you consider me in danger if I stayed here, then what does that make you?" I open my mouth to answer, but she cuts me off. "In danger! That makes you in danger too, Addie. Why would you stay here?"

I sigh and rub my hand down my face, growing frustrated. It's not Daya's fault. I'd be freaking the hell out and questioning her sanity too if roles were reversed.

But I refuse to run. I can't explain it, but it feels like I'm letting them win. I've only been back in Parsons Manor for a week, and already I'm being pushed out of it.

I can't explain why I have the need to stick it out. Test this mystery person. Challenge them and show them I'm not scared of them.

Though *that's* a big fat fucking lie. I'm absolutely terrified. However, I'm just as stubborn. And as already established—stupid, too. But I can't find it in me to care right now.

Ask me later when they're standing over my bed watching me sleep, I'll feel differently, I'm sure.

"I'll be fine, Daya. I promise. I'm sleeping with a butcher knife under my pillow. I'll barricade myself in the bedroom if I must. Who even knows if they'll come back?"

My argument is weak, but I suppose I'm not even really trying at this point. I'm not fucking leaving.

Why is it that being in public places and social settings make me want to light myself on fire, but when someone breaks into my house, I feel brave enough to stay?

It doesn't make sense in my head, either.

"I don't feel okay leaving you here. If you die, the rest of my life will be ruined. I'll live on in misery, plagued by the *what if* questions." With all the drama she learned from theater, she looks up to the ceiling and puts a contemplative finger on her chin. "Would she still be alive if I had just dragged the bitch out of the house by her hair?" she wonders aloud in a whimsical voice, mocking her possible future self and me.

I frown. I'd rather not be dragged out by my hair. It took me a long time to grow it out.

"If they come back, I'll call the police immediately."

Exasperatedly, she drops her hand and rolls her eyes, her mannerisms saturated with sass. She's angry with me.

Understandably so.

"If you die, I'm going to be so pissed at you, Addie."

I give her a weak smile.

"I'm not going to die."

I hope.

She growls, grabs my hand roughly, and pulls me into a fierce hug. She's letting me go, and all I can feel is immense relief tinged with a little regret.

"Call me if they come back."

"I will," I lie. She leaves without another word, slamming the door behind her.

I heave out a breath, grab a knife from the drawer, and tiredly make my way into the bathroom. I need a long, hot shower, and if the creep chooses now to interrupt me, I'll be happy to stab them for it.

May 16th, 1944

John has been questioning me lately. Always wondering what I'm doing when I'm home alone. I tell him I take care of the house, and crochet. Sera is fourteen and can do her own school work now. So I just make sure he comes home to a hot meal. My normal, mundane wifely duties.

He's suspicious of me.

He's starting to notice a change in my behavior.

I can't deny, I've been acting different lately. Ever since the strange man came into my life. Through my window.

He hasn't spoken to me yet. It doesn't matter how many times I beg him to. Asking him what his name is. Where he came from. How he knows me. What he wants from me. None of it successful.

I want to hear him speak so badly that I've begun to offer him things. Bad things.

A kiss. A touch. He smiles at me, but doesn't concede.

His fingers whisper across my cheek, and then he walks away, leaving me wanting for the next time he comes around.

Chapter Five
The Manipulator

he breeze coerces my body forward, as if urging me to jump. To take the leap and plunge to my death.

You won't regret it.

That little intrusive thought lingers. Somehow, I feel like crashing into sharp rocks would be regrettable, to say the least. What if I don't die right away? What if I miraculously survive the fall, and I'm forced to lie there, broken and bloody, until my body finally gives out?

Or what if my body refuses to give out and I'm forced to live the rest of my life as a vegetable?

All regrettable.

I'm snapped out of my musings when I hear a throat clear.

"Ma'am?"

I turn my head to see a tall, older man with a softness about him that almost comforts me. His grey, thinning hair is matted to his forehead from sweat, and his clothes are stained with dirt and gunk.

His eyes bounce between me and the edge of the cliff I'm standing on, emanating nervous energy. He thinks I'm going to jump. And as I continue to just stare at him, I realize I'm not giving him any reason to think otherwise.

Still, I don't move.

"We're heading out for the night," the man informs me.

He and his crew have been rebuilding my front porch all day, giving it the facelift it so desperately needed. While also ensuring that my foot isn't going to go through the rotted wood and probably give me sepsis.

He looks me up and down, his brow lowering as his concern seems to deepen. The breeze blows hard, swirling around us and stirring up my hair. I claw the strands away to see that he's still eyeing me closely.

When I was younger, Nana refused to let me near the cliff. It's only a good fifty feet from the manor. The view is breathtaking, especially when the sun sets. But at night, it's impossible to see where the cliff's edge is without a flashlight.

Currently, the sun is descending into the horizon, casting this lonely piece of land in dark shadows. I'm standing three feet away from danger, life and death separated by a rocky edge. Soon, it will disappear.

And if I'm not careful—I will, too.

"You okay, miss?" he asks, taking a single step forward. Instinctively, I take a step back—towards the cliff's edge. The man's brown eyes widen into saucers, and he immediately halts and puts up his hands, as if he's trying to keep me from going over with the Force. He was just trying to help, not scare me. And I've gone and scared the shit out of him in return.

I suppose I have been this whole time.

I look back, my heart lodging in my throat when I see just how close I was to stepping off. All I can feel in that moment is pure terror. And just like clockwork, the familiar heady feeling settles low in my stomach, like water circling down a drain.

Something is clearly wrong with me.

Sheepishly, I take a few steps away from the cliff and shoot him an apologetic look.

I'm on edge.

Red roses appear everywhere I go now. It's been three weeks since I found the whiskey glass and rose on my countertop.

After Daya left, I took a long, hot shower and during that time, I decided that I need to start making reports. Leaving some type of evidence behind. That way if I turn up dead or missing, they'll know exactly why.

By the time I got out of the shower, the empty cup with plucked petals was gone, depleting me of any warmth in my body.

I had immediately called the police that night. They humored me with a report, but they told me finding a rose in odd places around my house isn't sufficient evidence for them to do anything.

Ever since then, the incidences have escalated. I'm not sure of the exact moment I realized I had a stalker, but it's been made clear that's exactly what's been happening for the past three weeks.

I'll get into my car to go to my favorite coffee shop to write and waiting for me on my seat is a red rose. Inside a car that has been locked, and still was when I had approached.

There's never a note attached. Never any type of communication other than the red roses with clipped thorns.

My paranoia only heightened when renovations started two weeks ago. Numerous people have been in and out as they repair and replace the bones of the house. Electricians, plumbers, construction workers, and landscapers have all been here.

I've replaced every single window in Parsons Manor and installed brand new locks on every single door, but just as I suspected, it doesn't make a difference.

They always find a way in.

Any of the people coming through my house could be them. Admittedly, I've interrogated a few of the poor workers just to see if they acted suspiciously, but they all looked at me like I was asking them if they could sell me some crack.

"Ma'am?" the man prompts again. I shake my head—a sad attempt at focusing back on the conversation.

"I'm so sorry, I'm just really out of it," I rush out, waving my hands out in front of me in a placating gesture.

I feel like an asshole for my behavior.

Had I fallen, the poor guy probably would've blamed himself. The earth could've easily given out on me, or I could've just taken too large of a step and plummeted to my death just because he was concerned.

He would've lived the rest of his life with guilt, and who knows what would have become of him because of it.

"S'kay," he says, still eyeing me with a pinch of wariness. He hikes his thumb over his shoulder. "Well, we'll be back tomorrow to put the railing up."

I nod, twirling my fingers together.

"Thank you," I respond lightly.

The second he leaves, I'll cry about how I almost ruined his life, and even though he seems incredibly nice, I can tell he wants nothing more than to just leave. But his kindness perseveres. Or that insistent need to make sure he walks away guilt-free.

"You need me to call anyone?"

I smile and shake my head. "I know that looked bad, but I promise I wasn't going to jump."

His shoulders fall an inch, and his face smooths out in relief.

"Good," he says, nodding. He starts to turn but then stops. "Oh, there's a bouquet of roses waiting out there for you."

My heart stops for a solid five seconds before it kicks into high gear and climbs its way up my throat.

"W-what? From who?"

He shrugs a shoulder. "I don't know. They were there when we came back from lunch earlier. Forgot about 'em until just now. I can go grab the—"

"That's okay!" I cut in hastily. His teeth click shut, and another weird look passes on his face. This man definitely thinks I'm a nutcase.

He nods again with one last concerned glance before turning and walking back towards the front of the manor. Releasing a weighted sigh, I wait until he disappears from view before making my own way back.

It would've felt weird walking behind him—two people heading in the same direction that have no interest in talking to each other.

Gives me the heebie jeebies.

When I make my way around to the front of the house, I first stop to admire how beautiful the new black porch looks. The exterior has been refreshed— still all black, but with brand new siding and fresh paint. I kept the vines and cleaned the gargoyles, and though the stone is chipped and weathered, it only adds character to the haunting manor. Seems my taste isn't any more rainbows and sunshine than my predecessors.

Then my eyes jump to the bouquet of red flowers perched against the door. It looks like they were placed there by one of the crew members—assuming they didn't want to enter my house without my permission.

My eyes skirt the property. The sun's rays are nearly gone, and I can't see a damn thing five feet past the tree line. If someone is beyond that point, they could be watching me, and I would be none the wiser.

Feeling a tad more urgent, I scoop up the roses, rush inside, slam the door, and lock it. Nestled neatly in the bouquet is a single black card. From my view, I can see some type of gold calligraphy scrawled across it.

My eyes widen, wary of the note. It'll be the first real communication I've gotten from the stalker. Part of me has been waiting anxiously for it, hoping they'll tell me what they want from me.

And now that it's here, I want to tear it to pieces and live in blissful ignorance.

Screw it, I'll probably die from regret and curiosity if I don't read it.

Plucking the card out with shaking hands, I open it and read:

I'll be seeing you soon, little mouse.

Okay, I could've lived without seeing this.

I mean, *little mouse?* This is obviously a man stalking me, and he must be cracked in the fucking head. *Clearly*, he is.

Disgusted, I slide my phone from my back pocket and call the police. I really don't want to deal with them tonight, but I need to report this.

I'm not naïve enough to think they'll save me from the shadow that's attached itself to me, but I'll be damned if I become some unsolved mystery if I die.

A gentle, but firm knock vibrates my front door. It's almost becoming an instinct for my heart to skip a few beats whenever I hear any noise in the manor.

Surely, that can't be healthy. Maybe I'll eat some Cheerios. They say those are good for the heart, right?

I walk over to the window next to the door, peeking through the curtain to see who it is.

I groan. I *want* to be relieved that it's not some creepy ass dude outside my door, holding a gun and spouting about how if he can't have me, nobody can. Really, I do.

So all I am is a little sad that it's not the persistent shadow ready to end my life.

With a heavy sigh, I swing open the door and greet Sarina Reilly—my mother. Her blonde hair is tucked tightly into a chignon, pink lipstick painted on her thin lips, and icy blue eyes.

She's so prim and proper, and I'm so... not. Where she holds herself with regality and grace, I have a terrible habit of slumping and sitting with my legs open.

"To what do I owe the pleasure, Mom?" I ask dryly. She sniffs, unimpressed with my attitude.

"It's cold out here. Aren't you going to invite me in?" she snips, waving an impatient hand for me to move.

When I reluctantly step aside, she pushes past me, a wisp of her Chanel perfume trailing in her wake. I cringe at the smell.

My dear mother looks around the manor, distaste evident on her pinched face.

She grew up in this gothic house, and the darkness of the interior must've influenced the insides of her heart.

"You're going to get wrinkles if you keep looking at the house like that," I deadpan, shutting the door and brushing past her.

She huffs at me, her heels clicking against the checkered tiles as she makes her way to the couch. The fire is roaring, and the lights are dim, creating a cozy atmosphere. It'll start raining soon, and I really hope she leaves by then so I can enjoy my night in with a book and the sound of thunder in peace.

Mom sits daintily on the couch, her butt perched on the very edge.

If I poke her, she'll fall off.

"Always a pleasure, Adeline," she sighs, her tone high and mighty, as if it's just another day of her being the bigger person.

That *sigh*. The backdrop to my entire childhood. It's filled with disappointment and met expectations all at once. I never disappoint in disappointing her, I guess.

"Why are you here?" I ask, getting straight to the point.

"Can't I come visit my daughter?" she asks with an edge of bitterness in her tone.

Mom and I were never close. She was bitter because Nana and I were, resulting in me choosing her over Mom often. In arguments and where I spent most of my time growing up.

In return, I harbored resentment because I was made to feel like I *couldn't* choose her. Because if I did, I would only be rewarded with another underhanded comment about eating another cookie I can't afford.

She'd complain my ass would get too fat, but little did she know, that's exactly what I wanted.

To this day, the woman still doesn't understand why I don't particularly like her.

"Are you here to try and convince me that I'm wasting my life away in an old house?" I query, throwing myself into the rocking chair by the window and propping my feet up on the stool.

The same one my great-grandmother and I tend to get stalked in.

Sitting in this chair forces my thoughts back to last night, the creepy note and answering all of two questions from the police officer before he said he'd hold on to it for evidence and make a report.

Waste of time, but at least the police will know that it was foul play if I end up dead in a ditch somewhere.

"I have an open house today in town. I figured I'd stop by and see you beforehand."

Ah. That explains it. My mom wouldn't drive an hour to come to visit me just to have a tea party and play nice. She was in town, so she decided to come lecture me.

"Do you want to know why Parsons Manor deserves to be torn down, Adeline?" she asks, her tone dripping with condescension. She sounds like she's about to school me, and suddenly I feel very wary.

"Why?" I ask quietly.

"Because a lot of people died in this house."

"You mean the five construction workers in the fire?" I ask, recalling the story Nana told me when I was a child about Parsons Manor catching fire and killing five men. They had to tear down the charred bones and restart. But the ghosts of those men still linger—I just know it.

"Yes, but not just them."

She stares at me hard while my hesitance worsens. I turn to look out the window beside me, contemplating if I should just make her leave now. She's going to tell me something life-changing, and I'm not sure I want to hear it.

"Then who else?" I finally ask, my eyes glued to Mom's shiny black Lexus parked outside. Schmancy. So schmancy that it almost seems mocking. A stark difference to this old house, as if to say *I'm better than you.*

Being a real estate agent pays well. When I was born, she wanted to be a stay-at-home mom. But considering the turmoil of our relationship as I got older, that notion soured, so she threw herself into becoming one of the top sellers in Washington.

Honestly, I'm proud of her accomplishments. I just wish she felt the same about mine.

"Your great-grandmother, Gigi," she declares, pulling me out of my thoughts. My head snaps towards her, shock curling through me. "Not only did she die in this house, Addie, but she was murdered here." I couldn't keep my mouth from dropping open if I tried.

I shoot upward, the rocking chair slamming harshly against the wall behind me.

"She did not," I deny. But if my mother is anything, it's not a liar.

Nana spoke about Gigi often. Her mother was her entire world. But she definitely never told me Gigi was murdered. I had only asked once about her death, and Nana only said that she died too soon. Nana closed down after that and refused to say anything more.

At the time, I was too young to give it much thought. I just assumed she was still hurting and left it at that. It hadn't occurred to me that Gigi's death was tragic.

She sighs. "That's why your Nana always had this weird... obsession with the manor. She was young when it happened. Her father, John, no longer wanted anything to do with this place, but Nana threw the world's biggest temper tantrum and forced him to stay in the house his wife was murdered in." She glances at me, noting the droll look on my face from her insult. "Those were my grandpa's words, not mine. At least about the temper tantrum. Anyway, the second she was old enough, he gave it to her and moved out, and she lived on in the manor, as you already know."

I face the window again, the beginnings of the storm pattering against the glass. In a few minutes, it'll be a downpour. Thunder rolls, building to a crescendo before a loud crack shakes the foundations of the house.

It matches my mood perfectly.

"Do you have anything to say?" she pushes, her eyes boring a hole into the side of my head.

I shake my head soundlessly, scrambling for a response. My brain is numb to coherent thoughts.

There are no words.

Absolutely no words to describe the utter disbelief I'm feeling.

She sighs again, this time softer and filled with... I don't know, empathy? Mom may not be a liar, but she's also never been empathetic, either.

"My dad never felt comfortable raising me here, but your Nana insisted. She loved Gigi, and she wasn't capable of letting this house go. It's cursed. I don't want to see you do the same thing—grow attached to a house just because you loved your Nana."

I suck my bottom lip between my teeth, biting hard as another crack of thunder tears through the atmosphere.

Was Gigi killed by her stalker? The man she called a visitor, who would come into her home and do unspeakable things. Things that she tried not to want—but did.

Was it him? Was he playing her all along, sensing her growing attraction for him, despite what he was doing and took advantage?

It's the only thing that makes sense.

I turn back to her. "Do they know who did it—who killed Gigi?"

Mom shakes her head, her lips tightening into a thin line, causing the pink lipstick to crack. Those cracks extend far deeper than her lipstick. She's also been broken, though I could never figure out why.

"No, it still goes unsolved to this day. They didn't have sufficient evidence, and back then, it was easier to get away with things than it is now, Addie. Some thought it was my grandfather, but I know he'd never do such a thing. He loved her dearly."

Unsolved. My great-grandmother was murdered in this very house, and no one ever caught the killer. Dread sinks into my stomach like a stone in a lake.

I'm sure I know who killed her, but I don't want to open my mouth and say so until I'm absolutely positive.

"Where was she murdered?" I ask, my voice subdued.

"In her bedroom. Which disturbingly became your Nana's bedroom." She pauses for a beat before muttering, "And now yours, I'm sure."

She's not wrong. I took over Nana's old bedroom, and though it's been fully renovated, I still kept the chest at the end of the bed and the full-length ornate mirror propped in the corner of the room. Things that were passed down from

Gigi.

The bed is no more, having bought my own. But the same four walls that housed a horrific murder are the same four walls I sleep in at night.

It's chilling—a little creepy. But to Mom's dismay, it's not enough to get me to move out. Or even change rooms. If that makes me a freak, then I would only fit in with the family.

Gigi fell in love with her stalker. The very man who must've killed her eventually.

And now, I have one of my very own. The only silver lining is that I would never be so stupid to fall in love with him.

Mom stands, a signal that she's leaving. Her heels *click, clack* off the checkered tile as she slowly walks towards the entrance.

She gives me one last look.

"I hope you make the right decision and leave this place, Addie. It's... dangerous here."

Her staccato footsteps fade as the door softly closes behind her. I watch her car disappear down the mile-long driveway, leaving me all alone in this big, cursed house.

Suddenly, my stalker's last words are much more ominous now.

I'll be seeing you soon, little mouse.

May 25th, 1944

My visitor spoke to me today. For the first time since he started coming around. I was shocked when he did.

His voice is so deep. So alluring. Once he spoke, I had hoped he'd never stop.

I asked him why he kept coming around, watching me. He confessed his love for me. His desire to have me. I asked for his name, and he gave it to me.

Ronaldo. An interesting name, but it suited him perfectly.

He didn't stay much longer after that. But he did ask for a kiss. I was hesitant, but in the end, I let him.

I'm ashamed to admit I hadn't even considered John in that moment. All I could think about was what his lips would feel like on my own.

My imagination didn't do it justice. When he kissed me, I flew into the stars.

I don't think I've come back down yet.

Chapter Six
The Shadow

The crackle from the small device indicates my directions are about to come in. I shake out my fists, restlessness binding my nerves into tight knots.

"Five bodies in the main area, all of them armed. Three more on their six and four on their twelve."

I crack my neck, enjoying the feeling of my bones popping. Tension releases and my shoulders relax.

Twelve men won't be too hard to take down, but I'm going to have to be quick and stealthy. It was easier to pick off the guards surrounding the decrepit warehouse.

The sun has long since fallen, providing ample coverage. It took two seconds to find a spot hidden in the shadows, giving me the perfect angle for a sniper shot.

Their mistake was relying on their limited eyesight for intruders. My ability to hide in the shadows is what ultimately got them killed.

Should've had night vision goggles like me.

Maybe then I would've had a bit of entertainment.

I lick my lips, anticipation sharp on my tongue.

"Be careful, Z," says my righthand man, Jay. His hacking skills are nearly as good as mine—and only because I was his teacher.

I created an entire organization built solely around ending human trafficking. I started out as a hacker exposing the truths of our corrupt government. And then, as I became more aware of their true nature—the depravity of their sickness, it turned into personally snuffing out every single one of these sick bastards, starting from the bottom up.

Terminate all the worker bees, and the queen is left vulnerable and weak.

But I couldn't be both a hacker and a mercenary, and what I really enjoy doing is being the one to put the bullet in their heads myself.

So, I created my org, Z, from the ground up, recruiting a team of hackers to help the mercenaries with their job—get into the rings, kill them all, and get the victims out safely. I stationed my mercenaries in high-rate trafficking areas and assigned them their own team of hackers. Now, Z has become so big that there are teams in every state, and several outside of the country as well.

Jay is the only mouth I need in my ear—his skill levels out to the equivalent of what three hackers could do. And he's the only one I trust with my life.

I don't acknowledge Jay's sentiment.

I don't fucking need luck. Just skill and patience. And I have both in spades.

Slinking up to the door, I keep my body close to the wall and my footsteps undetectable.

When I reach the door, I hear the subtle click of the door unlocking.

Jay's doing.

Despite the decay of the building, it's still equipped with the latest technology where needed.

The ring leaders want to keep the appearance of a rundown, abandoned building to remain under the radar. But completely impenetrable for squatters and graffiti artists.

"It's clear. Systems are down for ten seconds, get in now."

Quickly, I turn the handle and slip through in a matter of seconds, opening the door just enough to fit my body through. The metal door shuts behind me soundlessly.

The old building is mostly an open concept. I came through the back door that leads into a dimly lit hallway. Straight ahead and to the left will open up to where the machinery used to be when this was a rubber factory.

That is where the girls are being held.

Muffled screams reach my ears—the sounds of girls crying and in pain. White-hot rage blinds my vision, but I don't rush in or lose my shit.

No one can do this job and lose their fucking shit, otherwise, these girls would never be saved.

It's hard not to, though. These assholes bring out the worst in me.

"Overrode the cameras. You have one hour before the system resets, and I'm kicked out," Jay informs.

I only need ten minutes.

Keeping to the shadows, I make my way through the hallway and peek around the corner. There are thin cots scattered across about a thousand square feet of space. Each cot is accompanied by a metal pole installed from the ground up. Each girl is chained to the poles by a metal collar that prevents them from moving only a couple of feet from their cots.

I flex my fists, tightening them until my hands go numb.

I pull my gun out of the back of my jeans.

Once they notice the first man is down, the rest will open fire, which is why I need to be careful and quick.

Whether they're going to be careless about the girls is impossible to say. The men know the risk if their leaders find out a virgin girl was killed. That means money taken out of someone's pockets and their head on a stake to set an example.

But some of these men care more about their own lives, even if it means they're walking around with a hit on their head.

Just as Jay said, three men stand guard in front of me, completely unaware of my presence.

Stupid fucks.

I'll never understand how people can't sense danger when it's right up their assholes.

Shit boggles me.

In one quick succession, I take out all three men. Their bodies drop, and a few of the girls jump. Some cry and hunker down, while others stay deathly silent. A normal reaction for a little girl would be to scream, but these girls have already been desensitized to murder.

The five men in the pit of girls turn their heads in tandem, their faces morphing from surprise to alarm to anger in a matter of seconds. Immediately, they scramble for their guns.

My body is still concealed by the wall I'm hiding behind. Two of them open fire, forcing me to back away. One bullet skids across the corner of the wall, right past my face. Chunks of concrete fly into my eyes as more bullets ping around me. I grunt, rubbing at my lids to clear my vision.

Right as I ready up again, one guy comes barreling around the corner. He's dead before he even spots me, a nice little hole right between his brows.

He was an ugly motherfucker anyway. World will do just fine without him.

Before his body can topple over, I grip him by the collar of his shirt and bring him in close. Wincing at the bad breath emanating from the rotting hole in his face, I step out of the hallway, using the dead man as a shield against the flying bullets still hurdling my way.

The dead body takes a few hits while I fire off two single shots. Two more bodies go down, and I step back inside the hallway, pushing away the bloodied man who's now riddled with bullets.

His head smacks off the concrete floor with a sickening thud.

I used his body as a shield for five seconds, but I still got lucky. It's not like the movies. Bullets can easily fly through bodies. Entry and exit point. Just to enter right back into my body.

I don't use other people for shields unless I have to, and it's only for a few seconds at a time.

A chorus of noises arise in the warehouse in the form of terrified screams from the girls, shouts of panic from the men, orders to *"kill the puta,"* and yells of outrage for the girls to stop crying.

There are still six men left, and I can feel the panic crawling off them.

"Come out, with your hands raised and gun on the floor, or I'll start killing these bitches!" one of them shouts, his voice echoing.

I sigh, roll my shoulders, and do as he says. I drop my gun on the floor and step out with my hands raised. The six men stand before the group of girls, keeping them safe from stray bullets. The knowledge that they're only doing so to ensure the product isn't damaged rather than giving a shit about hurting them burns hot in my chest.

"Come on, the fun was just starting," I croon, a smirk pulling my lips up.

"Shut up!" the man spits. He's a Mexican man with a shaved head, tattoos covering him from head to toe, and wearing clothes that look like they haven't been washed in weeks.

And look at that—quite the gnarly scar on his forehead.

Goddamn. It looks like someone took a bread knife and just sawed at his head.

This must be dear ol' Fernando. Just who I was looking for.

Fernando's eyes are wide with fear and based on the crack pipes sitting on the table behind him, I'd say most of them are high off their rockers.

Not so good.

They get trigger-happy when they're tripping on whatever substance they injected into their tired veins.

And I got six of those happy fingers on triggers.

"Who sent you?" Fernando shouts, emphasizing his question with a wave of his gun.

"I sent myself," I answer dryly.

Why do they always think I'm working for someone else? I don't work for anyone but myself.

The man holds his gun above my head and shoots it off, attempting to scare me.

See?

Trigger happy.

I don't flinch. Instead, I take the time to look at my surroundings better. There's a table to my left, littered with guns, ashtrays, empty beer cans, and another crack pipe.

Perfect.

"Don't make me ask again, *cabrón*," the man says, his finger caressing the trigger.

"You Fernando?" I ask, keeping my body as still as ice. The man's brows jump in surprise, and I see the paranoia leaking into his eyes from here.

He's not going to be much help like I had hoped. He's buzzing too hard.

"How you know that, huh? You following me?"

I smile, baring all my teeth. "It's what I do best after all. I heard you're the main man around here. Running the show and all that."

He shifts. The asshole can't help but feel a little pride, I just know it. Like he's doing something good in the world, when all he's doing is plaguing hundreds of little boys' and girls' nightmares.

"I was hoping you could help me out, man."

"Yeah?" he patronizes. "You think so? You think I'm going to tell you shit, man?"

He fires off another shot, this time next to me. Too close for comfort. Enough to feel the heat of the bullet. I still don't flinch, and if anything, that pisses him off more.

I sigh. With his current state of mind, he's useless to me. Just gonna have to kidnap his ass and wait till he comes down from his high.

A quick sweep of my eyes proves that I have about two seconds before the rest of the men start shooting, regardless of what comes out of my mouth.

Two seconds—that's all it takes to stick my hand in my hoodie pocket and fire off a shot through the material, downing one of the men to my left.

The surprise of *that* move gives me a small window of time to upend the table and roll behind it.

Glass shatters from the ashtrays, and a gun falls off the table and discharges, eliciting shocked screams from the girls.

Fuck. If that bullet ricochets and lands within an inch of those girls, I'm going to let them stab me for sure.

No cries of pain follow, so I blow out a deep breath. Relieved, but no less pissed at myself.

Like clockwork, a stream of bullets impales the thick, wooden table. Lucky for me, most don't make it through.

It's too dangerous for me to return fire. I won't be able to peek my pinky toe out without it getting shot off, and I refuse to endanger these girls even more and fire blindly. I don't take shots unless I'm positive they'll hit true.

The only thing I can do is wait.

It doesn't take long for them to empty their clips.

I hear the rustling of clothing and muttered curses as they scramble to reload.

It takes even less time for me to shoot the remaining four dead, sans Fernando. I'm going to save him for later.

The bullets rip through their brains in such quick succession that their bodies drop at the same time.

"You see that?" I ask aloud, already knowing Jay is watching through the cameras.

"Fuck, it only took you eight minutes," Jay groans through my earpiece.

"Five hundred bucks, fucker," is my smug answer. A string of curses leaves his mouth, but I tune him out.

Fernando is spitting out his own colorful tirade as he scrambles to find another gun. I shoot him in the knee, the angry man collapsing instantly. Screams of raw pain and anger fill the warehouse, and if I didn't know any better, I'd think he was a little girl himself.

No—the girls in this warehouse are far tougher than he could ever hope to be. He's just a whiny bitch trapped in a man's body.

I stand and saunter over to Fernando, enjoying the sight of him clutching his knee, blood bubbling from the wound and onto the floor. His face is red, full of murderous intent as he glares at me.

I ignore the look, instead surveying the copious amounts of blood streaking the cement floor. I don't want the girls to have to step through it.

"Jay, have Ruby make a pathway for these girls." Ruby is one member of the crew who comes in, explicitly assigned to handle the survivors and get them to safety. She's a redheaded spitfire but turns to mush when she's around any of the women or children we save.

"A pathway?"

"Yeah, I don't want a drop of blood on their toes."

The warehouse is full of about fifty girls, all deeply traumatized and broken. They will never have to wash blood from their bodies again if I have anything to do with it.

One of the girls stands, a fierce expression on her face. She can't be more than fifteen years old, but a pedophile ring will age anyone significantly.

"Are you going to hurt us, too?" she asks loudly. Her dirty brown hair is tangled around her face. She's filthy—they all are.

The extensive amount of skin showing is smudged with dirt and blood. She looks the oldest, and by her protective stance, she's pronounced herself the mother of the group.

All of the girls here were kidnapped within the past six days. Six days of unspeakable torture and assault that will stay with them for the rest of their lives. Six days of dirty men sexualizing, beating, and molesting them. The young girls would not have been deflowered, but that doesn't mean the monsters didn't find other ways to get pleasure out of them.

Jay and I have been watching this location for the past twelve hours, identifying both the girls and the men. Each second that ticked by felt like an eternity—knowing that they were enduring something horrific.

While Jay kept tabs, I allowed myself five hours of sleep before I came here, enough time to keep my mind sharp. I have to be at my absolute best if I'm going to get them out alive.

"I'm here to get you girls home," I respond, tucking my gun back in my boot.

She looks at me warily, as do some of the other girls.

None of them are going to trust me.

I get it.

I'm scarred from head to toe, have two different colored eyes—both on the dramatic spectrum—and I'm not a small guy. Not to mention, I just murdered a bunch of men in front of their faces.

"Backup is coming in," Jay informs, right before I hear the back door open and several people rush in.

"Young man, it's a bloodbath in here. These poor girls! Shame on you, Z." I wince at the sound of Ruby's voice. Can't make me flinch from firing off a bullet two inches from my head but Ruby... God help me.

"It couldn't be avoided, Ruby. I—"

"Not another word from you. If your mother were here, she'd have your ass."

I grunt but don't respond, letting her hem and haw over the survivors while still muttering reprimands under her breath. Ruby was a good friend of my mom's and likes to remind me—and the rest of the crew—that she used to wipe my ass when I was a baby.

If I could've killed the traffickers in private, I would've, and I hate that I added to their trauma. But when you have a warehouse full of armed men, there's no calling them back to your office one at a time like they're being fired from their job. They need to be taken down swiftly where they stand. Otherwise, there's room for error, potentially resulting in one of the survivors getting hurt or killed.

Necessary means to get the girls out.

The other two that came in with Ruby, Michael and Steve, take care of the bodies. Michael is dragging a struggling Fernando out, tossing me the keys to the girls' chains as he passes by. Ruby already found another set on one of the dead bodies and is currently unchaining the others.

I approach the mother hen of the group and unchain her collar, my hand nearly shaking from the fury of having to unhook a fucking collar from a little girl's neck. Welts and a large bruise encircle her throat, but I don't let her see the rage simmering beneath the surface. She stares at me silently, suspicion and tentative hope warring in her pretty light brown eyes.

Her eyes remind me of my little mouse, and something protective flares inside my chest.

"What's your name, kid?" I ask, keeping my eyes trained to hers. She's probably waiting for my leery gaze to travel the expanse of her body, but she won't ever get that shit from me.

"Sicily," she answers. I quirk a brow.

"Is that where your parents come from?" I question, noting her tanned skin peeking from beneath the grime on her face.

She nods her head tentatively. "Ma and Pa were born there, but they haven't been able to go back since they were in their teens. They said they named me after the island because even though they're homesick, I provide them with the only home they need."

I nod, eyeing her face. Purple blooms from her right eye, and another spark of anger ignites.

"You ready to give them a home again?"

She pauses, and then a small smile forms. "Yes," she whispers.

Tears flood her eyes, but I don't let her know that I noticed. I can tell she wouldn't appreciate it.

"Let's go then, kid."

This little girl will go back home, and though she has a long journey ahead of her, she'll heal.

We keep tabs on all the girls we extract to ensure they don't go missing again. If it can happen once, it can happen twice.

She huddles in close to me as we walk out of the building. Out of the corner of my eye, I see a girl step in blood. I pause, pointing at her but glaring at Ruby.

"Ruby! What'd I say? Not a drop of blood on the girls."

Ruby startles, roles reversing as she rushes towards the girl with shame.

"I'm sorry, honey bunny, let me clean you up," she coos to the little girl with way more than just a fucking drop on her foot. "Watch your step, okay?"

I turn, satisfied that she won't let it happen again.

I help Sicily navigate through the carnage, keeping one eye firmly on her feet and where she walks. When she's in the clear, I lead her to the van where they'll transport her safely to the hospital. There, her family will be notified.

I whistle an unnamed tune as I let my crew take care of the rest and head to my Mustang, hidden in another parking lot across the street. I'm eager to get the fuck out of here.

My hunt isn't over yet. I have to play with my little mouse now.

Chapter Seven
The Manipulator

"You need to get out of the house," Daya concludes, staring at me with fear and distress swirling in her sage eyes. I just told her about my mom's visit yesterday.

By the look on her face, I can tell that she's well and truly scared for me.

"I need to finish this manuscript," I argue, my thoughts straying to the massive plot hole I've fallen into. It doesn't seem to matter how many times I press the proverbial Life Alert—I can't get up. I'm going to have to roll out my whiteboard and sticky notes to map out the plot tonight, so I can figure out how to solve the issue once and for all.

Sometimes I wish I could just simplify my books and call it a day, but then I wouldn't have the readership I have.

"Uh uh," Daya snipes, shaking her head at me. "Get ready. We're having a girls night."

I slump, the whiteboard and sticky notes going *poof*. But I don't argue. I'm an indie author, so I publish when I'm ready to. I hardly set deadlines for myself because the pressure suppresses my creativity. I can't write when I'm too ridden with anxiety to get the book done by a specific time. And as great as my readers are, there's always that pressure to get the next book out.

Of course, Daya knows this and now wields this knowledge as a weapon.

Dick.

Groaning, I let her hurdle me up the stairs and into my bedroom, my eyes immediately finding the mirror and chest—they always seem to do that now after finding out what really happened in here.

Those two pieces feel like beacons in the room now, glaring at me as if to say *I know who killed her.*

It doesn't matter that I slapped some black paint on them. The bones are still the same.

The walls and floor are smooth black rock now, with white ceilings and large white rugs to lighten up the room. I also installed a heating system in the floors. Otherwise, getting up in the middle of the night to pee and stepping on ice-cold floors would just be cruel and unusual punishment.

I decided I love the sconces in the hallway so much that I wanted a few in my room, too. Placed artfully on the wall my bed is against, surrounding a massive, beautiful art piece of a woman.

Straight ahead of the bedroom door is my favorite part—the balcony. Black double doors open up to a terrace that overlooks the cliffside. It has a way of making you feel small and insignificant when you're standing before a sight as beautiful as that.

The entire house has now been modernized, though I kept most of the original style. The sconces, checkered floors, black stone fireplace, and black cabinets, just to name a few. Most importantly, I kept Gigi's red velvet rocking chair.

I'm living in a Victorian gothic dreamhouse.

"We're going to make you look hot and find you a delicious man to take home tonight. And if the stalker comes around, he can kill him, too."

I roll my eyes. "Daya, it's hard to find a man these days that can even fuck right. You think I'm going to find a man that will kill in my honor, too? That's cute."

"You never know, baby girl. Crazier things have happened."

The bass pumping through the speakers vibrates throughout my body. My black, ripped skinny jeans cling to my curves, and the plunging low cut red tank shows off my ample cleavage along with the small glistening beads of sweat between my breasts.

It's fucking hotter than Hades's ballsack, and the alcohol pumping through my veins doesn't help matters.

For a solid hour, Daya and I stick close to each other and dance. We both briefly separate to dance with a few men, but I tend to tire of the groping hands quickly and always find my way back to my best friend.

Suddenly, a heavy presence crowds into my back, his hands sliding around my waist and pressing in close. A whiff of spearmint and whiskey invades my senses right before I feel his breath on my ear.

"You're beautiful," he whispers, his spearmint gum stinging my nose now that he's closer. I wrinkle my nose and turn my head to see a tall, attractive man leaning over me.

He has strawberry blonde hair, pretty blue eyes, and a killer smile.

Just my type.

I grin. "Why, thank you," I respond sweetly. Social situations nearly send me into hibernation, but I've always been skilled at flirting. Too bad most times, I can't stand to do it.

Men have a unique way of killing my mood every time I come within ten feet of them.

"Come upstairs with me," he yells over the music. His voice isn't aggressive by any means, but it's not a question either. It's a demand that leaves little room for argument.

I like that.

I cock a brow. "And if I don't?" I ask.

His smile widens. "You'll regret it for the rest of your life."

The other brow joins its twin, hiking halfway up my forehead.

"Really," I say demurely. "What kind of plans do you have for me that I'd regret missing out on for the rest of my life?"

"The kind that leaves you naked and sated in my bed."

"Bitch, let's go already," Daya cuts in. My head turns to her, but I feel the man's eyes linger on my face, caressing my cheek like a feather tracing across skin.

Daya is standing in front of us, impatiently waving her hand towards the stairs that lead to the second floor. She must've been eavesdropping, and she doesn't look the least bit ashamed.

When we both just stare at her, she huffs and rolls her eyes.

"We get it, you're hot for each other. And she doesn't go anywhere without me. So, let's go already." She waves her hands at us more urgently, shooing us towards the stairs.

The man laughs and seizes the opportunity provided by my dear best friend. Grabbing my hand, he leads me towards the black metal stairs at the back of the club.

But not before I shoot Daya a narrow-eyed look. One which she dutifully cackles at.

Upstairs is for VIP members only. The stairs lead up to a balcony that overlooks the entirety of the club. It's where the rich, important people drink, staring out at us like a bunch of bugs trapped in a science experiment.

The atmosphere up here is darker, denser, and has a vibe that has my instincts flaring red. Walking up here feels like sticking my head into a hornet's nest. And the bastards won't stop stinging until they tire of you, or you're dead.

Four men are draped across a black leather booth formed in a half-moon. In the center is a black marble table occupied by several glasses of amber liquid, along with a few crystal ashtrays. There's barely a hint of color in here, the décor reminding me of Parsons Manor.

A man eyes the both of us with a predatory and calculated gleam. He looks eerily similar to the man who has his hand wrapped around mine. Same strawberry blonde hair and blue eyes, though this one appears younger and a tad more wicked.

The other three men are equally handsome, all sporting the same dark and dangerous type. One man appears European with white-blonde hair, fair, pale skin, and sharp angular features. His hooded icy blue eyes are locked on Daya as hers sweep across the small, intimate room. His gaze is already tracing the dips and curves of her body hungrily. My instincts spike again, telling me to pop the man's eyes out of their sockets and throw them over the balcony.

The remaining two men are twins with tanned skin, dark hair and eyes and killer bodies. Their suits can barely contain the muscles threatening to rip the expensive fabric at the seams.

One twin has long hair tied back in a bun and several rings adorning his fingers, while the other has his hair cropped close to his head and a diamond nose ring.

All four of them could easily ruin my life. And I would be hesitant to stop them.

"So, you finally grew the balls and got her," the blonde man says, grinning devilishly at me. He's the only one out of the four that isn't eye-fucking us. Honestly, he looks like he'd be far more interested in eating babies for dinner.

There's a dark aura around him. If I could guess, the unsettling atmosphere up here derives directly from him. His energy sprouts and festers until it makes you feel like you're trapped in a room breathing in black smoke.

"Quiet, Connor," the man says from beside me, his tone low and full of warning.

I nearly roll my eyes. He *looks* like a Connor. The frat boy that hangs around unoccupied drinks and sneaks his phone under girls' skirts to take pictures.

"Ladies, sorry for his rude behavior," my new friend says, his smile not quite reaching his eyes. "That's my brother, Connor. The twins, Landon and Luke. And then Max."

He points to each man respectively. Landon being the twin with the man bun, and Luke the one with a nose ring. I train my gaze on my companion with an expectant brow raised.

"And your name?"

"I'm Archibald Talaverra III. You can call me Arch."

"Sounds pretentious," I muse, smiling at the fact that he gave me his full name.

Who actually introduces themselves to a stranger that way? *Archibald Talaverra, the third. Just call me your Royal Highn-ass.*

His brother, Connor, laughs in response, seeming to agree.

Arch opens his mouth, but I cut him off. "I'm Addie. And this is Daya," I introduce, pointing towards my best friend. She offers a smile, but her stare is sharp and assessing. She's too keen and intelligent to get sucked into danger like I tend to do.

"Nice to meet you, ladies," Max murmurs, his attention still glued to Daya. Matter of fact, the twins have hardly looked away from her since the moment she walked into the room, either.

Every bit of me wants to step in front of her and protect her from the prying, feral eyes. But Daya can handle her own, so I stay beside her. Ready to attack if needed.

"Sit, please," Arch urges. There's plenty of room on the booth but the two of us decide to sit on the end, closest to Max.

My phone buzzes as soon as my ass hits the soft leather. Noticing that Daya has been immediately sucked into a conversation with Max, and Arch is filling up a glass of expensive bourbon, I sneak a peek at the text.

UNKNOWN: Sneaking off with random men, little mouse? If I catch his hands anywhere near you, they'll end up in your mailbox by morning.

My heart stills in my chest. This is the first time he has actually communicated with me outside of an ominous note.

My eyes snap up towards the balcony. No one can see us from here. We're too far back from the railing. But yet, someone is clearly watching me.

But how?

And how the hell did he get my number? Scratch that, that was a stupid question. He's a fucking stalker, for god's sake. Of course, he has my number.

Arch walks over and hands me a drink, a smile on his face. He thinks he's getting laid tonight.

Normally, he might have. But it looks like I might have to save his life instead and get the hell away from him.

An hour passes, and I grow more nervous as each minute ticks by. I haven't received another text, but it's sitting there, weighing down the back of my brain. I fear my brain stem will snap from the tension.

Arch's hands definitely touch me. One currently rests on my thigh, dangerously close to my center. I stare down at the star tattooed on his thumb, my mind conjuring images of holding it—without his body attached.

Yet, I let it happen, even though I shouldn't. And because I shouldn't, I can't stop staring at them, imagining them chopped off at the wrist and bloody. Sitting in my mailbox.

I don't even have a mailbox.

My house is too far back from the road, so my mail is just left on my front step.

Shouldn't a stalker know that?

What a shitty little shadow.

"You having fun?" Arch asks, nudging me with his shoulders. I nod absently as

I continue to abuse my lip trapped beneath my teeth.

I should run. I should tell this man to get his hand off of me if only it means it'll never be severed from his body and left in my nonexistent mailbox.

"You're tense," Arch observes quietly. I clear my throat and open my mouth, but another buzz from my back pocket interrupts me.

I can feel the color leech from my face. Arch's brows dip with concern, and it reminds me of the poor man that I nearly gave a heart attack by the cliff's edge.

He glances down towards the sound. "Are you okay?" he asks, his voice only seeming to quieten further.

I'm growing tired of the concerned looks, but yet, they feel like lifelines. Like there's people out there that will notice my strange behavior and speak out if something ever happens to me.

A news reporter will interview Arch, and he'll speak of how I seemed spooked by a text message. The construction worker who built my porch—his story will be broadcasted and talked about for weeks. A girl standing at the edge of a cliff, seeming to contemplate jumping and then nearly falling off.

It all connects to the fact that I had a stalker. And the police brushed it off when I made my reports of random roses. But it won't change anything for the next girl that's being stalked.

It never does.

In the end, I'll be another statistic but will fade away as just that. A beautiful girl stalked by an unhinged man. And no one bothered to help her until it was too late.

"I'm fine," I force out through a stilted smile. It feels wooden and disingenuous, but it does the trick nonetheless. His face relaxes, and the concern bleeds away.

Or rather, Arch is just letting it go because he doesn't actually care.

"Do you want to leave?" he murmurs, his voice now full of promise and intent. His bottom lip disappears between his white teeth, the act in itself primal.

The word *no* is on the tip of my tongue, like a little ballerina dancing precariously at the tip, dangerously close to falling off and breaking her ankle. Because if I say no to this man, I'll spend the rest of my night—week—possibly longer, regretting it.

Hating myself for letting a freak control my life and rob me of a good time with a delicious man.

He's beautiful, with a shade of darkness surrounding him that's as enticing and mouth-watering as chocolate cake. There's a promise that I would be ending the night with him entirely satisfied.

And what if it evolves into more? What if I'm saying no to something beautiful? Those are a little girl's hopes and dreams, but I can't help thinking them anyways.

He looks like a man that I could settle down with but dangerous enough to keep me excited.

"Yes," I say quietly—finally. "But after I know Daya gets home safely."

Arch smiles slowly. Salaciously. "I can see to that."

July 7th, 1944

Ronaldo likes to tease.

Only an hour after I send Seraphina off to school, he comes in and tells me to sit in my dining room chair.

I follow his orders eagerly. His fingers whisper across my flesh. When I talk to him, he doesn't respond.

He unbuttons my blouse, baring my breasts. Then onto my trousers. He pulls them down and leaves me in nothing but my undergarments.

He smiles when he sees the excitement in my eyes.

Yet he still denies me. He never touches me where I want him to. Where I need him to.

His fingers taunt me. And then he leaves.

And it takes everything in me not to beg for him to come back. One of these days, I won't be able to control myself any longer.

Chapter Eight
The Manipulator

Daya takes Luke home while I take Arch back to the manor. He asked me to go to his, but I felt much safer at my own home. More in control.

In retrospect, I shouldn't take him to a house that sits on a cliff, surrounded by woods and several miles out from civilization. Worst of all, with a stalker that lingers around and likes to break in.

God, this was stupid.

My house isn't safer by any means, but I couldn't bring myself to go to his place. I don't like being in unfamiliar places with strangers. Like I could be walking into a house that I'll never come back out of. It makes me feel far more vulnerable, though I'm in the most vulnerable position I could possibly be in right now.

"You have a beautiful home," Arch compliments, his eyes sweeping over the entirety of the living room and kitchen. I updated the wallpaper to a more modern black paisley, got rid of the tragic gold curtains, replaced them with red ones, and updated the couches to red leather.

But his eyes keep drifting back to the black wooden steps as if he knows they lead to my bedroom.

Except I have different plans.

"That's not the best part," I tease, grabbing his hand and leading him down the hallway to my favorite room in Parsons Manor.

The sunroom.

I don't go back here very often. It's where Nana and I spent most of our time together. It hurts to come in here when the room is still thick with her presence.

Breathing in deep, I open the double doors and step inside.

This room is a glass box. The ceiling, the walls, everywhere around us is one big window. It's also the best spot to be in. It overlooks the cliff edge, the waters glittering beneath the moonlight.

But the most notable part is directly above us. The stars are breathtaking to look at. Out here, we have no light pollution. The night sky is lit up with orbs of diamonds, glinting and shining against the black backdrop.

Arch's head slowly turns as he takes in the sight before him. And then he cranes his head back, staring up at the sky with his mouth hanging open.

I imagine it's one of the few moments where this man has looked unattractive. But to me, it's the most attractive he's been this entire night.

He's not concerned with controlling his face and movements, nor is he practiced and following a script. He's just a man in awe of the beauty surrounding him.

"Damn," he mutters finally, his voice deep with wonder. He turns his head back to me, the edges of his eyes round with delight.

The blue moons in his eyes are glimmering with an emotion I can't put my finger on. It isn't until that mask slides back over his face that I realize he looked sad. Melancholic.

And I want to know why, but with the way his eyes are heating like a burner on the stove, I know the opportunity has already passed.

"You got something special here," he says quietly, prowling towards me. The stars have long since faded, and the only thing he can't seem to look away from now is me.

"I do," I breathe, watching him come closer with bated breath.

There's a small tug at the back of my head—an instinctual feeling that reminds me that I'm in a glass box with a shadow possibly lurking outside. Provided with a full view of what's happening.

Part of me doesn't mind if he's out there. I want to prove something to the deranged man who thinks he owns me. I want to show him he *doesn't*.

The only person who will lay claim to my body is who I allow. I'll let Arch's hands touch me. Hands that will trace every inch of my skin, followed by his mouth. I'll let his tongue lick my pussy until I'm sated, right before he fucks me until I no longer know my name.

I'll let him because *I* said he could.

Arch towers over me, molding his front to mine and pinning my breasts against his chest. My breath stutters as warmth envelops me, his arm circling tightly around my waist and locking me against him.

I like the way he feels pressed against me. The softness of my body molding against the hard ridges of his. It feels... nice. Good.

Arch stares deeply into my eyes for a brief moment. And then he tilts his head and gently captures my lips between his.

I sigh, his soft lips moving against mine rhythmically, like the water at the bottom of the cliff, swaying against the rocks.

I moan into his mouth, needing more and deepening the kiss, prying his lips apart so I can dip my tongue inside.

He growls, his restraint slipping. His other hand sweeps into my hair, angling my head better so he can plunge his tongue in my mouth, exploring skillfully with little control.

I rise on my toes, pressing further into him. Shuddering at the feel of his hard cock digging into my stomach, the length of him only intensifying my desire.

He's not small. And that's really what I need tonight. Something that will blind me with pleasure and leave me breathless and satisfied.

His tongue fights against mine, swiping and licking as his teeth nip at my lips. Another moan slips free, bouncing in his mouth until he matches it with his own groan.

The hand in my hair tightens, jerking my mouth away, giving his lips freedom to trail down my jaw and descend to the juncture between my neck and shoulder.

I gasp when I feel his teeth scrape against my flesh, a small warning before he bites down. Sharp pleasure sends my eyes to the back of my head, and a long moan slips free.

"Fuck," he curses, licking at my neck with a feral groan. "That sexy voice of yours."

My eyes flutter as I succumb to the pleasure his tongue and teeth are drawing out of me.

His hands drift lower until I feel a firm tug on my jeans. The button pops open a second later, followed by the low purr of my zipper coming undone.

"Is your pussy wet for me, Addie?" Arch asks on a low growl, nipping a tad viciously at my neck. It smarts, and I can't help but wince from the pain. His tongue smooths across the bite mark, soothing the sting.

"Yes," I whisper as pleasure begins to override the pain.

His hand slithers down the front of my jeans and thong, his fingers drifting lower until the tip of his middle finger dips inside me. A low, deep growl arises when he feels just how truthful I was being.

"Fuck, baby, that's it. Let me hear you sing now."

And then two fingers are plunging inside of me, curling to hit that spot. My vision blackens and a yelp of pleasure is my only response. It's the only thing I'm capable of.

Instinctively, I roll my hips, grinding into his hand. He withdraws to the tips before driving them into me again. And again, until he's fucking me with his fingers and all I can do is hold on, my nails biting into his suit jacket.

Long, husky moans are drawn from my throat, singing for him just the way he asked.

"You sing so pretty," he whispers in my ear. A sharp nip follows his words.

The heel of his palm presses firmly into my clit. His skilled fingers lift me higher, the orgasm curling low in my stomach. But then he rubs just right, making my knees quake from the pleasure.

"Oh," I moan, my breathing erratic and breathless.

"Do you sing pretty when you come, Addie?" he asks in a dark whisper.

I think I nod, but I can't be sure because within seconds, my head is kicking back as my release builds to a fierce point.

"Let me hear it," he coaxes. His fingers slide out, and when they plunge back in, a third finger joins. My eyes roll and I plummet over the edge.

I cry out, the sound breaking from the pitch as deep-seated pleasure consumes me from the inside out. Shamelessly, I grind against his hand, riding out the endless waves.

"Such a pretty bird," he murmurs, satisfaction tightening his voice.

Breathless, but somehow even hungrier, I lift up on my toes and crush my mouth to his. He hums his approval, spearing my lips apart with his tongue. Then, his hand drifts up and breaks the kiss with a digit drifting across my bottom lip, spreading my arousal.

"You've left a mess on my hand, Addie. It'd be rude not to clean it up."

I hold eye contact while my tongue darts out, the tip sliding across his finger. He smiles wickedly, prompting me to open my mouth wider.

Just as his finger goes to slide in, an icy feeling washes over me. It feels like the waves I was drifting in have turned angry and are ramming my body into the unforgiving rock.

My mouth stalls and my eyes dart over his shoulder. It's dark in here, save for the moonlight and bright sky, but it feels like I'm in a room filled with stadium lights.

A movement straight ahead turns my heart upside down and sends it crashing to the pit of my stomach.

He's out there.

I can't see him, or even make out his silhouette. But I know he is. I can feel him.

Noticing the change, Arch pulls away, breathing heavily and looking at me like he can't decide if he wants to ask if I'm okay or just keep going anyway.

"What's wrong?" he asks, grabbing my biceps in an attempt to grab my attention.

"Nothing," I rush out, bringing him closer. "Let's go upstairs to my room instead."

I'm no longer feeling cocky enough to fuck a man in front of a crazy person. The high from my release has completely dissipated my confidence.

But I'm too stubborn to stop. I want Arch. I just don't want any voyeurs while I take him.

"You don't want to get your pussy eaten under the stars?" he asks incredulously, looking at me as if I've grown a second head.

"I do, but I..." I trail off when another movement draws my attention away.

Arch steps forward, pressing against me and pulling my attention back to him. I have to crane my neck to see him properly and the sight is one I'll never forget.

"I think you should strip off your clothes and show me that sexy little body of yours. Then I want you to lie down, spread your legs, and let me clean up the mess you made."

An entirely embarrassing squeak slips out. A sound that immediately brings a smirk to his face and blood rushing to my cheeks, the creep momentarily forgotten.

Real smooth, dipshit.

I take a step back, heat slithering across my body as I drift my hands down my sides and hook both thumbs into my jeans.

Just as I go to slide them down my legs, a loud bang disturbs the charged silence and sends my heart flying to my throat. I yelp, startled and way too close to pissing my pants from the angry knocking.

Arch's head snaps towards the sound, clearly just as startled.

"Expecting company?" Arch asks, his voice a tad breathless.

My own erratic breathing is uneven as I say, "No."

It's fucking de ja vu, and even though I saw it coming this time, I'm incredibly close to stomping my foot like a child. Unlike with Greyson, I was actually enjoying myself.

He rushes back into the hallway and down towards the front door with me hot on his heels. I'm buttoning and zipping my pants as I go, already sensing that this night is over.

The hallway leads straight back to the foyer, the entryway to the right of the staircase. Pausing before the entrance, he turns to me and grabs ahold of me.

"Stay in the hallway. Whoever it is, I don't want them seeing you."

He hesitates, a weird look passing on his face. Before I can decipher it, he's speaking again, his voice strained. "Call the cops if shit goes south."

I'm not capable of stringing together a coherent sentence, the panic stealing my sense.

I should've told him I have a stalker, and I thought I saw something when we were in the sunroom, but everything happened too fast and now he's actively putting himself in danger.

The situation turns me on just as much as it terrifies me. I need to check myself into a mental hospital if I survive this night.

Because my shadow is *pissed*. Just like he was when Greyson was here, and I have no idea how dangerous this guy is, but he could be here to kill us both.

Especially now that he watched another man make me come with the very hand he threatened to cut off and put in my mailbox.

I drop my head in my hands, instant regret filling up my body like a waterfall in a lake. I'm bursting with it because if the stalker is as insane as he says he is, then

I just possibly got a man killed. Or at least brutally mutilated.

I hear the door creak open. My head snaps up in response.

"Come on out, fucker. I know you're out there," Arch threatens loudly.

Peeking around the corner, I watch Arch step outside. But not before he pulls a gun out. Eyes bulging, my mouth falls open and I wonder just who the hell I let in my house. He shuts the door behind him, the resounding click of the door echoing in my head.

Looks like I was wrong and did happen to find someone willing to kill for me. Jury's out on the fucking part, but if his foreplay is any indication, I think he would've done well in that department, too. Now more than ever, I want to kill this creep myself.

I finally find a man capable of satisfying me, and this asshole is ruining it.

God? I know we don't always agree on my life choices, but please don't let this poor man die because of me. I'll stop drinking. I mean it this time.

And I also pray that Arch has good aim. If I walk out and find the weirdo with a bullet in his skull, I won't mourn his death.

For the next several minutes, I hear nothing at all. It's hard to when my heart is pounding in my ears, but there would be no mistaking a gunshot.

Fuck, I can't handle this suspense. No longer capable of waiting, I rush over to the window beside the door and peek out.

Arch's car is still sitting in my driveway, but I don't see anything else. No bodies. Nothing.

Shooting a quick prayer to my least favorite person at the moment, I open the door slowly, listening for any sounds of distress or fighting.

When I'm greeted with nothing but the chirping of crickets, I open the door wider and step out.

The crunch of something under my foot cements my body into stone.

I close my eyes, another prayer on my tongue. If I stepped on a body part...
oh my god—I'm going to *freak*.

Taking a few short breaths, I move my foot away and look down.

A rose, the petals crumpled from my foot.

"Oh, fuck," I mutter, bending down to pick up the rose. The thorns are
snipped, preventing it from cutting me, but it doesn't matter—this rose has not
been deprived of one's pain.

Dripping off the petals and onto my boot is fresh blood. Arch is gone, and all
that's left of him is a bloody rose.

Yanking my phone out of my back pocket, I unlock it to call the cops, hands
trembling. The phone lights up and that's when I see another text—the one that
came through in the club, and the one I dutifully ignored.

**UNKNOWN: Don't feel guilty, baby. I don't make idle threats, so
consider this a lesson learned.**

Red and blue lights brighten the world before me, and the flashing colors
make me feel sick. Dread is pooling in the pit of my stomach while police officers
and dogs search the surrounding area.

An officer has confiscated the rose, yet the blood has stained my hands—
physically and metaphorically. I rub my fingers together, watching the dried blood
flake from my skin.

A tear escapes, but I quickly wipe it away.

I killed a man.

I brought him here knowing someone dangerous was lurking, and I did it anyway.

And now he's gone.

"Ma'am? I need to ask you a few questions," Sheriff Walters says, walking towards the porch steps that I'm currently sitting on.

I've known him since I was a child. He went to school with my mother, and they were good friends. Every now and again, she'd invite him over for dinner. He's always been kind. Quiet and soft-spoken, he always seemed more interested in listening than speaking.

He's a tall, built man, towering to at least six-seven. I think his family descends from giants because his father and brothers are just as freakishly large. His father was a sheriff, and his father before. Pretty sure a couple of his brothers are cops, too.

One big family of gigantic cops. Just what the world needs, right.

Scruff peppers Sheriff Walters's cheeks, and his brown eyes are tired and wary.

I already gave the run down to the responding officer, but when I told him a man was missing and I was gifted a bloody rose, he was more concerned about getting a search party going.

Considering dense woods surround me, it's likely the man took Arch on foot until he managed to get him into a car somewhere and drive off.

I sniff, wiping snot from my nose and nodding my head.

"Yeah, sure."

"Can you give me the name of the man who was with you here tonight?"

"Archibald Talaverra," I answer robotically. I guess Arch being pretentious and giving me his full name paid off. I almost smile, yet it's anything but funny.

The sheriff doesn't speak right away. I glance at him and note his bushy black eyebrows are raised high on his forehead.

"Talaverra, huh? This man might've done you a favor," he says, muttering the last part.

"What?" I squeak out, the corners of my eyes rounding.

The sheriff sighs and runs a hand through his thick, dark hair. In his younger years, I'm sure he was attractive. But now, silver is invading his hair, and wrinkles line the edges of his eyes and mouth. He looks aged and weathered, and over the years, I've watched his eyes grow dull and tired.

"The Talaverra's are known criminals," he informs me.

My eyes pop, and in that moment, I realize my mother did a terrible job raising me. My life choices are questionable at best lately.

I'm going to need to have a long hard talk with the She-Devil from above. She's been trying to kill me off, I think. And I'm starting to wonder if I should just let Her.

"What kind of criminals?"

Sheriff Walters twists his chapped lips to the side, seeming to contemplate what he wants to say.

"Nothing has been proven. Never any sufficient evidence. But they deal in cocaine primarily. Allegedly," he tacks on at the end, side-eyeing me. "What I can say is Archibald has been accused of domestic violence by his ex-wife several times. He's gotten out of the charges unscathed, of course. But he's known to be a very violent man."

I turn my head and cover my face with my hands.

Sheriff Walters pats my back awkwardly, assuming I'm crying. But my eyes are as dry as the Sahara Desert. I'm too angry to cry. Angry at myself for being so stupid and taking a random man home.

Angry for getting that man killed. A man that is connected to a dangerous family.

"Will his family come after me?"

"No," he responds sharply. "That family has a list of enemies a mile long. They're not going to concern themselves with a random girl. They might look into you, but when they don't find anything, they'll start looking into whoever they pissed off."

I nod my head, slightly assured by that.

"That is, if they don't find out about the rose."

My heart sinks like a rock into a well. I lift my head and look at him, catching onto his meaning.

"That rose was personal, Adeline. Do you know what it means?"

"I... I have a stalker. I've made several reports lately about my house being broken into and roses popping up everywhere I go."

The sheriff's brows scrunch.

"I looked into your file. There are no reports made about a stalker."

My spine snaps straight as shock blasts through me.

"What do you mean?" I ask, my voice shrill and angry. "I've made several!"

"Calm down," Sheriff Walters says, splaying his hands out in a gesture that matches his words. "I'll take a deeper look when I get back to the precinct. Can you tell me now what's been going on?"

Forcing my heart to slow, I relay everything that's been happening. With the random glasses of alcohol being drunk while I was home alone. The roses. And the notecard with the ominous threat.

Sheriff Walters listens tentatively, pulling out a notepad and taking notes as I speak. When I'm finished, I feel even more exhausted than before.

"I'll look into it. But Adeline? You understand that if the Talaverra's find out you have a stalker, they might place blame?"

I rear back, completely baffled that a cop is warning me that a criminal family could come after me. But he's never been one to sugarcoat or hide truths. On several occasions, my dad would ask details about certain things, and the sheriff would always divulge whatever he was allowed to.

There were a few times Mom had to snap at the two men for grisly conversations at the dinner table—in front of a child, no less. Sheriff Walters would apologize, but he never actually looked sorry.

"I'll do everything in my power to stop that from happening," he assures. Somehow, that doesn't make me feel any better in the slightest.

Sighing, I turn away and stare out into the dense trees, the red and blue lights flickering and creating a shadow dance party.

I nod my head, accepting his help for what it is. This man isn't going to be able to do a damn thing to stop a criminal from walking up to my doorstep.

Whether it's a crime family or a fucking stalker.

September 10th, 1944

I haven't seen Ronaldo in three days.

Three days of wondering where he is. If something happened to him. My thoughts spiraled.

John and I got in a fight. He says I've changed. That I'm no longer the woman he fell in love with. I'm distant now. When he wants to have sex, I'm not interested.

I've begun to feel like my marriage is wrong and dirty.

I've begun to feel like I'm cheating, but not on my husband. It feels like I'm cheating on my visitor.

There wasn't much I could say to assure my husband I still love him other than those three words. They've begun to feel empty when I say them.

Based off the hollowness in his eyes, those three words have begun to feel hollow to him, too.

I'm losing my husband. Slowly, but surely.

And I'm ashamed to admit that I don't mind that too much.

Chapter Nine
The Shadow

I've committed homicide. Cold-blooded murder. On many men who have worn different faces of the devil. And I've done it for various reasons. Whether they raped a child, killed an innocent, or destroyed someone's life that didn't deserve it.

But I've never killed someone out of jealousy.

First time for everything, I guess.

Archibald Talaverra has his lips on my girl and his hands down her pants. He's touching her. Fucking her with his fingers. Saying dirty things to her that elicits a pretty little blush of color to her cheeks.

And at that moment, I decided he wasn't going to live tonight.

The second I saw them together it took all of my control not to storm into that club and drag her ass out of there.

Because not only was another man trying to lay claim to my girl, but Archibald Talaverra is a fucking psychopath.

A real one.

He beat his ex-wife to a bloody pulp on several occasions and made her life a living hell when she finally decided to divorce his ass.

The woman is still in a psychiatric hospital receiving treatment for severe PTSD. He literally broke the woman, and while she spends her days trying to heal from his abuse, he spends his nights in clubs and picking out a different woman to take home and fuck.

Last I heard, he's not a nice fuck either. His form of rough play isn't pleasurable by any means when the woman walks away with a bloody nose and a busted lip.

The asshole *deserves* to die. And I'm happy to get the fucking honor.

This man and his family's crimes were small crumbs in the grand scheme of things. His family gets involved in petty crimes and sees themselves as Seattle's mafia. But they're ants compared to the fucking dinosaurs walking around in this city.

I've left them alone because there are much bigger fish to fry than low-life criminals who think they're crime lords. Their threat to humanity is minuscule compared to the people I track and kill, and until they start trading in more than just powder, they've never been on my radar.

Until now, that is.

There's no stopping Addie from opening her mouth and telling the cops she has a stalker. Doesn't matter that I've destroyed all evidence of her police reports.

And if the Talaverra's get wind of that, they'll kill Addie for something way out of her control. It doesn't matter that the family has enemies. Any possibility will be eliminated when they find that the heir of the Talaverra empire has been murdered.

So tonight, I'll rid Seattle of the little pests that have been congregating so I can focus back on the bigger things. Making Adeline mine and dismantling the pedophile rings.

I crack my neck, storm over to the front door, and bang my fist into the wood as hard as I can. I pour all my anger into it, not giving a fuck if I crack the wood beneath my fist. Just like the night that small dick asshole was here. Running out of the house naked with only one sock on, cursing Addie's name.

I was relieved to see Addie kicked him out herself. It was the only reason I didn't kill him that night. But it doesn't mean I didn't cut out his tongue for the names he called her.

She still isn't aware of that since I ran him out of town and forbade him from contacting her again.

I duck back in the shadows beyond the porch.

I know Archie's type. He'll come storming out, ever the savior for the damsel in distress. Ready to take on the big bad wolf like he's not the old granny about to get eaten.

Really, he's just a rabid fox posing as a wolf. His bite hurts, but nothing compared to that of a real predator.

Right on cue, Archie whips the door open, his hands wrapped around a gun.

"Come on out, fucker. I know you're out there."

Come get me, Archie.

He hesitates on the doorstep, sensing the danger residing in the shadows.

But after a few moments, he develops a vagina and charges out the door and down the porch steps. His head turns, his eyes widening as he catches a glimpse of my face with a single red rose in my mouth, the stem caught between my teeth.

I bare my teeth, a feral grin that would chill even the devil. Before he can react, I dart out, grab his arm and twist him around. My hand slaps over his mouth as I pull his back to my front.

Twirling my knife, I stab him twice in the stomach. Both precise areas that won't cut through vital organs. He grunts beneath my hand, the shock rendering him mostly silent.

Before the situation catches up to him and he starts shouting, I push him off of me and deliver one sharp punch to the back of the head.

Done in a matter of ten seconds, not a single peep out of his mouth.

My arm snaps out and I catch him by the back of his suit jacket before he can face-plant the cold, muddy ground. Out cold and bleeding profusely.

I need to staunch the wounds before he loses too much blood.

But first, I slide the rose from my mouth, and dip the petals in the crimson spilling from his wounds.

Can't have my little mouse thinking there aren't consequences for letting another man touch what's mine. She'll find out soon enough that I don't make idle threats.

I rest his body against the porch for a second while I walk up and throw the rose at her doorstep. I'm too pissed to do much else.

And then I grab his body and start the brief trek through the woods where my Mustang awaits. By the time the cops get here, it'll be too late.

A blood trail will lead them to tire tracks, and they might be able to narrow down the make and model based on the tread impressions, but the evidence will run cold after that. It will all be destroyed soon enough.

The cops won't know which direction to look. And Archie's family will assume their enemies caught up to him.

And they wouldn't be wrong. They just won't be able to guess who until I'm standing in front of them with a knife in their necks.

"Let me the fuck go, you fucking prick. You think I'm someone to mess with? Do you have any fucking idea who I am and who my family is?"

His mouth is going to be stapled shut in point two seconds if he keeps running it, that I *do* know. I relay this to him, and he answers with a hyena laugh.

I turn and clock the fucker in the mouth, all the while keeping my Mustang straight.

Colorful words follow, but they're no brighter than the blood pouring out with them.

Pretty boy isn't so pretty now.

He's going to experience a lot worse once I get back to my place. He laid his mouth and hands on my girl, and there's consequences for silly mistakes like that.

He woke up about five minutes into the drive. Two strips of fabric from his shirt are tied tightly across each stab wound on his abdomen. His hands and feet are hog-tied—there's not a chance of him slipping free of those.

I've had too much practice.

He's been running his mouth since the moment he awoke, and it's been grinding my gears into dust. He throws out empty threats like bullets, but instead, they're paper in the wind. None of them make an impact. In fact, they don't land anywhere near me.

It's the mention of Addie that sends me into a murderous rage.

"Come on, man. Are you this worked over a piece of ass? Her voice may be cut out for porn, and her pussy tight as fuck, but shit, you can find that in other bitches too. I've fucked plenty of them."

What was going to be a fairly slow death is now going to be the slowest death to ever happen since the dawn of humanity.

It was bad enough that he spoke of my girl in such a disgusting manner, but then he went and topped it off by implying Addie isn't anything special.

She's the first of her kind to exist, and there will never be another like her.

I pull into the driveway leading into my warehouse. It's a smaller structure, used to manufacture cameras for some shitty company that went out of business within five years.

The building was foreclosed on, and I bought it for dirt cheap. And then spent hundreds of thousands of dollars transforming it into an impenetrable fortress.

I converted the main floor into my living space with state-of-the-art security. An ant will not be able to find its way into the building without me knowing about it.

The second floor is my workspace. Dozens of computers and illegal technology that make it possible to do what I do fill the space. And the basement is where I handle all of my business—meaning where I take the pedophiles to torture and kill them when they have information I need.

I built an underground garage that drives straight into the basement. Makes for an easier haul when I got a six-foot-two dickhead to carry to the table.

I'm a big man, but I'm just as capable of throwing out my back as the next person. I'm still a human fucking being.

Shutting the garage door behind me, I turn the car off and twist around.

I sigh at the sight. Usually, I'm more prepared when I kidnap people. They go in the trunk, and I don't have to worry about getting my car dirty. But by the time I carried him back to my car, I was in a hurry and just threw him back there.

He's already got blood everywhere, and I'm going to have to pay my cleaning crew extra to get those stains out. With that amount of blood, anyone would ask questions.

But they get paid way too much to ask stupid questions that'll get them killed.

"We can do this the easy way or the hard way. I can knock your ass out, or you can be a good little bitch and stay still."

His bloody mouth forms around the word *fuck,* and it doesn't take a genius to know what word is going to come out next. I punch him in the nose before he can get the first syllable out.

The crunch of bone beneath my fist is nearly orgasmic. By the time I'm pulling my fist away, blood is squirting from his broken nose. He spits, and a tooth flies out of his mouth and onto my floor.

I'm going to shove my foot up his ass just for that.

I get out, round the car, and swing open the door.

He starts protesting, but the words become garbled when I grab him by the collar and drag his ass out. With his limbs tied up, he feels every drop and bump as I drag his body out of the car and haul him towards the table.

He squirms like a worm on a hook, and I can tell by the panicked look on his face that he has that feeling. The sinking feeling that his life is balancing on the edge, and I'm about to fucking Sparta kick him off.

Despite his struggles, I wrangle him on the surgical table, and systematically untie specific ropes so I can strap him to the table while simultaneously keeping him immobile.

He looks over and sees a dead Fernando lying on the other table.

After I saw Sicily off, Michael dropped Fernando off at my place while I went to Parsons Manor to snoop around. Addie and her friend were leaving, so I followed them to a club.

It took all my willpower not to put a bullet in every man's head that grinded their dick against her ass. I decided to go home and take care of business before I did something stupid and actually kidnap her.

While I interrogated Fernando, I set up a monitor and kept an eye on Addie through the club's cameras. I'll admit, my torture methods became a lot bloodier once I saw Archie lead her up the stairs.

I got the information I needed from Fernando. Their process for extracting girls, names of some of the mules, and the name of who Fernando reports to. Turns out the guy is in Ohio, so I'm letting one of the other mercenaries handle him. He'll get the information on his boss and work our way up the chain.

The mules have already been located and targeted, so after I'm done disposing of these two fucks, they'll be getting a sniper shot to the head, then on to Archie's family.

"The fuck, man?" Archie spits, both terror and disgust evident in his tone. Fernando's face has started to bloat.

I shrug, unbothered. "I have a lot of bodies to dispose of tonight. It'll be easier to dispose of them all at the same time."

"Look, whatever my family did, we can work out a deal," Archie negotiates, his words a little garbled and misshapen from his broken teeth. His nose has already swollen and bruised, along with his split, puffy lips. He looks as if he went five rounds in a boxing match with his hands tied behind his back.

"I don't have any connections with your family," I say calmly. "At least not until now."

He's silent for a beat, staring at me incredulously as his brain processes that I'm not an enemy of the Talaverra's.

"Then why the fuck are you doing this? Because of that fucking girl?" he asks, his voice hysteric.

I lean close, letting him get a good look at my scarred face. If it's not the scars that warn people away, the deadly glint in my eyes usually does the trick.

"She fucking wanted me. Not my fault that your girl doesn't want you."

I sigh and straighten. I'm not going to bother explaining myself to this prick. He won't understand my obsession, and I don't give a shit enough to want him to.

What he doesn't know is that the minute I properly introduce myself to Adeline Reilly, she won't be able to think of anyone else.

I will devour her from the inside out, until every intake of breath will only stoke the inferno I've created inside her. Like oxygen feeding a fire, I will consume every inch of her sweet little body until she will think of nothing else but how to get me deeper inside of her.

She'll fear me at first, but that fear will only ignite her. And I will be all too fucking happy to deliver the pain when she gets too close to the flame.

Next to me is a tray of utensils lined up neatly. Without looking away, I grab the first tool my hand lands on.

A serrated screwdriver. Specially made for torturing. The military uses shit like this, unbeknownst to the public. Not that the government would ever willingly tell the country that they torture war criminals often and use pretty fucked up methods to do so.

The public isn't ignorant by any means, but they sure as fuck don't know the extent of the depravity of our government either.

His eyes widen comically when he catches sight of the screwdriver.

I smile. "Haven't gotten to use this one yet," I observe, twisting the screwdriver and giving us both a good view of each sharp point. Once this sucker goes in, it's going to hurt even worse taking it out.

I can't fucking wait.

"Bro, let's talk about this. That girl is *not* worth you killing me over. Do you realize what my family will do to you? To *her*?"

"Did you really think I was going to kill just you?" I volley back, quirking a brow to show how unimpressed I am with his warning.

His face turns beet red, like the apples my mother used to pluck for me from the orchard as a kid. Always loved those things.

Threats spill from his mouth, fueled by rage from his family's untimely fate.

"You're doing this because I almost fucked a girl?! I didn't even fucking know she was yours," he bellows, veins popping from his forehead.

Not a pretty sight.

In response, I stab the screwdriver straight into his stomach. He gapes at me, his mouth parted in shock. A moment passes, and then he's coughing up blood. An array of emotions filter through his eyes. Pretty sure I see the five stages of grief in there, too.

I bend down and grit out through my teeth, "What you and every sad motherfucker that even looks in her direction will learn is *no one* is safe when it comes to her. I don't care if you only breathed in her direction the wrong way, you will fucking die."

"You're fucking crazy," he chokes out, looking down at the screwdriver sticking out of his abdomen in disbelief. Definitely hit vital organs this time.

Slowly, I pull the screwdriver out, the suctioning noise quiet against the backdrop of his scream.

The unbridled anger pulsating through me is relentless—unstoppable. And the image of his hand in her pants, kissing her, whispering shit into her ear, and making her come. It all fuels the violent storm in my head. I plunge the screwdriver back in when the image flickers of her face. *Wanting* him back. Climaxing for a shitstain like him. I'll have to erase his touch from her.

And soon.

I rip out the screwdriver and take a deep breath. I have to remind myself she doesn't know me yet. She doesn't understand what true need is. Not yet, but she will. Because she's going to hate the way she needs me. She's going to fight it, rebel against the craving and attempt to search for something else that makes her feel even a fraction of what I will.

She'll never find it.

And I won't let her try.

Cracking my neck, I take another deep, calming breath. My temper got the best of me. I'm not usually a reactive person, but I've already accepted the fact that my little mouse brings out new feelings in me, too.

"How many women have you hurt, Archie?" I ask, licking my lips and circling his body until I disappear from view.

It's an intimidation tactic for the weak-minded. Makes them nervous when I vanish behind them for that brief moment. Their minds get away from them as they anticipate what I'm going to do. And then they get a little relief when they see me again.

Just to repeat the process.

It's torture in itself. Not knowing if I'm going to strike. Or when.

"Do *not* call me Archie," he snaps, seething as I stand behind him. He's tense.

I circle back to the front and his shoulders loosen, just an inch.

"You're evading the question, Archie," I point out, deliberately using the name. He snarls at my defiance but doesn't reply.

His mother always called him Archie. Up until she died of breast cancer when he was ten years old. That's when his father lost it and started dealing drugs to make money to pay off all the medical bills and funeral expenses.

He raised his children to be cold and ruthless, and Archie here never let anyone call him by his mother's nickname without stabbing them.

He's stabbed a lot of people for calling him that name, including his best friend Max. His buddy complained about it a time or two in a bar Jay frequents.

"Don't make me ask again," I warn, my voice lowering to convey just how serious I am.

"I don't know," he shouts, frustrated. "A couple, I guess. The fuck does it matter?"

"I read up on your ex-wife," I say, ignoring the stupid fucking question. "You beat her so badly, she was barely recognizable when she was taken to the hospital. Evidence indicated that you broke a tequila bottle against her face and then stabbed her with it. Not to mention the countless broken bones and bruises. You nearly killed her."

Archie sniffs, not the slightest bit of remorse reflecting in his cold eyes. The narcissistic assholes never are. Somehow, they twist it in their head that the victim deserved it and whatever injuries inflicted upon them were their own fault.

"She was cheating on me," he replies petulantly. Pouting like a child that didn't get a birthday cake.

"Did you cheat on her first?"

"That doesn't matter," he snaps back. "She's the wife and I make the money. If I feel like buying a stripper for a night, that's my goddamn right. All she ever did was sit at home on her lazy ass and spend my money."

I nod, accepting his answer for what it is.

"Would you have hurt Addie?" I ask after a pregnant pause.

He scoffs. "I would've fucked her how I like to fuck. If she ends up with a couple of bruises, so what? Bitches like that shit. They like it rough."

Renewed anger punches me in the chest. And it takes all my self-control not to plunge this screwdriver in his eye right then and there.

Archie wouldn't know how to have proper rough sex if he was given a fucking manual for it. He hurts women because he enjoys it. He doesn't know how to push women to the edge of pain and pleasure, balancing between the two and making them desperate for more.

He just hurts them. By the time he's done, the girl is thoroughly bruised and traumatized—maybe even bleeding. And he's walking away with a satisfied smirk on his face, as if he was the first man to prove a woman orgasming isn't actually a myth.

"You didn't hurt Addie," I observe, waiting for the answer I know he'll give. He isn't desperate enough yet—scared enough. He's still attempting to put on a false bravado act and die with dignity. But that will change very soon.

He smirks. "You gotta relax them first. The plans I had for her…" he trails off, licking his lips vulgarly. "Her cries would've been such a beautiful song."

Again, I nod my head in acceptance of the answer. I accept it because it fuels exactly what I have planned for him.

And I'm very much going to embody his method for sex. I will enjoy hurting him and making him bleed, and him? He will wish he had never met Adeline Reilly.

Chapter Ten
The Manipulator

"Have you heard anything?" I interrogate, my phone growing slick from the persistent anxiety since Arch went missing from my doorstep.

"No one has been able to locate him," Daya answers through the phone. She's been looking into Arch's disappearance herself since I told her what happened last night, never one to rely on the police to solve anything.

But Daya doesn't have much to go off of. She hacked into Arch's known enemy's systems—their cameras, phones, laptops, and the GPS on their cars. Just like we suspected, they had no connection to Arch's disappearance—at least not that we could find.

It was my shadow who took him. And without having any idea who he is, there's really no way to find Arch.

"I can't believe this is happening. I practically got this man killed," I say, tears pricking at my eyes.

"Babe, I hate to say this, but I don't think that's the worst thing that could've happened. I think this guy would've really hurt you. The things he did to his ex-wife… they're unspeakable. He wasn't a good man. None of those guys were…" she trails off, and I don't need her words to know she's thinking about Luke.

She said they had an incredible night together, but she ghosted him the second she found out what kind of guy Arch is—*was*.

She said anyone who is friends with a man like Arch isn't a nice man themselves.

Can't really disagree with that, either.

I take a deep breath. "I know, you're right. I guess I just don't like that he was hurt—maybe killed—because of *me*. I would've much preferred one of his many enemies caught up with him."

"Yeah, that would've been the best-case scenario," she allows.

"The best-case scenario would've been a wild night of hot sex with a hot guy where I orgasm multiple times and then send him off on his merry way," I interrupt.

She pauses a beat before saying, "Yeah, you're right. But that's not what would've happened. Not with this guy's history. He's violent."

"Well, apparently, so is my stalker."

"I know, which is why I'm hooking you up with a security system. You're not going to be another statistic, not more than you already are. If you die, I have to follow, and I'm quite attached to my body. God gave me a good one this lifetime."

I roll my eyes at her dramatics, especially because she's not even religious.

"Okay, just bill me for it," I agree. I like the idea of having cameras in my house. It makes me feel better about someone sneaking around when I can't see them.

"I'll be over later to set them up."

Getting cameras will be the first thing to happen in a month that gives me any semblance of safety. No matter how fragile it is.

I'm just finishing up another chapter when I hear the USPS truck pull up. The mailman has always been a pretty nice guy. He doesn't stick around long and spends most of his time glancing around nervously.

The last time I asked him about it, he said something evil happened here.

And since a man went missing off my doorstep last night, I'd say several evil things have happened here.

I open the door just as he's dropping off several cases of books. I have to sign these and get them shipped out to my readers.

Eight large boxes later, the mailman is panting, sweat running down his light brown face.

"Thank you, Pedro. Sorry for all the boxes," I say, waving awkwardly.

He waves a hand in acknowledgment before getting back in his truck and shooting off.

I sigh, staring at the boxes with a look of dread. These are going to be a bitch to haul in. I step out, but my foot knocks into the corner of something heavy.

Looking down, I notice a small, lidded cardboard box. There's no shipping label on it, which means Pedro didn't drop this one off.

My heart plummets, a burst of anxiety hitting me right in the gut.

I don't know why, but my eyes dart towards the woods as if I'm actually going to see someone standing there. I don't. Of course, I don't.

Sucking in a deep breath, I pick up the box. And then nearly drop it when I see a smear of blood where the box was sitting.

"Oh, fuck. Fuck, fuck, fuckity fuck. God? Please don't allow this to happen to me on this fine Sunday morning. Please let me not find what I think I'm going to find," I pray out loud, my voice cracking as a drop of blood lands on my toe.

Hands shaking, I set the box back down and just panic. There's a drop of blood on my toe. I knew there was blood on my hands already, but now my toes? I can't take this.

Before I can think about what I'm doing, I tip the lid off with my foot.

Hands.

Severed hands are in the box, just like I feared.

"Oh, fuck me. Fuck this shit."

I twirl and run back in the house, scrambling to find my phone to call Daya.

The line rings for all of two seconds before she answers.

"I'll be there in a few hou—"

"*Daya.*"

"What happened?" she asks sharply.

"A hand. And another hand. Two of them. In a box. On my porch."

She curses, but my panic mutes the sound.

"Don't do anything yet. Wait till I get there," Daya orders. "Go take a couple of shots and wait for me."

I nod, despite that she can't see me. But it doesn't stop me from nodding again and then hanging up without a word.

I do exactly as she says. Taking two shots of vodka to calm my nerves. And then take deep breaths, slowly, in and out until my racing heart calms.

The fucker actually did it. He sent me Arch's hands. A part of me knew he wouldn't lie, but somehow, I didn't believe it anyway.

"Shit," I mutter, dropping my head low between my shoulders, balancing my weight on the edge of the counter.

Twenty minutes later, Daya shows up, her car ripping through the driveway, based on the squealing tires.

Her car door slams shut. By the time I get to the door, she's approaching my gift still sitting on the porch, her gaze riveted on the grotesque sight.

"This guy is fucking deranged," Daya spits, picking up the box to inspect the hands closer. "Definitely Arch's too. He's got that stupid ass star tattoo on his thumb."

I blink, curious how she even knows that, but still too much in shock to open my mouth and ask.

"There's a note in here," she mumbles, plucking out a piece of paper covered in blood. Carefully, she opens it. It takes her two seconds to read it before she's sighing and handing it over.

Hesitantly, I reach out and grab the note by the corner that doesn't have blood on it.

While I will enjoy punishing you for every time you call the police, let's hold off this time. Wouldn't want to have to hurt them next, little mouse.

Is this guy shitting me? He's going to *punish* me? Don't you think sending me fucking *severed hands* is punishment enough, asshole?

"He's seriously going to threaten to kill a cop?" I hiss. Daya swallows, her eyes darting to the hands.

"I think you need to listen this time," she says quietly. I look up at her, having come to the same conclusion. This guy is dangerous. Very dangerous.

As much as I *want* the police to handle this, there are two problems. I don't have any faith whatsoever that they'd be able to catch the guy. And secondly, I don't want anyone else to get hurt because of me.

I don't know if I will be able to bear it.

"I don't know what to do, Daya," I whisper, my voice cracking. Daya sets the box down and rushes to me, enveloping me in a tight hug.

"I have a friend coming over to help install the security cameras and alarm system. Listen, normally, I would say call the cops anyway. But I don't know, Addie. You know how I feel about cops as it is, but I truly don't believe they will be able to help you. I have some connections, and maybe we can hire a personal bodyguard or something."

I'm shaking my head before she can finish her last sentence. "So he can die, too?"

She gives me a droll look. "This isn't just going to be some guy off the streets, Addie. Whatever you're up against, they can't be more badass than a trained killer, right?"

"Maybe," I concede. "But I don't know about any of that yet. Having a bodyguard follow me everywhere just makes me feel like a damsel in distress."

I can tell by the look on her face that she thinks I'm being stupid. I mean, I *do* have a hand-chopping, possible murderer stalking me. But then what? I have some random guy following me around until my shadow is caught, and who knows if that'll ever happen.

I grind my teeth, overwhelmed with frustration. I don't want to live my life with an extra attachment—an extra limb. And in both scenarios, I have one. One is there to protect me, while the other is there to… I don't know. Hurt me? Love me?

Either way, I don't want either of them.

"Do you think Arch is dead?" I ask, failing to keep the tremble out of my voice.

She twists her lips. "I don't know. It's definitely a possibility. But it's also possible he chopped off his hands and let him go as a warning. We won't know until Arch either shows up… or doesn't."

I nod. "I'll let you know about the bodyguard thing. Let's just see how this alarm system thing works out first."

"Okay, in the meantime, I'm going to dispose of these hands. I'll be back in an hour, and then we're getting hammered."

My eyes widen. "Daya, you don't have to do that. This is morbid enough, and I don't want you to have to—"

The severity of her expression stops me short, my words trailing off.

"I see worse every day, Addie. Go inside, I'll be back soon."

Swallowing, I nod and turn towards my door, shooting one last lingering look at my best friend's retreating form, wondering what the hell she's involved in if she sees worse than chopped up body parts every day.

"They're all dead." The words are a bomb going off in my ear, like that judge in *Law Abiding Citizen.*

"What?"

"Arch's entire family was reported dead. His father, two brothers, an uncle, and two cousins. I don't know the details because the crime was fucking smooth as hell. No witnesses. No evidence. Nothing."

"Oh my God. Do you think it was the stalker?"

She sighs, and even through the phone, I know she's twirling her nose ring. "That's a pretty hefty crime, but not impossible. There's been word that when Arch was reported missing after you called the police, Connor started throwing some serious accusations around to their rivals. The police seem to think it was them, but with lack of evidence, there's no one to pin it on."

I squeeze my eyes shut, a headache blooming in my temple. "So the stalker *did* kill Arch, then."

"Probably," she hedges. "If Arch made it back home before the family was wiped, he would've said who mutilated him and Connor wouldn't have gone off on their rivals. So, I think it's plausible that Connor's accusations are what got the rest of them killed."

There's so many emotions swirling in my head, and I can't make heads or tails of what I'm feeling. I'm fucking horrified that my shadow murdered somebody.

But he was an evil man.

That shouldn't matter, should it? And to be perfectly honest, I think his true intentions for killing Arch were because he touched me, not because of his crimes.

"Honestly, Daya, I'm a little relieved. Arch's family won't come for me now, and I feel so selfish saying that."

"Then we're both selfish bitches because I'm happy as hell." I snort at her enthusiasm. "Look, the Talaverra's were bad people. Arch wasn't the only one with a bad history. Connor had rape allegations against him, and their father must've taught them how to rape and beat a woman because his rap sheet... even worse."

I nod my head, forgetting she can't see it.

"I certainly won't mourn their deaths," I mutter.

After that, we hang up, both needing to get some work done, but my mind keeps wandering.

Truly, I'm not sad to hear about the fate of the Talaverra's, but there is still that niggling worry in the back of my head that my shadow is the one who delivered it to them.

It's been a week since Arch went missing and still no sign of my shadow. Not to say he still isn't sneaking around, but he hasn't made his presence known.

Daya's friend set up my new alarm system and cameras, and I'm ashamed of how obsessive I've been with checking them since.

The naïve part of me is hoping now that I have a security system, he'll stay away. But while I make a lot of stupid decisions—and I mean *a lot*—I'm not stupid enough to believe he isn't going to show up here soon.

I stretch, groaning as my muscles crack, the barstool in my kitchen doing little to support my back while I write. I've been working on a new fantasy novel about a girl escaping slavery, and the deadline I set for myself is quickly approaching.

Right as I begin typing again, a creak from above snags my attention. The sound immediately has my heart kickstarting into overdrive. I pause, listening for any more noises. Several beats pass with no disturbance. The only sounds are the furnace and the low pattering of rain against the window.

Just when I begin to think I'm losing my mind, I hear another creak from directly above me.

Holding my breath, I slowly get up from the stool, the metal legs screeching against the tile. I wince, the eruption loud and unpleasant.

Well, goddammit, good thing I didn't become a spy. I would so die on the job.

Quickly, I walk over to the silverware drawer, slide it open and grab the butcher knife. Holding this weapon is starting to become a daily routine, and I'm becoming bored with it.

I don't stop to think about what I'm doing. I clamber towards the stairs, whip around the railing, and quietly make my way up the steps. Briefly, I consider the movie title of the horror movie they'd make after my life.

Making my way down the hall, I peek into open rooms, holding the knife out in front of me. The hallway is long and wide, with five of the bedrooms up here.

Just as I step out of one of the empty bedrooms, I hear a small thump. It sounded like it came from my room.

With bated breath, I creep down the hallway, holding all my weight on my toes.

No fucking idea how ballerinas do it.

My bedroom door is shut. Adrenaline steadily releases into my bloodstream, like injecting heroin in a vein.

It wasn't shut before.

I stand outside my door, staring at it as if it's going to grow a face and warn me of what's inside. That'd totally be beneficial right now.

Because not knowing what I will find on the other side is the worst part. That's what makes my heart pound viciously in my chest and tightens my lungs.

Will I open the door and see the shadow from my nightmares? Going through my things?

My eyes widen, realization hitting that the sick fuck could be going through my underwear drawer. The thought sends a tsunami of anger washing over me, and before I can consider the ramifications, I barrel through the door.

No one is inside.

I charge through the room, checking every corner before storming out onto the balcony. No one.

Chest heaving, I whip around and scope out the room, trying to figure out where an intruder could hide. My eyes pause on the closet.

I aim for it, sliding the door open so forcefully, it nearly comes off the track. My arm lashes through the clothing, searching for someone that isn't here.

But I know I heard something.

My breath catches when I turn, and my eyes sweep across my bed, forcing me to backtrack. Right under my bed is Gigi's diary, lying on the floor and flipped open.

That must've been what the thump was, but how the fuck did it fall? My blood freezes when I look on my nightstand and see the diary I've been reading still there.

I had put Gigi's other two diaries in my nightstand for safekeeping until I got to them. So how did one of them end up on the floor?

With another suspicious sweep of the room, I walk over to the book and pick it up, leaving it open. Skimming my eyes across the page, I pause when I take in the words.

Judging by the dates, it's the last book she wrote in before she died. The three books span across two years, Gigi having died on May 20th, 1946.

The book was open on an entry two days before Gigi's murder, May 18th. She's expressing fear, but she doesn't say of who. Clearly, she's terrified of something. My heart thumps harder as I ingest her rushed words.

She talks about someone being after her. Scaring her. Who, though? Forgetting about everything else around me, I sit on the edge of the bed and flip to the beginning.

With each passing entry, her words become clipped and fearful. Before I know it, I'm nearly ripping through the pages, trying to find any inkling of who her murderer is.

But on the very last page, her last words are: *he came for me*. No lipstick kiss on the page. Just those four daunting words. I turn the page, looking to see if there's more. Desperate for it, actually.

There are no more entries, but I do notice something strange.

A jagged piece of paper sticks out from the spine. I trace my fingers over it. A page has been ripped out of the diary.

Did she write down something important and decide it wasn't worth the risk of anyone knowing? All three of these books are risqué, full of cheating and sex. Above all, full of love for a man that stalked her.

I look up, staring ahead but seeing nothing.

When Mom left, she left with the hopes that I'd listen to her advice and move out of Parsons Manor. But when she walked out of that door, the sickening smell of her Chanel perfume lingering in my nostrils, I decided I didn't *want* to move.

Did Nana have a weird attachment to the manor? Possibly. But if this house meant so much to her, it doesn't feel right to give it away. Even if that means I have an unhealthy attachment, too.

And now, that decision is only solidifying. There's no way this book could've ended up on the floor. Yet it did. And I don't know if it was Nana's doing, or Gigi's, but someone wanted me to read these entries.

Do they want me to find the person who killed Gigi? God, I can't imagine how difficult it would've been to solve a murder in the 40s with such underwhelming technology. Is her murderer even still alive?

Maybe it doesn't matter if he is or not. Maybe Gigi wants justice for her murder, and for the man that ended her life too soon to be exposed—dead or alive.

I exhale a shaky breath, my fingers tracing the four daunting words.

He came for me.

"Can you please explain to me why you're making me hack into the PD's database to look at crime photos of your murdered grandmother?" Daya asks from beside me, her fingers hovering over her mouse.

I'm tempted to reach over and push her finger down for her so she'll finally click the damn button. Once she does, it'll pull up Gigi's records.

I sigh. "I told you already. She was murdered. And I think I know who did it, I just... well, I don't know anything about him but his first name, and the fact that he stalked her."

Daya eyes me, but eventually relents. She clicks the mouse—finally—and pulls up Gigi's crime scene photos.

They're pretty disturbing. Gigi had been found in her bed, with her throat slit and a cigarette burn on her wrist. They never found the killer due to insufficient evidence.

A lot of blame pointed towards the officers that responded to the call, citing that they trampled all over the crime scene. Evidence was lost or contaminated by the police force, and fingers were pointed, but ultimately, no one was held accountable for it.

Daya clicks through the photos, each one more disturbing than the last. Close up pictures of the wound on her neck. The burn on her wrist. Gigi's face, frozen in fear as her dead eyes stare back at the camera. And her signature lipstick smeared across her cheek.

I swallow, the sight a stark contrast to the picture that concealed her safe. Her wide, smiling face so full of life and fire. And then her dead, cold body frozen in fear.

Whoever had killed her had scared her pretty bad. A niggling feeling tugs at the back of my head. Based on Gigi's entries, her stalker didn't scare her. In fact, it sounds like he did the exact opposite.

I shake the thought from my head. He was obsessed with her, and there were several entries nearing her death that indicated they weren't getting along due to his jealousy over her marriage.

His obsession must've been of the deadly variety.

Daya then clicks over to the police reports. Not just the ones released to the public, but documents from the investigation that were confidential.

Technically, the investigation is still open. It's just gone cold.

We took our time reading through the documents, but in the end, the only thing we learned was the time of death, and the fact that Gigi fought and fought hard.

My great-grandfather, John, was immediately ruled out due to having several eyewitness reports seeing him at the grocery store during the time of the murder.

I bite my lip, the thought eliciting guilt, yet I can't help but think it.

What if he was still an accomplice?

I shake the thought from my head. No. There's no way. My great-grandfather loved Gigi, despite the fact that their marriage was falling apart at the seams.

It *had* to be her stalker.

It's the obvious explanation. The stalker gained Gigi's trust—somehow—made her feel comfortable enough that she relaxed around him. And then he killed her.

"There has to be significance to that ripped-out page," I murmur, growing frustrated from the lack of evidence. I could never be a detective and do this shit every day.

"Maybe the killer did it," Daya guesses, scrolling mindlessly through the pictures.

I twist my lips, considering it before I shake my head. "No, that wouldn't make sense. Why would they rip only one page out and not just dispose of all the journals? They're all incriminating. Whether it was the stalker or someone else, Gigi speaks of being hunted. And if it wasn't the stalker, then they could've easily pinned the blame on Ronaldo and been done with it. Whoever it was, they can't have known about these. Gigi had to have ripped the page out before hiding the books."

Daya nods her head. "You're right. Whatever is on that missing page is important, but we can't rely on that."

"We need to figure out who Ronaldo is," I conclude.

Daya nods her head, appearing a little exhausted from the thought. Can't say I'm not either.

"And we have nothing to go off of. There's no mention of his last name. Barely any physical description."

"He had a scar on his hand," I offer, recalling mentions of those things in Gigi's diary. "And wore a gold ring."

"Did she mention his social standing? Job? Anything that could lead us to who he might be?"

I twist my lips, "I'll have to look again. I remember she said he was involved in something dangerous, but I haven't gotten the chance to read through everything yet."

She nods and heaves out a weighted sigh. "Until then, I think we're going to be stuck until we find Ronaldo or that missing page."

I sigh, my shoulders drooping. "That could literally be anywhere, or it not even exist anymore."

Daya looks at me then, sympathy in her eyes. "We'll keep trying different avenues. I'm just as invested as you at this point."

I shoot her a grateful smile before looking back at the crime scene photos.

This was undoubtedly a crime of passion, and if I know anything, stalkers tend to be deeply passionate about their obsessions.

I bolt upright, a gasp lingering on the tip of my tongue. Sweat coats my skin, and my hair is plastered to my cheeks, neck, and down my back.

I can't remember what I was dreaming about. But something woke me.

Heart pounding, my sleep-riddled eyes drift over the dark room. Just enough light from the moon filters in through the balcony doors. The furniture casts shadows across the room, creating figures that aren't really there. I don't mind the phantoms dancing across my floor, but whatever woke me has a presence. A *soul*.

The floorboards creak from my right, outside my bedroom door. My head snaps in the direction, and I suck in a sharp breath. The hair rises on the back of my neck, like a scared dog backed in a corner.

I hold the air in my lungs, careful not to make a sound should I hear the noise again. Stillness settles around the house. Too still. My fingers clench the duvet on my lap as my heart rate increases.

Someone is outside my room.

But how?

How the fuck did he make it past the alarm system?

Another creak followed by heavy footsteps. A methodical walk, slow and purposeful. Intentional.

I slowly slip out of bed and tiptoe backwards until my back presses against the cool stone wall, creating distance between the intruder outside my door and me.

Despite my best efforts, I release a shaky breath. My chest heaves with small, fast pants as the footsteps come closer.

I'm frozen. My back is pressed so deeply into the stone that I'm becoming a part of it, preventing me from moving. From hiding.

The footsteps stop outside my door.

Desperately, my eyes search across the expanse of the room. They land on a lone screwdriver sitting on the chest at the end of the bed. I had carelessly tossed it aside after assembling my vanity chair, and now it sits there like a beacon of hope. Possibly the only thing that could keep me alive tonight.

Move, Addie. Goddammit, MOVE!

My limbs unlock, and I rush to the screwdriver, gripping the tool in my slick hands. My eyes are glued to the door handle, waiting for the knob to turn. Quietly, I slink over to the door and mold myself to the wall.

I'll wait for him to come in and then attack. Hopefully I can get the screwdriver lodged in his neck before he knows what's happening.

So with bated breath, I wait. The knob doesn't turn, but I can feel deep in my bones that someone is out there. Are they waiting for me? They're out of their mind if they think I'll open that door. I suppose they must be, though, if they're breaking into my house and lingering outside my room.

The longest minute of my life passes. It feels like it's been hours before I hear another creak. And then I hear the footsteps retreat. Further and further they fade, until eventually I no longer hear them at all.

My ears prick, and just like I suspected, I hear my front door shut. A soft click that feels like thunder in a silent house. Instantly, I rip open the door and run across the hall into the bedroom with windows that face the driveway.

Hunkering down, I peek through the curtains and wait for the person to emerge from the front porch.

It feels like an eternity passes, but I imagine it's only been seconds before I see movement. An audible cry leaves my lips when a large man saunters off the steps and walks out onto my driveway. He's wearing all black, with a deep hood settled over his head.

He's tall—very tall, but not bulky. Even beneath his clothing, I can tell his body is fucking lethal. Lean, but packed with muscle. His hoodie clings to his body, showing off his broad shoulders, thick arms, and trimmed waist.

God, he could crush me if he wanted to. His hand looks big enough to cover the entirety of my face. Or wrap around my neck.

Would he do it to cause pain or pleasure? Does my shadow want to hurt me or love me?

He stills, his back facing me. He can feel me watching him, just like I felt him outside my door.

I find myself curling deeper into the shadows, out of sight. My heart is still racing, though now for an entirely different reason.

Something about him has me wanting to press my face into the window. I want to see him. I want to see the man that's been creeping inside my house, leaving me flowers, and mutilating any unsuspecting soul that dared to touch me.

Was his hand on the knob, ready to come in? What stopped him?

As if hearing my thoughts, he cocks his head slightly. Intently, I watch him slowly turn his head to the side. And ever so slightly, he raises his chin, the moonlight revealing his wide mouth and a sharp jaw.

I huddle deeper into the wall, feeling his eyes on me. There's no way he can see me. Yet somehow, I feel his gaze piercing me anyway. Like little, sharp knives grazing my skin before digging inside me.

And then he smiles, his mouth stretching into a wicked smirk. My breath hitches, and my lungs fill with fire.

Oh, this is funny to you, asshole?

Before I can process what to do—what I'm feeling—he turns and walks away, disappearing into the tree line. Slow and purposeful, as if he doesn't have a care in the world.

September 18th, 1944

He came back. Ronaldo came back.

He was bruised and hurt when he did. Cuts marred his beautiful face. Bruises discolored his skin. I was so excited to see him, I threw myself at him. Only then, did I notice the grunt of pain. I nearly cried when I saw his hurt.

He wouldn't tell me what happened. But I think the distance got to both of us. Because we...

I lied with another man. A man that was not my husband. And I'm finding it very hard to find the regret. There's shame. I feel that. But not regret.

In fact, all I want to do is do it again.

Chapter Eleven
The Manipulator

Daya said Nana was the freak, but I'm starting to wonder if it was *her* mother that was the freak. I skim through the diary, reading over her words.

I'm sitting in the same rocking chair Gigi used to sit in to write in her diary while her stalker watched on. While she let him feast his eyes on her, and got off on it too, apparently.

Snapping the book shut, I throw it on the footstool before me, the furniture rocking from the movement of the heavy book.

I sigh heavily, pinching the bridge of my nose to ward off the blooming headache.

I mean, what was she thinking? Letting a strange man watch her, come into her home, and touch her? That's insane. Certifiably insane.

What's truly insane is the fact that I found this diary, and a stalker found me on the same night. I don't want to think about what that means.

The wind blows outside the window, rattling the glass. Storm clouds are rolling in, the ever-present weather that plagues Seattle like bad acne. Just when you think we're going to have a lovely sunny day, a storm cloud pops up, ready to burst.

Okay, gross, Addie.

A loud thump sounds from the kitchen, causing me to nearly jump out of my seat. Heart pumping heavily in my chest, I look towards the direction and find nothing amiss.

"Hello?" I call out, but no one answers.

Attempting to even my breathing, I turn back right as movement from the corner of my eye snags my attention right outside the window. My head snaps in that direction and my eyes zero in on whatever it was I just saw. It's nearly pitch-black outside save for the moonlight and a single light outside my front door.

Another flash of movement causes me to nearly plant my face against the glass. It's a person, walking towards my house, having emerged from between two large trees. My eyes narrow into thin slits as the person's shape becomes more apparent.

He's back.

After two nights of nothing, the son of a bitch actually came back.

My hand drifts over to the end table next to me, snagging the butcher knife I've been carrying around with me since he broke into my house last. Turns out my security cameras are useless with him. The second he left, I checked them just to find out that they didn't catch sight of him.

When Daya looked into it, her face dropped, and her eyes went wide with terror. He spliced the cameras. Hacked into them and made it appear as if nothing was happening while he was walking through my house while I slept.

She said not only did he splice the camera feed, but he did it so well, it was untraceable. The only reason Daya was even able to come to that conclusion is because she knows how technology works and she does the same thing herself for her job.

This guy is dangerous—in more ways than just his violent tendencies.

I grip the handle in my fist and settle it on my lap. As he nears, my heart pounds in my chest, matching each step he takes towards me.

I stand and close in on my window. I don't know what I'm doing exactly. Provoking him? Daring him to come inside my house again? If he does, I have every right to defend myself.

The man stops about twenty feet away, his face once again hidden deep in a hood. He widens his stance as if getting comfortable, plunging a hand into his hoodie pocket and pulls out something I can't see. It's not until I see him flick a lighter, defining his impossibly sharp jawline and a cigarette sticking out from his mouth. He lights the cigarette, and then the flame goes out, leaving nothing but his moonlit silhouette and a blaring cherry.

He stares.

And I stare back.

Without looking away, I grab my phone from the end table. I listened to him and didn't call the cops when he sent me that fucked up box of hands, but he didn't say I couldn't call them when he's standing twenty feet outside my window.

I look down to unlock my phone, and when I glance up, my thumb freezes.

The moonlight spills over his silhouette. And with perfect clarity, I watch him slowly shake his head at me. Warning me not to do what I'm about to do.

I glance at my front door, fear steadily trickling through my body at an alarming rate. It's locked, but he's already proven that it's futile. I calculate the distance between him and the door. How long would it take him to run to it, break through, and get to me? At least a solid thirty seconds.

That's enough time to dial 911 and tell them someone is trying to hurt me, right? But it would be pointless. It's going to take the police no less than a half-hour to get to me.

As if hearing my thoughts, he takes a few steps closer, his hand periodically pulling the cigarette from his mouth as he puffs.

Is he... challenging me? My spine snaps straight, and white-hot rage fills my vision. Who the hell does this dude think he is?

Growling under my breath, I storm to my door, unlock it and whip it open. He turns his head to face me, and for a moment, I almost develop a brain and run back inside.

Steeling my spine, I angrily stomp down the steps and charge towards him.

"Hey, asshole! If you don't get off my property, I *will* call the cops."

Later, I'll ask God why She made me the way that I am, but right now, all I can do is plant two of my hands on his chest and push when I get close enough. I don't allow myself to register the defined muscles under his hoodie—because only psychos would focus on that right now.

The behemoth of a man doesn't move back an inch.

Nor does he speak. Or react. Or do anything.

Harsh, angry breaths huff from my nose like a bull as I glare at the hooded man. I can't see much of his face except the bottom half, but I can feel his eyes burning into me. Soon, my body will smolder until there's nothing left but ashes dancing in the cold wind.

"What do you want from me?" I hiss, curling my hands into fists, only to abate the shaking. My whole body has begun to vibrate from anger and fear. But also from something else. Something so disturbing, I refuse to put a name to it.

He doesn't answer, but he does grin—a slow, sinful twist of his lips that sends sparks skittering down my spine.

With deliberation, his tongue darts out and licks his bottom lip. My eyes zero in on the movement. The act primal. Animalistic. And fucking terrifying.

My heart starts to claw its way up my throat. Swallowing it back down, I narrow my eyes and open my mouth to yell at him some more.

Before I can, he takes a single step back. And though I can't see it, I know he's giving me a once-over. Then he turns and walks away.

Just like that.

Not a single word spoken. Not an explanation offered. Not even a crazy confession of how he wants us to be together or some shit.

Nothing.

I stand there and watch his retreating form, going back to whatever portal from Hell he crawled out of. I stare until he's gone, and I begin to contemplate if I really have lost my mind, and just imagined the whole thing.

Surely, I wouldn't be so stupid to *confront* a psychopath. The very psychopath that cut off a man's hands and left them on my doorstep.

But that's precisely what I did. And he did nothing in return, except lick his lips at me like he plans to feast on me.

Oh no, what if I have a second-coming of Jeffrey Dahmer stalking me?

Heart back in my throat, I turn and rush back inside, feeling like Lucifer's

hounds are nipping at my asscheeks. And when I shut and lock the door behind me,
I look back to the rocking chair I was sitting in and see the knife lying haphazardly
on the floor, next to the footstool.

Oh my God.

I confront a psycho and I *drop* the knife on the ground instead of bringing it
with me.

*God, why did you make me the way that I am? Next lifetime, can you not do such
a shitty job?*

As a reward for finishing my manuscript and sending it off to my editor, I'm
treating myself to a nice murder investigation.

Daya sent over more notes that she found from the PD's database. Emails
pour in by the minute with more details. Most of it is handwritten reports by men
with atrocious penmanship.

And with the mishandling of the crime scene, we essentially have nothing to
go on.

My great-grandfather mentioned in a report that she was acting strangely for
several months leading up to her death.

She was distant. Not as talkative. Paranoid. Short-tempered with Nana, and
she was late picking her up from school several times with no explanation as to
why.

Gigi wouldn't talk about it with her husband, which led to several arguments
between them. In the reports, he admitted their relationship had been declining
for the past two years. He had begged Gigi to talk to him about her change in

behavior, but she claimed nothing was amiss.

I spend hours dissecting Gigi's diary entries, looking for hidden meanings in everything she wrote. Searching for the entries where she expresses fear and discomfort.

But whatever scared her, scared her so much that she couldn't even write it out in words.

Part of me wishes these journals had been found during her investigation. I might've never gotten to read them if they had been, but maybe then they might've been able to solve her case.

I sigh and run my hands through my thick hair. My shoulders are starting to burn from my hunched-over position and my eyes are growing bleary from all the reading.

A headache blooms in my temples, worsening my vision until I can't see or think straight anymore.

I sit back in the rocking chair and look out the window.

My strangled scream pierces the air when I see the stalker is back—standing in the same spot as before, puffing on his stupid cigarette. It's been three days since I confronted him, and I've been on high alert ever since. Waiting for him to break in again, and this time, come into my room while I'm sleeping.

My heart lobs around in my chest, pumping erratically. A low heat sparks in the pit of my stomach, my mouth drying as the burn descends between my thighs.

I'm glued to the chair, panting from the heady mix of fear and arousal. My cheeks burn from shame, but the feeling doesn't dissipate. I should close the curtains—do myself a favor and cut us both off from our silent war.

But for some unknown reason, I can't get myself to move. To pick up the phone and call the police. To do anything that would classify me as intelligent and having common sense.

Those things are nonexistent as I stare out at the man. Whatever ghosts haunt these walls are no longer relevant, not when there's something much more dangerous haunting the grounds.

As if the ghosts heard me, light footsteps sound from above me. I turn my head and lift my eyes to the ceiling, tracking the phantom footsteps until they fade away.

And when I turn back, my stalker is a few feet closer. As if he's wondering what I'm staring at. Questioning what could've possibly turned my attention away from him.

He's wondering if it's another man, I'm sure. Maybe he thinks Greyson is back, occupying the house somewhere. Calling out for me and asking me to join him in my bed, naked and hard for me.

Maybe he even thinks we just fucked, my thighs still slick with another man's seed.

Does that piss him off?

Of course it does. He mutilated and killed a man for touching me. What would he do to a man for fucking me?

What would he do to me?

Doesn't matter that it's the furthest thing from the truth. The fact that those thoughts could be running through his head and driving him crazy brings a small smile to my lips.

Just to fuck with him, I turn my head and pretend to shout something out.

"What are you doing?" I say aloud, aiming my words towards a ghost that'll never reply.

Looking back at my shadow, I see him pull out his phone, the blue light getting lost in the depths of his hood as he looks at something. Several seconds later, he tucks it away in his pocket, slides out another cigarette from the pack, and lights it up. Chain smoker. Gross.

He sticks around for another fifteen minutes. And during that time, I scarcely look away. It feels like a game almost, and I've always been a sore loser.

I'm thanking Jesus I don't have to travel for this book signing event. Another big romance author is hosting it, and luckily, it takes place in good ol' Seattle.

A thin layer of sweat coats my skin as I look myself over one last time in the mirror.

"You've done a million of these, girlfriend. You're going to be fine," Daya assures from behind me. I'm wearing a flattering red blouse that shows off my body nicely without looking too racy or inappropriate and ripped black mom jeans. I painted my lips red and slipped on comfortable checkered Vans.

My cinnamon hair is curled into loose beach waves, completing the casual but chic look. I don't usually like to dress up for these things. I'm sitting in a chair all day, so I make sure to look nice enough to take pictures with and leave the rest to comfort.

I sniff my armpit, double checking that my deodorant didn't lie to me and doesn't fight against tough odors.

"I know, but it doesn't make them any easier," I grumble.

"What do you call yourself?" Daya asks, quirking a brow at me.

I sigh. "A master manipulator."

"Why?"

I roll my eyes. "Because I manipulate people's emotions with my words when they read my books," I grouse.

"Exactly. So that's all you do, except your mouth says the words instead of your fingers. Fake it till you make it, baby."

I nod my head, looking at my underarms in the mirror from all angles. My deodorant may claim to fight tough odors, but the shirt didn't come with a tag that said it was pit stain resistant.

Sighing again, I drop my arms. "It's not that I don't love meeting my readers, I just don't do well in crowds and social situations. I'm too awkward."

"You're also a great liar. That's what you do for a living. Just smile and pretend you're not having one big panic attack."

Another roll of my eyes as I grab my purse from the bed. "You're such a great pep-talker," I say dryly. She snorts in response.

Daya sucks at pep-talking, and she knows it. She's the logical person in our friendship, while I'm the emotional one. She's all about offering solutions, while I'd rather roll around in my dread and anxiety and wax on about it.

Guess I'm more like my mother than I thought.

I'll still never admit it out loud.

The event is a blast, as usual. Every time, I work myself up for these events, and I always end up never wanting to leave by the time they're over.

Getting the chance to meet up with other author friends and attempting to run away with all their signed books while laughing maniacally is what truly brings me peace in life.

What truly brings me happiness is seeing the many smiling faces eager to meet me and get signed books of mine.

I love my career as a professional manipulator. I'm fortunate to do what I do.

I'm a tad tipsy from getting drinks at a bar after the event, so Daya is driving me back home in my car. We laugh and giggle over funny moments and even gossip about the crazy drama that always circulates the book community.

We're riding a high from having such a good time, but our smiles bleed dry as she pulls up to the house.

A lone light is on, shining through the bay window. I turned off all the lights before we left.

I go to scramble out of the car, but Daya's firm grip around my hand stops me.

"He could still be in there," she says urgently, her grip tightening almost painfully.

"He fucking better be," I growl, wrangling my arm from her grip. I slip out of the car before Daya can try to stop me again and charge towards the manor.

"Addie, stop! You're being stupid."

I am, but the alcohol has only made my anger more potent. Before Daya can stop me, I'm unlocking the front door and barreling into the house.

A single light is on over my kitchen sink, too weak to illuminate the front of the house properly.

No one is waiting for me, so I start flipping on lights to diminish the ominous tone in the air.

"Come out, you freak!" I yell, storming into the kitchen and grabbing the largest knife I can find. When I turn, Daya is standing in the doorway, looking around the room with an alarmed expression on her face.

I was so intent on killing the bastard, I didn't even bother to look around.

The entire living room is covered in red roses. My mouth pops open, and the words on my tongue stutter and evaporate.

I turn and spot an empty whiskey glass sitting on the counter, a dribble of alcohol at the bottom of the glass, and a distinct mark on the lip.

Lying next to the glass is a single red rose.

My widened gaze clashes with Daya's. All we can do is just stare at each other in shock.

Heart in my throat, I finally choke out, "I need to check the rest of the house."

"Addie, he could still be here. We need to call the police and leave. Now."

I bite my lip, two halves warring inside me. I want to look for him, confront him, and stab him in the eye a few times. But I can't endanger Daya more than I already have. I can't keep being stupid about this.

Relenting, I nod my head and follow her out of the manor. The brisk air doesn't even penetrate the ice settling in my bones.

What else did he do? A snarl forms when I realize that he probably went into my bedroom. Touched my underwear. Maybe even stole some.

The operator's voice cuts through my thoughts. I was so zoned out, I hadn't realized Daya called the police for me.

She describes the situation, and after a few minutes, the operator dispatches an officer and lets us know it'll take him twenty minutes to get to us.

I know the stalker isn't here anymore. I know it in my bones. But I'm hoping he's a criminal and in the system, that way his DNA from the whiskey glass will identify him.

But just like I know he's no longer here, I know it won't be that easy to catch him either.

"Come home with me tonight," Daya says. We're both tired and stone-cold sober after talking to the police for two hours.

They searched the house, and he was nowhere to be found. They did take prints from the whiskey glass to see if they could get a match.

I'm exhausted, so I nod my head.

Her house is twenty minutes away, and it's a good thing I tailed her the entire time, or else I might have lost focus and drove without direction.

Daya lives in a quaint house in a nice, quiet neighborhood. She parks the car and we both slump our way into the house.

Her house would be fairly empty if it weren't for the furniture and the thousands of computers everywhere. She takes her work seriously, and while she doesn't talk much about her job, I know she deals with some pretty heavy matters.

She's mentioned before that she deals with the dark web and human trafficking. And that alone is enough to give someone night terrors.

Apparently, her boss is strict with keeping the details confidential, but there's been times where Daya has looked more haunted than Parsons Manor.

When I had asked what she gets out of it, she had said saving innocent lives. That was all I needed to hear to know that Daya is a hero.

"You know where the guest bedroom is," Daya says, lazily pointing her finger in the direction. "Do you want some company? I'm sure you're really freaked out."

I force a smile. "I love you for offering, but I think we both just need sleep right now," I say.

Daya nods, and after wishing me goodnight, retires to her room.

I flop on the white duvet in her guest bedroom. Just like the rest of her house, it's pretty bare in here. Light blue walls, decorated with a few oceanic pictures and white, gauzy curtains.

My eyes snag on those.

Not the curtains themselves, but what's in between them.

For the second time tonight, my heart lodges into my throat, pulsating against my voice box and preventing me from making a sound.

Outside the window is the silhouette of a man. Staring directly at me.

I take a step back, ready to turn and call for Daya. When my phone buzzes, I flinch, freezing me in place and nearly choking me on the fear.

Keeping one eye on the man, I slide my phone out of my pocket and see a new text message.

UNKNOWN: You didn't like my flowers?

November 19th, 1944

I can't get enough of him. I'm embarrassed to even admit it. It's been months but yet it feels like each time is new.

Frank and John are going fishing today, and I'm ashamed to say that I can't wait until they leave. Despite my change in attitude, John hasn't suspected me of cheating.

It's terrible, but I don't regret this love affair.

Ronaldo makes me feel beautiful. Cherished. Something I haven't felt since before I had Sera. He treats me like a woman, not someone to do his bidding and make him food.

And certainly not like fine china, but a woman who lvoes to be properly ravished.

I try my best not to think about it when John is home. I can't seem to control the smile on my face. And it's been so long since John has made me smile, I fear he'll grow even more suspicious.

Chapter Twelve
The Shadow

"There's another video," Jay says through the phone, his voice solemn. I scramble up from my couch and make my way into my office.

An array of computer screens line the ten-foot-long desk, and all my other illegal devices in here. Jammers, trackers, buttons that set off explosives in a number of places should someone betray me, and so on.

This room alone is worth millions with all the shit I have in here.

It's both my happy place and my living nightmare.

This is where I make a difference in the world. Where I find women and children who need saving, while also witnessing the torture those sick individuals put them through.

It takes money to infiltrate high-security buildings, rescue the girls and give them sanctuary and safety off the grid.

Big corporations pay me an ungodly amount of money to hack into their rival's systems for whatever bullshit reason, whether it be because they're competing and want to know what the other is cooking up, or because they have a lawsuit against one another and trying to find information.

I don't give a fuck what their problems are with each other. It's only my concern that they get what they hired me for.

In the end, someone wealthy gets fucked over, my client makes a massive profit from it, and I collect interest on it. It's dirty, but I've never been in the business of keeping my hands clean.

And it allows me to dedicate my life to ending human trafficking.

"Where?" I bark, my fingers already flying over the keyboard.

"Already encrypted and sent to your email."

I roll my neck, cracking the muscles and gearing up for something that's going to make the steak I just ate settle in my stomach like a wrecked ship in the ocean.

The video starts playing, and despite my instincts screaming at me not to, I turn up the volume so I can hear.

It's a grainy video of a fucked up satanic ritual. The person recording is breathing heavily, more than likely from the risk of being caught doing something extremely dangerous.

Four robed men stand over a stone slab with a squirming little boy tied down to it.

Over and over, he's screaming to let him go. His little voice breaking as he cries for help.

I run a hand over my face when they plunge a curved knife into his chest.

They fill metal goblets with his blood and drink the entirety of the cup in one swallow.

I force myself to watch and endure the pain alongside this boy. Because even though this innocent soul is now gone, that doesn't mean I won't do everything in my power to find justice for him.

When the video is over, I have to turn away and breathe through the urge to vomit.

"Z?" I had forgotten Jay was even on the phone.

"Yeah?" I respond, my voice hoarse and barely there.

"I... I couldn't watch it, man. I couldn't do it."

I close my eyes and breathe deeply.

"That's okay," I say. "You don't need to."

Jay knows how hard I take these things, but he also knows I refuse to turn away from them. That's what most people do when it comes to human trafficking. Everybody knows it exists, and most will educate themselves on how to avoid it, but they can't watch when it comes to the reality of it. Can't listen. Can't see the depravity. Because if they don't look, then they can go back to their normal lives and live on as if there aren't thousands of people out here dying every day.

Jay isn't one of those people, he's doing what he can. But he also doesn't have the stomach for it, and I can't blame him.

Because I don't either. And to be honest, the people who do are the ones who are trafficking them and committing the crimes.

"Is it the four we've been tracking?" I ask.

Jay sighs. "No, Mark was spotted at a restaurant last night with his wife during the timestamp of the video. Looks like different men, but these ones aren't identifiable. I imagine they only do the ritual once."

I nod my head, my mind racing as I try to figure out what the fuck I'm going to do.

About six months ago, a video leaked on the dark web of four men in black robes performing a ritual on a little girl. I'm not sure if it was arrogance or what, but the men kept their hoods down, unfazed with onlookers seeing exactly who they were.

Even with the low-quality video and dim lighting, I was able to identify them immediately.

Senators Mark Seinburg, Miller Foreman, Jack Baird, and Robert Fisher.

They surrounded the little girl on a slab of cement, stabbed her and then drank her blood. The girl was still alive, wriggling and screaming at the top of her lungs as the men chanted around her.

The same exact ritual the little boy just went through, still looping on my computer screen. Except in this one, the four men surrounding the little boy have tall, sharp-pointed hoods drawn over their heads, concealing their identities.

I can already feel myself slipping back into that black hole it took weeks to crawl out of six months ago. It put me in one of the darkest headspaces I've ever been in.

I locked myself in a room and didn't come out for twenty-six hours after watching that first video. I was physically unable to go on living my normal day-to-day with the knowledge that this was being done to children.

That helplessness grew as I explored the dark web and found thousands of videos of parents raping their own children. Alongside the millions of other videos of torture, cannibalism, and even necrophilia. A lot of those videos take place in red rooms, where buyers can direct how exactly they want the victim to be tortured, raped, and killed.

And those are just the ones involving children.

Those videos in particular are what drove me to create Z five years ago. Since I was a kid, I had a knack for computer science, and my skills have surpassed even the top hackers in government organizations.

Finding myself on the dark web and stumbling upon those videos was by accident. But it changed my fucking life.

I haven't been able to sleep since then. Knowing sick people pay to view hundreds of thousands of children being subjected to those things. Even worse, knowing that the people committing the acts do it both for their own pleasure and monetary gain.

And that just as many women and children continue to go missing every day so they can be subjected to those same things.

Since then, I made it my mission to find and kill them all. I've killed hundreds of people at this point. Locating predators that I have one hundred percent proof of their involvement in human trafficking.

Now I'm going to make my way through the government, starting with the four politicians from the first video, and then making my way through the rest.

I know exactly where they live. What they eat, where they sleep, shit, and work. But what they haven't led me to is where these rituals take place.

And every day that goes by without that information, these rituals will be performed more.

"Did we get a hit on an IP address from who leaked the video?" I ask Jay, though I already know the answer.

"No, they covered their tracks. Whoever leaked it knew what they were doing," Jay answers. I roll my neck again, gritting my teeth against the flaring pain radiating from the tightened muscles.

More than anything, I'd love to feel my little mouse's hands working out the near permanent knots in my neck and shoulders. But it'll be a little while before she agrees to that.

"Alright, I'll see what I can find out with this new video," I say, before ending the call.

Fuck. I need a drink.

And my little mouse happens to have a bottle of my favorite whiskey in her house.

A bone-chilling cold settles on the back of my neck. I hiss through my teeth and turn my head, convinced I'll find someone standing behind me. But no one is there, despite the persistent cold surrounding me like dense fog.

I've already experienced a few unexplainable things while perusing Parsons Manor.

But whatever ghost that's floating up my ass has bad fucking timing.

"Back off," I mutter through gritted teeth, turning back around. Surprisingly, it does. Whatever it is.

And I go back to staring mindlessly into my whiskey glass.

Whoever's whiskey this is, it's divine. A citrus flavor lingers on my tongue as I sip from the crystal cup. Addie's upstairs sleeping, none the wiser to me being down here, drinking her whiskey, and stewing in the hornet's nest buzzing throughout my skull.

Two of my employees installed security systems throughout her house, unknowingly to keep their boss out. I basically invented these systems, so I'm more than capable of disarming them with a click of my phone.

In the beginning, I just picked her locks to get in, then reverse-picked them after I left. The only predator I'll allow in her house is myself. Despite her shit locks, I'd never leave her vulnerable.

I was relieved when she installed the security system, even if it was meant to keep me out. Breaking past those barriers is just another lesson to teach. Eventually, she'll learn that she can't shut me out any more than she can fuck another man.

She tried to convince me of that the other day, but with one look at her cameras, I knew she was bluffing. Trying to get me riled up. It almost worked until I remembered that I'm taking it slow with her.

In the beginning, I tried so hard to forget her. I tried to run. But I couldn't get her out of my mind. I went home from that bookstore and attempted to talk myself down. But it seemed the more I struggled to convince the beast inside of me to leave her alone, the more it raged.

And the second I started looking into her life, digging up anything I could find, the obsession only grew. She became an inoperable brain tumor that plagues every waking moment of my life.

Sometimes it feels like if I tried to cut her out of me anyways, I wouldn't survive it.

Taking another swallow of whiskey, I twirl a red rose between my thumb and forefinger, a drop of blood pooling from where the thorn pricked me. Ignoring them, I keep rolling the dangerous stem between my fingers, a vortex of anger and anxiety swirling in my stomach.

Children are being tortured at this very moment. This second—this *millisecond*—while I sit here and drink liquor from a crystal glass.

There are children being sacrificed right now. Hurt. Maimed. Raped. Killed.

While sadistic fucks circle around them and drink the blood from their bodies.

My phone rests on the island, the screen lit up with the grotesque video playing on a loop.

I haven't been able to stop watching it—or rather, stop torturing myself. It's a small price to pay for the absolute horror this poor kid suffered from. My need to find where these rituals take place digs deeper, and it's driving me fucking insane.

There's nothing I can do at this moment. I've attempted to trace the source of the video, but whoever is leaking them has done their homework. No hits came through, leaving me feeling utterly fucking powerless.

I may be the best, but technology has limitations. I've learned how to bend and coerce information from almost nothing, but sometimes the tracks don't exist. The numbers just aren't there.

My thoughts spiral downward, like the amber liquid sliding down my throat.

I roll the rose harder through my fingers—faster. The sharp thorns slice through my flesh. The small amount of pain offers me a semblance of release.

Sometimes witnessing the torture these kids go through makes me want to slice open my own skin and feel the pain alongside them. I want to ease their pain by creating my own. Maybe if I'm bleeding out on an altar next to them, they won't feel so fucking alone.

But I don't. The urge is unfounded and I recognize that. I recognize that I need to be strong, not weakened from blood loss and my mental state hanging on by a fraying thread.

If I'm going to save these kids and destroy the skin trade, then I need to be at my best. They need me to be strong and capable because they can't be.

The video restarts. I snarl, the cries of the boy renewed, filling the otherwise silent space around me.

I've studied the video closely, just like I did the last one, searching for any type of clue. But I could detect nothing. Nothing significant that would lead me to where exactly these rituals are taking place.

Just four people dressed in black robes, surrounding a stone slab. From what I can see, the entire area is rock, emulating a cave of sorts.

But I'm not stupid enough to believe these men have found some cave in a mountain to sneak off into. This is a manmade cave, somewhere deep in the underbelly of Seattle. Someplace that no random civilian could accidentally stumble upon.

The whole reason I moved to Seattle six months ago was because of this dungeon. Originally, I was born and raised in California. But when the first video leaked, I was able to get a ping from the person's IP address that revealed Seattle as the original location.

They haven't made the same mistake twice.

This job gives me the freedom to live wherever I want, so it took only a day to settle on moving to Washington, where I could find the hellhole and destroy it.

And times like these, where I'm at my lowest, I can't help but feel like it also changed my life in the best of ways. It brought me to Addie, after all.

My head drops low between my shoulders, tension threading throughout my overused muscles.

The black cloud surrounding me darkens, sucking me in deeper as the video loops around again. I curl the rose, crushing it tightly in my fist. My hand trembles from the pain and the force in which I'm squeezing the flower.

I continue to crush it until it's nothing but crinkled petals and a crushed stem painted in the blood pouring from my hand.

I grit my teeth, just barely holding onto the sorrowful wail that threatens to leave my lips.

This—this is the destruction from what I do.

Some days, it's hard to live with. Some days, I can barely stand from the weight of this cruel world resting on my shoulders.

But I know if I don't, my life would be worthless, and those kids would have died for nothing.

Chapter Thirteen
The Manipulator

"I just got back the first round of edits," I say to Marietta through the phone. "I'm starting on them tonight."

"Wonderful, let me know if you need anything," she says.

I'm walking down my dimly lit hallway towards my room when a flash of movement catches my eye. I freeze, my finger just pressing the red button when I see what looks like a woman disappearing through the attic door.

A smile forms on my face before I can stop it.

In all the years I've been in this house, I've only seen an apparition a few times. More often, I've heard voices, footsteps, doors slam and felt the freezing drafts, but rarely anything visual.

But I know what I just saw.

A woman in a white dress with tight blonde curls. I didn't see her face, but there's a distinct feeling that it was Gigi.

Nearly dropping my phone rushing after her, I run down the hall and swing the attic door open. It's pitch black leading up the stairs, and there's that nervous tickle in the back of my brain, but it doesn't stop me.

I tap the flashlight on my phone and quickly make my way up the stairs. A heavy weight of foreboding presses down on my shoulders, but I trudge through it. Whoever that was, they wanted me to see something. I shiver from the feeling, both in fear and delight.

The moment I step on the landing, it feels like breathing in water. The air up here is stifling and heavy, rife with negativity.

It feels like something dark has consumed this space. And it doesn't like me up here. I can feel it staring at me from every angle.

There's a single bulb up here somewhere with a long string attached to it. I swivel my flashlight around until I spot the string.

It's swinging back and forth in an attic with no airflow and where the atmosphere feels denser than the woods outside of this manor.

Rushing over, I grab the swinging string and yank on it, clicking on the light bulb. A whirring sound breaks through the silence, adding an extra note of spookiness.

I squint my eyes, readying myself to see some scary monster hiding in the corner, but nothing is up here.

At least, not that I can see.

"Why did you lead me up here, Gigi?" I ask aloud, looking around the area and trying to figure out what I could possibly see up here.

Of course, I don't receive an answer. It's never that simple.

My eyes track over every dusty item cluttering the space. I have completely avoided coming up here and even opted out of renovating this space. I don't know what it was, but I felt like if I did, then something evil would be unleashed.

I already have enough monsters haunting me.

There's an old, cracked mirror in the corner with a white sheet hanging partially over it. I make sure to avoid looking at it at all costs. I love to be scared, but I still don't have any desire to see a demon standing behind me in the mirror.

Loads of dusty boxes and totes are scattered throughout the area. It's a fairly big room, so there's a lot of places to look.

Stuffing my phone in my pocket, I take a deep breath, feeling like I just filled my lungs with toxic waste. And then, I head over to one of the boxes and start digging.

They're covered in cobwebs, and I almost consider going down to the bottom floor and finding a pair of gloves. But I don't want to stop when I'm already committed. I might convince myself not to come back up once I'm no longer sharing space with something malicious.

Ignoring the spiders scattering from the boxes, I keep digging. All I find are old clothes, shoes, trinkets, and knick-knacks.

Nothing of importance, but maybe a few of these things could be valuable.

A loud bang sounds from behind me, and this time I scream loudly. The echo of my scream rings out as I whip around and face whatever made the noise.

Nothing's there but a dangling wooden board, hanging on by a single nail. The entirety of the attic is made up of wooden boards, most of them rotted and chewed up by mice. Where the wooden board once was is a bottomless black hole.

"You want me to stick my hand in there, don't you?" I say dryly, glancing around to see if I spot another hint of Gigi. Still not looking in that fucking mirror, though.

Hand over my pounding heart, I carefully walk over to the still swinging wood. Grabbing my phone and turning on the flashlight once more, I shine the light inside the hole.

It's a platform, and deep in the hole looks like two pieces of crinkled paper.

I groan aloud. "Fuck, you're *really* going to make me stick my hand in there?"

Bugs don't usually creep me out. There's not a lot of things in this world that genuinely scare me to my core. But that doesn't mean I enjoy sticking my hand in a bug-infested hole. Furthermore, I wouldn't be surprised if whatever negative energy resides up here decided to fuck with me and grab my hand.

I can admit I'd probably pee a little then.

Sighing, I plunge my hand in, snatch the papers and rip my hand out, all in under a second.

I almost open my mouth and gloat but decide it's better not to piss anything off when we're sharing the same house.

I turn, run over to the string, click off the light and dash down the stairs like the girl from The Ring is chasing after me.

Slamming the attic door shut, I take in a deep, cleansing breath of air. It's so much lighter down here. It feels like the entire house collapsed on me, and I just crawled out from beneath it.

I smooth out the papers, squinting my eyes to make out the neat scrawl on the first one.

I did what I was told to do. Because if I didn't, I know I'd be next. So this is my confession. I helped him cover up her murder. I'm so sorry.

My heart quickens as I read the note over and over. Whoever wrote this, they're speaking of Gigi's murder. They must be. *Who* helped him cover up the murder? Who is *him?*

Switching to the other note, it takes only a second to realize it's the page ripped out of her diary. I smile triumphantly, but the smile quickly drops as I read the messy words.

I have to be quick, he said he's on his way and I'm terrified. If I run, he'll catch me so I'm writing this note down in hopes someone will find it. If something happens to me, John, it wa

The note ends there, not even finishing the last word. My mouth drops open in shock as I stare down at it in utter disbelief.

"Are you fucking *kidding* me, Gigi! You leave it off *there? That's* what you wanted to show me? A note where you're about to say who it is BUT DON'T?" I finish my rant on a loud shout, stomping my foot and flaring my arms wide.

Of course, she doesn't answer me.

Growling dramatically, I stomp my way into the bedroom and slam the door shut.

I'm mad at her now. She better not come in here, or I'm kicking her right back out.

He's outside again. Watching me, a bright red cherry blaring in the moonlight.

I stare back at him. The familiar tendrils of fear have me tightly in their grip. But also, the bricks are settled in my stomach, sinking lower...

I chew my lip, contemplating if I should confront him again or not. Picking up my phone and reporting him would be the logical thing to do.

But the police won't be able to do anything. By the time they get here, he'll be gone again.

And what good will a police report do when they come up missing like last time? With his apparent breaking and entering skills, not to mention hacking skills, he's obviously tampering with shit. But maybe that doesn't matter. Sheriff Walters knows I have a stalker, despite him saying they had no record of it.

Maybe that's all the more reason *to* call.

He's probably planning on murdering me right now, just like Gigi's stalker murdered her. I've read over that note and combed through her diaries for the past three nights, but I haven't seen any evidence of her stalker being the murderer yet.

But I'm sure I'm right.

Eyeing him, I pick up my phone, stand directly in front of the window, and put the phone to my ear. I haven't even dialed the police yet; I just want to see what he'll do.

Because evidently, there's something wrong with me.

I'm playing with fire. The more I provoke him, the more likely he is to come after me. But I can't stop myself. I can't stop the sharp thrill that I get every time I push back.

It's as addicting as it is stupid.

I can't see his face under the deep hood, but I know he's smiling at me. Knowing that doesn't give me the reaction it should. I *should* be repulsed. I *should* be scared. I suppose I *am* scared, but what I'm really feeling is the urge to smile back.

My phone chimes in my ear. Brow plunging, I hesitantly pull the phone away from my ear and look at the incoming message.

UNKNOWN: Am I supposed to believe that you're on the phone with the police? I think my little mouse is a liar.

Oh, no, he didn't.

I angrily type back my message.

ME: Want to find out?

UNKNOWN: Yeah, I do, actually. I'd love to punish you later for it, too.

My thumbs freeze over the letters. The last punishment was gruesome and sickening.

ME: What, you gonna send me toes next?

UNKNOWN: Depends, are you still pretending to fuck other guys? Or would you rather yell at the ghosts in your house again?

My head snaps up and I stare into the depths of his hood. His phone is perched in his hand, waiting for my response. The lighting from his phone is set to low, the dim glow casting enough light to show me his wickedly sharp jawline and a portion of his smirking lips.

I lift my hand and flip him the bird.

Fuck you, asshole.

In response, his thumb starts moving, his smile growing wider.

UNKNOWN: I plan to.

I growl at his audacity. Like hell, he'll fuck me.

ME: You come near me, I will stab you. I'm calling the police if you don't leave right now.

UNKNOWN: So do it, little mouse.

I can't tell if he's telling me to stab him or call. I'd be happy to do both. I don't like his insinuation that I'm the mouse and he's the cat. That would mean he's hunting me. The last thing I want to be is hunted.

Fuck. I hesitate. I need to call the police. I have to. But I can't convince my fingers to move. He's challenging me, and I hate that I'm scared to find out what he's going to do if I do. I hate that I want to.

Heart pounding, I dial the numbers. He watches me closely as I press the call button and bring the phone to my ear.

"911, what's your emergency?"

I breathe in deep.

"There's a man that's been stalking me. He broke into my house a week ago. And now he's standing outside watching me."

"He's standing outside right now?" the operator asks. I hear typing in the background, accompanied by the smack of her gum.

"Yes," I whisper.

"Ma'am, is he doing anything? Does he have any weapons on him?" she asks.

"Not that I know of. Can you send someone out?"

More typing. "What's your address, ma'am?"

I recite the address to her. She asks a few more pointless questions and informs me a cruiser is about five minutes out. She asks me to stay on the phone, but I don't.

I click the phone off. My little shadow isn't going to stick around long enough for the police to show up and catch him. He'll disappear off into the woods he came out of, and never be found. I know this.

I can't see his eyes, but I meet his gaze anyway. With one last smile, he types out a quick message. My phone buzzes, but I don't look right away.

I'm too scared to.

And without a concern in the fucking world, he slowly turns and walks away. The darkness reaches out and grabs ahold of him, swallowing him into its depths until he's vanished completely.

When the cruiser shows up, I already want him to leave. For reasons I can't quite explain, I regret calling the police. I just… want him to leave.

The cop is an overweight man with short blonde hair and a ruddy face. He looks like he wants to be anywhere but here.

I feel the same exact way.

"What's going on here, ma'am?" he asks, huffing and puffing as he makes his way up the front porch.

"A man was outside my window," I say shortly.

"O-okay," he says, drawing out the O. "Has this happened before?"

I tell him that I've made several police reports that came up missing, but that this man has been coming around and breaking into my house for the past couple of months. After telling him of the previous experiences, he pulls out his pad and starts writing out the report.

"You said your name was Adeline Reilly, correct?"

"Yes."

He pauses from writing and looks at me as if he's seeing a different person.

"Aren't you the one that had Archibald Talaverra go missing off your porch?" he asks, looking me up and down, pausing on my chest for a second too long, as if my tits are going to give him the answer.

"Yes," I bite out, growing impatient.

He hums in response and goes back to writing his report.

"You think it was the same guy?"

"It'd be pretty fucked if it wasn't," I mutter. When the cop just side-eyes me, I sigh. "Yes, I do."

He stops writing after that and asks me a few more customary questions. Do you have a description, do you know who he might be, and so on. I give him all the information I have, except what's most important.

I don't tell him about the text messages. I don't know why, but they feel... private. Which is fucking stupid. Makes no sense, but I can't bring myself to say anything. The police officer leaves with absolutely no helpful information. But he still leaves with a police report, and that's what's important.

It's not until after I take a hot shower and settle into my bed that I read his message.

UNKNOWN: The more you disobey me, the harder your punishment.

"I'm going to find this little dick prick," Daya declares angrily, practically slamming the keys through her laptop as she types god knows what. I just finished telling her the details of last night.

I take a sip of my drink. It's not enough, so I take another. And then end up chugging the whole thing.

We're both doing our respective work, but she didn't want to leave me alone in the house now that my shadow is starting to interact more.

"Dick and prick are the same thing," I say. She looks up, her face reflecting my exact thoughts since last night. *What is wrong with you?*

I shrug a shoulder. "I'm just saying. You just called him a little dick dick."

She rolls her eyes, ignores me, and starts typing on her laptop again. Probably hacking into something. Though I can't imagine what she could possibly be hacking into. Better not be my phone. I have nudes on there.

My face pales. Oh, god, what if *he* hacks into it and finds them? I scramble to pick up my phone, delete every single racy picture, and then delete them a second time from the Trash folder.

Some of my anxiety eases, but not all of it. He could've already hacked into it for all I know.

I'm going to be obsessing over this for the rest of my life now.

Noticing my internal crisis, Daya focuses on me, her brow pinched with concern. "You okay, girl?"

I clear my throat. "How likely is it that he can hack into my phone and find my nudes?" Her lip twitches and I'm two seconds away from smacking it off her face.

"Baby girl, that man has probably watched you get naked in your room a thousand times now."

My eyes widen further, having not considered that yet, either.

"Oh my God."

"Why do you ask?" Daya asks, her voice full of suspicion.

I roll my lips together, debating. At this point, the only thing holding me back from telling Daya about the texts is her impending anger.

Finally building up the courage, I rush out, "Would you be able to trace an unknown number?"

Her eyes slant. "Did he text you from one?"

Shame creeps in. I should've told her this sooner, but I had a weird protective need to keep the texts to myself, just like with the police officer. Now, I realize how stupid that is when Daya is one of the best hackers in the world. Or so she says, at least.

I nod sheepishly and hand her the phone, the thread already pulled up. She snatches it from my hand, shooting me a heated glare, and reads through them.

Her eyes draw back to my own, fire licking at her pupils. "You're just now showing me these?"

I groan. "I know, I'm a stupid bitch. I just... I don't know, Daya. I honestly don't. Can you trace them?"

"I don't forgive you yet, but let me see."

I don't worry about her anger. Daya could get bit by a snake and immediately forgive it. She's just playing hard to get right now.

What looks like frustration settles over her face. Her lips curve down, and as the seconds pass by, her frown deepens. She leans closer to the screen, still typing a mile a second.

After a few minutes, she slaps her palms on the granite and leans back, obvious anger now on her face.

"Untraceable," is all she says.

My anxiety resurfaces. "So, this man can hack into my security cameras, override them, and can clearly text me from an untraceable number. Which means he probably hacked my phone and got my nudes."

She looks up at me, and I already know my answer.

"It's possible," she says, though her tone conveys that it's *probable*.

I drop my head to my laptop, surely pressing a bunch of keys, but I don't care right now. A creepy ass dude potentially has my nudes. Worse, he probably has video footage of me naked. I suppose it's not the worst thing in the world to happen—my body is fabulous. But I'll definitely be mortified if they get leaked.

What if he uses them as blackmail? Never thought I'd think this, but hopefully, he's too obsessed with me to leak them. He's already proven to be highly possessive.

If another man can't even touch my thigh without getting his hands cut off, then surely he wouldn't show the world my naked body?

"Did you delete them?" I nod, my forehead grating against the keys. I cringe at the noise. If I don't stop, my big ass head will ruin my laptop.

I lift my head, pick up Daya's glass of vodka and pineapple juice, and start chugging. She doesn't complain. In fact, she slides over the entire bottle of vodka.

"Don't obsess over it. If he hasn't said anything about them yet, then there's a good chance he doesn't have them."

Her words do little to make me feel better, but I appreciate the sentiment anyway.

"Who did you even send your nudes to?" she asks, snatching the bottle of vodka from my hand after I take a hefty swig.

"I haven't sent a nude since I was twenty. I take nudes because I like my body and want to stare at it all day."

Daya laughs. "I fucking love you."

Sadly, she might not be the only one.

Her phone lights up. Instinctively, my eyes flash towards the screen, but it's her snatching it up like the phone caught fire is what draws my attention to it.

I quirk a brow, watching her glance nervously at me.

"You don't forgive me for keeping secrets, but yet you're doing the same thing," I state dryly.

She deflates, now looking like a dog caught with the toilet paper in its mouth.

"I didn't want to worry you," she mumbles.

"About what?" I bark, holding my hand out expectantly for the phone. She groans, tucking it further into her chest.

"Luke... he's been texting me," she starts. My eyes widen, alarm stark in my eyes.

"Texting you about what? Just to hook up again?"

Slowly, she shakes her head. "He's been bugging me about you and what happened that night with Arch. I told him what you told the police. That someone pounded on the door, and he went missing after that. I guess he's trying to figure out who it could've been."

"Fuck," I curse, dropping my head in my hands.

"Apparently, Max is going on a rampage," she admits on a sigh. "Not only did his best friend die, but the entire family. They haven't said it, but I'm not sure they believe it was the Talaverra's rivals that killed the family. I told Luke you have nothing to do with it. And I think he bought it."

Words are left unsaid, so I say them for her. "For now."

Her lips tighten in response, and I realize that my shadow has just made me some dangerous enemies.

January 14th, 1945

The cold, dreary weather is putting me in a mood that rivals the ice clinging to my windows.

Frank even noticed my sour state when he stopped by today. He tried to cheer me up with bad jokes. I'll admit I laughed at one or two, but I can't seem to muster much more than that.

Ronaldo and I argued yesterday.

He said he can't stand that I'm still with John. He's growing incredibly jealous. And I can't say I entirely blame him. Not when the thought of him with another woman nearly makes me blind with rage.

But Ronaldo's life is still a mystery to me. He said that he refuses to involve me in his dangerous lifestyle, and I'm not even sure what that means.

How could I give up stability for my daughter, for a man whose life is still mysterious and dangerous?

I'm at a loss.

Chapter Fourteen
The Manipulator

Daya put some type of block on my phone to prevent further hacking. While my brain kept circling back to the nudes, Daya's concern was the guy having access to my phone in general. He'd be able to see all my messages, have access to my bank information, track my phone and find me wherever I go.

It seems every day, my appreciation for Daya grows. She gave me a sense of safety I didn't realize I was missing.

I'm going to have to propose to her soon or something.

Still, I will never take another nude in my entire life, but that's a small price to pay in the grand scheme. I've decided to remove the camera from my room to allow me at least some semblance of comfort. I'll just have to hold off on walking around the house naked until something is done about this creep.

Now, if only Arch's best friends weren't up my asshole, then maybe I'd get an extra hour or two of sleep at night.

The rest of the day was spent in silence, both of us lost in our work.

While Daya did whatever she does, I pulled out every picture in this house and picked through them. I've no idea what I'm actually looking for. Maybe Gigi with another man besides my grandfather.

After an hour of looking, I realized that she tended to write the names of the people captured in the photo and the year on the back of each picture.

I searched for the name Ronaldo, but never found it.

"Halloween is coming up. We're going to haunted houses this year, right?" Daya asks. She's standing at my front door, about to head home for the night.

I give her a droll look. "Halloween is my entire life, Daya. Of course, we're going to fucking haunted houses."

For as long as I can remember, Halloween fascinated me. The creatures and creepy faces. The jump scares and impending dread that something horrific is going to happen. I've had an unhealthy obsession with it all.

Mom sent me to therapy specifically for my fascination with gory horror movies. She thought I was a psychopath. And really, I just get off on being scared.

I think it's a step up from being a psycho, but the therapist disagreed.

Too often, I'd hear my mother telling my father that I was a freak. That something was wrong with me. No one in their right mind *likes* being scared.

But I do.

I love it.

Which is why having a stalker is the worst thing for someone like me. I'm susceptible to enjoying the fear a bit too much. My love for horror is going to get me killed one day. It's like I was meant to be hunted.

Little mouse.

That name is going to haunt me.

I'm not prey. I'm not.

"Satan's Affair is coming to town again, and they have new haunted houses," Daya reminds, bringing me back to the present.

Satan's Affair is a traveling fair that comes to town every year, staying for two nights before moving on to the next town. They set up loads of haunted houses and thrill rides. Daya and I go every year religiously.

After the first few years, the haunted houses became predictable. Since then, they change them every year, and now the traveling fair has some of the best haunted houses in the country.

"You already know I'll be the first one in line."

"Yeah, we know, freak," she teases. Despite the fact that it used to be my mother's favorite slur, I don't let it bother me anymore.

Plenty of men have called me the same, followed up by desperate begging to fuck me again. Being a freak took on a whole new meaning a long time ago. I tend to enjoy the name now.

Daya leaves once we confirm plans for the fair night. It's not for another few weeks, but the event has garnered a loyal fanbase and sells out every year. It got to the point where so many people would come, they had to limit the number allowed in.

They treat it like a concert to avoid lines forming outside the fairgrounds. Once tickets sell out, you won't be able to enter. Luckily, I have a computer genius on my side, and she gets tickets for us before they even go live.

The moment the door clicks shut behind Daya, my phone buzzes. Thinking it's Daya texting me that she forgot something, I slide my phone out and open the message without registering who it is.

The second I see the text, my heart drops.

UNKNOWN: Ready for your punishment, little mouse?

I look up and storm over to the window. He's not standing outside. Daya is just now pulling out of the driveway and speeding off, her taillights disappearing through the trees.

I turn around, nervous he found another way inside my home. Or that he's already in the house with me and has been the entire time.

ME: Why are you doing this?

His text doesn't come through right away. I wait with bated breath, and when I realize I'm glaring at my phone, I nearly throw it across the room. He's probably making me wait on purpose.

Finally, my phone buzzes. I force myself to wait a minute before opening it, just to spite him.

UNKNOWN: You haunt me. It's only fair I return the sentiment.

I swallow, nervous energy coursing through me as I decide how to respond.

UNKNOWN: You're so beautiful when you're scared.

I drop the phone. Embarrassed and praying he didn't see my blunder, I look out the window again. Still not there.

Where the fuck is he?

As if reading my thoughts, another text comes in.

UNKNOWN: I'm so close, I can smell you.

My hands tremble as I read his text over and over again. The words begin to blur as panic sets in. He's here in my house somewhere. I run over to the kitchen, grab my handy dandy knife and storm back into the living room.

He hasn't come out yet, but I imagine he will.

Heart racing and hands shaking, I perch myself on the edge of the rocking chair, sealing my fate.

ME: Quit being a pussy and come out then.

The second the message shoots off, I regret it. I want to snatch it back.

Footsteps sound from above me. I swallow and look up as if I'll be able to see through the ceiling and spot him. The footsteps travel further away from me, towards my room.

My phone buzzes.

UNKNOWN: Come find me.

At this exact moment, I'm questioning my sanity. Without thought, my ass lifts off the seat and I take a single step towards the staircase. My instincts are to run towards the danger, not away.

God? Me again. We really need to talk about your life decisions when you made me.

I'm not even sure I believe in Her, but if She is real, then someone needs to smack Her hand for making me the way that I am.

Thankfully, common sense kicks in, and I stop myself from going up and finding a crazed man in my house. The smart thing would be to call the police.

There's no way he'd be able to get out without being seen. The only way out of this house is down the steps. He can't hide forever. At this point, I don't even care if the officer can't catch him. As long as someone else has proof that they saw him, too, that'll be enough for them to take me seriously.

Another buzz.

UNKNOWN: Too scared, little mouse?

As if challenging me, a door slams shut. I startle from the noise, my heart jumping up into my throat. Even if I wanted to scream, I wouldn't have been able to make a sound.

My chest pumps erratically as the fear grows more potent.

ME: I'm calling the police.

I can feel the judgment through the walls. Here I am, calling him a pussy and challenging him to come out. Then when the tables turn, I threaten to call the police.

Because that's the smart *thing to do, dumbass.*

Then why the fuck do I feel so stupid for saying it? How is that possible?

UNKNOWN: Do you remember what I said last time?

How could I forget? The more I disobey him, the harder the punishment. I bite my lip, seriously contemplating going upstairs and finding him. I release a shaky breath.

I have a choice to make, and I already know I'm going to make the wrong one.

I resign myself and start typing.

ME: Here I come, asshole.

I keep my phone clutched in one hand and the knife in the other. No way am I going to be an idiot again and drop the knife. It's staying firmly planted in my grip, just like it'll be firmly planted in this dude's face once I find him.

I make my way up the steps quietly. Though I'm not sure it really matters if he hears me coming or not. I have a dreadful feeling that even though I'm coming to find him, he's going to find me first.

That familiar heady feeling settles in my gut. It churns like alcohol in an empty stomach. Sweat breaks across my forehead, and my mouth feels like I swallowed sand.

I'm fucking terrified.

A row of sconces on each side of the hallway provides just enough light to see that no one is there. I click the flashlight on my phone and start in the first room.

I slowly make my way into each room, checking immediately to my left and right before entering any further. I check behind the doors and in every corner of the room.

The closet is the worst part. Opening the door and knowing that I may come face to face with a man.

A man that wants to punish me.

Tears gather in my eyes when I discover the first closet empty. My poor heart is suffering from extreme palpitations right now. I don't think this amount of fear in my bloodstream is healthy.

Still, I forge on, finding the following two rooms completely empty as well.

There are only two more rooms and a bathroom left in this hallway. And lastly, a door at the very end of the hall that leads to the attic.

If he's up there, he can stay there. There's no way I'm going up in the fucking attic to find him. I will gladly admit defeat.

Sucking in a deep breath, I face my bedroom. Aside from the attic, it's the only room left in this hallway with a closed door.

What is he feeling right now? Standing on the other side, waiting for me to enter. Our roles are reversed, this time with me lingering outside the door. Still, I'm the one left terrified while he calmly awaits me. Anticipating all the things he's going to say to me. Do to me.

How he's going to hurt me. *Punish me.*

Steeling my spine, I turn the knob and push open the door. When it swings open, a scream climbs up my throat.

He didn't even try to hide.

My balcony doors are wide open, the moonlight spilling in. And there, a dark figure shrouded in white light, is my shadow. Staring at me with a wicked smile on his face and a blade in his hand.

March 13th, 1945

Ronaldo took me out on a mini vacation. I told John that I was having a girls weekend with a friend from Sera's school. Considering I've gone out on weekends before, he didn't question me.

I feel so guilty. But not enough to come home.

I'm so happy with Ronaldo. So enthralled.

This weekend has been absolutely magical. I just wish Sera were here to enjoy it with us. But that's awful of me, isn't it?

I love John, and I would never want Sera to not have him. He's wonderful to her and my Sera would be lost without him. I would never take her away from him.

But sometimes, I wish she had Ronaldo too.

Chapter Fifteen
The Manipulator

I'm completely immobilized beneath his stare. I can only imagine the look on my face when I see him standing there, waiting for me.

The sconces behind my bed are lit, offering dim lighting. Enough for me to get a clear view of him. He's clad in all black. Leather boots, jeans that wrap tightly around broad thighs, and a matching hoodie that looks a size too small with the way he fills it out.

Still, I can't see much of his face—that damn hood.

My tongue darts out, wetting my dry lips.

"Take off your hood," I say, a slight tremor in my voice. He doesn't. Nor does he speak.

Anger begins to build beneath the fear.

"You wanted me to come find you, kitty cat. I did. So take off your fucking hood and show me your face," I demand, my voice rising alongside my anger.

A sinful smirk tugs at his lips when he hears his new nickname. He thinks this is a game of cat and mouse. If he wants to debase me with a nickname, it's only fair I return the favor.

Slowly, he reaches up and slides the hood off his head, the knife glinting as if to mock me. I have my own knife, too.

Any triumph I felt over my little jab dissipates like butter in a hot skillet.

And all the fear I've been feeling triples. His face is... unlike anything I've seen. But that's the thing—I *have* seen him before. The mismatched eyes give him away.

In the bookstore, I only saw portions of his face. At the time, he seemed mildly attractive. But now that I see those pieces as a whole, he's devastating.

His right eye darker than the midnight sky, and the other the exact opposite. His left eye is so bleached of color, it's nearly white. The scar starting from the middle of his forehead, slashing straight down through his white eye and to the middle of his cheek, is something I haven't been able to forget since I saw him in the bookstore.

Despite the ugly scar, it only serves to heighten his utter beauty. A jawline so sharp, he could cut diamonds with it. A straight, aristocratic nose. Full lips. And short black hair, just long enough to run your hands through.

This is wrong. *So* wrong.

I shouldn't be attracted to a stalker.

His presence is so overwhelming, it feels as if he's ten feet tall with a shadow crawling up the ceiling, slithering toward me. This room feels tiny with him in it. *I* feel tiny with him in it.

He takes a step toward me, a hint of that smirk remaining on his face—just the slightest curl in his lips.

I take a step back. Finally, my instincts aren't completely jacked sideways, and I make my first smart move of the night.

"Cat got your tongue, little mouse?"

Briefly, I close my eyes. His voice washes over me, leaving goosebumps in its wake. The sound is as deep as his black eye.

I swallow again, nearly choking on the very muscle. It feels like my tongue has swollen to double its size.

"What do you want from me?" I choke out.

He prowls towards me. My spine tightens, and despite the gallons of fear pumping through my heart valves, I stay still. When he gets close enough, I'll stab him.

Aim for the throat, Addie.

My eyes lock with his, and all thought escapes me. He presses the entirety of his body against mine. No shame. No shyness. No, *let me buy you a drink first before I press my man pecs into you.*

The boldness of it has me nearly biting my tongue in surprise.

It takes several seconds for my body to unlock. Before I can think about what I'm doing, I swing my knife towards him, but meet resistance when I attempt to lift it.

I look down in confusion, just to see his bare hand wrapped around the blade. Blood pools in his hand, a small trail heading straight towards my own.

I gasp, my eyes widening and snapping back to his. Not a single iota of pain shines in his eyes. Not even a glimmer.

He jerks on the blade once, ripping it from my weak hold, blindly tossing it behind him.

The knife clatters loudly against something before toppling to the floor, the sound reverberating in the otherwise quiet room. Nothing but my heavy panting breaks the static of silence surrounding us. His presence is a vortex, steadily depleting the oxygen from the room—and even from my brain.

Because I cannot think straight with his body so close to mine. With the fear coiled tightly around me, the force of it turning my body to stone. I'm useless. Powerless. The inability to fight rages in my head, my survival instincts tell me to just *move*, yet my body refuses to.

And then his bloody hand is wrapping around the back of my neck and bringing my body flush with his once more. I cringe at the feel of his life's essence dripping from his hand. The blood feels like menacing fingers crawling down my spine, staining my skin as if to mark me.

To my horror, he lifts his other hand—the one still gripping a much more wicked-looking knife than mine—and brings the tip of the blade to the underside of my chin.

He applies enough pressure to force my chin up further, the metal biting into my skin. The slightest curl to his lips stalls the breath in my lungs. The act speaks of something daunting. Something condemning.

"You're even more beautiful up close," he murmurs, his sinful eyes devouring my face.

I scowl and plant my hands on his chest, ignoring the pure steel beneath his flesh, and attempt to push him away. But he resists the force, his lip curling into a snarl.

Tears rim my lids as frustration grows.

"Please, just leave. I-I don't want you here. I don't want *you*. Just leave me alone," I beg. It feels like reaching a hand inside my chest, yanking out my pride and throwing it onto the floor. But I don't give a fuck about my pride in this moment.

I just want this man to fucking *leave*.

He presses in closer. "Are you going to cry, Addie?" he taunts. My hands are still pressed firmly against his chest. His heart is racing beneath my palms, giving me pause. If I didn't know any better, I'd think he's not as unaffected as he's appearing to be.

"No," I lie.

I will absolutely have no problems crying my eyes out *after* he leaves. But I refuse to show him any more weakness.

He flashes me a feral, toothy smile, pulling the blade from my chin and dropping his hand from behind my neck.

The second he steps away, I feel a mixture of coldness and relief. But then he's coming right back.

The intensity in his eyes holds me in place as he walks to stand beside me, his chest brushing against my arm. He smells like leather and smoke. It's intoxicating. *He's* intoxicating.

Fear has a taste. Acidic, burnt metal. It numbs my tongue. Not just my tongue, but my entire being.

I'm so, so scared.

But yet, so... consumed by him.

I keep my head straight but don't let him out of my line of sight. He leans into me, pressing his weight against me. I combat his strength. Rather than being pushed away from him, I'm being absorbed by him. Hot breath warms my skin as his lips trace the outer edge of my ear. Another shiver wracks my spine.

"I want to devour you," he whispers.

My lip trembles. I suck the traitorous lip between my teeth, if only it stops showing my weakness. When I risk a glance at him, his eyes have zeroed in on my lips.

"Are you here to kill me?" I ask lowly, trying my best to mask the tremors wracking through my body.

I'm failing.

Slowly, he shakes his head. "Why would I do that?" I'm not sure how to answer that. He continues, "I wouldn't kill you, little mouse. I want to *keep* you."

"What if I don't want you to?"

He smiles. "You will."

I open my mouth, ready to tell him about himself *and* his momma, but the words die on my tongue when he reaches up a hand and swipes his thumb roughly across my bottom lip.

"Mm," he growls in delight. "Here's what's going to happen. I'm going to allow you the opportunity to run and hide. If I find you, then I will deliver your punishment. If I don't, you go unpunished and I will leave."

I pinch my eyes shut, a small single strand of hope threading throughout the hysteria. I know this house like the back of my hand. I know where the good hiding spots are.

There are two bedrooms down there in the hallway on the bottom floor. The first bedroom has a tiny little nook in the back of the closet. Just barely able to fit my body in, but I used to hide there all the time when Nana and I would play hide-and-seek.

"Fine," I whisper. "How long will you search for me before I win?"

He smiles. "I'll give you five minutes before your ass is bent over my knee."

I huff, jerking my face away from his hand. He lets me go, but the smile on his face grows.

"Your time starts now, Adeline. Better run."

I don't hesitate any longer. Turning, I bolt out of the room, slamming the door shut behind me. I don't miss the amusement on his face when he watches me do so, but I don't give myself time to care.

I head straight for the stairs, keeping my steps light as my little legs carry me down the steps at an alarming speed. Halfway down, I nearly pitch forward and face plant, barely catching myself on the railing and keeping the loud squeak from escaping.

I feel like throwing up, the adrenaline and fear intense and biting at my nerves.

Making a left turn, I aim for the hallway and slip into the first bedroom just as I hear heavy footsteps from above.

My heart races impossibly faster, and my hands tremble fiercely as I slide open the closet door. The metal rattles from my sloppiness. A slight, insignificant sound that feels like thunder rolling throughout the bones of the house.

Heaving in a deep breath, I force my body to slow as I glide the closet door closed and hurry into the nook.

I'm panicking.

My chest is tight, and I have the strangest urge to cough. Could be because my throat is dry and steadily closing. I want to claw at my neck, force the muscle to open back up, and let in the oxygen I so desperately need.

It's all in your head. Breathe, Addie, breathe. He's not going to find you in here. Nana never could.

His footsteps have disappeared from above me, meaning that he's made his way downstairs most likely. I bite my lip hard, tangy copper filling my mouth. And still, I keep biting down.

Shuffling and distinct noises filter through. And as the minutes pass, my breathing begins to slow.

But then I hear the door slowly creak open, and my breathing stutters. I clamp my hand over my mouth, refusing to make a sound, even if it literally kills me.

The closet door slides open, and his scent fills the tiny area. Leather. A hint of smoke. And something else. Something that would ordinarily make my eyes roll if it wasn't so goddamn suffocating.

"You can come out now, baby," he breathes, the sound of his voice gravelly and deep.

Oh, no. No, no, no.

I don't move, hoping that he's just guessing.

"I can smell you," he says. And if that's not the creepiest thing I've ever fucking heard, I don't know what is.

Risking a peek around the corner, I see him standing at the entrance of the closet. He's not looking in my direction. His head is down, staring off at a random spot on the ground.

"You have ten seconds before I come drag you out." He takes a step back, and I decide to just go for it.

I dart out, slipping past him and heading towards the door. He lets loose a deep, cruel laugh. It's a sound I'll hear in my nightmares for the rest of my existence.

But I don't stop. I run down the hallway and head for the front door, gasping when I find it locked.

"You unlock that door and there will be consequences," he warns. I startle at his proximity. There's not enough time to unlock the deadbolt, knob, and chain. He's too close.

Sunroom. It has a back door that leads outside. I turn, and out of the corner of my eye, I see my shadow round the corner of the entranceway to the hallway I came from.

I bolt through the living room, then the kitchen, and towards the door that leads into the backside of the hallway. Praying that he didn't stay in the hallway, I fling open the door to find it empty. At least within five feet of me, I can't see past the darkness beyond that.

Heading straight for the sunroom, I barrel through the door and find him already there, leaning against the door that I need to escape out of.

I skid on my feet, halting my momentum before I crash right into his waiting arms. I back up, chest heaving and mind racing.

He tsks. "You're very predictable, little mouse. We're going to have to work on that."

I just stand there, frozen in place as I process the fact that I won't be able to get out of this house. He's incredibly fast, but the scariest part is that I didn't hear a single fucking footstep from him. I sounded like an elephant and he was quieter than a mouse.

"You're not touching me," I hiss, my voice wobbly and rife with unshed tears.

"A deal is a deal, little mouse." He looks up at the night sky. "It *is* beautiful in here. I think it's only fitting that the punishment occurs here, don't you think? It feels like we've come full circle."

Growling, I finally force my body into action and run right back down the hallway towards the stairs.

Maybe I can find a spot to hide again. Somewhere he won't find me this time. My mind turns over every possibility as I swing myself around the banister and charge up the steps.

A whisper of wind brushes against the back of my thighs, and when I glance behind me, I see him right on my heels.

I let loose another scream, quickening my steps. I make it up the stairs and barrel down the hallway, my desperation and pure panic clouding my head. I can't think, I can only act.

I'm halfway down the hallway before a steel arm bands around my waist and lifts me up.

"NO!" I scream, kicking at air as I fight his hold.

"Oh yes, baby," he growls, swinging our bodies towards the wall. I grunt from the impact, leaning my back against the wall and using it as leverage to kick against the bastard of a man.

"Let me go, you fucking creepy-ass fuck—"

"Keep talking and you'll just make it worse."

I screech, out of breath and growing weaker, as he pins my flailing body against the wall.

"We had a deal, did we not?"

A tear spills over my lid. And then another and another until I'm on the verge of sobbing.

"Don't cry, little mouse," he coos. "It's going to get so much worse."

His breath skates over my cheek as he presses himself deeper into my body. He's so much bigger, his body enveloping me until all I can see, feel, and smell is him. Warmth, leather, that unique scent that belongs to only him, and his black-clad body surrounding me.

"I like you scared," he whispers, sending shivers down my spine. "I like you begging and pleading. Crying out for God to save you." I feel the touch of his hand on my face, and I flinch away. His fingers lightly trace over my cheekbone to my hair, tucking the loose strands behind my ear. "I like you trembling beneath my touch, uncontrollably."

"You're sick," I snap, doing just that. I'm shaking from head to toe, and I can't seem to stop it.

"You think you're only going to beg because you're fighting for your life, but that's where you're wrong. The only way I'll be sending you to heaven is with my cock." He grunts out a deep laugh. "And definitely my tongue and fingers, too."

"That will never happen," I hiss, glaring at him with all my might. Or at least I think I am.

His eyes are shadowed by the dim light radiating from the sconces. It feels almost like being far-sighted. Your face is so close to something, but clarity evades you. The shadows are a part of him. He carries them with him.

"It's time to punish you, and I've thought of the many ways I could do this," he says, ignoring my jab. It only infuriates me more that he finds my lack of consent is so inconsequential. So... *worthless.*

"I'll be nice this time." I open my mouth, but he cuts me off with a deep growl of warning, "But only if you are too, Adeline."

The click of my teeth snapping together is audible, pulling another grunt of amusement from him. My pride takes a hit, and I want to knee him in the balls for it, but I couldn't lift my leg an inch if I tried.

"What are you going to do?" I choke out, the stutter of my words in sync with the beat of my heart.

His hot breath fans across my cheek, and I feel the glide of his lips alongside my jaw. I swallow, but I nearly choke from how dry my throat has become. Those lips descend to the column of my neck, skittering along until he pauses on the spot right below my ear.

"I'm going to claim you," he says, right before his teeth clamp down.

My back arches involuntarily, repulsion and pleasure marrying in my nerves, sending misfires to my brain. All coherent thoughts escape from my mind as a result, leaving me with nothing but basic instinct.

He groans, his teeth piercing as his tongue laps at my flesh. My mouth opens, a silent scream suctioned away just as his mouth does the same, drawing in deep like he's drinking the essence from my body. And then he's pulling back, dragging his teeth along my skin as he lets go, leaving the spot smarting with pain.

My hands press into his chest for stability or to push him away, I am not sure. Though my question is quickly answered when instinct coerces my hands to curl, gripping his hoodie tight and anchoring myself to him as if he's my lifeline. When really, he's the one who's killing me.

Severe shivers wrack my body when he licks a wet trail down to the juncture of my neck. He pauses, and it feels like my body is hanging over a pointed knife. I hold my breath, the anticipation rattling my bones.

And then he's biting down again, pulling an animalistic sound from the depths of my chest. He does this, over and over, leaving a trail of bruises down my neck and across my shoulder.

I'm breathless by the time he pulls away.

"Good girl," he breathes, his own voice airy. Somehow, that makes me feel worse. I want him to hate it as much as I should've.

I can't explain why I do what I do next. I'll ask God later. But in that moment, I'm so overcome with a tsunami of emotions that I reach up and bite his cheek.

Hard.

Blood spurts into my mouth, but I don't care, I just bite harder.

Maybe I want to hurt him back. Give him a taste of his own medicine. Make him feel whatever I feel.

Regardless of the reason, he doesn't take kindly to it. His hand wraps around my throat, pushing me back while he rips his face away. My head thumps against the wall, a dull throb radiating from the spot.

He's squeezing tightly, but I don't care. I feel justified. If he kills me here and now, at least I can say I left one last mark on him.

He growls low, a sound of frustration and something else that I can't put a name to.

I stare up at him, blood coating my tongue and trailing down my chin. It's a small amount. I didn't get the chance to rip his face to shreds like I wanted. But the small dots of blood on his face leave me feeling invigorated all the same.

"I'm beginning to think you like to be punished, which means I'm just going to have to do better."

Before I can react, he's lifting me up and tossing me over his shoulder like a sack of potatoes.

"Fucker!" I snap, banging my fists against his back. I am *not* a potato.

A sharp slap to my ass is his only response.

He carries me down the steps, takes a left turn into the hallway and down towards the sunroom. The entire time I fight, kicking and punching, but he acts like a butterfly is attacking him.

As if he hears my frustrations, he says, "Baby, the wind can do more damage than what you're doing."

"Want to see my teeth again, asshole? I'll keep making your face uglier."

"Keep telling yourself that, but we both know my scars make you wet," he retorts, amusement coloring his words. I growl, frustrated by how fucking unruffled he is. And because he's not entirely wrong.

No, dumbass, he is wrong.

More curses flood out of my mouth, but they're cut short when he drags my body down his front until my legs are wrapped around his waist, and he's cradling me to his chest.

Oh, *fuck this.*

I lift my hands to scratch his face, maybe do a little eye-gouging, but instead, I just squeal. He swoops me backward, my stomach bottoming out as he sets me on the ground, flat on my back. He kneels before me, his arms on either side of my head as he braces himself over me.

Above him, the stars are twinkling bright, and the nearly full moon is casting a soft white glow down in the room.

It's almost dooming that the sky happens to be completely clear of clouds tonight. Overcast skies constantly plague Seattle.

I swallow, tears pricking my eyes.

"Such a gentleman, letting me look at the stars as you murder me," I mouth off, forcing the words through my tightened throat.

I really need to shut the fuck up. But I can't seem to stop myself. Apparently, when I'm in a life-threatening situation, all I can manage to do is make it worse.

Some might call it fearlessness, but I just call it stupidity.

He supports himself on one hand as the other reaches behind him. I open my mouth, gearing up for more insults, when his arm reappears, a gun in his hand.

Another audible click of my teeth later, and I'm back to being choked silent with fear.

"You let a man touch you in here. Make you come," he states, his tone bled dry of emotion. "Normally, I'd replace his fingers with my own, but I think you need something else to teach you a lesson."

"Okay, I'm sorry," I rush out, my eyes widening as he points the gun to my chest. "I-I'm really, rea—"

"Shh," he hushes. "You're not sorry yet, little mouse. But you will be."

April 14th, 1945

John and I are accompanying Frank for a dinner he has with the police department. We usually have a good time on these outings.

Frank is picking us up soon, and John and I are waiting around in stilted silence. Sera is off with her girlfriends for the night, and right now I wish she were here.

Lately, she's been a good buffer between the two of us. I don't know if she's noticed the difference. John and I aren't fighting. We're just coexisting.

I broke his heart. I know I did.

But why does it feel like mine is healing?

Frank is here now. Thank God.

Chapter Sixteen
The Manipulator

illions of thoughts run through my head on what I could possibly say to get out of this. *I'm sorry* clearly wasn't good enough.

"You're going to shoot me?"

My bladder is threatening to explode, and the knowledge that I might die in a puddle of pee brings tears to my eyes.

"I've already said I'm not going to kill you," he responds, his tone dripping with impatience. He punctuates his response by dragging the tip of the gun down through the valley of my breasts. The gun continues its path down my stomach, stopping at the edge of my leggings.

"Take these off."

My lip trembles and a single tear slides down my temple.

"Please, don't do this."

He cocks a brow, and the act is damning. He looks so damn unimpressed with my pleas, causing another tear to trace the path of the first.

"Now, Adeline."

Sniffing, I finally listen. Hooking my thumbs in the band of my leggings, I pull them down. I'm only able to reach mid-thigh before his body gets in the way.

He takes the hint, lifting up and ripping the leggings down the rest of the way. More tears follow suit.

"T-shirt next," he orders, jerking his gun to signal his order. I lift up and slide the shirt over my head, laying back down with a huff.

"Fucking beautiful," he murmurs, his eyes tracing over the curves of my body. Fucker is lucky I'm wearing my black lace set tonight.

He doesn't fucking deserve it, either.

He leans over me again, his mouth kissing the last bruise he left on my shoulder.

"Do you know what these mean?" he whispers, kissing another spot. I shudder beneath his touch, electricity sprouting from the point of contact and dancing across my skin.

I don't answer, but he doesn't seem to mind.

"They mean that I own you. Marked you as mine."

The tip of his tongue darts out, trailing my flesh as he moves down towards my breasts.

"Don't—"

His teeth pierce the swell of my left breast before I can finish my pointless demand. I gasp, squeezing my eyes shut as he leaves another mark on my skin.

Once he's satisfied, he renews his path with his mouth, leaving hickeys on both of my tits and several across my stomach. And all I can do is just take it. Because that gun in his hand is keeping me pliant—just like he planned.

When my body is well and abused from his teeth and tongue, he lifts up and forces my thighs open. I strain against him, but it only hurts me in the end. He's too strong.

His pointer finger curls in the edge of my thong, tracing the lining from the juncture of my thigh, down towards my center. Before he reaches my clit, he pulls the material out and runs his finger up and down the fabric, his finger a mere inch from my pussy.

I want to cover my face because I know he's feeling my body's betrayal.

"These are soaked," he rasps out, his lips still wet from his saliva.

"That's called discharge," I snap, hoping my lie turns him off. He smiles in response.

"As much as I hate to say this to you, I'm no stranger to a woman's pussy and what it feels like when it weeps for me."

I curl my lip in disgust. "Last time I checked, most girls weep because they're upset. Take a hint."

He chuckles. "Little mouse, that's exactly what I'm doing." He then pulls my thong to the side, baring my pussy to him, and the arousal glistening from within. He mutters a curse under his breath as his eyes devour every inch of me. Another tremble of my lips has me biting down on the traitorous flesh.

Keeping one finger hooked in my underwear, he points the gun in my face with the other. I recoil, pinching my eyes shut and letting loose a startled yelp.

"Relax, I just want you to suck on it."

It takes several seconds for his words to process. To process that he didn't pull the trigger, and I'm not dead. When they do, my eyes snap open, and I glare at him.

"Why the fuc—" He taps the tip of the gun on my mouth, effectively cutting me off. The rest of my words dissipate as he slides the gun across my lips, as if he's painting them with lipstick.

"Suck," he orders, his tone deepening with finality. Closing my eyes against more tears, I open my mouth and let him guide the gun between my teeth. I squeeze my lids tighter as I twirl my tongue over the cold metal, cringing from the nasty taste.

"Such a good girl," he says, pulling the dripping gun out, a trail of saliva following until it snaps.

My entire body locks when I feel the cool metal slide against my clit. I flinch against the foreign touch of an incredibly dangerous weapon.

Pure terror washes over me, and it takes all of my strength to keep from full on sobbing. Holding a gun to my head is far less intimidating than it being held between my legs. A gunshot to the head is instant death, but this? This would be slow and painful. Torturous.

He leans down, close enough for his hot breath to fan across my core. I lift up for a better view just as he looks up at me through long, thick lashes, his mismatched eyes sparkling with delight. Right when I open my mouth to ask what he's doing, he sticks out his tongue, saliva pooling to the tip and dripping off onto my pussy.

"Can never be too wet, can you, little mouse?"

Sitting up, he circles my entrance with the tip of the gun, the metal slipping against my skin.

"Oh my God, please do—" This time, my words are cut off from the feel of him dipping the gun past my folds. Just the tip, but enough to close my throat, only allowing a startled squeak to escape.

He laughs cruelly. "You even sound like a mouse."

I'd snap at him if I wasn't frozen solid. I can't look away. I just watch him push the gun inside me, my rounded eyes barely processing what I'm seeing. What I'm feeling.

Slowly, he works the gun inside me, drawing out both pleasure and pain. I clench my jaw, shuddering from his ministrations but refusing to make a sound. I won't give him that satisfaction.

He works the weapon halfway in before the gun retreats to the very tip. I'm allowed a moment's breath before he buries the entire barrel inside me. I suck in a sharp gasp and let my head fall back, no longer having the strength to watch.

This is so, so fucked up. Beyond fucked up.

But when the gun pulls out and sinks back in again, a noise does slip through as a wave of pleasure rocks through me.

"Good girl," he breathes. "Open wider, baby." The hand still holding my thong to the side nudges against my thigh. Without thought, my thighs instinctively fall further apart.

Another praise, but I barely hear it over the beating of my heart.

"I can feel how tight your pussy is. The way it grips onto my gun when I slide it out—so fucking pretty."

I bite my lip, but it isn't enough to hold in the next moan. Or the one after that. I can hear the suctioning and slurping noises as he fucks me with his gun, and shame fills me in response.

The embarrassment nearly overrides the fear. But neither of them is more potent than the pleasure my body is being forced to succumb to.

When he angles the gun in a particular way, he hits a spot inside me that sends my eyes to the back of my head and an unchecked moan to slip free.

He growls in response, my back arching as he continues to hit that spot. My thong grows impossibly tight, biting into my flesh before it's ripped away from my body, the sound getting lost in another cry.

The tattered fabric is tossed aside, freeing his hand to grip my thigh in a bruising hold.

My heart jumps when he leans down, but he only clamps his teeth on my inner thigh. I cry out from the sharp bite, but it quickly morphs into pleasure when he hits that spot again.

His mouth sucks and his movements quicken until I feel the beginnings of an orgasm settle low in the pit of my stomach.

"Please," I beg, but I don't know what for. He tears his mouth away just to clamp down again, lower this time, but still far away from my center.

Too far away.

"Tell me what you learned, Adeline," he demands, looking up at me, his mouth wet from his biting. The sight makes my heart drop deep into my belly, right to where the gun is driving into me.

"Not to bite your cheek?" I guess, my voice trembling.

He answers by biting my thigh in a punishing grip. I cry out, the pain blinding. He loosens his jaw, allowing the pain to bleed into pleasure. A primal noise slips out as he pushes the gun deep.

"Are you going to make me ask again?"

I open my mouth, but no answer comes out. My silence allows for me to hear his warning loud and clear. He cocks the gun.

"Okay, okay, *fuck*," I relent on a terrified hush. "I-I learned not to let another man touch me."

Those words bring tears to my eyes. Because saying them out loud makes me feel well and truly trapped by this man.

"Who's the only one allowed to touch you, Adeline?"

I close my eyes, hating the lie that's about to slip from my mouth just like the tears are from my eyes.

"You," I whisper, the bitter taste of the words clogging my throat. A battlefield rages in my body. The side that wants him to make me come, and the other side that wants him to turn the gun on himself and fire it.

I glance down at him and note the way he's staring up at me. And I have the terrifying realization that he doesn't believe my lies.

"You have ten more seconds to come, little mouse. No more after that," he warns before nipping at my thigh again. "Rub your clit, baby."

I hesitate. The last thing I want to do is allow this man the satisfaction of making me come, and even worse, helping him do it.

He doesn't fucking deserve it. And though my body is strung tight with desperation for it, my brain revolts against the thought.

"Now," he growls, his eyes blazing with something carnal and dangerous.

Muttering a curse, I reach down and twirl my fingers over my clit, too scared of the repercussions. If it's between orgasming and getting shot, I'm going to have to choose the option that will cause the least amount of damage.

"Good girl," he whispers. It takes two more thrusts of the gun before I'm tipping over the edge, my ass shooting clear off the ground as the orgasm rips through me.

I'm screaming. I can feel the sound vibrating the muscles in my throat. And I can feel how hoarse it's becoming. But I can't hear it. Not when my entire being is consumed in fire and ice, and the only thing I can see is heaven.

The gun works inside of me faster and deeper, drawing out the orgasm until

I'm literally begging for it to stop.

He rips the gun out of me, and my thighs snap shut instantly as the last of the orgasm dies.

I'm left a shuddering mess from the aftershocks, while he stands, his body towering over me.

I look up through half-lidded eyes, still jerking from the little shocks, when he lifts the gun and swallows the barrel. It feels like an out-of-body experience as I watch him lick the weapon clean, and then stick it in the back of his jeans.

My body is full of rage, humiliation, and shame—I know this. But it's like my brain can't process those emotions, so it's just choosing to feel nothing at all.

Is this what trauma does? Knowing you've been violated but your body chooses to go numb instead?

Like a magic trick, his hand comes back into view with a rose that must've been in his back pocket. The petals are crushed, likely from our struggle, but he doesn't seem to care. He twirls the rose in his hand before tossing it on me, the flower fluttering to my stomach.

With one last lingering look, he turns and walks out without a word.

And finally, the dam bursts as emotions crash through my body and flood out of my eyes.

For the next three nights, my shadow stood outside my window. Watching me, a red cherry blaring in the night as he puffed on a cigarette. What I wanted to tell him is how fucking disgusting it is that he smokes.

But the heat between my thighs likes the way he looks. I think my asshole of a vagina might've even been jealous of the cigarette. Apparently, it has a thing for inanimate objects.

And *that* reminder royally pissed me off. Enough to storm into the kitchen and pour myself an entire cup of wine. Wine cures everything for a little while.

Anger.

Trauma.

But now, with a glass of wine absent, rage causes my hands to tremble with the reminder of how he left me on the floor, tossing a rose on me like discarded trash and then leaving. I had never felt more debased as a human until that moment. Never more humiliated.

He hasn't messaged me since. Hasn't tried to come to me and wave another gun in my face. He just lingered outside the window.

And I stared back.

It's become our fucked-up routine.

He doesn't come around during the day, and as long as I'm not letting men feel me up and stick their hand down my pants, he doesn't text me any more threatening messages.

I don't tell Daya about our confrontation, and especially not about how that night ended. If my shadow doesn't murder me first, Daya will.

I was incredibly stupid. A fact I've never tried to deny. Especially now.

There's just no explaining the reactions he pulls from me. I'd love to pretend like confronting a scary man is so like me, but it's the exact opposite. I work myself into a panic attack if I have to ask a complete stranger a question.

So why is it every time he comes around, I slip into insanity?

"Why are you wearing a turtleneck?" Daya asks with disdain, shoving a bite of her salad into her mouth. We met at Fiona's to grab a bite to eat.

I needed to get out of the house. Desperately. The smallest things would bring me back to that night. And every time I looked in the mirror, I was overcome with the memory of his teeth sinking into me. And the bite of metal soon after.

I clear my throat. "I'm trying something new," I mutter. It was the only thing that would cover the marks staining my body. I had to order several of them in different colors through Amazon Prime, the need for them dire.

I can never let Daya see those marks. Nor could I ever confess the new meaning my stalker gave to finger-banging.

She shrugs her shoulders, looking down at her salad. "Only you can make a turtleneck, mom jeans, and a belt look fashionable."

I frown down at my outfit, disagreeing with her assessment. I hate this outfit, but maybe I only hate what it represents. Something designed solely to cover the bruises covering my body. Beneath these clothes is a map of purple hickeys.

"What about lover boy? Anything else happen with him?"

I hope the flush crawling up my neck stays down. If it doesn't, maybe I can blame it on the goddamn turtleneck.

"I'd much rather talk about Gigi," I say, eyeing the mozzarella sticks sitting between Daya and me. I've had four already and I want the last one. Noting my stare, Daya rolls her eyes and flaps her hand, urging me to take it.

I do so with a big smile on my face.

"I have some news on Ronaldo." Both brows shoot up, urging me to continue. "Last night I was picking through the diaries to see what I could find on him. Gigi would often mention him wearing nice suits and that gold ring, indicating that he was middle to upper class. And there was one entry where he seemed to have gotten jumped. Came in bruised and bloodied but wouldn't speak about it.

"So, I'm thinking he was involved in crime of some sort. He was very secretive about his life and told her at one point that he wouldn't allow his dangerous lifestyle to affect her."

"You think he was like a mob boss?"

I shake my head. "No, I think *his* boss was a mob boss. When Gigi spoke of him when he was beat up, she made it sound like he was punished for something. She quoted him saying, "it was nothing I didn't deserve," and that's all he would say.

"Gigi had noted several times in entries that she kept asking anyways, concerned for his wellbeing. The last thing he told her was that he had a very strict boss, and he couldn't know about her."

Daya nods her head, a spark of excitement in her sage eyes. "I'll look into crime families in the 40s. See if I can find anyone that might match his description."

I smile, feeling the same spark of hope. The high lasts for a total of five seconds before Daya's eyes widen, her gaze locked behind me.

My heart drops and the hairs on the back of my neck rise. My shadow wouldn't show up here now, would he? In front of Daya?

"Hello, ladies."

My eyes widen along with Daya's. Her gaze clashes with mine and a million things are said in the span of two seconds. Like that we need to be very fucking careful.

He sits down next to me, his body relaxing back into the chair as he stares at me with a wide smile that stops miles from his eyes.

I clear my throat and force a smile. "Hello, Max. Arch's friend, right?"

"The one and only," he responds, his stony blue gaze glued to my face. I can feel a blush creeping up my neck from the intensity of his glare.

"What can I do for you?" I ask casually, sipping on my quickly depleting margarita. I'm going to have to flag down the waitress soon because I'm going to need another to get me through the conversation, and one more to get me through the aftermath.

I'm going to need to call an Uber tonight, I already feel it.

He leans forward on the table, crossing his fingers and looking at me like he's really curious about something. His entire demeanor is hostile.

"I'd like for you to tell me exactly what happened when Arch went missing." His lips curl into a cruel smile as he tacks on, "From your doorstep."

I frown. "Didn't you already hear about it from the police reports?"

He narrows his eyes, that smile frozen on his ice-cold face. "I want to hear it from you, Ms. Reilly."

I do my best to keep my face blank, but I'm not sure how well I'm doing. Can't say I'm practiced in the art of handling a criminal. Matter of fact, three nights ago pretty much proved that I *suck* at handling criminals.

He said my last name to show me he looked into me. But that would be the one thing I'm used to by now. Being stalked.

"We went back to my place and had some fun," I start. A glimmer shines in Max's eye when I say that. "We were actually in the middle of having fun when someone banged really hard on my front door—"

"Has that happened before?"

My nerves flare because this is a question I don't know how to answer.

"No," I say finally, refraining from gulping like I really want to. I also really want to pick up my margarita again, but my hands are shaking, and I don't think I'll be able to hide that.

So, I act like an imbecile and lean over to suck down more of the margarita with it on the table.

"Hmm," he hums.

Max has to know I have a stalker now. It was something Sheriff Walters told me that would bite me in the ass with them, but I couldn't *not* report someone stalking me. Max must've seen those reports. But one thing is for sure, I didn't report his hands appearing on my doorstep.

"You see, Addie, I just can't quite figure out the motive, ya' know? Like, say, why would an enemy of Arch show up at *your* doorstep in the middle of Arch getting his dick wet?"

I flinch from his crass words, feeling almost ashamed that I let Arch touch me at all.

"Max," Daya snaps. His cold eyes turn to her, but she doesn't cower. "I've told ya'll a million fucking times. Addie had nothing to do with it."

His gaze thins again, and he leans further into the table, pinning Daya with a steely glare.

"That's the problem, Daya. I don't fucking believe you."

She snarls, her hands clenching into fists.

"If you want answers, Max, you're looking in the wrong place," I cut in before this conversation blows up and Max murders us right here and now.

"I don't think I am," he responds, facing me again. "Because Arch's hands ended up on your doorstep the next morning. And if I didn't know any better, I'd say that's personal. So why would Arch's hands be personal to *you?*"

He smiles in victory when my eyes round with surprise. "How did you know that?"

"Something didn't sit right with Arch going missing at your house of all places. The morning after, we sent a man to scope out your property. Just in time to see Daya here picking up a bloody box and driving off with it. They tailed her and after she buried it, they simply unburied it. Imagine our surprise when I saw my best friend's hands in that box. And imagine my surprise when my men told me it was gifted to *you*."

I don't look to Daya. I don't want Max to see just how alarmed I truly am.

My eyes thin. "Maybe it was put on my doorstep because whoever it was assumed I was connected to Arch's *dealings*."

He laughs then. "You think our rival assumed you were Arch's bitch? And that you were involved with our work?"

"Maybe," I snap. "Would they know if I wasn't?"

He doesn't answer. He just stares, sussing me out. And I stare back, letting him see the anger in my face. The frustration.

"Why did you have Daya bury them, Addie? Why not tell the police?"

I weigh my options and decide that telling the partial truth is my best bet. "Because there was a note in it threatening my life, along with any police officers involved if I called them. I was made aware of Arch's... *work* by then and thought it best to listen and not get further involved. In something I have *nothing* to do with, by the way."

Again, he just stares. My heart is beating out of my chest, and by the look in Max's eyes, I'm still not sure he believes me innocent.

Part of me just wants to confess to him that I'm being stalked. What difference would it make at this point, anyway? Now that Max discovered Arch's hands, there's no reason to keep it a secret.

But there is.

If Max discovers I have a stalker—one who is clearly violent and dangerous—he might use me as leverage to draw him out to get his revenge.

I'd become collateral. And I'm not sure I'd make it out alive.

At least this way, there's a chance that Max will leave me alone if he thinks I'm just some random girl who got caught in the crosshairs of gang activity.

Max hums again and stands, straightening his suit jacket and rebuttoning it. The suit drips class and money, and something tells me Max has taken over the Talaverra's dealings.

There's a new crime lord in town, and he's pissed. At me, no less.

"Enjoy the rest of your dinner, ladies."

He walks away, taking all of his bad juju with him. The air instantly feels lighter now that he's gone, but he managed to still leave an ashy taste in my mouth.

"They're going to be a problem," Daya says quietly.

I nod and flag down the waitress. "Add it to the fucking list."

April 15th, 1945

This evening was awful. John drank too much, and when he does, he gets mean.

Finally, the dam broke and he accused me of cheating. Frank was there and looked at me as if I killed his dog. This happened in front of Frank's work associates.

It was mortifying. But nothing I didn't deserve.

I denied his claims of course, more worried about calming him down. We left right after, and I could feel the stares searing into my back as I walked out.

Frank had to carry him in the house and put him to bed. I was too angry to even help undress him.

After Frank got John to bed, he asked me if it was true.

I said no, but I don't think he believed me.

He stormed out of the house after that. And I'm not sure what I said to upset him so badly.

Chapter Seventeen
The Shadow

Fuck. She's so pretty when she thinks no one is watching.

My little mouse trudges into her bedroom, her tattered slippers dragging against the smooth stone floors. She's tired. Dark circles are beginning to form underneath her eyes.

I want to smooth them away, just to bring them back again. But I want her to be tired from staying up all night, taking my cock into her body until she's depleted of all her strength. Even then, I'll still fuck her.

I deprived myself last time. Refused to touch her with my own hands when she hadn't earned that from me yet. But watching that gun slide in and out of her pussy was just as torturous for me.

I barely made it to my car before I was coming in my hand, the sweet melody of her smoky cries echoing in my head.

That woman's voice alone can bring any man to their knees.

And now, she's wearing nothing but a long white t-shirt, the soft cotton ending mid-thigh. Her rosy nipples poke through the thin material, and my mouth waters with the need to take one into my mouth and suck on it until she's wriggling beneath me.

I lick my lips. Soon.

Her tantalizing, creamy skin is on full display, and I get hints of her red cotton panties anytime she bends over. Like when she pulls the covers back and pounds her tiny fist into the pillow to fluff it up.

I get a full view of her ass when she slides her feet out of her slippers, and then bends down to arrange them neatly before her nightstand.

My cock hardens, her perfectly round ass overflowing her underwear. Her pussy is on full display. Just a thin piece of fabric separating her from my tongue.

I close my eyes and work to regain control.

I have to be quiet.

She doesn't know I'm hiding in her closet. Waiting for her to fall asleep so I can stare at her beauty in peace.

Right now, she fears me. Rightfully so.

I'm a dangerous man, and I kill people daily. Not only that, but I enjoy it too.

She should fear me, but only because once she ultimately submits to me, she'll have no chance of escaping me.

She's already started to and hasn't even realized it yet.

I've never been in love with anything other than my job. I haven't even bothered fucking a woman for over a year. I just don't have time. They were always a quick fuck, and then I'd be off again, the release rarely easing any tension.

After dealing with enough tears and desperate attempts to get me to stay with them, I grew tired of the hassle.

The moment I saw her sitting in that bookstore, working to hide her nerves and anxiety, there I was—a grown-ass man, falling in obsession at first sight.

And now, I feel like a fifteen-year-old boy who just discovered what pussy feels like. Every time I set eyes on her, I'm ready to bust in my jeans just from looking at her.

I want to touch her, kiss her, and make her mine in every sense of the word. Marking her body wasn't enough. But I get the feeling I will never feel like I've had enough of Adeline Seraphina Reilly. At least on paper.

And I have no fucking shame. I never claimed to be a good man.

She slides into her bed, curls up under the duvet, and picks up an old leather book.

Her great-grandmother's diary.

After Addie had left one day to run errands or some shit, I flipped through the pages.

Her great-grandmother also had a stalker. It made me smile when I realized history was repeating itself.

Addie flips through the diary for an hour, her face pinched with an unreadable emotion as she inhales Gigi's deepest, darkest secrets. It looks like she's searching for answers, and the only thing that will give her clarity is her great-grandmother's words.

Part of her looks disturbed by the diaries. But a bigger part of her seems fascinated. Enthralled. Like she's trying to picture falling in love with her stalker, and the thought both excites her and makes her deeply uncomfortable.

I want to laugh at that. Because that's exactly what's going to fucking happen.

I'm going to make her fall in love with every single fucked up part of me. I want this girl to see me at my most depraved. I want her to experience the true darkness residing in my soul.

When you make someone fall in love with the darkest parts of you, there's nothing you can do that will scare them away.

They will be yours forever because they already love all the fucked up bits and pieces of you.

Her eyes start to droop, her head lolls, and the diary begins to slip from her black-painted fingers.

She jolts awake, her eyes rounding before she settles down. I bite my lip, too many feelings invading my chest.

Giving up pretenses, she snaps the journal shut, slides it on her nightstand and clicks off the light. Instantly, the room goes black. The moonlight filtering through the balcony doors casts shadows across the room, creating monsters out of wooden furniture.

The only real monster in this house is me.

Once her breathing deepens, I slowly slide the closet door open and wait in the shadows, making sure she hasn't awoken.

Just as I go to take a step, a burst of ice blooms across the back of my neck. Goosebumps rise on my skin as I turn my head and look around in the closet, fighting against the urge to chatter my teeth.

It's an unnatural cold, and it's not the first time I've felt it. But whatever is breathing down my neck isn't going to deter me. I feel its eyes on me, and I hope I meet its stare so it can see I'm not the least bit afraid.

Seeing nothing, I turn and step out into the room. The chill recedes as I make my way over to her bed. I'm tempted to brush her hair away from her face, but I know it'll wake her.

She senses danger easily, and I know she's going to catch me soon.

A large part of me wants her to. There's a depravity in my mind that enjoys seeing her scared. I want to see her scream because I know every time she gets scared, my little mouse gets turned on, too. It makes the blood rush straight to my cock, and I want more than anything to show her exactly how hard I can make her scream.

But the softer part of me wants to watch her sleep in peace. Especially because I know I'll bring her so little of it when she's awake.

Slipping the rose out of my pocket, I lay it on her nightstand. She'll freak out in the morning, and I'll make sure to play the video back so I can see it and find joy in her terror.

She stirs, and a loud noise disturbs the air.

Something between a snore and snorting like a pig.

I bring my fist to my mouth, biting down hard to keep the laughter from exploding out of me. Immediately, I turn and exit the room, struggling immensely in keeping quiet.

I don't think I've ever heard a noise like that come out of *anybody*, let alone someone that looks as cute as Addie does. I've tortured and killed a lot of people, and that was... that was unlike anything I've ever heard.

It's only when I'm out of the house that I let loose a bark of laughter.

But my laughter is cut short when my phone buzzes in my pocket. I pull it out, seeing Jay's name flash across the screen.

"Yeah?" I answer, my steps quickening as I make my way to my car.

Jay only calls me for work purposes. And usually, that results in shooting one or twelve people dead.

"Mark Seinburg is in town," he starts, diving right in. It's what I like best about Jay. He gets straight to the point. "Along with his colleagues Miller Foreman, Jack Baird, and Robert Fisher."

I open my car door and sink into the leather seat. I turn on my car, but don't make a move to leave yet.

"Where are they?" I ask.

"I've gotten hits in casinos, a couple of high scale bars and a private gentlemen's club. Members only. All places that are heavily guarded."

"Guards mean they have something to hide," I say. "They're of no concern to me."

It's not cockiness, it's just facts. My confidence in my skills is the only thing that keeps me alive.

You can't go into a lion's den with the confidence of a gazelle. You go in knowing that you're going to walk back out with their blood on your hands and their heads rolling on the ground.

It's the only way you'll ever survive.

"They're not," Jay acquiesces. "It's too soon to storm their hangouts, though. I got you access to a couple of the gentlemen's clubs they attend. I think they're going to be our best bet for information. Just go there, scope them out, start making more appearances there, and gain their trust. See if there's anything amiss."

The laughter from Addie is long gone. It almost feels like I never felt such a... *happy* emotion only minutes ago. Dickheads trafficking innocent children will do that to you.

"Fuck, Jay, you want me to mingle with a bunch of rapists? I can hack into their cameras."

"Hacking into cameras only gets you so far."

I sigh, rubbing at the tightening muscle in my shoulder. He's right. Their cameras won't have audio, and there's a lot more to learn when listening in on conversations.

"And right now, we have nothing," Jay continues, driving home his point.

I nod, though he can't see me. Making friends with the pedos means I could be invited into the ritual. Based on the video, it's definitely deep underground. Gaining access will be incredibly difficult, but nothing is ever impossible for me.

Not only that, but it'll put more people on my radar to take down.

It's a fucking network of pedophiles and once you meet one, you meet a hundred more. It's fucking exhausting—the never-ending list of people to kill.

But I'm a very patient man.

"I know," I agree. "I'll make the necessary connections."

I *will* find this place, and once I do, I will kill every single motherfucker associated with that hellhole.

By the time I'm done, the entire government will be dismantled.

Chapter Eighteen
The Manipulator

UNKNOWN: You're so pretty when you sleep.

My heart drops when I read the text. I already knew the fucker was in my house from the rose on my nightstand, but his lack of shame enrages me. I feel the blood rush to my cheeks as fury and embarrassment rise inside of me.

I was knocked out cold last night, and I hate that while I was peacefully sleeping, a man was standing over me, watching and just being an all-around freak of nature. The thought sends cold shivers down my spine.

After Max crashed our dinner, Daya and I felt considerably on edge—the mood soured and rotted. We combated that feeling by bar-hopping. We picked a random drink off the menu for each other, and by the end of the night, we were both pretty toasted.

I tried to avoid thinking about Max the entire night, but his threats plagued me anyway. Lingering at the back of my mind, there to remind me when I had a moment to think.

And it hasn't gotten any better.

I spent this whole day trying to write, but I barely managed over a thousand words. I've long since given up and have retreated to my room to watch mindless TV.

ME: You'll look pretty after I stab you.

I don't even know why I reply to him. I should stop and report this to the police. They'll think I'm antagonizing him.

Jesus, I *am* antagonizing him.

But after Max's threat, I don't need any more reason to make him suspicious by reporting a stalker. And for the ones I already made after Arch's disappearance, I hope those went missing too.

Never thought I'd wish for my only evidence against my shadow to disappear, but the threat of Max oddly frightens me more.

Maybe I'm kidding myself with a false sense of security with the former. He's scared the absolute fuck out of me, but he hasn't seemed inclined to physically hurt me. In fact, he's done the exact opposite, and that knowledge makes me sick.

Max, on the other hand, I know would hurt me.

UNKNOWN: A gun wasn't enough for you? Interesting.

I drop the phone on my bed, and then my head into my hands. But then my head snaps up when I remind myself that the fucker was watching me sleep last night. Which means he got in my house *again*.

All the blood in my cheeks drains like a whirlpool when I realize he could've been in my house before I even went to bed.

That's what he did last time, and I was pretty out of it last night. I know I read Gigi's diary for a little while, but I don't think I retained a single word I read.

My gaze draws to my closet doors, like a magnet on a refrigerator. It's a large closet with two doors that slide apart. My eyes thin, narrowing on the tiny crack between the two.

My body moves on autopilot. I'm scrambling out of my bed and storming to the closet door before I can think it through. I have no idea what I'd do if he's standing there.

Probably shit myself.

I tear the doors open and stop short when I'm met with nothing but way too many clothes that I don't wear.

There's nowhere for him to hide in here. It's not a deep closet and certainly not big enough to hide a six-foot-too-many-inches man. My hands tear through my clothes anyways, searching for him. And even when I'm positive he's not there, I stare harder, swiping my clothes aside with heightening aggression.

Get a fucking grip, Addie. It's like you want *him to be there.*

I sigh and turn away, the adrenaline rush diminishing. There's nowhere else in this room for him to hide. As immense as the room is, it's an open concept with minimal furniture.

Now, I just feel like an idiot.

I plop on the bed, crisscrossing my legs as I stare at my phone like it's a mousetrap with a big ass block of cheese in it. Gourmet smoked gouda fucking cheese, to be precise.

The phone lights up with an incoming text, the vibrations in the bed traveling straight up my legs.

I snatch it up. I fucking love gouda cheese, goddammit.

UNKNOWN: I'll be seeing you tonight, little mouse.

I snarl.

ME: From outside my house, and preferably in a cop's handcuffs.

UNKNOWN: You don't need a cop to get me in handcuffs, baby. I'll let you do anything you want to me.

I'm going to suffer from a heart attack with the severe directions my blood keeps rushing to. My pussy pulses from the illicit thought of him handcuffed to my bed, a smirk on his face, dripping with sin. And those goddamn mismatched eyes looking up at me the way he did when he was fucking me with his gun. Like I'm a little mouse that he wants to devour, stuck in the trap with the gouda cheese puffing up my cheeks.

Fuck.

My hands shake as I try to force the thought from my head. But it's taken hold and I can't get it out.

I straighten my legs, squeezing my thighs together. But it doesn't ease the steady throb between my clenched thighs, nor the wetness pooling between them.

My heart races as another ping vibrates my phone.

I don't want to look, but I have no fucking self-control.

UNKNOWN: Are you playing with yourself, little mouse? Touching your sweet little pussy to the thought of me handcuffed to your bed?

ME: You're disgusting.

But that's exactly what I've begun to do. As soon as I read the words, it was like he possessed my body to do exactly what he was asking. My hand snaked down into my panties, my finger gently swiping at my engorged clit. Even as I wrote back my scathing reply.

I'm wearing nothing but a long t-shirt and comfortable underwear.

I feel bare and exposed beneath the thin cotton. When my legs begin to fall apart, I rip my hand out like I touched a burning stove, hissing at my own stupidity.

UNKNOWN: And you're a liar.

ME: Fuck. Off.

UNKNOWN: Next time you tell me to fuck off, your clit is going between my teeth.

My bottom lip goes between mine. I suck my lip in sharply, shocked by his nerve. By the pure *audacity* this man possesses. Yet just as turned on.

I squeeze my hand around the phone, hating myself more and more as this conversation progresses.

My fingers twitch with the need to tell him to fuck off again. The asshole probably doesn't even know how oppositional I am.

Tell me not to do something, and I'll only want to do it more.

And with a threat like that, I'm so fucking tempted. I feel my heart tumble in my chest again, beating against my rib cage as my thumb travels over the letters.

I stare at the two words on my screen, my thumb hovering over the Send button. My shadow has proven to follow through with his threats.

So why do I want to do it so badly? I mean, who instigates their fucking stalker? And to put his mouth on their pussy, no less.

I throw my phone as soon as my thumb skates across the button. The message swoops away, and I know I just did something idiotic.

Fuck, fuck, fuck.

My head is in my hands again, my fingers clenching my hair tightly until I feel the strands pulling taut, tiny stabs of pain following suit.

Ping.

The racing muscle inside my ribcage bursts free and climbs up my throat.

I can't look. Abruptly, I stand, restless energy coating my nerves until I'm nearly convulsing. I need to... do something. Distract myself.

Snatching my phone, I hurry down the hall, down the creaky wooden stairs, and into my kitchen.

It's dark in here. Eerie. But my stubbornness prevents me from turning any lights on.

Ping.

Shakily, I pour two fingers of my grandfather's whiskey into a glass. And then I hold up the decanter, noting how little is left.

Asshole.

I shoot the alcohol down in one swallow. The taste is smoky, with a hint of citrus. It burns on the way down, turning the insides of my body into an inferno.

As if I wasn't already burning up.

After I pour myself another two fingers and swallow that down, I work up the courage to look at my phone.

UNKNOWN: Oh, little mouse.

UNKNOWN: I can't wait to eat you. There will be nothing left of you once I'm done.

Goddammit.

Shivers wrack through my body, and I drop the phone. It clatters loudly against the island, disturbing the stilted air.

"God? Why do you fucking hate me?" I ask aloud, my voice ringing out into empty air.

Of course, she doesn't answer me. She never does. I'm not even talking to God. I'm talking to myself and the ghosts inside this house.

Not even they will answer me.

Fuck it. I'm going to bed.

I storm up the stairs, turn off the T.V., and slip back into my bed, connecting my phone to the charger, and then toss the blanket over my head.

Under here, the monsters can't get me. I'm safe. Untouchable.

I ignore the throbbing between my legs and close my eyes, willing myself to sleep.

And despite the sporadic thoughts floating around in my head, I manage to drift off into a restless sleep. I toss and turn, the blanket keeping my body too warm, but my subconscious won't allow the blanket to go past my eyes.

Sometime in the middle of the night, I feel rough flesh skate across my arms. My subconscious slowly starts to drift away from my dreams, but it feels like I'm weighed under a heavy fog.

Something rough glides around one wrist, jolting me further into consciousness. When I feel the rough texture tighten around my other wrist, I finally start to slip back into reality. My surroundings rush in, and even in my half-asleep state, I know something is wrong.

My face feels tight, and my body is exposed.

I feel the blanket drift past my breasts, down my stomach, and past my hips. When the cool air settles, tightening my nipples into sharp buds, I jerk awake.

My eyes open wide, and my breath lodges in my throat when I see a dark figure settled between my legs. Immediately, I panic. My heart races and my adrenaline surges.

I go to scream, but something constricts my mouth. My eyes round when I realize my mouth is taped shut.

Several realizations hit all at once. My arms are above me, tied to the headboard with thick ropes. I tug against the binds, desperately trying to slide my wrists out of the loops to no avail.

I struggle hard, but my body can only move so much. Thick thighs trap me into a firm hold as my stalker props himself above me, his face concealed by the shadows.

I continue to fight against the rope but only succeed in rubbing my skin raw.

"What did I tell you, little mouse?" he asks, his deep voice barely above a whisper. I don't even spare him a glance, my panicked gaze glued to the ropes that are rendering me completely fucking helpless.

Fuck what he told me.

"Let me go!" I shout beneath the tape, but the words are muffled and indistinguishable.

He plants his hands on my hips and roughly pins me to the bed. Electric shocks travel from his skin to mine, the feeling making me tremble beneath his calloused hands.

Panic sends my mind into a complete tailspin. I no longer think rationally. My body goes into survival mode, and I fight against his hold with all the strength I can muster.

But it's useless. He's too big. Too heavy. Too fucking imposing.

I scream with frustration, attempting to buck him off. He laughs at my attempt, the rich sound of his amusement sending ice down my spine.

I still, huffing and puffing against the tape. My hair is in disarray, with several tendrils scattered across my face and constricting my view of him.

Not that I particularly want to see his face anyways. It's a goddamn weapon.

Gently, he brushes the tendrils out of my face, tenderness in his touch.

"Fascinating that you have yet to learn, I always follow through with my threats," he whispers.

"Fuck. Off!" I shout, enunciating my words as clearly as possible beneath the tape. They're muffled, but he heard what I said loud and clear anyway.

He grabs my face in his hand roughly and brings his face down into mine. Minty breath and a hint of smoke washes over me.

"Keep pissing me off, Adeline. I do enjoy hurting you. It's music to my ears when I hear you cry."

I struggle against him, muffled curse words spilling from my taped mouth.

Another chuckle reaches my ears.

"You've been a very bad girl, little mouse," he drawls, his deep tenor vibrating through his throat. "And I do enjoy showing you what happens to bad girls."

Sweat pricks at my hairline and trails down my back. I'm still panicking—absolutely shaking with fear.

But I have no idea how the hell I'm going to get away from him. Tears prick at my eyes when I realize that I can't.

His words from before filter through the panic. *You can't escape me.*

His calloused fingers lift up my t-shirt, exposing my black lace panties and flat stomach. I can't see them, but I feel his eyes devouring me. He continues to lift the shirt until my breasts are bared to him.

I hear a sharp intake of breath, revealing his desire. My nipples are tightened into hard peaks. But the asshole is cracked if he thinks it's because of *him.*

"You are absolutely exquisite," he breathes, his hands trailing across my stomach reverently. Over the fading marks, he forced on me four nights ago.

"Fuck. Off," I growl again.

"Don't mind if I do," he tells me, his voice shadowed with desire and anticipation.

My eyes round when his fingers skim beneath the waistband of my underwear, teasing my sensitive skin and warning me of his intentions. I suppress the shiver, determined to maintain my dignity, even as he pulls them down to my knees in one move.

My fight renews, kicking at him harshly and landing a good kick in his chest. He powers through the kick, pushing back into it and sending painful shockwaves up my leg.

It stuns me long enough for him to slip my underwear the rest of the way down my legs. Instead of discarding my underwear, he bundles them in a ball and slides them in his pocket.

Oh… that's *gross!*

I growl, deep in my chest and desperately kick at him again. I use both legs, putting every bit of force behind them. He snatches both of my feet before they can connect with his face.

Dammit.

I squirm, upending the upper half of my body as I struggle.

Quickly, he works his hands around both ankles while avoiding a foot to the face. And then he forces my legs apart, pinning my knees to the bed as he bares my pussy.

What felt like forever only took fifteen seconds.

I force myself to still, my chest heaving wildly. If I continue to buck, I'll only be putting my pussy right in his stupid face. And the asshole would just *love* that.

Rage unlike anything I've ever felt floods me, replacing the fear and helplessness. I scream beneath the tape, raging and cursing him as his eyes eat up the expanse of my center.

The moonlight doesn't provide enough light for him to see much, but it doesn't matter to him. He's seen it before.

He inhales deeply. "Fuck, you smell just like I remember. So fucking sweet."

He leans down and places a gentle kiss on my pelvic bone. I arch my back, pushing my body deeper into the mattress and away from his kiss. I'm panting harshly through my nose, imitating a pissed-off bull.

Self-hatred wars against the hatred for him. I did this to myself. I know I did. I instigated him—pushed against him when he warned me what would happen.

It didn't matter. I was too fucking stupid and hard-headed. Too high off whatever sick thrill I can't seem to get enough of.

He grips my hips and roughly yanks me down, tightening the bonds on my wrists and giving him full access to my pussy.

Another soft kiss, an inch above my clit. I can't stop the whimper that releases from my mouth, sticking against the tape, just as my lips are.

But the tape doesn't mask the sound like it's masking my words. I feel him pause, and then he smiles against my skin.

I shudder beneath his touch, his hot breath fanning across my most sensitive area. My knees jerk inward, another useless attempt to close my legs.

And then I feel them. A stubborn tear slips free as his teeth scrape against my mound. I scream and thrash against the feeling, dislodging his teeth from my skin only for my body to jerk right back into his mouth.

I gasp, feeling far more than just teeth this time. His tongue slides against my clit, a feral groan releasing from his throat as he tastes me. Uncontrollably, my eyes roll and my head kicks back as the most delicious feeling envelopes me.

But I refuse to let that cloud my judgment. Riding alongside pleasure is disgust.

Disgust at myself—my body—for feeling anything else. And disgust that he is taking something that I didn't willingly give.

"*Fuck*," he growls against me, the vibrations forcing me to suck in a deep breath. The sound of his deep tenor sends a burst of butterflies into my stomach.

"You're so fucking creamy," he rasps. I squeeze my eyes shut, hating how I feel my pussy throb from his words and the attention he's giving me. More so, I hate that he's right. I can smell my own arousal, feel the juices sliding down my asscheeks.

I shake.

I shake because I don't know what else to fucking do right now.

Now more than ever, I hate *myself*, and the reaction my body has to adrenaline and terror.

He licks the entirety of my slit, his tongue moving leisurely all the way up to the bundle of nerves before he sucks my clit between his teeth and clamps down.

Just like he said he would.

I scream with both fright and bliss. His bite is hard enough to send a wave of pain scattering across my clit, but not hard enough to truly hurt me.

He pulls his head away slowly, my clit dragging between his teeth until it slips free, a burning sensation radiating from the bud.

I try to wriggle away, but all it does is cause him to slide his hands behind my knees and forcefully push them back to my ears.

I squeeze my eyes shut again, another traitorous tear slipping free as I thrash against my bonds, desperate to slip free. In this position, I'm far more exposed and vulnerable to him.

But just as it always does, the thrill of danger sends an uncomfortable feeling straight to my core.

He has my body curled so far inward, my ass is no longer on the bed. As if I wasn't already ashamed enough, I feel my arousal sliding down my stomach.

He growls, noting the desire flooding from my entrance. I can feel his body tightening with need, power rippling through his body.

He doesn't waste any more time bringing his mouth back to my pussy and sucking my clit back into his mouth.

I jerk, the pleasure renewed as he tugs and sucks at the bud. He doesn't lick me again, refusing to use his tongue against me—only his teeth.

Every time I move, he clamps harder. So I force myself to stiffen, but the pressure doesn't lessen. If anything, it only heightens until sharp pain is sluicing from my clit.

I squeal from the sting, screaming muffled curses at him through the tape. And just when it becomes too much, he lets go. I pant through the relief and the lingering pain, my clit throbbing and sore.

But he doesn't allow me to suffer for long. His middle finger slides inside of me, curling to hit that sweet spot. My hips buck against his hand, a different type of pleasure swelling inside of me.

A bliss that stings and burns but yet, feels fucking incredible.

"Did that hurt?" he asks softly, tilting his head as he watches his finger slide in and out of me, juices collecting in the palm of his hand.

Now that one of my legs is free, I'm tempted to drive my foot into his face. But the reminder of that bite keeps my leg still.

So I just fume silently, glaring holes into him. The anger feels like it's burning me from the inside out.

He hums, disappointed by my silence. Leaning down, he captures the abused nub between his teeth, sucking in but keeping his bite minimal. Combined with his finger curling up to hit that spot, I can no longer breathe.

Gently, he scrapes his teeth over the sensitive flesh. Over and over until it drives me mad with both the need for more and the need to kill him. Maybe I can cut his hands off like he did Arch. Knock his teeth out so he can't turn my body against me anymore.

"Remember this, little mouse," he murmurs in between nips. "Remember that your disobedience brings you pain." Another sharp nip. My hips jerk away, but the action is futile. "I know you remember how good it felt when my gun was fucking your pussy. Imagine my tongue inside of you—my cock. The pleasure you'd feel would be blinding."

His finger curls and proves his words true, sending that blinding pleasure racing throughout my body.

I feel the break. The moment when my body decides it needs what he's giving me more than the need for him to stop.

I fight against the dark part of me that wants to beg for more. A dark part that has found a voice and is trying to break free. Take over and give in to this man so we both can find relief. I thrash against it, entering a silent battlefield and trying to choke the life out of it so it never comes to light.

But then he withdraws his finger to the very tip, swiping his finger along my entrance, and when he sinks back inside me, he adds two more fingers. My eyes roll as he stretches me, caressing that sweet spot over and over while his teeth bite into my clit anew.

The dark side of me wins while I watch helplessly as my body renews its struggle. But this time, I'm shamefully grinding myself against him. He's not giving me what my body has begun to crave—to *need*—in order to assuage the pleasure building deep in my belly.

He continues to scour my clit with his teeth. Nipping and biting, but refusing to give me his tongue.

Frustration mounts until I'm brimming with it. I'm so, so *angry*, but now it's because he's denying me pleasure.

"Asshole!" I screech against the tape. The answering smile against my pussy is evident that he heard me.

Giving into the anger, I kick my leg out with unrestrained force. He dodges the kick by a mere inch.

A feral growl tears from his chest, and he pushes my knee back down with bruising force. The sound wasn't of desire like before—but anger.

Even if I were forced in front of a priest tomorrow, no fear of God would convince me to confess how fucking sexy that growl was. Or how hard my pussy pulsed in response.

I'll *never* confess that—not even to myself.

He tightens his grip to a punishing hold. Tomorrow, I'll have handprints on the underside of my thighs. They'll go nicely with the hickeys smattering my body.

"What did you learn, little mouse?" he taunts, blowing hot breath directly onto my clit.

I growl, another frustrated tear leaking down my temple and into my hairline.

"Are you going to tell me to fuck off again?" he asks, darting out his tongue for a sharp lick. It's there and gone before I can get any satisfaction from it.

I shout at him some more until he finally reaches up and rips the tape from my mouth. I curse against the flaring pain in my face, and then keep cursing now that he can finally fucking hear me.

"You fucking psycho motherf—" my tangent is cut short due to another painful bite to my clit.

"Try again. Are you going to tell me to fuck off again?"

I heave, trying to calm myself down but failing.

I don't even know how to begin to name the emotions swelling inside of me. I could explode from the force of them converging all in my chest.

"Probably," I grind out through gritted teeth. He chuckles, a musical sound so dark, it must come straight from an Edgar Allan Poe flick.

He nips at me again, but this one lighter and more playful.

"Do you understand what's going to happen from now on when you do?"

I clamp my mouth shut, refusing to answer such a stupid fucking question. I understand perfectly what's going to happen. It's just a matter of *listening*.

In response to my nonverbal answer, he withdraws his fingers, leaving me bereft. But before I can complain, he licks me again, this time slower and more languid. He flattens his tongue and licks me from the bottom up, going particularly slow over my pulsating clit.

My eyes close against the sensation, a breath whooshing from my throat. There's no stopping the shivers that encase my spine. No stopping the bliss radiating from where his tongue laps up my cunt.

I arch my back, growling from how easily my body turns to jello beneath his unfairly skilled tongue.

But just as I start to grind against his mouth, shamefully and unabashedly, he stops.

"Do you. Understand?" he asks again, his tone lilted with superiority.

A frustrated sob works its way up my throat, but I swallow it back down. It takes several swallows before I feel confident to speak levelly, though the words taste like battery acid on my tongue.

"Loud and fucking clear, kitty cat."

A dark chuckle skitters across my core, and I'm ashamed of how my body responds. My ass curves towards his mouth without permission, seeking what it needs.

His tongue dives into my pussy, licking the insides with ravenous strokes.

A cry leaves my lips, breathless and embarrassingly loud.

The pressure builds as he finally does what I've been silently begging for. His tongue swirls up to my clit with the perfect amount of pressure, paying special attention to the abused bud before dipping lower again and spearing the muscle inside of my pussy.

Cries of pleasure echo throughout the room, and now I regret the tape ever leaving my mouth. Because I don't want him to hear what he's doing to me, but I can't seem to contain myself either.

I just lose myself. To him and the thrashing of his tongue on my clit. It's impossible to resist as the coil deep in my stomach curls painfully tight.

I can't stop him from sucking my clit into his mouth any more than I can control the orgasm from reaching its peak.

I suck in a sharp breath, a strangled cry escaping as my body falls over the edge. He plunges two fingers inside me just as I do, and the bliss is catastrophic. I no longer care to hold back the sharp screams, nor do I stop my thighs from clamping his head firmly between them.

Drown in my fucking pussy. Die there for all I care.

Euphoria consumes me, wrapping me so tightly in its clutches, all five of my senses are lost to it.

This isn't a climb to heaven. It's a fall from grace.

I'll never recover—not when my soul has been ripped from my body and dragged down to hell. I fell so deeply that I've found myself in the devil's lair, being feasted on from the dark god himself.

Moans wrack from my throat, and I feel his answering groan. His hands clutch at my thighs, prying them apart just enough to continue to lap at my throbbing cunt, riding out the orgasm for longer than my body can handle.

He rips his mouth away and crawls up my body while continuing to fuck me with his fingers. I'm still delirious, my mouth still parted as I continue to moan. So, when he pinches my cheeks, holding my mouth open, I hardly care. His fingers feel too good.

His mouth skates over my lips once before I watch a trail of saliva drip from his mouth into mine.

"Swallow your juices," he rasps.

And I do. My throat works as the unique taste blooms across my tongue. He growls deep in his chest before he crushes his lips to mine.

I let him. Later, I'll ask myself why. But with his fingers still drawing out pleasure, despite my orgasm having faded and the fog clouding my judgement—I fucking let him.

Not only that, but I kiss back.

His tongue dives into my mouth, swirling with my own. Fire and electricity spark from our connected lips, and it feels like planets colliding. Like the energy is astronomical, and with every brush and every lick, a new star is being born.

Time ceases to exist as he kisses me until my lips are bruised, and I'm sure I'll come out of this with a permanent stutter in my breathing. At one point, he withdrew his fingers and cupped my face with his hands almost sweetly. A stark contrast to… well, *him* and the way he devours me.

He yanks himself away when our bodies begin to grind ruthlessly and moans slip free, and I'm glad for it. The second he retreats, it's like time and clarity come rushing back in, hitting me over the head like someone just clocked me with a bat.

I don't open my eyes, I just suck in deeply, breathless from that kiss. His body slips out from between my thighs, and I immediately snap my knees inward and drop my feet, hiding myself from his ravenous eyes.

Being consumed by him feels like drowning in water with a live wire in it. Electric currents ravish your body until you're overcome with it. No oxygen. No thought. No control.

And when it's over, he yanks you out of the water. The electricity still dancing across your skin, currents sparking between your bodies, but you can see and think clearly again.

All you can feel is like you've been ripped to shreds. Like your body chemistry has been completely rearranged, and you've come out of that water an entirely different person.

I *hate* him for it.

I hate him more than I've ever hated anyone. The bliss fades, and the familiar feeling of fury and hatred reawaken.

He doesn't speak, but I feel the power bubbling beneath his skin.

I can feel the desire. The thirst. The absolute ravenous beast threatening to tear from his skin.

If it does, I can no longer trust myself to stop him from consuming me from the inside out. And the realization makes me want to cry.

I let it fucking happen again. With the gun, and now this, *why* do I keep letting this happen?

He's forcing himself on me, we both know that. But in the end, he had me wanting it just as much as he did. He had me nearly begging for it. Whether it was his gun fucking me or his tongue, my legs fell open by the time it was over.

Not to mention we just made out like two horny teenagers about to lose their virginity.

I don't know what the fuck to do with that information. Or how the hell to even process it.

A moment of silence passes, the air disturbed only by our heavy breathing.

I'm not strong enough to open my eyes and face what happened. I'm scared of what I'll do—what I'll say.

For the first time, the asshole in the sky finally listens to my pleas and compels this man to reach over, untie the ropes and walk the fuck away.

I force my eyes open and watch him go, swallowing the venom that threatens to spew from my mouth. If I let it loose, I know it'll just result in him carrying out another threat.

He pauses at the door, turning his head just enough for the moonlight to reveal his sharp jawline, the wetness coating his skin, and a hint of a scar.

He doesn't speak, but he does bite his bottom lip hard, trapping whatever meaningless words on his tongue. Right along with the taste of my pussy.

Finally, he turns, the door gently clicking shut behind him. For the second time, I'm left alone. Decimated and in ruins. And again, I let the tears fall freely while I work to pick up the pieces.

June 19th, 1945

John is drunk again. I told him that I needed space, and of course I sneaked off to see Ronaldo.

I know, I know.

My husband is hurt and angry, and to escape his harsh, but validated words, I run off to cheat.

God, I'm terrible. I truly am.

But I don't know how to stop. And lately, I haven't been feeling the safest. John is drinking more, and though he hasn't hurt me yet, I fear he might.

He seems to grow angrier as the days pass.

He comes home from work and yells at Sera for the simplest things. He's even made her cry a few times.

I've tried to explain to her that we're going through a rough patch. She's fifteen now and old enough to understand that marriages aren't all sunshine and rainbows.

She begged me to work it out with him. But I'm not entirely sure I want to anymore. Even if it's for Sera's sake.

And I know that makes me incredibly selfish.

Chapter Nineteen
The Shadow

I don't regret it. Not any more than when I stuck a gun in her cunt and made her come.

And I know how fucked up that is—to take something without consent. I know that's what I'm fighting against every day.

She hasn't given it to me yet, but she will. I know my little mouse better than she knows herself. She's in too much denial to see how drawn she is to me. If she wasn't, she wouldn't instigate, pushing to get her clit bitten, knowing damn well I stay true to my word.

If she genuinely wasn't intrigued, she wouldn't have texted me back in the first place.

Her actions speak an entirely different language than her words. A language filled with desire and pleas—she just hasn't learned to translate it yet.

Doesn't make it right, nor does it justify it. But I can't make myself regret tasting something so fucking sweet—so fucking perfect. Even if she didn't want to want it. Because that's what that was.

She *knew* I was going to follow through with my threat if she told me to fuck off again, and she kept doing it anyways. And that tells me that my little mouse can't control how she *really* feels. This means that whatever she feels, it's fucking addicting.

She fought me so hard initially, her anger and ire only turning my blood to molten lava. The harder she fought me, the harder my cock fought against the confines of my jeans.

I wanted so badly to release the zipper and plunge myself deep inside that sweet little pussy. I was close—too fucking close to doing it. Once those cries of pleasure reached my ears, and she gripped me in her hold, shamelessly grinding against my face—I was nearly done for.

The only thing that stopped me was the look on her face.

When she was coming on my face, she was unashamed. But as soon as the orgasm drained from her body and the kiss was no longer consuming us, she felt nothing *but* shame.

It's going to take time, I remind myself.

I crack my neck, releasing a shuddering breath.

I'm sitting in my Mustang, my dick still painfully pressed against my zipper. Just as I decide to say fuck it—jacking off in a car is the *least* of my sins and wouldn't be the first fucking time—my phone blares in the console next to me.

I curl my hand into a tight fist, my muscles straining as I fight the overwhelming urge to bash it into the fucking window.

I don't think I've had blue balls like this since high school when Sarah Forton jacked me off in the locker room. It was the first time a girl touched my dick, and I didn't even get to finish because Coach walked in before I could shoot my load off on her pretty tits.

I snatch up the phone and bring it to my ear without even looking.

"Yeah?" I snap, my frustration boiling to dangerous levels.

"Didn't get laid tonight?" Jay croons through the phone, his voice laced with mocking amusement.

I crack my neck again, growling when my muscles don't pop and give me any relief.

"Jay," I growl.

I refuse to touch my dick while on the phone with him. As much as I need to lessen the pressure, Jay's voice would make me feel sick.

"Satan's Affair is coming to town," he starts. I open my mouth—gearing up to ask him why the fuck that would matter to me.

"And I got confirmation there're tickets with four little birdy's names on them," he continues. I snap my mouth shut.

"Why would they go there?" I ask, completely confused why four grown-ass men would go to a haunted fair.

"Prime girls for the pickin', my friend. And now there's a ticket with *your* name on it."

I sigh. "When?"

"Three weeks from now. Plenty of time to go to the clubs a few times and start showing that pretty face of yours."

Sighing again, I pluck the pack of cigarettes from the console, bring it to my mouth, and slide out a cigarette with my teeth.

I grab my lighter and flick the flame, inhaling deeply as the cherry blares red.

"You're smoking, aren't you?" Jay says. I offer a noncommittal confirmation as I roll down my window and blow out smoke.

The raging hard-on is gone, but my dick still hurts.

"You said you were going to quit," he whines. "Do you know how many chemicals are in that? According to the—"

"Jay," I snap, cutting off his tangent. If I let it go on, he'd list off the ingredients in a cigarette like he's listing off all the components in the periodic table.

Nobody. Fucking. *Cares.*

He sighs like an angry teenager on their period. "Whatever," he mumbles.

"Update me if anything else comes up," I say before clicking off the phone.

I drag in another inhale of smoke and turn my attention to my laptop.

The inside of my Mustang is decked out in gadgets. A laptop sits on a platform, a mechanical arm attached to the dash so I can push and pull it towards me for convenience. Dash cams, an alert system for law enforcement, and other illegal shit decorate the interior of my car.

I pull the laptop towards me and fire it on. The bright screen stabs at my sensitive eyes. Squinting against the light, I pull up my programs and get to work.

In pure curiosity, I want to know who is attending this haunted fair.

It comes to town every single year, and I've never bothered to go. Haunted houses don't scare me. Not when I see true horror every day.

There's nothing a couple of made-up monsters can do to horrify me more than the actual monsters polluting this world.

Humans don't need to decorate themselves in gory make-up and fake blood to be scary. It's the insides of us—the darkness that lurks *beneath* the surface—

that's what's truly fucking terrifying.

That's what leads people to commit heinous crimes every single day. That's what leads innocent little kids to die horrific deaths for no fucking reason at all.

The insides of us—that's what keeps me alive. It's the only purpose I have in life, and without it, I'd be nothing.

I scroll through the list of names and stop short when I see one in particular that has my heart pounding.

Adeline Reilly.

I smile. Well, that *used* to be my only reason for living. But now... now I've discovered a new meaning to life.

ME: I can still taste you, little mouse.

I stepped back for all of two days before I could no longer resist.

I've beat my dick like it was an opponent in a boxing match, and I'm so fucking tired of the feel of my own hand.

There are zero expectations for her to reply today. I'm sure she's still nestled comfortably in that corner of her head where she hates herself and is convinced she'll never give me the time of day again.

But that corner is a farce, and we both know it. The feel of my gun inside her scared her. But the feel of my tongue on her pussy, and how hard she came will fucking haunt her.

She'll cry about it for a little while, but soon she'll fall right back into temptation.

ADDIE: Did you know a stalker killed my great-grandmother?

My brows shoot into my hairline at her text.

Not only was I not expecting one at all, but the fact that she replied with real words and not some empty threat. Hers don't necessarily hold weight like mine do.

ME: Do you have proof of this?

Based on the few journal entries I read, she and her stalker had a passionate relationship. And he was also tossed up with some bad people according to the entry of him visiting her with unknown injuries. It didn't seem like he showed signs of aggression or violent obsession. But who really knows?

Addie's great-grandmother could've just been seeing what she wanted to see, and he really did kill her.

Or maybe her husband caught her having an affair and flew into a fit of rage.

Both possibilities are equally likely, just as it's likely that whatever shit her stalker got mixed up in could've bitten him in the ass. And bite they did—right where it would've hurt him most.

His obsession.

After I poked through the diary, I became curious and looked deeper into her great-grandmother's story. The pull of history repeating itself was too intriguing.

The crime scene was trampled over, and the detectives handling the case were complete imbeciles.

ADDIE: Not yet. But I'm going to find it. And I'll be proven right. All stalkers are just fucking psychotic freaks.

I purse my lips, a smile threatening to take over. I'll let her stew on her response for a few minutes. Let her think she pissed me off or hurt me. Whatever she's convinced herself my reaction would be.

She thinks she knows me already, but my little mouse couldn't be further

251

from the truth.

I stalk her because I'm fucking addicted. I'm fascinated with every move she makes, every word that comes from her pretty pink mouth. And now I'm addicted to her scent, her taste, and the way she sounds when she's scared for her life—just as much as I'm addicted to the way she sounds when she's begging for more.

It's not something I can explain. When I saw her, I fucking nearly fell to my knees with need, and I *will* have her.

But not because I'm psychotic and delusional. I'm not going to make a goddamn shrine of her and convince myself that we were destined to be together by the gods or whatever weird shit people believe in these days.

I'll have her because she's the first thing that made me feel something good in so long, and I've become obsessed with keeping it.

I don't have very many something goods in my life, and I don't care if it makes me selfish for wanting to hold on to it.

The only way I'll be able to truly keep her is if she sees me at my worst.

I would rather just off myself than trick Addie into loving me as a good man, just to break both of our hearts when she realizes I'm not a good man at all.

So, my obsession with her is just… is what it is.

ME: Well, that's pretty judgy, don't ya think? Your great-grandmother loved her stalker last time I checked.

She's going to be pissed when she sees that I snooped through her great-grandmother's diaries.

Smiling, I pull up the camera feed of her house on my phone and click through until I find Addie sitting on her bed, staring at her phone. I was alerted when she took out the camera in her bedroom, and it wasn't hard to sneak in while she was out and set up my own. Though I can't see her face very well, it doesn't take a telescope to see she's glaring holes into the screen.

She's pretty fun when she's angry.

Her thumbs start moving a mile a minute, and I can't help but laugh when she slam dunks the phone on her pillow after she hits send.

My phone buzzes a second later.

ADDIE: He tricked her, just like what you're trying to do to me. And then he killed her. Just like I'm sure you'll eventually try to do too.

I roll my eyes at her dramatics and hit the call button.

She picks up the phone but doesn't speak. I hear her breathing softly through the receiver, and I wish I were there to lick her pulse. To feel it drumming against my tongue.

I love that I scare her.

"You done being dramatic?" I ask, letting her hear the amusement in my voice.

She huffs, and I can picture the scowl on her face. My cock hardens in my jeans, swelling to the point of pain in a matter of seconds.

"Dramatic? You think Gigi being murdered by her stalker is *dramatic?* Do you think being stalked at all is something to take lightly?"

"Well, of course not," I reply. "People die all the time from crazed stalkers."

My honesty stuns her into silence.

"Addie, baby, you're smart for being scared. Very smart. But why would I want you to fall in love with something fake?"

She snorts. "You really think I'd fall in love with you?"

"You're really going to act like you wouldn't? If I approached you in that bookstore and asked you on a date, I'd woo you, charm you, show you a pretty fake smile and treat you like a queen, all while lying to your face. Is that really what you want?"

Silence greets me again. She can't say no, and she knows it.

"Why can't you just be *decent* and not feel the need to stalk me?"

"Because then I wouldn't be true to myself, little mouse. I love that I scare you. I love that you try to run from me. The push and pull. The cat and mouse game. I fucking *love* it. And I think a part of you does, too."

She scoffs at me. "You're fucking insane if you think I love you scaring me. But then again, I already knew you were."

I smile. I can't remember the last time I genuinely smiled before I inserted myself into this beautiful creature's life.

"Don't you, though? I see how you try to hide how wet your pussy gets when you're scared. Your nipples get so fucking hard, and you clench your thighs tight as if that's going to lessen the need to feel my cock inside of you."

She gasps, a quiet inhale of breath. I grind my teeth against the raging urge to go to her house and bring that noise out of her some more.

"Did you do it?" she asks suddenly, as if the question burst out of her. Her breathing escalates. "Did you kill Arch?"

I bite my bottom lip, a smile forming. I've been waiting for this question. Surprised it took her so long to work up the nerve when she's got plenty of it to disobey me.

"I think you already know the answer to that, Adeline."

"I do. His family is dead, too."

I'm not surprised to hear that she knows. It made national news, after all. Bodies are gone without a trace, and a bit of a war has begun now that there's a power vacuum.

"Do you know what that caused, kitty cat?"

I chuckle at the nickname. I'll correct that little bad habit of hers soon.

"It gained me some pretty fucked up enemies."

My smile fades. I've been keeping an eye on Arch's friends. But apparently, I haven't been keeping it close enough.

"Max?" I guess. I've heard he's been strong-arming his way to the top.

"Yup," she says sassily, popping the P.

"Hmm," I hum, my mind wandering to all the ways I'm going to teach Max and his crew a lesson. I had hoped they would be smart enough to leave Addie alone with her police reports disappearing. She listened and didn't report the hands to the police. In retrospect, Max has no reason to target Addie.

Which means he had to have found out about the hands.

"That's it? That's all you have to say? *Humm?* Some pretty dangerous men are after me because of you, ya' know? If I end up dead because of your psychotic jealou—"

"Let me stop you there, baby. Because you seem to forget that I had a gun in your pussy not too long ago. Did you think teaching you how to act right is the only lesson I'm teaching with that?" She quiets. "If you think low-life criminals are scarier than me, then I haven't been clear enough, have I? Next time you place them above me, I'll be sending their heads to your doorstep next."

I crack my neck, the flare of anger residing now that Addie has closed her pretty little mouth. She's starting to learn, but I hope to God she never stops talking back.

I do like to punish her.

"I-I don't even know why I'm talking to you," she finally stutters out. "You're a sick, deranged individual. And I already made another police report against you, asshole."

Lies. The last report she made about me was the night she pretended to call when I stood outside her house. She was attempting to scare me away, but once I called her out on it, she followed through with the threat. My girl doesn't back down from a challenge.

I walked back to my car with a stiff cock and a smile on my face. I don't back down, either.

A bark of laughter bursts from my throat before I can stop it.

"That's funny?"

"That's sexy. But we both know that's not true."

I've been deleting them since she started making them and sent a guy in to destroy any physical evidence. The policemen will recall going to her house, but the second they try to investigate—if they ever got off their asses, that is—they would have nothing to go off of. Not that stalking cases are ever taken seriously anyways, which is why so many women end up murdered.

She growls and hangs up on me, and I can't keep in the fucking laughter. Especially when I pull the feed up and see her stomping her cute little feet around the house mumbling to herself, probably berating herself for even picking up the phone.

The fun has only just begun, little mouse.

Chapter Twenty
The Shadow

The bass from the music is all-consuming. It feels like the beat is coming from inside my chest. I never quite got used to the volume in clubs.

I make my way through the throng of grinding couples, drunk girls shaking their asses, and obnoxious douchebags wearing too much cologne with a mountain of gel in their hair. Oh God, one even has his button-up parted so he can show off the gold chain dangling on his hairy, overly tanned chest.

Scarface is a role model very few manage to do justice to when they imitate him. They can stick their faces in a pile of coke but don't exhibit the same finesse while doing so.

My hood is pulled over my head, concealing my identity as I make my way up the metal stairs. The same metal steps Addie climbed up not too long ago with another man's hand wrapped around hers.

I enjoyed sawing off that hand and would definitely do it again.

When I reach the landing, I stop short. On the half-moon couch is Max with his legs spread and a waitress bouncing up and down on his lap while his head is kicked back with his eyes closed. Her skirt is hiked up, and her thong pulled to the side, baring her pussy eating up Max's cock for all to see.

I arch a brow, unimpressed with how low she has to bounce. Addie would never have that issue.

A pair of twins sit on either edge, receiving their own treatment from a girl.

Sighing, I step back in the shadows, pulling out my gun and screwing on the silencer piece. The bass is milder up here, but a bullet zipping by your ear will draw anyone's attention.

I take aim and shoot, the bullet an inch away from Max's head.

Immediately, he dives for cover, pushing the poor girl off him and onto the floor. She yelps, covering her body as she scrambles up and makes a run for it.

"Hey," I say calmly. She freezes, while the twins move into action, reaching for their own guns while Max quickly yanks up his slacks to cover his now flaccid dick.

"I'd appreciate it if you tuck the guns back in your pockets along with your dicks. None of you are my type. Unfortunately for you, I only have one, and she's got pretty light brown eyes and a penchant for dangerous men."

When one of the twins doesn't listen, continuing to pull out the gun and take aim, I fire off one shot next to his head too. He drops the gun and raises his hands.

I turn my eyes to the three girls. "I want you beautiful ladies to see yourselves out and never speak of this again, yeah? I have the memory of an elephant, especially with faces."

These women will never see the wrong end of my gun, even if they do tell, but it sure as hell would make my life a lot harder if *they* knew that.

They all nod and run out of the room like there's a Rottweiler nipping at their bare asses.

"Who the fuck are you? Where the fuck is security?" Max spits, a hand resting on the gun in the back of his pants.

"Security from this club?" I laugh. "You know, for someone who has some pretty seedy business dealings, you're a cocky son of a bitch for not having your own damn guards."

Max sniffs with indignation. I smile wider, realizing that he's still struggling with loyalty and that pesky power vacuum now that the Talaverras are wiped out.

"Couldn't get any loyal guards?"

"Mind your fucking business," he snaps. "Who are you and what do you want?"

I trot over to where he's sitting and take a seat next to him, sighing as if I just sat on a beach chair on a private island with a piña colada.

And then I press the cold metal of my silencer to his temple. I'm riding on the fact that at least these two bozos will show him a shred of loyalty.

"Does it freak you out when someone pops up out of nowhere and threatens your life? I'll admit, I was a bit more direct, but the intention is the same."

The twins' eyes shift to each other.

"What the fuck are you talking about, man?"

"I'll tell you why I'm here when the three of you set those purdy little guns you got riding up your assholes on the table there," I say, nodding my head towards said table.

The twins look to Max for direction, and when he nods, they listen.

Oh. Goodie. He *does* have two people that have a shred of loyalty. Let's see how long that lasts when someone who is clearly in over their head is running the show.

A bead of sweat drips down Max's forehead as he follows my directions, nearly throwing the weapon on the table from his anger. The other two follow suit, one twin picking his up from the ground and the other sliding his out from the back of his pants before setting them on the table with Max's. Slowly and gently. Indicating this isn't their first rodeo where a gun is in their face.

"Adeline Reilly and Daya Pierson. Those names ring any bells in those empty heads of yours?"

Max's eyes round at the edges slightly, enough to reveal recognition.

"Never hear—"

"Here's the thing about liars," I cut in. "I really don't fucking like them. They kinda make me twitchy actually. Do you want me getting twitchy when my finger is on a trigger?"

Max's lips tighten into a hard line.

"Your girl was involved in my best frie—"

"And here's the thing about assumptions," I cut in again, grinning when Max snarls with irritation. "They're baseless, and most of the time, you're really fucking wrong. Addie doesn't have anything to do with Archie's death. But I do."

Max's head jerks towards me but is deterred by the gun still firmly pressed against his temple. He grits his teeth, his chest heaving with fury. I smile as his body trembles.

"What, is Addie an ex or something? You get jealous she wanted Arch instead?" Max hisses. Man, those two really were besties. They sound exactly alike when laid on their deathbed.

I shrug, unbothered. "I did get jealous, but she's certainly no ex. Your best

260

friend was a shit person. You sorry pieces of shit may get off on slapping around women but can't say I find enjoyment out of that."

"I will fucking kil—"

"You're not going to do shit," I interrupt for the third time. "You're a tadpole in an ocean of sharks and you have no fucking idea who I am, but you're about to learn."

When Max's eyes meet mine, I flash my teeth, pull out my phone and click the play button on the awaiting video.

Max's father sits in a chair with a gag in his mouth. Sweat and tears run down his face as he looks at the camera with all the fear humankind has ever known.

The two of them are as close as a father and son can be, sharing the same interests in drugs and tossing around women for the hell of it.

His father rambles behind the gag, pleading for his life. I have no plans to kill the man. While he's a shitty human, he wouldn't be any good to me dead. Not when he's going to be the leverage hanging over Max's head.

I came awfully close to walking in here and shooting them all dead, but then I'd have to kill all their families too, and my girl doesn't like it when I do that.

Now that Addie's on their radar, the more of them I kill, the more enemies I make not only for myself, but her too.

Exhibit A—the dickhead who has my gun pressed to his head because I killed his best friend.

I don't have the goddamn time to deal with small fish when I have Great Whites floating around in my ocean. Too bad for them, I'm a fucking Megalodon.

"What did you do to him?!" Max shouts, jerking forward towards the guns. I grab his arm and haul him back against the booth, a breath of air puffing out of his chest from the force.

"He's not dead, so settle down. No need to yell, my ears are sensitive."

Colorful expletives spill from his mouth, but I ignore them and tap the silencer on the underside of his chin hard enough to make him bite his tongue.

"As long as you leave Addie and Daya alone for good, daddy dearest will continue to live a long, healthy life. I don't want to see a goddamn hair out of place on either of their heads, you feel me? I know everything about you, Max, and your two helpers over there too. I know where you eat, sleep, and shit. And I will watch you until some other sorry asshole puts a bullet in your brain. You pickin' up what I'm puttin' down?"

His blue eyes narrow into slits, glaring at me heatedly. It's the equivalent to throwing a bunny at me, but whatever makes the asshole feel like Elmer Fudd.

I stop the video of Max's sniveling father and stand, keeping my gun trained on him. Specifically on his dick. Most men would rather die than live without a dick.

"We have a deal, Elmer?" His brows plunge at the name, but he doesn't question it. Having a gun pointed at your family jewels changes your priorities sometimes.

"Yes. As long as you let him go."

I flash a wide smile. "He's already on his way home."

I turn to leave, walking back over to the staircase before his voice stops me once more.

"Hey! You never said who you were," Max calls from behind me, his voice still packed full of unbridled anger.

Turning to look over my shoulder, a feral grin curls my lips, and I say with a wink, "You can call me Z."

And then I see myself out, laughing from the look on their paling faces.

"Mr. Forthright, welcome to *Pearl*," the blonde woman says, ushering me into the dimly lit foyer. She's dressed in a plain black blazer and skirt, with nondescript heels and her hair pulled back into a tight bun.

Shit looks painful.

A serene smile is on her face, but her bright blue eyes are missing their sparkle. The baby blue color is lifeless, and it's my first clue that she's seen too much in this place.

I enter into what looks like a foyer with gold tiled flooring, black walls, and an obscene chandelier. Gold framed pictures of the founding members of the gentlemen's club line the walls.

Or, in other words, a bunch of fucking rapists line the walls.

Men in business suits, smiling at the camera and probably still riding the high from raping a little girl or boy. They all look the fucking same to me.

I walk down the hallway, the creepy men staring at me from either side the whole way down, while music with a heavy bass emanates from somewhere ahead of me.

I'm keeping the earpiece tucked safely away in my jacket until it's needed.

It took five minutes to get in this godforsaken place because Detective Fingers from security wanted to thoroughly investigate my asscrack. I had to spend several minutes lecturing him about what would happen if his fingers brushed up against my asshole one more time.

After walking down Rapist Alley, I walk into a massive room filled with couches and poker tables. Men lounge on the couches with women draped over their laps and shaking their asses or tits in their faces.

At the back of the stage, a woman is currently humping a pole while men are throwing dollar bills at her. A full bar is off to the left of that, where several men in business suits sit, drinking glasses of alcohol. Probably fifty-thousand-dollar Scotch that tastes like ass.

Then again, they probably enjoy that taste since they think their own farts smell like flowers.

Women in scantily clad clothing roam the room, delivering drinks, and pretending to laugh at their lame jokes and—what the fuck?

Ten feet from me, a woman stands at a poker bar holding out her bare arm while an asshole stubs out his very lit cigar on her skin. My face drops when I see that asshole is Mark fucking Seinburg.

Goddamn it.

Smoke sizzles from her flesh, but she doesn't move an inch. In fact, she doesn't even flinch.

Anger punches through my chest. I force myself to stay calm as I walk over to the table, acting more interested in the game than I am in the girl.

As I get closer, I notice she has a blank look on her face, much like the hostess that greeted me.

The smell of burnt flesh fills the area. One dickhead even waves his hand in front of his nose dramatically, as if it's *her* fault it smells. She drops her arm and just stands there, a glazed look in her eyes. After closer inspection, I notice that the entirety of her arm is covered in burn scars. Old and fresh. All in different stages of healing and plenty of fresh burns from tonight.

Mark shoos her away, and she robotically turns and walks off, as if she didn't just have a cigar stubbed out on her flesh.

She's drugged.

And after looking around at the women, I realize they all are.

Not only does it keep them compliant, but they probably won't remember the majority of the shit that goes down in here.

My mask stays in place, refusing to crack from the anger swirling in the depths of my chest. Keeping my eyes on the table, I approach the men.

"Gentlemen! Who's winning tonight?"

Five pairs of eyes turn to look at me, all with snide looks on their faces. I can tell what they're thinking without them even saying it.

Who are you? What gives you the right to speak to us?

"I am," Mark chirps, and I literally couldn't have planned that better myself. It's like God opened up His hands and dropped that fine piece of blessing in my lap Himself. "Do you play, boy?"

What I really want to do is smack the shit out of him for calling me 'boy' when I'm a thirty-two-year-old man, but instead, I offer a devious smile.

"Sure do," I say.

Mark looks over at a bald man and tips his chin up. "Let him have your spot."

The table seems to go silent. I keep my expression calm as the bald man stares back at Mark with a blank expression. But he doesn't have his eyes on lockdown. Anger sparks in his brown pools, and he looks at Mark much like how I really want to. Like he wants to kill him.

It's for the best really. He wasn't a good poker player anyways if he couldn't even keep his anger in check.

Calmly, the man stands and places his cards down. Royal Flush.

He would've won that round.

I keep my face blank, not unveiling the smile that's threatening to emerge. I would feel bad for him if he didn't get off on hurting women.

Who am I kidding? I wouldn't feel bad at all.

While Mark was burning his cigar on the waitress's flesh, this bald man over here was adjusting himself. He wasn't the only one, though, and I made sure to note every one of their faces for later.

The man gives Mark and me one last look before walking off without a word.

The valuable little lesson that came out of that embarrassing spectacle was that Marky-Mark here has power. Whatever weight he pulls, it's enough to give him superiority over the common folk.

Wonder how many little boys' and girls' lives it took to get that far.

"What's your name, boy?" he asks.

"Zack Forthright," I lie easily.

"Name's Mark Seinburg. I'm sure you already know who I am, though. How long have you been playing poker?" Mark asks as they restart the game, brushing over his narcissism like the notion of me *not* knowing who he is isn't an option.

I know exactly who he is, but not for the reasons he thinks.

"Since I was a kid," I answer truthfully.

My father was a professional poker player, and he taught me how to master a poker face. Something that has been crucial to my field of work.

He'd sit me on his lap as a little boy, teaching me the game, and then show me his cards as he played with his friends. Testing me to see if I could keep a blank face. He lost a lot of games doing that.

But he truly believed I wouldn't learn how to master a poker face unless I knew what it meant to play the game. He'd whisper in my ear, point out my tells, and teach me how to not only read and understand facial expressions but micro-expressions.

During that time, my father never truly lost any money. After my lesson, I'd run off and play, and he'd win all his money back plus some. It took me a couple of years to master a poker face and even longer to master the game itself, but he made me play against him once I did.

I beat him in the first game, and I don't think I've ever seen pride in a man's eyes shine brighter since that day.

"Well, boy, let's see what you're made of then."

He'll find out what a bullet is made of when it's lodged in his throat. But I don't say that.

Throughout the next several hours, I purposely stay neck-in-neck with him. I understand a narcissist's ego enough to know that it would've only angered him if I cleaned him out. And if I'm horrible, he won't respect me. So, I keep the playing field even.

You win some, you lose some. Back and forth until he slaps his cards down with a hearty laugh.

"I've met my match," he chortles, taking a drink out of his whiskey glass.

I smile prettily at him. "You're a lot better than I gave you credit for," I praise.

He offers me a cigar and I take one, but I'd let Detective Fingers finger blast my ass before I put it out on a girl's arm. I'll have to figure out a way to stop him without breaking his neck if he tries it again.

"How come I haven't seen you here before?" he asks, eyeing me closely as he lights his cigar. Not necessarily suspicious, but every man in these types of clubs looks at a new member with an air of wariness. "I'd recognize those nasty scars anywhere."

That was fucking rude. But he's not wrong.

I shrug a shoulder. "My money is new," I lie.

Zack Forthright is a self-made millionaire from web design and branding. If that name is googled, there will be a Wikipedia page and social media posts with fake followers and engagement, but everything is a blanket site.

Once I start gaining a reputation here and showing my face more, I'll be looked into, and I'll have little enough to raise an eyebrow or two, but nothing that would make someone think I'm trying to take down the club.

"How'd you get them?" he asks, nodding his head at my face.

"Bully in middle school. Pretty fucked up kid that liked to play with knives," I lie again, flashing a grin. And then I shrug. "The ladies seem to like them."

He chuckles. "Oh, I bet they do. The young girls have always liked that—oh, what do you call it? Bad boy look?"

Before I can respond, a waitress approaches with refills of our drinks, the same glazed look in her eyes.

"Come here, sweetie," Mark says to the girl, patting his hand on his knee for her to sit on. The wedding ring on his finger glints in the light, as if to shine a light on the fact that he's a skeevy son of a bitch.

Addie won't ever have to worry about that shit when I marry her, that's for damn sure. She doesn't even have to worry about it now. The only pussy I want wrapped around my cock for the rest of my life is hers.

The waitress looks at him like he's merely an apparition. She's looking through him.

Robotically, she sits on his lap, a toneless smile gracing her bright red lips.

Mark cuddles her closer, looking at her with a smarmy grin. From here, I can see his cock growing in his pants. Normally, I'm not one to judge another man's dick, but when it's hard for an abused girl and the tent is lackluster, well... that's just disgusting on many levels.

He pulls her back directly onto his dick, gripping her hips tightly and guiding her ass to grind against him. I sigh, keeping my composure.

Carefully, I swallow the last of my whiskey and purposely set it on the edge.

I raise my nose in the air, sniffing dramatically.

"What is that delectable smell?" I ask aloud. Mark looks over to me, his grin growing, while I stare at the girl. "You smell delicious. Lean over, let me smell you."

The girl doesn't hesitate. We both lean towards each other, and once her body is hovering over my empty glass, I flick it.

The glass tips and it goes crashing to the black tiled floor. Thousands of glass pieces shatter, the sound ringing out loudly despite the heavy music in the room.

Chatter ceases and heads swivel towards the commotion.

Reminds me of high school when a kid farted in class, and the whole room went silent and stared at him until his face turned purple.

The girl jumps up, tiptoeing her platform heels through the glass as planned.

"I'm so sorry," she apologizes, the first hint of inflection in her tone. "I'll clean this up right away."

"Are you fucking kidding me?" I shout, glaring at her like she's the one that knocked it over.

Her mouth falls open, and I stand.

"Come to the back with me," I snarl, my eyes flashing with fury. She curls in on herself, while the other men snicker.

"Clumsy bitch," one of the men mutters, looking at her the same way you would if you accidentally touched the week-old gum stuck to the bottom of your desk.

"I'll be back once I take care of her," I say directly to Mark.

He laughs heartily, enjoying the thought of an innocent woman being punished for something so trivial. The old fuck probably falls over once a week and needs LifeAlert to get back up. Asshole can't talk about glass falling when he can't even keep his body vertical.

I grab the woman's arm firmly, jerking her against me and dragging her away.

She doesn't fight too hard. Self-preservation is kicking in, fighting its way through the cloud of drugs in her system. But she has long accepted her fate.

As soon as I get her into a quiet room, I turn to her. She's already dropped to her knees, her green eyes looking up at me with sorrow and acceptance.

She's a beautiful girl, with bright red hair, grass-green eyes and freckles dotting her nose.

Something about her reminds me a little of Addie, and I nearly walk right back out and crush my fist in Mark's face just for touching her.

"Get up," I say firmly. She gets to her feet unsteadily, looking much like a baby giraffe walking for the first time.

"I'm going to get you out of here," I say. Her brow puckers and she frowns.

"Sir—"

"What's your name, sweetheart?"

She stutters over the question. "Cherry."

I shake my head. "Is that your real name or stage name?"

She rolls her lips. "Real."

Her parents are really fucking unoriginal. Like might as well have a second child and name her Strawberry or Watermelon.

Anyway, besides the point. "How would you feel about getting a fresh start in life, yeah?"

Her eyes widen, and it seems like the prospect of escaping this one has some of the drug-induced fog receding from her gaze. But then she turns wary, and then resigned. Tears line the edges of her lids, and the sight will forever haunt me.

She looks down, seeming to collect herself. "I know what that means. I-I'm really sorry. I didn't realize I was leaning that far down."

"I'm not going to hurt or kill you, Cherry," I cut in. "I'm going to help you, but I need you to listen to exactly what I say."

She shifts on her feet, peering up at me through her lashes and bobbing her head frantically. I slip out the Bluetooth earpiece I had hidden deep in my inner suit pocket. All of my jackets have a special lead lining in them that deflects radiation. Meaning I can walk through any body scanner without the devices being detected.

I pop it in my ear, press the button that immediately calls out to Jay, and wait for him to answer.

When he does, I explain the situation. It takes fifteen minutes before he has a car ready to pick her up. In that time, Cherry tells me about her family. About her younger sister that has cancer and her poor single mother. She works this job to pay the medical bills, but she confesses that she doesn't know if it's worth it if she's killed and the extra income stops.

She won't ever have to worry about taking care of them again. Or being killed because of a broken glass.

Jay watches the camera feed and directs me towards a back door exit without detection.

I grab her wrist before she walks out of the door. The nondescript black sedan is waiting ten feet away, and the door already open for her.

"I know," she says softly. "I don't know your face. I've never seen you before," she guesses.

I shake my head. "Cherry, you're not going to a place where you'll ever be questioned about something like that. You and your family will be taken care of and safe. I promise. All I ask is that you do something meaningful with your life. That's all."

A single tear slips from her eye. She hurriedly wipes it away and nods. Her brightened eyes shine with hope, and doing this shit, involving myself in the worst of humanity—it's all worth it when I have a survivor look at me like that.

Not like I'm a hero, but like they can actually envision a future.

She stumbles off to the car, and I make my way back inside, making sure no one spots me.

"Jay, clear the cameras," I say before taking the earpiece out and slipping it back in the hidden pocket.

The cameras will be spliced. If anyone reviews them, they'll see me dragging a dejected Cherry into a room and us walking out separately.

It's one of my specialties that I mastered and then trained Jay in. Taking parts of a camera feed and manipulating them to look exactly how you want them to, without even the best hackers being able to detect manipulation.

I crack my neck, and ready myself for a very long night of shooting the shit and becoming BFF's with a fucking pedophile.

July 4th, 1945

4th of July is always one of my favorite holidays. I spend all day setting up for guests while John grills.

And then we let off fireworks in our backyard over the cliff. It's always incredibly beautiful and my favorite part of the whole night.

But right now, I'm in my room crying.

John is drunk again. And he's been yelling at Sera and I all day. Nothing is done right and he even went as far as throwing a glass plate against the wall.

I'm thankful our guests haven't arrived yet.

Frank is on his way here, and I'm thankful for it. He's been a little distant since the dinner where John finally exploded.

But I imagine he doesn't want to be involved in our marital disputes. Still, I'm glad he's coming. He'll be able to keep John busy while I entertain the rest of our family.

I only pray John doesn't embarrass me tonight. I don't think I'll ever forgive him for it.

Chapter Twenty One
The Manipulator

I'm stewing.

Nana used to make this god-awful stew when I was young. It smelled like a dumpster fire and tasted even worse. My attitude is about as foul as that stew right now.

"I don't even know his name," I groan, my voice muffled by my hands. They've been glued to my face ever since Daya got here, and I confessed he broke in again.

I haven't gotten around to what happened yet. There's not an ounce of courage in my bones. She's been patiently waiting, knowing that I'm holding something back. Something terrible and shameful. And something I can't stop fucking thinking about.

"You fucked him, didn't you?" she asks calmly.

My eyes bulge, and I unglue my hands from my face so I can pin her with a glare.

"*No,* I did not fuck him," I snarl, as if she's suggesting something insane and I didn't come really damn close to it. I can feel the blood rising in my cheeks and my left eye twitches.

Fuck. Daya knows that's my tell.

"You did!" she bursts, standing up from her chair and looking down at me with shock.

"I didn't! I promise," I rush out, grabbing her hand. "But… something did happen."

She puffs out a breath and settles back down in her chair, scooting back into the island in my kitchen and grabbing her margarita. She sucks down two huge gulps, trepidation on her face.

"You sucked his dick?" she guesses, lifting a hand to fiddle with her nose ring.

The images those words just put in my head have my blood pressure rising to dangerous levels. I bite my lip and shake my head slowly, the guilty look still present on my face.

"*He* sucked *you?*"

When I just stare, the guilt in my eyes burning brighter, her mouth pops open and her eyes round.

"Bitch, what the fuck!" she shouts. She leans in closer, an unreadable emotion flaring in her eyes. "Was it consensual?"

And this is where I get tripped up. Because it wasn't. But had he kept going, had he stripped his clothes from his body and fucked me—I can't say with absolute certainty that I would've stopped him. Or that I would've wanted to.

Still, I shake my head no.

Fury flares in her sage eyes, and her lips twist into a snarl. I lean back, honestly a little afraid of her.

I put my hand on hers. "Daya... I-well, it wasn't consensual... at first?" I say the last part like a question, embarrassed that I'm even admitting something like that.

She blinks. "At first," she echoes. "Meaning what? He was that good that he changed your mind?"

My hands cover my face, but she forces them away, nearly bumping her nose into mine as she intently waits for an answer.

"You have such pretty eyes," I tell her.

She snarls at me. "Spill, slut."

I close my eyes with a resigned sigh. "That man ate the soul out of my body, and I don't think I've gotten it back yet."

She jerks back, surprise in her pale green irises.

"I know, you can judge me. I'm judging me too," I say pitifully. I slide her margarita over to me and finish it off. Mine's been gone since I first told her he broke in.

"Baby girl, I am *not* judging you. But let me get this straight. You egged him on in a text because you felt like a bad bitch. And then he broke in to make good on his promise, tied your ass up, and you freaked out at first, but then ended up riding his face?" she summarizes slowly.

Several emotions swirl in her eyes. Confusion, shock, maybe even intrigue. But not judgment. And that's only because I didn't confess to her about the gun incident. I don't think I'll ever be able to talk about that one.

I roll my lips. "Pretty much."

Without taking her eyes off me, she leans over and grabs the bottle of tequila we used to make the margaritas. She pours a shot into both of our empty cups and then hands one to me.

We take the shot, cringing at the taste, and then stare at each other in silence.

"I'm just not even sure what to say."

I groan. "Daya, I don't know what to do. He didn't hurt me, but he did. He definitely forced himself on me. But I would've let him go farther had he tried. I'm so fucking confused. And I feel dirty and wrong, but when it was happening, it felt..."

I trail off with another groan, and this time I just bang my head against the granite countertop.

"Really good?" she fills in. "Amazing? Out of this world?"

"All of the above," I confess. "I have never come so hard in my entire life."

"Damn," she breathes, a note of awe in her voice. "Has he contacted you since then?" she asks gently, running her fingers through my hair in a comforting gesture.

I lift my head, a frown on my face. "Yes. He just... he said he didn't want me to fall in love with something fake. He pretty much said he's showing me who he really is, instead of lying to me about it. The fact that he thinks he can make me fall in love with him in the first place goes to show how deranged he is."

"That's... oddly nice? But really fucked up. There's something wrong with him. But we knew that from the chopped-off hands."

I snort. "Yeah, just a bit."

"Have you, uh, asked him about that yet?"

I nod. "Yeah, he basically played his usual macho man act and said not to worry about it and that he'd take care of it." I roll my eyes, but in all honesty, I'm glad for it. If I can count on my shadow for anything, it's to fuck someone up.

He's made that more than clear.

I sit up and bring Gigi's journal back towards me. "Anyhoo, let's just focus on figuring out what happened to my great-grandmother."

It's not hard to put Daya back into hacker mode. She slides her laptop towards her and immediately starts tapping away on the keyboard. The quickness of her fingers gives me a run for my money when I'm in a particularly good part in writing my book. She's been known to have to replace a few keys from how hard she types.

"So, time of death for Gigi was estimated about 5:05 P.M. Your great-grandfather claimed that he had run to the grocery store and when he came home, he found her dead in their bed. I found some witness reports claiming they did see John in Morty's grocery store around 5:35 P.M. But they didn't specify if they had seen him walking in or out of the store, or if they just saw him shopping during that time."

I nod my head, twisting my lips in contemplation. "In her last few journal entries, she was frantic and kept saying that he was coming for her. She never said who *he* is. But it has to be Ronaldo, right?

"So, maybe he waited until John left and snuck in and killed her while he was gone. He stalked her after all, he'd know exactly when my great-grandfather would've left."

Daya shrugs a shoulder, looking a little unconvinced.

"But don't the diary entries say that John was getting aggressive, and Gigi said she was going to divorce him, right?" she questions.

I frown. "Well, yeah, but I don't think he would've killed her. He loved her too much."

"Couldn't the same be said for her stalker?"

278

Noting my expression, Daya sighs and rests her hand on mine.

"Addie, I love you and I'm going to say this with all my love. But don't project. I'm starting to get the feeling that you *want* Ronaldo to be the killer because in your head, that will criminalize your stalker, too. Please tell me that's not why you're seeking justice for Gigi. Because you're looking for a reason to hate your stalker when in actuality, you don't."

I pull my hand from under hers and look away. Uncomfortable feelings invade my body, preventing me from speaking right away.

"I don't need to look for a reason to hate him," I grumble.

Daya cocks a brow, unimpressed with my attitude. I sigh, a headache blooming right between my eyes. I rub at the spot, stalling as I try to figure out what I want to say.

Because she's not entirely wrong.

Maybe I just want to be able to say that all stalkers are crazy, and that it's not possible to fall in love with one. I want to be able to say it's never happened before. And I want to say it's absolutely impossible to find myself in a loving, passionate, and healthy relationship with a person who invaded every aspect of my life unapologetically.

As much as I hate to say it, my shadow might not be wrong either. The man has a magnetism about him that rocks me to my core. He's shifted my entire life out of balance.

He scares the fuck out of me. But just like watching a horror flick, it thrills me too. He was right when he said that if he had approached me in the bookstore and took me out like a normal man, I would've fallen for him. The way he carries himself, the way he speaks, and his passion are irresistible.

And he's also right that if I had fallen in love with a lie, I would've been devastated. I just *wish* he wasn't such a bad guy.

But then he'd be a different man—a man you might not be able to love.

Doesn't matter.

I refuse to love my shadow. And I'm not going to fuck him, either. What happened two nights ago was sexual assault and I'm not going to spin it any other way.

"That's not why I want justice for her," I say quietly. My hand drops and I meet Daya's soft gaze.

Never one to judge me. Even when I probably deserve it.

"I obviously never met Gigi, but Nana loved her to a million pieces. And I don't think she ever quite got over it. Not only do I want justice for Gigi, but for Nana, too."

That seems to placate her. "Good. Because I did find a lead on one of Seattle's most notorious crime families in the 40s."

I perk up, leaning over to look at the laptop screen. She turns it towards me for a better view.

"Back in the 40s, the Salvatore family ran the streets. Angelo Salvatore was the crime lord." She points towards a picture of five men.

In the middle is what you would expect from an Italian mafia boss. Deeply tanned skin, large bulbous hooked nose and incredibly handsome, with his wide smile and sparkling brown eyes.

Surrounding him are four men, their ages ranging from what looks to be eighteen to late twenties. Based off the white hair peppered through Angelo's black hair, these must be his sons.

They all look like him and are equally good-looking. Two of them are wearing military fatigues, most likely having been drafted in WWII.

"Those are his four sons," Daya confirms. "But they're irrelevant, sexy as they are. Look in the background behind them. Do you see him?"

She points to a grainy, slightly blurred image of a man looking off in the distance behind the Salvatore family. Most of his body is concealed but what can be seen is a handsome face, part of a nice suit, and a top hat.

"This is the only picture I could find but I think there's a possibility that's Ronaldo."

My nose is nearly smushed into the screen, I'm staring so hard. It's a reach. Any man could be in a suit and a top hat in the 40s. But something is different about him.

"You see what I see?" Daya questions, excitement in her tone.

"He has a black eye, and his lip looks busted..." I trail off when I note Angelo's right hand, gripping a glass of alcohol. "Angelo's hand is busted too!"

I look to Daya and it's like looking into a mirror. I know the excitement burning on her face reflects my own.

"And guess the date on the picture," she says, smiling wider.

My eyes round. "Bitch, just tell me. "

"September 22nd, 1944. Four days after that entry from Gigi saying Ronaldo came in beat up."

My mouth pops open, and I look back at the picture. Staring at the man that could've possibly been Gigi's stalker.

And her murderer.

I'm drunk.

I ended up drinking two more margaritas, and Daya had the bright idea to take more tequila shots.

My world spins as I stumble up the stairs, a giggling Daya on my heels. We're both on all fours, our hands planted on the dirty wooden floors so we don't fall.

"Bitch, why did you make me drink this much?" I ask, giggling harder when I almost topple sideways.

"I felt it was appro-ahh—appro—priate while we're inveshtigating a murder," she stutters, her voice wobbly and filled with giggles.

I snort in response, my vision still playing tilt-a-whirl with my head.

I walk her to the guest bedroom and help her get to bed. I'm not much help, considering I nearly send us both crashing to the ground a time or two when I try to help her get her jeans off.

"How are you going to get yours off?" she asks, staring at my jeans.

I wave a hand. "I'm sure the stalker will help me," I retort. She widens her eyes comically.

"If he puts his peen in you, record it. I want to watch it later."

Right now, the prospect of fucking my stalker seems hilarious. We'll both regret it later, I'm sure. If we even remember.

We giggle like schoolgirls, her laughter following me out of the room. I lean heavily against the wall as I stumble my way to the bedroom.

I don't even bother trying to take my jeans off. I just plop on the bed, on top of the covers and everything, and I'm out seconds later.

A brush of skin across my cheek wakes me. I groan, my world still spinning as I open my crusted eyes and see my shadow standing by my bed, brushing the hair from my face.

"Oh, great," I grumble. "You're here."

"Little mouse, are you drunk?"

"Way to ask the obvious," I mumble, slurping up some drool that's leaking out of my mouth.

I'm still too drunk to be embarrassed. Shakily, I sit up and stare around the room. The lights are still on—I guess I forgot to turn them off—and it feels wrong to see my stalker in anything but the darkness.

It makes him more real, and I don't like it.

"Turn the light off," I demand, refusing to meet his eyes. I much prefer when I can only see shadows of his face.

He turns and does what I say. I'm so surprised that he listened that I almost snap out another demand when the light clicks off, just to see what he'll do.

He's once again hidden in the shadows. When he walks through the room, it's like the darkness clings to him. He *is* darkness.

I can't figure out what scares me more—him in the dark, or him in the light.

"I need to take my jeans off. I suppose you're going to watch me, aren't you?"

The alcohol is making me feel bold right now. I'm not thinking about consequences or his threats. Even the fear I feel swirling around is muted.

Right now, I feel like I can say or do anything. Like being drunk somehow gives me a protective armor, when in reality, it just makes me more vulnerable.

He leans against my door, his arms crossed as he watches me unbutton my jeans and slide them down my thighs.

"You know," I start, stumbling as I try to get the pant leg around my foot. Who the fuck invented skinny jeans, and why am I wearing them? "I don't even know your name."

"You never asked," is his reply.

"I'm asking now, kitty cat."

Finally, I get my foot through the hole and slide my leg out. I straighten and look at my freed leg in victory. One down. One to go.

"You know," I say again, before he can even open his mouth. "I do quite like calling you kitty cat."

"But it wouldn't sound so good when you're screaming it," he taunts, his voice a little closer than it was before. I look up to see he's stepped away from the door, his form creeping through the darkness.

I snort. "You don't think so? I bet I could make it sound good," I challenge.

It looks like his entire body turns to stone. And that makes me feel even bolder. I slide the other pant leg off, this one going a little smoother than the other.

And then I climb up on the bed, in nothing but a bra and t-shirt and my purple thong.

He gets a good view of my ass, but that's the least of my concerns. I grab a pillow and straddle it.

"Addie," he growls his warning. The deep rumble has dampness gathering between my thighs. It's unfair how his voice has a physical effect on my body, but I guess right now, it works for me.

I grind on the pillow, tip my head back and moan out, "Kitty cat."

I squeak when I see his hand flying towards my face from my peripheral. The alcohol has sucked away all my reflexes, so when his hand grabs my hair roughly, I can do nothing to stop it.

My back arches as he yanks my head back. His beautifully scarred face appears above mine. Those goddamn yin-yang eyes, with thick lashes framing them.

He's terrifyingly beautiful. And right now, he looks pissed.

"What?" I breathe out innocently.

He leans down and softly brushes his lips against mine. Electric shocks ignite from where our lips touch. I suck in a sharp gasp, appalled by the reaction his body creates within my own.

"Zade," he whispers against my lips. "That's the only name that will ever leave your lips from now on, especially when you're making that little pussy feel good. And when *I'm* making that pussy feel good, then you can call me God."

All the oxygen in my lungs evaporates. If he had given my soul back, it would be gone again.

"I think Lucifer would suit you better," I whisper, my lips sliding against him as I speak.

A sinful smile flashes across his mouth, baring his straight teeth for a brief second. The one second was a stark reminder in my drunk-addled brain that I have someone very dangerous in my face right now.

And I need to get him away from me.

I arch further back, pulling my face away from his.

"You gonna assault me again? Is it going to be you forcing your dick in my mouth this time?" I spit at him, narrowing my eyes in thin, hateful slits.

"I thought about it," he admits in a contemplative murmur. "I would love to see you swallow my cock tonight."

There's a *but*, and in my drunken state, I'm almost offended.

I quirk a brow, but even I know it doesn't have the same effect as him doing it.

"But you're still inebriated. And you'd vomit all over my cock the second it touched the back of your throat."

Okay, now I'm really offended.

My mouth pops open in shock. "I would not, you asshole!" I squirm away from him, but he reinforces his hold in my hair and keeps me still.

Always fucking forcing me.

Who could love this man?

He laughs—a dark, cruel laugh. But it also transforms his face right into the devil's. Handsome and ruthless.

"Are you saying you want to try?" he taunts, his eyes glittering in the moonlight.

I scowl at him. "Never. You know what, you're right. I *would* vomit, but not because I can't handle your puny dick. But because I would be so disgusted by it." The venomous words spew from my mouth without preservation.

My fear is muted so my mouth is uncensored.

He arches a brow, and my mouth dries.

Fuck. Why does it look so scary when he does that?

He stares at me, and I hold my breath, waiting for him to snap. To murder me. Hurt me. Do something.

When his free hand reaches to his zipper and slowly pulls it down, I know I fucked up.

You just couldn't keep your mouth shut, could you, Addie?

I stare at his hand movements like he's about to open up a jar of spiders. He pops the button on his jeans and then stills for a beat.

A gasp bursts from my throat as he wrenches my head roughly to his pelvis right as he pulls out his cock.

Fuck. Fine. Okay.

So, *maybe* his dick is the exact opposite of puny and would surely kill me if he did decide to choke me on it. And *maybe* it wouldn't be the worst way to die when it's the most mouth-watering thing I've ever seen.

It's *otherworldly.*

He holds his cock in his hand, and my pussy weeps in response.

I'll never tell him how glorious he looks because right now, I want to fucking chop it off. Just like he did Arch's hands. He wouldn't be a man without his cock, and I wouldn't have to worry about him using it as a weapon and crushing my windpipe.

He yanks my head closer until it's inches from my face. Musk and the scent of leather and spices waft to my nose. Of course, he smells as tempting as he looks.

"You think you can handle this?" he asks darkly.

I swallow, desperate to lubricate the dryness in my throat. The false bravado is steadily slipping away, and now the fear is coming back full force.

"Yep," I say, my voice wobbly. "But I will bite it off if you try it."

I'm too busy staring at his cock to notice the smirk glide on his face. The tip caresses my jaw, the soft skin sliding against me, sending shivers down my spine.

I stare at him in disgust, but my face is a mask of lies. And the fucker knows it.

He starts to pump his cock, gripping it tightly, the veins bulging beneath his grip. Even swallowed in his large hand, it looks intimidating.

"What are you doing?" I snap. He slaps the head of his dick on my cheek in response, silencing me with a sharp gasp.

The *asshole.*

He continues to pump his cock, and when I realize that he's jacking off on my face, I start to struggle.

His hand tightens painfully, needle-like pricks of pain blooming along my scalp.

"Let me go," I hiss, pushing both of my hands against his thick thighs.

He lets go of his dick and darts his hand up to my face, squishing my cheeks painfully together. My teeth bite into the sensitive flesh, but he doesn't let up. Tears line the edges of my lids, threatening to spill over as he leans down and bares his teeth in a vicious snarl.

That fear holds me completely immobile. Finally, I feel the terror penetrate my thick skull. Because this man could easily kill me. My bravery is sucked out of me like a vacuum, and I melt into a puddle of fear and hatred.

"You want to act brave, then I'm going to show you exactly what happens to smart mouths. You're going to swallow my cum like the fucking bad girl you are, and I don't give a fuck if you don't like it."

He roughly lets my face go, and the hand still tangled in my hair yanks me back to its previous position. I glare up at him through blurred eyes, but if anything, the sight only spurs him on.

He pumps his cock in quick, rough tugs. It doesn't take long before he's growling again, the veins in his neck tightening.

"What's my name?" he growls.

"Kitt—" he briefly lets go of his dick to deliver a sharp slap to my cheek. It stings, but it wasn't enough to actually hurt me.

I snarl. "*Zade.*"

He sucks in a sharp breath. "Open your mouth, little mouse. Now."

When I refuse, he slaps his dick across my face again, this time harder. I'm getting tired of him slapping me. Rage burns hotter, and I'm tempted to reach over and bite the tip of his dick until it's severed completely.

"You really want to test me right now?" he challenges, cocking that damn brow and breathing heavily. Desire shines in his yin-yang pools, and although he's punishing me, he's staring down at me like I'm a priceless jewel.

With reluctance, I open my mouth, hatred spewing from my eyes. He flashes a sinister smile before he says, "Now thank me."

I go rigid, fury spiking hot. He wants me to do *what?*

"Fucking thank me for letting you swallow all my cum, Adeline."

A dark edge creeps into his tone, and I just can't let go of the fear, even as I work up the nerve to deny him. Images of him holding a gun to my face and pinning my tied-up body to the bed as he took what he wanted flash through my mind, fortifying the terror in my bones.

"Thank you," I choke out angrily. As soon as I say the words, ropes of cum are spurting from his dick and right into my mouth.

A deep, rumbling growl releases from his throat, traveling straight to my core. I clench my thighs as my tastebuds are invaded with the flavor of his saltiness. Desperately, I want to spit it out right in his face.

"Fuck, that's a good girl," he breathes.

In response, a tear slips from my eye. I shiver from the words, just as my hatred for him burns brighter.

When the last bit of cum drops from his tip and onto my lips, he grabs my face again, pinching my cheeks together and preventing me from spitting it all back on him like I planned to.

"Swallow," he demands, his voice dark and full of warning.

I do because I have no other choice. His seed slides down my throat, alongside a mouthful of hateful words I want to spit at him.

I refrain for now. The situation has cleared the alcohol-induced fog, and at the moment, I feel stone-cold sober.

He tucks himself back into his jeans and stares at me as if he can't tell if he wants to eat me or hurt me.

"Your pussy is wet for me, isn't it?"

"Fuck you," I snap back, my tone uneven and filled with unshed tears. So much for refraining.

"Let me see, little mouse."

My brow plunges, and I stare at him in confusion.

"Stick your hand in your underwear, dip one of those fingers into your pussy, and show it to me."

I open my mouth to tell him to fuck off, but he squeezes my cheeks again. Another tear slips free.

"Did you not just learn your lesson about having a smart mouth?"

My fists curl, bleaching my knuckles white from the force.

And to think this man believes I'll fall in love with him? I want to laugh in his fucking face. No, I want to add my own scars to his face. Cut it up until he's nothing but ugliness, just like he is on the inside.

Again, I do as he says. I slide my thong to the side, plunge my middle finger in deep, and present him with the only *fuck you* I can give, my arousal glistening on the digit.

He smirks at my dig, not the least bit bothered. Embarrassment clouds my vision, but I don't let him see it. He's getting nothing but poison from me.

He grabs my hand and brings my finger to his mouth. I resist his hold, but I'm powerless against him. His warm, wet mouth wraps around my finger and sucks off my juices in one swirl of his tongue. I hiss through my teeth, those electric waves shooting from where he licks me and throughout my body. His eyes roll backwards, acting as if he's sucking on the best lollipop he's ever had.

I can't control how my stomach tightens, and thighs clench in response. I'm drenched and embarrassed.

He pops my finger from his mouth, and it takes massive strength not to send my fist into his dick.

He finally releases my hair from his grip, and I scramble away from him.

Zipping up his jeans, he looks down at me. I can only see a sliver of his face from the moonlight, but what I do see makes me feel murderous.

He's not looking down at me smugly like I had expected. His face is arranged into a blank mask as if what just happened didn't affect him at all. And that—that is so much worse.

"You want to know the best part?" he asks quietly. "I was going to tuck you into bed and leave you alone tonight. But you seem to forget that just because I am wholly yours, little mouse, I am not a nice man."

September 27th, 1945

The world has seemed to relax now that WWII is over. Soldiers are coming home, and though many have fallen or have been injured, I think we're all thankful it's over.

But the war has not ended in Parsons Manor.

Ronaldo is taking me out today while John is at work and Sera is at school. It'll be nice to get out of the house and get some fresh air before the weather starts to chill.

He's taking me on a lovely picnic and then out to a movie.

With John's growing aggressiveness, I'm not sure how to tell Ronaldo. I've only been able to see him about twice a month lately. He said his job is demanding.

And I haven't confessed to him about John and our demise.

I'm sure he'll be glad to hear that we might be heading towards a divorce. But I fear what he'll do when I confess just how angry John is.

I pray he keeps his temper. Ronaldo has a short fuse. Maybe even shorter than John's.

Chapter Twenty Two
The Shadow

y little mouse decided to get a change of scenery today. Maybe she wanted to get away from the house that I seem to keep popping up in.

As if sitting outside of a bar and grill is going to keep her safe from me.

I'm just walking down 5th street, passing a lawyer's office, when Mark comes barreling out of the door. We both stop short, inches from colliding with each other.

"Oh, Zack! Didn't see you there. Were you just coming in…" he asks, trailing off and looking behind him at the door to the lawyer's office.

"No, I was on my way back to my car," I lie smoothly, resuming my walk. My car is in the opposite direction, but I will sit in a random ass car if it means keeping Mark away from Bailey's.

"Let me walk with you," Mark smiles, inviting himself on what would've been a pleasant and peaceful stroll to spy on my girl.

Now I have to deal with this fucktwit.

Mark walks alongside me, prattling on about this and that—nothing that I deem important. He must not have many friends. He's a fucking chatterbox and enjoys the sound of his own voice. I bet money he's one of those guys who stand in front of a mirror and give themselves daily pep talks about how he's still got it goin' on.

Bailey's is straight ahead. Right as we come up to the intersection right before the bar and grill, I veer left, deciding to cross the road so we're on the opposite side of the restaurant. But when I go to press the button to signal for the lights to change, Mark stops me.

"Hey, Bailey's is a good place to get drinks. It's been a little while since I've been here."

I keep from gritting my teeth, though all I really want to do right now is grind them to dust. The main reason I don't is because I would no longer be able to bite Addie's clit.

And I really enjoy doing that.

"It's pretty crowded in there. You sure you don't want to go somewhere else? I know a perfect place a few blocks from here."

Mark waves a hand, already walking across the road towards Bailey's.

Fuck.

I follow after him, opening my mouth and readying to find another reason to opt-out of the restaurant, but he's turning back to me.

"I actually really enjoy the drinks and food here. I come here every so often, and I usually get in no problem. The hostess loves me," he says, ending his statement with a wink.

Yeah, and how many times did you ask her, "Do you know who I am" before she found an empty table?

My guess is at least four times.

Sighing internally, I force a grin as Mark approaches Bailey's restaurant, walking in and right up to the hostess.

And just like when an ex walks in unexpectedly, the hostess' smile drops an inch before forcing the most strained smile known to mankind.

"Hi, Mark. Table for two this time?"

"It would appear so," Mark responds with a smartass chuckle. I keep my face blank and pleasant, even as she sighs and leads us to a table out on the patio.

Right where Addie is.

Thankfully, she doesn't notice us when we arrive, even though we're seated only five tables down. Our table is perpendicular to her, providing the perfect view of her heart-shaped face, abused bottom lip, and the long lashes fanning her cheeks.

She's writing on her laptop, wholly focused on her task and not the world around her. Her bottom lip rolls between her straight teeth. I have the fiercest urge to walk over and take that bottom lip between my own.

Despite my obsession with my little mouse, I keep my eyes off of her. In fact, I make a point to never look in her direction in front of Mark. I got a single look walking in while Mark was ahead of me, and that's the only privilege I gave myself.

If he sees me looking at her, she'll be targeted. And the last thing I want is Addie on any of these shitheads' radars.

As Mark drones on about some bill he doesn't want to pass, a couple and their kid walk past us, the little girl talking animatedly. She looks to be about five years old—cute girl with a ponytail, big doe eyes, and dimples.

I see the sly look on Mark's face before he even registers what he's doing, and it takes physical restraint not to reach across the table, point his butter knife upright and slam his head down on it.

Instead, I make a split-second decision. The family is walking past Mark, beyond his view. When his head swivels back to me, I lean to the side and pretend to check out the little girl. I look just to the right of her at a plate of food—I'd rather slit my own throat than look at a child in a sexual manner—but it looks authentic to Mark.

I let the predatory look linger on those chicken tenders for a few seconds before I'm straightening and feigning innocence. But I feel Mark's gaze burning into me.

As much as it sickens me, I need him to think I have an interest in the depraved things he does.

An hour passes while I continue to pretend to show interest in underage girls, looking right above their heads, at their food or whatever else that's close enough to feed the illusion. Nothing too obvious, and I don't do it every time as not to be suspicious. Just subtle glances here and there.

During the hour, Mark continues to grow more inebriated. At the gentlemen's club, I noticed that he sucks down whiskey like it's life support.

I'm sensing alcoholism alongside his sadism.

And of course, that's when the fucker decides to really look around and catch notice of a still-working Addie, tucked in her little corner and typing away like her life depends on it. I've kept an eye on her from my peripheral, and whatever she's writing, she's invested.

"Now, that's a beauty," Mark says, staring straight at Addie. Her mouth is wrapped around her straw as she finishes off a margarita. I watch her from the corner of my eye, but I don't slide my gaze over right away. I have two seconds to make a decision. Act like I don't know her or claim her.

Before I can open my mouth, Mark slides out his phone and snaps a picture of her, his thumbs moving quickly as he goes to send it to someone.

Fucking ballsy to do that shit in front of me. I'm not sure if it was leering at children together or the alcohol, but it was far bolder than I would've expected.

My hand lands over his phone, halting his progress.

He looks up at me, his eyes wide and cheeks flushed.

"Whatever you're about to do, stop it. That's my girl."

Somehow, Mark's eyes get even wider.

"That girl over there? She's yours?"

I nod my head once.

"She likes to be left alone when she works, and I respect her space."

Mark's white, bushy brows plunge down.

"Why didn't you say anything? Introduce us at least?"

"I was planning to after she finished with her work."

Mark's eyes thin, confusion swirling in his blue eyes. He's an older man, with sagging skin, liver spots, and knee problems from how he groans every time he stands up. But he's also an astute man for his age, and his mind is still sharp.

"You were going to pass the restaurant without saying hi to her?" he interrogates, referring to my lie about walking to my car. "And go to a different restaurant?"

I stare him dead in the eye, making sure he can see just how unconcerned I am with his questioning.

"My girl lives in a peaceful little bubble when she writes her books. She doesn't like to be bothered when working, and I respect her space. Especially because it allows me the freedom to do whatever I please without her worrying about what I'm doing."

Add a sprinkle of adulterous implications in there, and Mark immediately relates. He laughs, his yellowed teeth on full display.

"I knew I liked you," he chuckles, his crow's feet deepening.

I squeeze his phone, the device still trapped between both of our hands.

"Delete the picture, Mark."

Mark's eyes bug. "Oh, of course! I'm terribly sorry, Zack. I didn't mean to offend. I had no idea," he says hurriedly, trying to laugh off the fact that he was looking to kidnap my mouse. He hastily deletes the picture from his gallery.

I'll be hacking into his phone later to confirm it has been permanently deleted. Asshole thinks I'm dense and don't know what a Cloud is, or that you can access your trash and reload the picture.

I'll also be ensuring that he didn't actually send the picture to anyone.

"S'all good," I say calmly, sitting back in my chair and appearing casual.

I'm anything but.

The need to slice him open from ear to ear is vibrating through my tense muscles. Beneath the table, I flex my hand, fighting the urge not to drive it down Mark's throat.

I want to kill him.

Scratch that.

I'm *going* to kill him.

Slowly.

"Let me go introduce myself then. She's been hard at work for an hour. I'm sure she won't mind."

Before I can tell the old fart to sit his ass down, he's up and heading towards Addie.

Fuck. Me.

I hurry after him. Sensing the incoming danger—whether it's from Mark or me, I'm not sure—she looks up and her gaze clashes with mine.

Instantly, her eyes widen into caramel marbles, and her face pales about five shades lighter. I'm ready to squirt some spray tan lotion on her if it means she doesn't make it so damn obvious that she's not happy to see me.

With Mark ahead of me, I quickly give her a severe warning look. Her brows plunge, but she doesn't have time to react before Mark sticks his hand in her face.

"Young lady! What a pleasure to meet you. I'm sorry, Zack here didn't tell me your name. But I'm Mark Seinburg. I just had the pleasure of meeting your boyfriend here not too long ago, and he's quite the catch, but I must say, you're much more impressive."

Addie opens her mouth, but nothing escapes, her equilibrium thrown off from the sudden intrusion, alongside Mark calling me Zack and claiming her as my girlfriend.

"Addie," I say. Both eyes snap to me. "Her name is Addie. Sorry, baby, I didn't mean to intrude. I told you about Mark here already, he's the guy I met at work." I side-eye Mark, letting him think I told Addie we met under different circumstances than we did. He smiles wider at that.

Gentlemen's clubs aren't necessarily a secret, but they're definitely not a place you go to visit when you have a beautiful wife or girlfriend waiting for you at home. At least if you're not a narcissistic prick.

"Oh, uh, hi Mark. Pleasure to meet you," she finally says, clasping Mark's hand in her own.

I feel so many things right now.

Namely, the urge to fucking kiss her for going along with something she doesn't understand.

She's definitely getting rewarded later.

But I also feel the possessive beast rise. Not only to claim Addie as my own, but to protect her from the real monster. The moment Mark registers Addie's beautiful smoky voice, his eyes droop. And if I see his khakis start to tent, I *will* kill him here and now.

She glances at their entwined hands with a hint of trepidation, but she smooths her face out quickly. Mark doesn't notice her subtly wiping her hand on her jeans when he lets it go, but I do.

"The pleasure is mine. You have a beautiful name. What is it short for?"

She clears her throat, throwing me another *what the fuck* glance. "Adeline."

Mark's face is animated as he marvels over her response. "A beautiful name for a beautiful girl."

A red blush stains her cheeks prettily. She pretends to act bashful, but I can feel the nervous energy emanating from her in waves. My little mouse doesn't do well in social situations, especially when she's thrown in one unprepared.

"Alright, Mark. Let's leave my girl to get back to work."

Her eyes narrow into slits briefly when I say *my girl*. I subtly quirk a brow, daring her to defy me. She knows I'm not saying it for Mark's benefit. She's going to hear me call her my girl for a long fucking time.

Next, we'll graduate to my wife and then the mother of my children.

One day she'll get it in her head that she's *mine*.

"Nonsense!" he bellows, attracting a few curious eyes. "You don't mind, do you, Addie?"

For the first time, my face slips, and I let loose a snarl. Mark doesn't notice, but Addie does. If anything, my anger relaxes her by an inch. The knowledge that I'm not liking this situation must bring her some sort of comfort, compared to her thinking I'm purposely involving her in something dangerous.

Addie shakes her head, closing her laptop gently and sliding it into the case at her feet.

"Please, go ahead," she says, a single note in her tone wobbly. I sit next to her and wrap an arm around her tense shoulders, hoping that my presence will bring her some semblance of safety and comfort.

"Please, tell me how you two love birds met," Mark says, settling in his new seat. He waves to the waiter for another drink, and internally, I groan.

"At a book signing," I respond. "Super amazing author was there signing books. I saw her and instantly fell in love. I sought her out afterwards, asked her on a date and the rest was history."

She smiles, though it doesn't reach her eyes. "Yeah, he's a persistent one," she says with an awkward laugh.

"Fascinating!" Mark says, his eyes pinballing between us. His phone vibrates and when he slips it out of his pocket, his face drops.

Clearing his throat, he looks up at us with a sheepish grin. "If you don't mind, I'm going to head to the restroom and take this call. Addie, please order yourself another margarita. It's on me."

Mark gets up and walks away without a backward glance, his stagger uneven from the copious amounts of alcohol he consumed and his gaze pinned to his phone.

Addie starts packing her belongings frantically within a millisecond, hands shaking as she throws the rest of her stuff in her bag.

"If you think you're leaving, you're sadly mistaken."

She freezes, glancing back at me before she resumes. Keeping my movements calm and fluid as not to raise any alarm from bystanders, I slide my hand to her neck.

She pauses again when she feels my touch, and then whimpers when I squeeze tight.

"Look at me. Now."

Her eyes pinch shut for a moment before they open, and those pretty caramel eyes glide to mine. They're full of fear, and I'm almost surprised.

In the dark, she comes alive with fire. As if it's the night that feeds her flames and not oxygen. And in daylight, she's timid and scared. She becomes her moniker—a meek little mouse.

"If you've never taken me seriously before, then do it now, Adeline." Her eyes widen at the severity of my tone. "You're going to sit there like a good little girl and play along until I can convince Mark to leave. Then and *only* then, you can pack up your shit and go home. Do you understand?"

There it is.

The fire sparks and ignites.

"*Fine.* At least tell me what the *fuck* is happening, Zade. Or Zack. Which is your real name? You know what, I don't care. I don't know what game you're playing, but after this, you need to leave me out of it."

I lean forward and give her a warning look. She snaps her mouth shut, but the flames never dull.

"I. Tried," I bite out. "I will try to leave with Mark as soon as I can, but until

302

then, do as I fucking say. We're super in love and you're my doting little girlfriend. That's all you need to know right now."

Her eyes widen gradually until she's staring at me like I've lost my mind. What she doesn't realize is I *did* lose my fucking mind the second I laid eyes on her, and I haven't gotten it back yet.

"What is this, Zade?" she asks quietly. "Is Mark dangerous? Why are you lying to him?"

I sigh. "Yes," I concede. "He is dangerous, and he set his sights on you."

Before she can question me further, Mark returns, a jolly smile on his flushed face.

"No drink?" he questions, sauntering up to the table with his arms outstretched.

"My fault. I got a little carried away with my hello kiss," I lie, grinning a cheesy smile. The thought of me making out with my girl in public clearly gets him hot and bothered by the flash of heat in his eyes, but he covers it well enough with a hearty laugh.

Addie clears her throat, elbowing me hard in the side and offering an embarrassed smile.

"What is it you were working on, Adeline dear?" Mark asks, settling back into the chair and gulping down a large swallow of his bourbon.

"Uh, a few things. I was researching a cold case from the '40s," she answers.

Mark cocks a brow. "Really? Why's that?"

The red in her cheeks brightens. "Uh, well it's my great-grandmother's actually. Genevieve Parsons."

"Oh, I know that case!" Mark exclaims. "My father was a detective during that time, though he wasn't allowed to work the case."

By the way her brows raise, her interest has been piqued. "He wasn't allowed to? How come?"

"Conflict of interest. He and John Parsons were best friends for twenty years, and Gigi was a good friend of his. His sergeant said it'd be too personal, so he had to stand by and watch them butcher the case." He shrugs. "Dad always thought John was the one who did it."

Addie leans forward, hanging on Mark's every word. "Your father was Frank?"

Mark quirks a brow. "Yes, he was."

Addie clears her throat. "My Nana mentioned Frank a time or two."

He chuckles. "Yeah, we played together when we were younger."

"So, why did your father think John did it?"

Mark shrugs a shoulder. "Not sure, to be honest, but I do remember that Gigi and John were fighting a lot. He was real adamant, but there wasn't any evidence to prove it. I was pretty young back then, so my memory might be a little sparse. But there were a few nights he would drink an entire bottle of Jack, always muttering under his breath about making "him" pay for what happened." He finger quotes the word *him*. "I know their friendship fell apart after her murder. John was a raging alcoholic, and my dad was devastated that he lost two good friends."

Addie's eyes are wide with excitement. Clearly, she cares. Solving Gigi's murder means a lot to her. But I know she's only trying to prove something to herself.

If it wasn't for the fact that she has her own stalker, I don't know if Addie would've even bothered figuring out who murdered her great-grandmother.

It's not about finding who did it, it's about proving that it was Gigi's stalker and no one else. I get the feeling that if she can one hundred percent prove it, then it'll cement the fact that all stalkers are murderous psychos, and she can finally hate me and shut me out for good.

And all that tells me is I'm getting through the diamond-encrusted fortress surrounding her heart.

She wants something concrete to believe in because her morals and fundamental beliefs are being challenged.

Mark's phone rings, cutting off any further questions Addie was gearing up to ask. Mark glances at his phone and silences it, but from the way his face has turned serious, I know something is calling him away.

"That was my associate. I gotta head out for some business," he starts, swallowing down the rest of his drink and standing. "But listen, I'm hosting a charity event at my house next weekend. It would be my absolute honor if you both could attend."

"Oh, I don't know..." Addie says, the discomfort renewed. Last thing she wants is to pretend to be my girlfriend any longer than she has to.

Wonder what she's going to do when we're married, and her belly is swollen with my child.

Quite the predicament she'll be in there.

"Please, I would be insulted if you didn't show. Zack here has been a wonderful friend, and I would be heartbroken not to see you two there." Noting the trepidation in her eyes, he tacks on, "If you'd like, we can talk further about your great-grandmother's case. With my father being so close to your family, I was around John and Gigi quite a bit growing up. In fact, Sera and I played together all the time. I'm sure there's some potential information rattling around in my head."

Fucker.

He's manipulating her, and that's a big no-no. No one manipulates my girl but me.

"I have a few business meetings that weekend," I cut in, keeping my face controlled but growing a tad angry by the reluctant interest in Addie's eyes. She wants that information and Mark damn well knows it.

Mark places a hand over his chest. "Not possible to reschedule?"

"I'll get back to you tomorrow," I promise. He acquiesces, satisfied with that answer. Dickhead is confident I'll say yes, and I'm not even sure if he's wrong anymore now that he's fucking hooked Addie.

He slaps a hundred-dollar bill to cover the tab, says his goodbyes, and heads off. With his presence gone, it feels like the air opens up again and I can breathe. He sure has a way of sucking everything good out of the world when he's around.

I look to Addie, and she's already staring at me. She doesn't say anything, waiting for me to explain myself.

Sighing, I push out of my chair and hold out my hand, prompting her to grab it. Unsurprisingly, she ignores it. Grabbing her laptop case, she stands and follows me.

I walk her to her car in silence, and she doesn't push.

"I'm not letting you within ten feet of that place. Him even knowing about you was never supposed to happen," I say firmly. We arrive at her SUV. She unlocks the door but doesn't move to get in it yet.

"I don't want to get involved, either," she snaps. She looks away, contemplating something as she chews her bottom lip. The urge to suck it between my own teeth reemerges. "I don't know what the hell you're involved in, Zade, clearly something I probably don't want to know about, but I think keeping me away from it is a bit too late." She sighs, gearing herself up for whatever she's going to say next.

"You already got dangerous men on my ass, so what's one more, right? I'll go with you this one time. I'll get the information I need, and you get whatever you need from him."

I never told her I needed anything from him, but I think she can sense I'm involved with this man for a reason.

"Afterwards, we can pretend to break up. You can *actually* get out of my life while you're at it, maybe take Max and them with you, and that will be the end of it."

I cock a brow, and her eyes latch onto the movement.

It's not that simple when it comes to the underbelly of society. When you're dealing with seriously evil people, you don't just *get out*. Mark has his eyes on Addie, whether she realizes it or not. And if we "break up"—which would never fucking happen—she's free game.

Instead of saying all that, I just nod. "You'll come with me just this once. You'll be safe and protected. And afterwards, I promise that Mark will never see you again."

Because I'm going to kill him.

I just need to ride this out a bit longer until I can get the information I need.

"And the rest?" she pushes, thinning her eyes.

"If you're expecting me to say that we're going to break up, you're more delusional than *you* believe *me* to be. There will never be an end to me and you. But I can assure you Max is not going to be a problem any longer. He and I had a nice little talk, and he's promised to be a good boy."

Her eyes round. "Did you threaten him?"

"Well, what else would I do, baby? Ask him nicely and say pretty please?"

Her lip curls. "You probably just made him angrier."

"If he miraculously develops a pair that are bigger than the ping pong balls he's got swinging between his legs and tries to hurt you, he'll be taken care of."

She wrinkles her nose, and I don't think she can decide if she wants to question how I know what size his balls are. I'd rather not relive that nightmare.

"Taken care of how? You're going to murder him too?"

"Of course I am. Slowly, too. Start with snipping the Achille's heel so he can't run, and then—"

"That's fucked up, you're going to jail," she cuts in, disgust curling her lip. "Actually, I hope you go to prison and are sentenced to death."

She turns with a snarl, but she doesn't make it a step before my hand snaps out, capturing her arm and whipping her back around, directly into my chest.

Addie inhales sharply, her eyes dilating as I seize the back of her neck with one hand and grab her delectable ass with the other, lifting her up against my body.

"Will you be my last meal, baby?"

Her mouth parts and her breathing hitches. Those light brown eyes are wide and swollen with emotion. Shock. Awe.

Desire.

I lean in close, my mouth hovering a mere inch from hers.

"You taste like heaven. I could feast on that sweet little pussy for hours and still die a starving man. It'll be the closest I will ever get to God before they inject me with that needle, don't you agree?"

She's speechless, so I take advantage and capture those sweet lips with my own. She tenses beneath my hold but doesn't pull away. The taste of fruit from her margarita blooms on my tongue, and I can't help but groan.

"You taste like fucking nirvana," I rasp, before sucking her bottom lip into my mouth. The faintest little moan slips free, and it's enough to drive me wild with hunger. I'm ravenous and only the depths of her body will feed the monster.

Addie's hands clench the front of my hoodie as I devour her. The hand cupping her plump ass slides lower until my fingers are brushing across her jean-clad pussy. Cupping her from behind, I lift her higher, grinding my rock-hard cock into her.

Her next moan is free of restraint, ringing loud and clear as it vibrates across my tongue.

"Mommy, are they having sex?"

The loud voice of a little girl breaks the shroud of lust. Addie jerks violently and scrambles back, bumping into her car to get away from me.

"Penny, get in the car," the mother snaps from somewhere behind me. Addie's rounded eyes drift over my shoulder, and whatever she sees has her face reddening to a concerning color. She's panting heavily and flushed from both embarrassment and desire.

I turn my head to the side, glimpsing over my shoulder to see a blonde woman ushering her small child into the car. Her own face is red. She catches me looking and shoots me a scornful glare. I just smirk and turn back to my trembling little mouse.

She clears her throat, embarrassed and soaking wet by the flush of her cheeks and clenched thighs. She looks around, burning from the harsh wake-up call that we're in a parking lot in broad daylight.

"That was inappropriate, don't... don't do that again. Just text me the details, okay?" she snaps, stuttering over her words. She goes to turn but stops. "Oh, and can you just text me from a normal fucking number? I know it's you now. Quit trying to be cute."

And with that, she gets in her car with an irritated huff and slams the door behind her.

Despite the clusterfuck we've just found ourselves in, I laugh, biting my swollen bottom lip between my teeth. She does a double-take through the window, her eyes locking on my mouth.

Then she seems to shake herself, start her car, and speed off, tires squealing from the urgency to get away from me.

I fucking love it when she runs.

Chapter
Twenty Three
The Manipulator

"**Y**ou're going *where* to do *what*?" Daya barks through the phone. I sigh, closing my eyes in resignation. "And with who? Zade? That's your stalker's name?"

"Yeah." I bite my lip, "I don't know if I really had a choice…" I trail off. Because that's not entirely true. Zade was going to say no to Mark. But I made him say yes. Mark has information on Gigi and supposedly has valuable information for Zade as well.

"Look, I don't know what this man is into, Daya. But whatever it is, it's really fucking serious. And I can say that he really did try to avoid the situation."

"How the hell did this even happen, Addie?" Daya asks, frustration evident in her tone.

"I was working on my manuscript at Bailey's when Zade and a fucking *senator* approached me, introduced himself and said he wanted to meet *Zack's* girlfriend. Zade was staring at him like he wanted to murder him. And he asked me to go along with it until he could get rid of Mark. Long story short, Mark's father was best friends with my great-grandfather, John. He said he'd tell me more if I agreed to go to the party."

"So the man manipulated you," Daya deadpans.

I sigh. "Pretty much," I say, before rubbing my lips together.

Daya stays silent, and if it weren't for her angry breathing on the other line, I'd think she hung up. Wouldn't blame her if she did.

I am going to a party with my stalker.

All for some information that might not even help me.

"Addie, what does this man do for a living?"

I blink. "I'm not entirely sure, to be honest," I answer truthfully.

"He's not Z, is he? Because that would be fucking insane, but it would also make sense."

I frown. "What makes you think he is? Do you know a lot about that organization or something?"

Daya hesitates before she admits, "That's who I work for."

My mouth pops open.

I've heard of Z from social media and news outlets. It's a massive vigilante organization built around destroying the government. A *we for the people* type of org, and basically the government's public enemy number one.

I knew Daya was a vigilante of sorts, I just didn't know she did it for Z. In that case, it doesn't sound like she is aware of a connection between Mark and the organization.

And if Zade is indeed who she thinks he is, that means I'm now involved in something so much more than I thought it was, if even Daya is ignorant to it.

God, could Zade really be Z? It would explain his inexplicable ability to get past my security cameras. But more than that, it would explain him befriending and hiding his real identity from a goddamn senator. How the hell did I get so unlucky that the ultimate hacker would stalk me?

I never really stood a chance.

"I don't know, Daya. I honestly don't. I just... really want to solve this case. Gigi didn't deserve what happened to her. And I think Mark might be able to give us some insight on the case."

"Addie, I love you, but you're crazy. There are other routes to look at, you don't need to go to a goddamn senator's party with a fucking stalker to get a bit of information. A stalker that might be a world-renowned hacker and vigilante."

She's right.

Totally valid point.

But I'd be a liar if I said going to the party tonight didn't stir something in my chest that feels sublime. The thrill. The adrenaline rush. The danger. It stirs something deep in my core, too.

It calls to me and I'm too weak to ignore it.

But that's something that I can never explain to Daya. She's logical. Reasonable. *Smart.* And she's not an adrenaline junkie like I without a doubt am. She doesn't get a thrill out of danger.

I should've been a stunt double or something.

"I know you're going to think I'm even more insane than I already am, but at least for this occasion, I really feel like Zade will protect me. In fact, I know he will."

It's Daya's turn to sigh. "Honestly, I don't doubt that, Addie. If he is who I think he is… he's doing some good in the world. And he's clearly obsessed with you in a very unhealthy manner, but from the sounds of it, he's not the typical stalker where he's out to murder you. I think he just really, really wants to be with you and is handling it in a very creepy fucking manner."

I laugh even though it's not a funny situation. It's not necessarily something to make light of, considering we don't know if he'll just turn around and kill me, but it makes me feel better.

"Just please keep in mind that you don't know this guy, and he might not have good intentions."

I laugh dryly. "Trust me, I haven't forgotten."

"When is this party?"

I twist my red-painted lips and give myself a slow perusal in the mirror. I'm wearing a red strapless gown, the top half encrusted with thousands of tiny diamonds throughout the lacy material. The bottom half molds to my body like a second skin with a large slit slicing all the way to mid-thigh. Diamond strappy gold heels adorn my feet, while my hair is curled into beach waves, the tendrils falling around my shoulders.

It's both sexy and elegant.

Zade sent it to me, and the rebellious side of me almost threw it out to go and find my own damn dress. But then my imagination got away from me.

And I couldn't stop myself from picturing the look in his eyes when he sees me wearing the dress and shoes he chose for me. I was horrified by the butterflies that were set free in my stomach with the incessant desire to bring that image to life.

"Tonight," I say quietly, a frown tugging at my lips.

What are you doing, Addie?

Zade picks me up in a classic Mustang. The metal gleams in the moonlight, glinting off the rock in the sky as if it was built to be seen after sundown.

Shakily, I make my way down the porch steps. I wrap my long trench coat tighter around my body, partly to ward off the chill and partly to ward off the anxiety stirring in my gut.

I can't tell if I have a bad feeling about tonight or not. What I do know is that whatever happens, I'm going to see Zade in an entirely new light and discover new things about him. Things that might make me hate him more... or less.

And the latter is what I'm scared of most.

Before I can make my way to the car, his driver's side door is swinging open, and a suit-clad leg is stepping out.

Oxygen crystallizes in my lungs as Zade takes one last hit of his cigarette before flicking it to the ground and stomping it out. Smoke billows from his mouth as he looks at me from beneath hooded eyes.

Jesus Christ.

"You shouldn't litter," I say hoarsely, earning a slight grin in return. He bends and picks up the cigarette butt and deposits it in his pocket.

"Sorry, baby," he rasps. "Won't happen again."

I can hardly say thank you when I'm too enraptured by the dark God before me.

He's absolutely breathtaking. And I'd like to blame the cold autumn air on the ice in my lungs, but I know better.

Zade is adorned in an all-black suit. Every single inch of the fabric stitched to the exact millimeter of his body. It fits him impeccably, molding to his muscular arms, trimmed waist, and thick thighs.

My knees weaken, along with my resolve.

I have the most insane urge to turn around, walk back in that house, bend over the couch and let him fuck the rest of whatever sanity I have left out of me.

I want to be delirious from his cock, and to make matters worse, I know he would absolutely surpass every one of my expectations if I let him.

God?

I don't even get to finish that thought before he's walking towards me, a sinfully dark smirk on his face.

The black suit does nothing but darken his aura. Zade is Hades, stepping out from the underworld and wreaking havoc on my quiet little life. The wicked scar cutting through his nearly-white eye, with his other nearly-black eye is a combination that could only be forged in Hell.

It's just not fucking *fair.*

"You're fucking magnificent," he growls as he stalks towards me, his shiny shoes reflecting the moonlight. His voice is deeper than normal—smokier. Deadlier.

It's only when his hand rises towards my face that I notice the single red rose in his hand. He slips the flower behind my curls, biting back a smile as he does.

I hold my breath. I feel just like a mouse caught in a trap, with my predator licking his lips, ready to eat me alive.

Before I can open my mouth, he's pressing into me and grabbing my trench coat, wrenching it apart and down my arms. I gasp, both shocked by his actions and the cold licking against my skin.

"What the he—"

"You wore the dress I bought you," he interrupts, his mismatched eyes roving over the entirety of my body.

I swallow and give him a look. "I wore it out of convenience. I hate dress shopping."

He barely acknowledges me—we both know that's not why I wore it—and focuses his attention on every inch of my body. Flames lap at his pupils as the heat in his gaze intensifies.

My coat dangles in his hand, and I glare at it, willing it to magically appear back on my body.

A cold sweat breaks out across my forehead. I feel exposed, and the way he's looking at me is searing me from the inside out.

I'm just… really fucking uncomfortable right now.

I hold my hand out expectantly. "Are you done holding my coat hostage? I'm freezing."

His eyes finally draw back to my own. A shiver snakes down my spine, slithering against my shot nerve endings.

God, the way he's looking at me should be fucking illegal.

Instead of doing as I ask, he grabs my outstretched hand in his own and inspects it closely, his brow lowered as he concentrates.

"The hell are you doing, Zade?"

The slightest curl to his lips and my mouth instantly dries. I'll never get over how easily he morphs from man to beast.

"Just trying to picture what ring would look best on your finger," he says lightly. As if he didn't just send my heart flying into my throat.

Swallowing, I slide my hand from his. "What if I don't want one? I would say no."

Slowly, he drags his eyes up to mine, and the intensity of his stare has me questioning why I just can't be agreeable for once. It would save time and spare me from his smooth lines that never cease to fail. At least not completely.

Maybe I'm just addicted to the fear and excitement he awakens in me when he looks at me... just like that.

Like the beast readying to consume its prey, painfully slow. And I hope he does go slow. Drags out the torture of being caught between Zade's teeth.

His hand drifts slowly up past my chest, gently grazing his fingers across the column of my neck. And then, in an instant, his hand is snapping around my throat, gripping tight.

I gasp, my eyes widening as his lip curls into a sinister smile.

"I can put a collar around this pretty neck of yours instead. Then you wouldn't have the option to say no. You would just be my good little girl that does whatever your master says. Would you like that better, baby?"

"No," I snarl, but it tastes like a lie. "You don't own me. You never will."

His eyes narrow, and my heart drops.

"Take off my belt, Adeline." I gape at him, and when I don't make a move, his hand tightens. "Make me ask again and see what happens."

Clenching my jaw, I reach out and undo the black belt around his waist. I rip it off, not caring if it breaks. The movement jerks him, and he only grins in return.

He's evil.

I dangle the belt between us like I'm holding a dead snake. With the grin still on his smug face, he grabs it from me and lets my throat go.

Just as I suck in a deep breath, he's wrapping the belt around my neck, looping it through the buckle, and pulling tight. My eyes bulge like a fish, the metal biting into my skin as the belt constricts.

The snake wasn't dead—it's become a python wrapped around my throat.

My hands instinctively claw at the belt, but Zade swats my hands away. "You can breathe, little mouse. Don't panic."

It takes several seconds of hyperventilating to realize he's right. I can breathe. Just not very well.

When I calm, tears spring to my eyes as I glare heatedly at Zade. His grin only widens.

"I think this will do for now," he murmurs, observing my trembling body. Icy wind gusts, and I shiver in response, goosebumps smattered across my exposed flesh.

"Now get on your knees."

Again, my eyes widen, though this time in outrage. "You've *got* to be fuck—"

He tightens the belt again, and I cough from the strain. Glaring at him some more, I snap my mouth shut, lift up my dress and crouch down, making sure the fabric is gathered on my lap and away from the muddy ground.

I'm *not* ruining this dress so he can get his power trip in.

Keeping hold of the tail of the belt in one hand, Zade gestures to his pants. Growling, I unbutton and unzip him, nearly choking on my tongue when his cock springs free.

God, I don't think I'll ever get used to it. It's far larger than what's considered human. Getting fucked by that is just *inhumane.*

Seething, I don't even wait for him to spout more orders out of his stupid fucking mouth. I grip his cock and swallow it in one go.

Or try to.

I don't even get halfway down before he's clutching my hair, strands breaking free from my scalp as he sucks in a sharp breath.

"*Fuck*, Addie. I didn't sa—"

Fuck him.

Fighting against his hold, I swallow him again, lathering my tongue against the silkiness of his cock and running the tip along his veins and up to the underside of his head.

Now he's the one choking.

I glare up at him, tears still lining the edges of my lids as I take him deeper. He's staring down at me with awe and an intensity that makes him look just a little insane.

Snarling from the pleasure, he tightens the belt until my vision blackens. But if he thinks that's going to stop me, he's delusional.

Hollowing my cheeks, I suck harder. Fighting against his power even as he bleeds the life from my eyes.

I use my hand to wrap around the length that my mouth can't reach, even as I feel him breaking past the barrier of my constricted throat. I'm swallowing him as deep as he can possibly go, and my hand still doesn't fully cover his length.

Twisting my hand as I slide my red-stained lips along his cock, I think of all the ways I want to kill him. And as my vision blurs, darkness licking at the edges, I wonder who will die first.

One from lack of oxygen, or the other from lack of blood when I bite down.

He groans deeper, his eyes sparking before igniting into a blaze. "Looks like that mouth knows how to do more than make useless threats."

Seething, I graze my teeth along his dick, making sure he reads the intention in my eyes. He bares his teeth.

"I fucking dare you, little mouse. You think I won't be able to snap your jaw before your teeth break skin? Try me."

I'm tempted. But I believe him. The second my teeth dig too deep, my jaw will end up on the ground and my neck will probably snap if he pulls the belt hard enough.

I make sure he sees the rebellion in my eyes. I don't withdraw my teeth, but I don't try to hurt him either. Instead, I do the complete opposite of what he's expecting.

I roll my eyes to the back of my head like I just took a bite of the most delectable dessert I've ever had and moan around his cock, vibrations traveling through his length.

He curses, the belt loosening a fraction. I work him harder until he's growling deep, the sound feral and surely sending the animals in these woods scattering.

A predator is on the loose, but I'm the one bringing him to his knees.

"You're putting on an act, Addie," he pants, calling me out. "But don't pretend like your pussy isn't salivating just as much as your mouth is."

As much as I want to tell him how wrong he is... I can't. The slickness between my thighs is proof enough. But he doesn't get to have that, too. He doesn't get to strip me of power and turn me into a puddle of desire and desperation. So I clench my thighs and ignore my body's need.

Eyes locked on his near crazed eyes, the hand in my hair flexes until I can no longer move of my own volition. My only warning that his control has snapped. The belt tightens again, and my head is held immobilized as he drives his cock down my throat.

I gag, tears spilling over my lids, but it only seems to incite him further. He withdraws nearly to the tip before he's driving his hips forward until my mouth is stuffed full.

"Are you going to swallow my cum like a good little girl?" he bites out. I can't move, or actually answer him. The only thing I can do is brace myself as he buries himself deep and spills down my throat.

"Fuck, *Addie,*" he roars, growling as he floods my mouth faster than I can swallow. His seed slips from my lips and drips down my chin.

I can't breathe. Can hardly think anymore. My lungs are deprived of oxygen, and just when I think I'm going to blackout, he jerks himself out with another grunt, releasing the belt as he does.

I suck in a deep breath, coughing and hacking as I try to regain everything I lost. Air. Morals. Even some of my hair.

But I didn't lose my damn dignity. Not when *I* took control of that situation. That was on my terms, not his.

Sniffing, I wipe my mouth and thank God that I wore the lipstick that will take a bucket of oil to even smudge. I stand and wipe the underside of my eyes, clearing them of mascara and eyeliner while he tucks himself back in and slides his belt back around his waist.

And then I straighten out my dress, slip the rose from my hair and walk past him, snatching my coat from his hand and shoulder checking him on the way.

His dark chuckle follows me, but somehow, his long legs manage to eat up the space faster. He beats me to the car, opening the door with an amused grin on his face.

"Your chariot awaits, baby," he says, his tone low and sinful.

Oh, what a fine gentleman you're pretending to be.

I sneer at him as I slide in, refusing to be embarrassed. The door slams shut, and the smell of Zade envelops me. Leather, spice, and a hint of smoke.

The entire interior of the car is black, buttery soft leather. But what renders me speechless are the gadgets decorating his car. There are so many switches, screens—a *laptop?*—and so on that I don't even know what the hell I'm looking at.

When he slides into his seat and lurches the car forward, I shrink against the door. We descend into a stilted silence. It's not awkward necessarily, but it's tense. Charged. The sexual tension in the car has fingers trailing along my flesh and raising the goosebumps on my skin like zombies from their graves.

What happened outside felt like a prelude to something I'm not sure I'll survive. I'm breathing in the static air, and it feels like with every inhale, I'm pulling apart articles of clothing fresh from the dryer.

"How far away is it?" I ask, my voice hoarse and rough. My throat is going to be sore for days.

He glances at me, his hand tightening around the wheel. I never knew the act of driving a vehicle could look so pornographic until now.

"Twenty minutes if traffic behaves."

"I think now would be a great time to explain what this whole thing is about. What do you even do for a living?" I question, the conversation with Daya still fresh in my mind.

"I hack into government and military databases and expose crimes against humanity. I also take things a bit more personal and infiltrate the lives of officials who have proven themselves corrupt or evil."

My mouth opens, but no sound escapes.

Oh, fuck.

"You're Z."

The smile widens. "You finally figured it out. Daya tell you that?"

My eyes bulge. "You know her?" I ask incredulously.

He shrugs a shoulder. "She's one of hundreds who work in my organization," he explains simply. "I don't know her personally. And I've certainly never met or talked to her. But I know everybody that works for me."

I shake my head, dumbfounded. "You're her boss?"

"I guess you could say that. I started my organization from the ground up, and once it got big enough, I took plenty of people on. They have their objectives and the people they report to. But we all have the same goal."

"Which is?" I press.

"Bring the girls home."

My chest constricts, and I have the sudden urge to... I don't know, do something. I don't know how I'm feeling—completely bewildered, for starters.

I turn my head to look out the window, contemplating his words. He's being upfront, but I get the feeling he's still holding back.

"So, you're helping to save children and women from sex trafficking," I conclude. While it doesn't seem like a lie, it just seems too... simple.

"Yes," he confirms. "I do my own work on the side to bring in the funds to support the organization. Luckily, it's something that allows me, my employees, and every survivor we rescue to live comfortably. But that isn't the only thing we do. The government takes advantage of the public in more ways than stealing their kids. The enslavement of children and women is just my primary focus."

"Okay," I say slowly, trying to ignore the fluttering in my stomach. "What exactly is Mark involved in?"

He sighs, curling his fingers tighter around the steering wheel. "He performed a sadistic ritual on a child. A sacrifice of some sort. Someone recorded and leaked a video of it happening, and another one just leaked."

I cringe, closing my eyes against the pain in my chest. How could anyone do something so vile?

"Does Daya know about what's happening with Mark?"

"No. The rituals and Mark's involvement have been kept under wraps. I'm not ready to expose that until I take them down. It's something I've been handling mostly by myself."

I nod, understanding the implication. Don't tell Daya.

"So that's why you're under a different alias. Why not give me a different name?"

"Because you're an average citizen and finding out who you really are would be so incredibly easy, it's almost laughable. Me, on the other hand, not so much," he answers, shooting another smirk my way.

Ugh. The *arrogance.*

His face turns serious. "This is why I didn't want you involved. But I'm afraid Mark has already taken notice of you and I'd rather you be close to me. At least this way, I know you're safe."

I face him, eyeing him closely. He's relaxed into his seat, his long legs spread, one hand draped over the wheel and the other resting on the armrest between us.

I force myself to focus and ignore the way my chest is clenching from just one look.

Just because the sun is pretty doesn't mean it's not dangerous to stare at, Addie.

"I believe that you'll protect me from Mark, but who's going to protect me from you?"

His gaze sweeps the entirety of my body, and his eyes blaze with possessiveness. "Whoever tries is going to end up dead."

My eyes thin. "How can you work to save women while actively stalking another?" I challenge, cocking a brow.

He has the nerve to look amused. I have no idea what could possibly be so funny about stalking someone.

"I've never stalked anyone before you," he says simply. "Not outside of my job, at least. Definitely not for romantic purposes."

I give him a face, my expression full of incredulity.

"Is that supposed to make me feel special?"

A slow, wicked smirk glides across his face, unbothered by my increasingly burning stare. "I wouldn't mind if it did."

I want to slap him. But the asshole would probably like it, and then turn around and slap me back. And my dumbass self would probably like it, too.

I'm fucked in the head. And dealing with this man—I am beyond stressed. This just *can't* be good for my skin.

Scoffing, I turn my head out the window and spend the rest of the car ride in tense silence. The atmosphere has only worsened, and I can't tell if it's because I now know he's some vigilante, saving children and women from evil people, or if it's because he confessed that he's only ever turned into a psycho for me. Still, both prospects have shifted the way I look at him.

The latter shouldn't by any means, considering he just lodged his dick down my throat while strangling me with a belt five minutes ago.

But it fucking does.

September 28th, 1945

Ronaldo didn't take it well. In fact, he completely exploded and threatened to kill John.

I didn't know how to handle a threat like that. Ronaldo has mentioned before that he has killed men. But I had no idea how to handle it being directed towards someone I still hold love for.

Suffice to say, I didn't take it well and yelled at him. He accused me of taking my husband's side while really, I'm just growing tired of the threat of violence.

When I told him so, he immediately drove me home.

And I must admit, the look he gave me scared me half to death.

The car ride was awful.

He dropped me off only an hour ago, and I haven't stopped crying since.

What was supposed to be an escape just turned into a bigger nightmare.

Chapter
Twenty Four
The Manipulator

"Is there anything I need to know before you bring me into the pit of snakes?" I ask as Zade drives up to the valet parking.

Valet parking at their own damn house. This shit should be illegal.

"In here, my name is Zack Forthright. I'm a self-made millionaire and have my own company for web design. We live in Parsons Manor together and are a happy couple, but I sneak around on you and go to gentlemen's clubs without your knowledge."

My eyes snap to his. He's been going to *gentlemen's clubs?* As in, the clubs that offer up women on a silver platter for men to get their rocks off to? Rich people gentlemen's clubs at that—ones occupied by corrupt sadists. Who knows what happens in those places to those poor women?

Sensing my thoughts, he smirks. "Before you judge, I have not and will not ever indulge in what they offer there, and eventually, I'll get all those girls out. But *they* don't know that. Don't be jealous, little mouse. No one will ever be capable of getting my cock hard except you."

The heroism wars with his imprudent assumption. Part of me wants to melt, while the other stiffens into granite at being accused of such a thing.

I roll my eyes. "I'm not jealous," I snipe. "And it sounds like you just have erectile dysfunction to me."

He bites back a grin, a knowing look gleaming in his eyes. His voice deepens as he drawls lazily, "Keep it up, and you'll be choking on those words when my cock is filling up your throat again. Everyone passing by will see me fucking your filthy little mouth, and there won't be a single person in that house that won't be aware of it by the time I'm done."

I scoff, turning my head away from him. Only to hide the blush that I feel creeping up my cheeks and the sharp thrill chasing the nerves down my spine. I still feel the phantom bite of metal from his belt buckle around my neck, and I know with absolute certainty that Zade would follow through on his threat if I pushed.

Dickhead.

He continues as if he didn't just serve me the most delicious threat I've ever heard. "Don't speak of your personal life. Nothing that means anything to you anyways. You're here to get information on Gigi, and that's incentive enough."

"Incentive?" I interrupt, whipping my head back towards him.

"You're walking into the viper's pit because Mark found something that you care about and is holding it over your head," Zade explains plainly. I snap my mouth shut, contrite and a little worried.

"If he finds out anything else you care about, that will be something he'll use to his advantage if he's given the chance."

My mouth falls back open. "But don't worry," he says, cutting in before I can demand that he take me home. "I'll flay his skin from his body before he can even think to do anything to hurt you."

With that, he opens the door, gets out and throws his keys at the waiting valet, shutting the door firmly and cutting off any questions I had on the tip of my tongue.

For starters, *can I go home now?*

I'm asking myself if solving Gigi's murder is worth involving myself with dangerous people. But it's too late. I'm here, and I'm bound and determined to get at least a few more of my questions answered before Zade takes me home.

I have the feeling that not only am I putting my safety in Zade's hands tonight, but my life.

Because I'm walking into a house owned by an evil man, I don't need Zade to spell that out for me.

Zade opens my door and holds out a hand for me to grab onto as I slide out of the car. Electricity explodes from where his hand grips mine, and all I really want to do is guide his hands to other parts of my body.

I suck in icy air, the cold offering a balm to my insides, and allowing me enough clarity to concentrate on everything else besides the domineering man beside me.

Mark's house is ostentatious. A massive white monstrosity with five huge pillars and a million windows. In my opinion, the house is ugly, typical and downright boring.

The inside is even worse. I walk into a large, wide hallway with picture frames lining either side of the wall of who I assume is Mark's family. My heels click against the ivory tile, and I can't help but think it's going to turn brown after all the shoes that'll be treading across it.

We're ushered by a butler down the hallway, past an all-white kitchen and into a ballroom.

An actual fucking ballroom.

The kind you see in movies set back in the 1800s, when finding your future husband or wife depended on going to a ball.

Three massive chandeliers dangle from the gold ceiling, arches of intricately carved wood between each fixture. The floor is a sparkling ivory, the little flecks glinting off of the chandeliers nearly blinding me. It's like looking into the damn sun.

"Fix your face," Zade murmurs from beside me. It's not until he speaks that I realize my face was screwed up into a look of disgust.

Not because the room is ugly, but because it's so damn... pretentious and flashy. I don't need to see the rest of the house to know that the place screams *look at me, I have a gazillion dollars and have no intention of sharing the wealth with the millions of starving families around the world.*

But what do I know? I've always wondered if the people who have the money to feed the entire world population are *allowed* to. All governments are corrupted. Maybe if you try to save the world and actively steal money from the rich's pockets, you'll wake up dead one day.

I smooth out my face, donning a blank mask as I look around at the hundreds of people occupying the ballroom. Everyone is dressed to the nines, the guests ranging from young adults to people who look like they're on their deathbed.

Zade holds out his elbow to me, and every signal in my brain tells me to snub the request. But that's pride speaking, and I'm not in a good position to let pride get the best of me. I loathe to admit it, but I'm safer attached to Zade.

Stiffly, I grab onto his elbow and lean into his side. It feels like hands smoothing into wet clay. No matter the divots in our bodies, we mold together perfectly.

Ugh.

For the next hour, we mingle around the ballroom, talking to random people, many of them familiar faces I've seen on the news, arguing over bills and laws that usually do nothing but flatten Americans further under their thumbs.

Zade is charming, his demeanor calm and slightly reserved, but still manages to draw people in until they're hanging on every word he says.

Most of their eyes linger on his scars. Questions on the tip of their tongues that never see the light. You'd think it's because it's a rude question to ask, but really, it's because Zade carries intimidation around with him like a woman with a designer purse.

Despite that, he's a sight to behold as he works the room, gaining these people's trust and interest in a matter of minutes.

I've no idea who's involved in Zade's mission and who's not, but he looks at each and every one of these people as if he knows exactly who they are and their entire life story. Maybe that's how he sucks them in so profoundly—he makes them feel like they've known each other for years.

I, on the other hand, am not a natural. The social anxiety licks at my nerves, keeping my heart rate well above a normal pace. I smile at the strangers and laugh at everything they say, doing what I do best and manipulate people's emotions with my words. I pretend they're all avid readers, and the words I'm speaking are printing on blank sheets of paper for their greedy eyes to consume.

Somehow, it works to the point of discomfort as all of their eyes are ensnared on me as I answer their questions about my career. I heed Zade's advice and keep it all vague and surface-level but find pretty words to make my life seem more interesting than it is. Even Zade appears to struggle with looking away, and the notion gives me a small bit of confidence.

But on the inside, it feels like my stomach is a black hole, crumpling my insides like a wadded-up piece of paper.

On several occasions throughout the hour, Zade wraps his arm around my waist and squeezes, his grip firm and reassuring. Those small touches are anchors, leveling my head and reminding me that I'm not alone.

Mark seems to appear out of thin air, joining the two couples gathered around Zade, listening to him speak about some interaction he had with another senator. I guess the story is supposed to be funny as the couples are both tittering out laughs, but I can barely digest a single word he says.

"Zack! Adeline! I'm so glad to see you two made it," Mark announces boisterously, interrupting Zade's story. He doesn't seem the least bit bothered. I have a feeling the tale was fabricated entirely anyway.

Seems I'm not the only one good at bullshitting.

"Mark," I croon joyfully, as if this man's face brings me any type of delight. He eats it up as he shakes hands with Zade and offers me a warm hug.

Or what's supposed to be warm. It feels like hugging a cold-blooded reptile.

Next to Mark must be his wife. An older woman with beautiful red hair—the color of ripe cherries—matching red lipstick, and a black dress that seems to hang on her frail body.

She widens her lips into a beautiful smile as Mark introduces her to Zade and

I. What irks me is he doesn't tell us her name, he just says *my wife*. As if she's merely a possession and not her own person with her own fucking identity outside of her marriage to this wretched man.

"Pleasure to make your acquaintance, Adeline. I'm Claire," she says, gripping my hand in a light handshake. She offers the introduction to Zade as well, and the devil takes it a step further and kisses her hand, trapping her gaze into his own.

It wasn't sensual by any means. Something about it seemed comforting, like he was making her a promise that even she didn't know she needed.

Claire's smile wobbles and she gently pulls her hand from Zade's grip. No one except my shadow and I seem to notice her hand curling into a tight fist to abate the shaking.

She's nervous. Scared. And whatever that moment was with Zade, it shook her.

It doesn't take a genius to figure out this woman is abused. My eyes subtly search her body, but the high neck, long sleeves, and full-length dress hide her body. It's a beautiful dress, but one clearly designed to disguise the bruises that I'm sure are staining her skin beneath the silky fabric.

The other couples meanders off, sensing that Mark is now expecting a private conversation.

"I have a few more guests to greet, but please, I insist you meet me in my study in about an hour and join me for a drink. My butler, Marion, would be happy to show you the way when the time comes."

Zade smiles, appearing relaxed. Maybe it's because I've become acquainted with the monster settled between his bones, but I can feel the intent beneath his fabricated ease.

"Of course, be happy to," Zade responds smoothly.

"Great!" Mark bursts, smiling wide. "And Adeline, I look forward to speaking with you about your great-grandmother."

He smiles one last time, casting me a lingering look before walking off with Claire in tow.

Zade wasn't wrong. The man is definitely exploiting the one weakness I have, solving Gigi's murder. And something tells me he's going to hang information over my head until he gets whatever he wants.

Problem is, I don't know what he wants from me. But whatever it is, I have a feeling deep in my bones that it's capable of ending my life.

November 15th, 1945

I'm so livid, I'm shaking.

Lately, I've noticed John's gambling habits. He comes home late now, drunk and angry. He goes on rants about being swindled out of money, though it sounds like whoever these people are know John can't play poker very well.

Regardless, I got a letter today saying that our house is going into foreclosure.

Normally, John is the one that handles the bills since he brings home the money. But then I found out that all of our savings has been depleted. All of it.

That was going to pay for Sera's schooling. And it's gone. I broke down in tears.

He gambled away all of our money, and part of me can't help but realize that this is all my fault.

Before Ronaldo came into the picture, we were happy...

And now. Now we're a ship wreck.

Broken, and with no home.

Chapter Twenty Five
The Shadow

I f I spend another moment in this stuffy ballroom, I'm going to start shooting people just to release some tension. There are plenty of heads in this room that I wouldn't mind embedding with a bullet.

Addie stands beside me, her tiny hand gripping onto my arm like her life depends on it.

It's fucking addictive.

"Let's get out of here," I whisper in her ear. Her sweet jasmine smell wafts from the juncture between her neck and shoulder, and I have to grind my teeth against the urge to take a bite.

Flashes of her on her knees, that red rose in her hair as she sucked me off with a belt around that dainty neck... *fuck.*

A growl slips free, and it takes monumental effort to bite back the satisfied grin when I feel her tremble.

Her reaction is more potent than a drug. It drives me deliriously insane, and the need to wrap my hand around her throat and fuck her until neither of us can breathe is overwhelming.

This woman is going to reduce me to an animal.

Her head snaps towards mine, her brows scrunching in confusion and what almost looks like anger. She probably thinks I mean to leave this place entirely and deny her the chance to get information on her great-grandmother.

"Calm, sweet little mouse. I just meant this *room*."

She relaxes, her shoulders dropping an inch.

It goes without saying that all guests are expected to stay inside the ballroom. But if staying on the safe side of rules and laws was something I did, I wouldn't be where I am now.

In a senator's house with a girl who's not supposed to want me.

I grab her hand, basking in the feel of her skin against mine as I guide her out of the room. I wait until it seems all eyes have turned away from us and slip through the door and out into a grand hallway.

Now would be a perfect time to search the house, see what I can discover in a pedophile's safe space. But selfishly, I want to ease some of the building tension swelling in Addie's shoulders.

She's doing fucking amazing so far. Despite the obvious nerves, she's managed to make every single person in the room fall in love with her. If anything, her shy, innocent demeanor and suave words are these people's daily dose of whatever prescription pills keep them sane.

I'm equal parts impressed and perturbed by her. Because all this woman has managed to do is make these people want to see her again. And that's the last thing both of us want.

I slide out my phone and shoot off a quick message to Jay, asking him to take care of the security cameras. I've spotted dozens just from the entrance to the ballroom, and I'm sure Mark has a team actively watching to make sure no one does exactly what we're doing now.

Mark would be alerted immediately and we would be caught before we even got a chance to have fun.

Jay confirms the cameras are set, and Addie and I take off. Her heels click against the tiled floor as we sneak through the maze of hallways and rooms.

Occasionally, I open up doors and peek inside, finding nothing of interest. That is until we get somewhere far enough away that the noise from the ballroom no longer penetrates the walls.

At the end of another hallway are wide double doors, the cherry wood standing out against the champagne walls.

I head towards the doors, Addie barely keeping up behind me. "Zade, we shouldn't be sneaking around. We're going to get in trouble," she pleads, glancing behind her as if someone is hot on her heels. It's the fifth time she's said that since we left the ballroom, yet her eyes are dilated with excitement.

She's not fooling me when she wears her arousal on her sleeve. She's scared. Nervous. And that feeling never fails to make her pussy dripping wet.

The girl gets off on fear. The moment I realized she was turned on by the terror I instill in her—there was no chance of me ever letting her go. She was fucking made for me.

"Shh, baby girl," I whisper, silencing her weak protests. Her mouth audibly clicks shut, and this time I don't bother restraining the smile.

Too easy.

Gently, I open the doors, sticking my head inside to look around. It takes a moment for my eyes to adjust, but my smile widens when I get a good look at the darkened room.

I look back at Addie, allowing her to see my shit-eating grin. Her eyes round and another protest builds on her sharp little tongue.

Yanking her inside, I quickly shut the door behind her and let her take in the room, once more silencing her objections.

A movie theater.

Ten rows of comfortable red chairs line the walls and in front of it is a massive screen, the sides curving to the adjoining walls to fill the viewer's peripheral vision. It gives the effect that you're inside the movie, and I know just the type of movie to watch.

I note the padded walls and tightly sealed doors. This room is soundproof, and I'm nearly weak in the knees with how perfect this night is turning out to be.

"Zade, whatever you're planning..." her voice trails off when I make my way to the projector in the back of the room.

There's a display screen, showing the controls of the projector, along with thousands of options of movies to watch. Some of these haven't even hit theaters yet.

I select the latest horror movie, set to come out in a couple of months. Which means Addie hasn't seen it, and the experience will be entirely new.

Hopefully, it's a good one and has the desired effect I'm looking for.

"Zade, we shouldn't be in here," she says, backing away towards the door.

I chuckle. "Always following the rules," I observe, messing with the buttons on the screen. "Tell me, little mouse, are you close with your father?"

She sniffs. "Why would you even ask that?"

"Your father is an attorney, is he not? A rule follower. I imagine you got your desire to follow the rules from him, no?"

She scoffs, "No. I didn't learn that from him."

I pause to look over my shoulder, giving her a wicked smile.

"You got daddy issues then?"

"I don't have daddy issues," she snaps. "I mean, I don't *really*. My father has always kind of just... been there. My mother was such a force that he usually faded in the background." She finishes with another sniff, looking every bit uncomfortable.

"Well, if you didn't before, you do now," I drawl, my smile growing as I watch a pretty blush stain her cheeks.

Her eyes round and her mouth drops in shock. I want to stick my cock in it again just to give it a better use. Her skills are very refined in that area.

And thinking of *how* she refined those skills makes me murderous for a brief moment.

"Are you saying you're my daddy?" she sputters out incredulously, bringing my attention back to her.

"That's right, baby. And you're my good little girl," I croon, sliding my tongue across my lower lip and looking at her like... fuck. The things I want to do to this woman. Things that would show her just how insane I can be.

"I am not," she hisses, though the protest is weak.

Leaving the movie for now, I stalk towards her, enjoying the sight of her stumbling away from me and into a wall. If she had the power, she'd burn me to a crisp from the heat in her glare. Good thing she doesn't realize what power she truly holds yet.

I don't stop pursuing her until my body is pressed into hers, relishing over the feel of her nipples cutting through her thin dress.

Watching her on her knees for me earlier, sucking my cock like her life depended on it, but yet angry as hell about it—was the most magnificent sight I've ever seen.

She wanted her power back in that moment, and I was more than happy to show her that she never lost it. This beautiful woman holds my life in the palm of her hand, she's just incapable of seeing it that way.

The only one who's truly in danger is me.

"No?" I whisper. I tip her chin up, brushing my lips softly against hers. The sharp intake of breath has my cock straining against my slacks.

"If you were my little girl, I would worship every inch of your body for as long as our souls are tethered to this earth. My tongue would leave no part of you untouched." I nip at her bottom lip, wringing a whimper from her throat. "Untasted," I murmur, my tongue darting out, sliding along the seam of her lips.

My hand slides up to grip her dainty throat, and I can't stop the deep growl from forming. My fingers nearly wrapping around the entirety of her neck.

I could snap it so easily. Bruise it. Leave my mark with my tongue and teeth.

"If you were my little girl," I breathe, desire growing dangerously high. "Your sweet little pussy would be so full of me, you would forget what it means to feel empty. I would be inside of you so deeply, you would have to cut me out."

Then, I bare my teeth, squeezing her throat until her face pinkens, overcome with the thought of her trying to do something so futile. "You would bleed out before that could ever happen."

"I would do it," she croaks. I loosen my hand just enough to allow her to continue. "I would take a knife and cut every inch of my skin from my body. So nothing would be left of your touch."

I cock a brow and grunt my amusement, both turned on and angry from her insolence.

"We'll see about that—" I lean down, making sure that my lips brush against the shell of her ear. "Little girl," I finish on a whisper.

Grabbing Addie's hand, I drag her towards the touchscreen to push play on the movie, and then grab a seat smack in the middle of the front row, forcing her onto my lap.

She tried to sit *two* seats down from me, but that only pulled a deep laugh from me. Expletives spilled from her mouth in the five seconds it took to wrangle her little body on top of mine.

The surround sound booms with the opening credits, causing Addie to jolt against me. I wrap my arm tightly around her waist, sliding her back until she's molded into me. Her perky ass sits nicely against my straining cock, and the second she feels how hard I am, she stiffens.

"Zade," she warns breathlessly, though the effect is lost on both of us.

I keep quiet, letting her slowly relax into me as the movie starts to play. Despite the loosening of her muscles, she's still on edge. I would bet anything right now she's high on endorphins from the mix of fear of being caught, the conversation that just transpired, and the movie.

The opening scene is already creepy, setting the tone immediately. Addie wriggles in my hold, her thighs clamped tight.

I let twenty minutes pass, the movie subtly getting scarier. I pay it no attention—all of it has been routed to Addie.

Her wide eyes are hooked onto the screen, her breathing is escalated, and heart pounding against her chest. The first jump scare has her yelping, nearly jumping out of her own skin.

Beneath the flickering light, I watch her skin grow flushed with desire and a small bead of sweat forms on her hairline.

"Are you even watching?" she asks, her voice a mere octave above a whisper.

"Yes," I murmur, my voice deeper and hoarse with need.

Her breath stutters and her eyes slowly slide towards mine. Those rosebud lips are parted as she stares at me with unbridled heat.

Gliding my tongue across my bottom lip, I wait until her gaze has been hooked onto the act before I fist the soft fabric of her dress and hike it up until it's pooled around her hips.

"Stop it," she pants, but I don't listen. She swats at me, but those tiny hands are no match against mine.

With wicked intention, I slide both of my hands in the crease of her thighs and jerk them apart.

Her hands snap to my forearms, gripping tightly as if to stop me. But she doesn't fight against me, even as I spread her thighs so far apart, each leg rests on either chair beside us.

"What are you doing?" she gasps, staring at my creeping hands with trepidation. I lift one to grab her by her jaw and force her face to the screen.

"Watch the movie," I growl.

A creature in the movie pops out, diverting Addie's attention enough to scare her again. A startled scream rings out as she shrinks away from the screen and deeper into my hold.

I groan, the feel of her ass digging into my cock nearly blinding me with pleasure and need.

The tips of my fingers glide across her creamy thigh, causing her to shift against my touch with restless desire. The creepy music from the movie builds to a crescendo, sending her heart rate to dangerous levels as a person is chased down by something from your worst nightmares.

"Zade," she pleas breathlessly, desperate for something that she's not capable of putting a name to.

I glance down, biting back a groan when I see her bare.

"This might not end well for you," I muse.

She stiffens. "Why?"

"Your cum will be leaking down your legs when we're done," I hum. "How scandalous."

"I'd rather have wet thighs than have panty lines with a dress like this."

My fingers softly brush against her folds, reveling in the cream gathering on my fingers. I keep my touch light, depriving her of truly gaining any pleasure.

"Zade," she bites out, her voice more forceful and demanding. I smile, refusing to give in.

"Are you watching the movie, Adeline?" I ask harshly. "Don't make me tell you again."

Her eyes snap to the screen, another gasp pulled from her painted lips when the creature brutally slaughters a person.

Her pussy pulses, juices gushing from her slit and over my fingers. I groan, fighting the impulse to plunge my fingers into the depths of her pussy and feel her come all over me.

My tongue darts out, licking along her neck and inhaling her jasmine scent. Tasting the saltiness from the thin layer of sweat coating her skin.

She tastes so fucking delicious. My mouth waters with the need to lap up the arousal soaking my hand. I deny myself the pleasure, keeping my hand glued to her weeping little cunt.

Giving in to her silent plea, I swirl the pad of my middle finger on her clit, giving her just enough pressure to cause her head to kick back with bliss.

This time when she whispers my name, it's full of pleasure.

A scream from the movie startles her, and her head snaps upright once more.

"S-someone could come in," she croaks, my ministrations steady and firm. When I pinch her sensitive clit between my fingers, her eyes cross, a sexy moan releasing from her parted lips.

"Does that make your pussy wet?" I implore, continuing to rub her clit with my finger. "Does the knowledge that someone could come in any second and see you spread open for me turn you on?"

She shakes her head, denying the truth as much as she denies how much she wants me.

"The fear of being caught with my fingers deep in your pussy—" I pause to drive home my point, plunging my middle finger inside her and wringing out a sharp cry— "it makes you want to come so badly, doesn't it?"

I add a second finger, fucking her in quick hard strokes. Her breath sharpens, and her moans heighten as she draws closer to an orgasm.

My eyes shift back and forth between what my fingers are doing to her and her face. Her eyes have long since dropped to my hand, defying my orders once again.

Mid-stroke, I withdraw my fingers and grab her face with my other hand, roughly squeezing her jaw in my grip. She mewls, crying from both the loss and the pain lancing through her face.

I deliver one quick, sharp slap to her pussy, enjoying the startled cry of pain that sneaks past her lips.

"What. Did. I. Say?" Her chest heaves, and her hips buck against the air, desperate to feel my fingers filling her up once more.

"Watch the movie," she answers, sucking her lip between her teeth as her glazed eyes focus back on the screen.

"Were you listening?" I growl, refusing to touch her needy pussy.

"I—no. I'm sorry," she says quietly, a deep crease forming between her brows. Her apology didn't settle right with her, so to abate the sobering thoughts, I plunge my fingers back inside her.

A long moan releases, but her eyes stay glued to the screen.

"Good girl," I praise, feeling the answering clench around my fingers. "If I catch you disobeying me one more time, you won't get to come. Am I understood?"

She nods, the movement choppy and strained against the force of my fingers clutching her cheeks.

Releasing her face, my hand drifts to the front of her dress, tugging down harshly. The fabric holds tight beneath her tits, forcing them to swell. Groaning, I cup a full breast in my palm, squeezing tightly before kneading the sharpened point of her nipple between my fingers.

I resume my ministrations with the hand between her thighs, keeping my thrusts slow and languid. Drawing out her pleasure and wringing more delicious moans from her mouth. Her eyes droop into a half-lidded state, but they don't stray from the screen.

Loud, wet noises war with the sound from the movie as my fingers dip in and out. She's so fucking wet. She's creating a pool on my slacks and the seat beneath us.

I trade between biting and licking at her neck and whispering words of appraisal in her ear. This time, I want her orgasm to build at a slower, more painful pace. It'll gradually creep up while feeling so far out of reach.

"This sweet little pussy is so fucking needy for my fingers, isn't it? Do you feel how tightly you're gripping me? I have to fight just to withdraw my fingers so I can fuck you with them."

A sinister vibe emanates from the screen, and Addie's pulse seems to become even more erratic.

"Zade, please," she begs, her nails biting into my arms. My sleeves alleviate the sting, but the pressure increases until I fear she's going to start breaking her red painted nails.

My free hand grips her throat and squeezes firmly until her face pinkens, and her breath grows short. Staccato moans bursts from her lips as I increase my pace and firmly rub her clit with my thumb.

"Oh, God—" she sucks in a sharp breath.

"That's right, I *am* your God."

"Zade!" she screams a moment before her pussy clenches onto my fingers so tightly, I can hardly move them any longer.

Her back arches and her head kicks back, past the point of caring about my demands and the movie. A sob wracks her throat as I continue thrusting, riding out her orgasm until her entire body is convulsing and she's desperately trying to pull my hand away.

"Oh my god, oh my god, Zade, *stop*," she chants, her juices flooding so heavily from her core that I feel them spilling past my hand.

Finally, I ease my fingers out, licking them clean as she watches me with a colorful expression. She's satisfied, but embarrassment, shame, and anger are slowly creeping back in.

Now that she's coming down from her high, reality is setting in.

I laugh as she scrambles from my lap and rearranges her dress back to its previous state—a tad more rumpled than before but no less beautiful.

There's a slight wet spot between my legs, but luckily my black slacks conceal it, and most of it got on the seat. I feel the need to leave a hundred-dollar bill for whoever has to clean that.

"I can't believe we did that," she mutters under her breath, seemingly to herself as her hands drift over her hair, checking to make sure nothing is out of place.

"You look beautiful," I say, cutting off her continued muttering and rendering her silent. Subtly, she glances over her shoulder at me, but doesn't acknowledge my words.

"So, not only do you only fear me in the daylight, but you only love me when I'm making you come."

That gets her attention. She whips around, fire in her eyes as she spits, "I *don't* love you."

"Not yet," I counter, topping it off with a grin. Her eyes narrow into thin slits.

"Come on, little mouse. You've wasted enough time getting your pussy worshipped, let's go get some answers."

I slip past her, walking ahead of her and towards the doors. Yet, I still hear her mutter *asshole* under her breath, and it does nothing but bring me joy to know I get under her skin so deeply.

Chapter
Twenty Six
The Manipulator

I'm seething, and my thighs are slick with my own arousal as I rush after Zade.

He doesn't bother turning the movie off. We just slip from the room and quickly make our way back into the ballroom.

It's like no one even noticed us gone. But I'm sure people have, right? Zade has worked this entire room by now, and as much as I loathe to admit it, the man is unforgettable.

To say the fucking least.

All of two minutes pass before a man approaches us, his black uniform and white vest signaling his position.

"Mr. Forthright, Ms. Reilly, please follow me," the butler, Marion, instructs.

Just like that, I'm stone-cold sober and the lingering orgasm has been completely eradicated.

Marion leads us through a series of hallways, pointing out certain pictures and historical artifacts Mark managed to get his hands on.

I nod and hum my appraisal, but my mind is drifting back towards Gigi and the potential information I could garner tonight. Mark might choose to give me breadcrumbs and keep me coming back for more, but it'll be futile.

He's not getting me back in this house again. I'm not entirely sure if coming here was even worth it yet or not.

At least I got to watch an unreleased movie, even though I didn't get to see how it ended.

Whatever, I don't remember much about it anyways. My gaze was sightless when all I could focus on was—

Stop it, Addie.

My stomach drops from the fresh memory, and it takes entering Mark's study to pull my attention firmly back into the present.

"My two favorite people," Mark greets loudly, a lit cigar poised between his fingers and a glass of amber liquid in the crystal cup dangling in his other hand.

He looks drunk. His ruddy face is flushed red, and his eyes have begun to glaze over a bit.

"Please, sit," he directs, pointing to the plush leather couch beside his desk.

Zade and I take a seat, and the two men immediately engage in a conversation about the party. I add my two cents in when required, noting how beautiful the chandeliers are and the fascinating artifacts decorating his house.

He beams at the compliment, a smile stretching across his face.

"All thanks to my wife, of course. She does enjoy spending my money, and if decorating this house is what keeps her happy, then I can live with that," he jests. His tone is joyful, but the words are condescending and meant to be an attack.

"I'm sure you know how much the ladies love our money, huh, Zack?"

And there's the cherry on top of his sundae of misogyny. I bet his sundae taste like bruised skin and a bleeding heart.

Zade smiles, the act nearly primal and ripe with danger. "Small price to pay when they give us something so priceless every day. And if you ask me, I'd tell you I'm not worthy of it, but I'm a selfish bastard and will accept it anyways," he answers cryptically. I don't know how I know, but I know exactly what he's speaking of.

Love.

Love is priceless. As Mark's nefarious dealings have proven, pussy can be bought and is plentiful, whether they're forcing it or getting consent. And despite all the ways Zade has forced me to my knees for him, the only thing he's ever really wanted from me is to return his addiction. Because that's the one thing he can't take or force.

He can force my body to succumb to him, but he can't force my heart to beat for him.

And ironically, it seems that's the one thing he wants most from me.

Mark takes it the direction most men would. He laughs and offers me a wink, as if he knows without a doubt how priceless my pussy might be. But if I had to guess on what type of man Mark is, he'd put a price on me in a heartbeat.

"I know exactly what you mean," he chortles.

Do you, asshole?

I shrug a shoulder. "I think you're the lucky one, Mark. One look at Claire, and you can see she is a strong, capable woman. Those are the most dangerous." I add in a wink, but I know it's falling on deaf ears. Mark is too comfortable in the patriarchy to consider that Claire might not shove a knife through his neck while sleeping one night.

Mark scoffs, but he takes the hint and shuts his mouth. At least he's not dense enough to feel the plummeting mood.

Zade appears relaxed and collected, but I know that beast in his soul is pacing back and forth, just waiting to be set loose. I can tell by the subtle flexing of his fist, and that way his smile appears threatening and feral. I can just *feel* the energy radiating off of him despite the serenity he exudes.

Why does Zade wanting to kill a man over a sleazy comment most men would say make me want to repeat the favor he stole from me in my driveway? This time I'd be much more... willing.

I hate him.

"So, Adeline, about your great-grandmother. Gigi was a beautiful woman. Even as a little boy, I remember that clearly," he continues.

Climbing a mountain would take less energy than what it does to keep my eyes from rolling at his remark.

That *would* be something Mark latched onto. Gigi was beautiful, but who the fuck cares about personalities, right?

I clear my throat and paste on a smile. "Yes, she was."

Mark tips his head back, seeming to retreat into a memory. "Yeah, I remember her signature red lips. Don't think I ever saw her without that lipstick on."

"Do you remember anything about her murder?" I ask, trying to keep the hope at bay.

"I remember how absolutely devastated John was when he found her. Was in near hysterics, and it took my father hours to calm him down enough to tell him what happened."

"You said your father thought it was John, but do you think it could've been anyone else?" I press. I already know my great-grandfather freaked the hell out. There was a comment in the police report that they threatened to sedate him.

What I really want to know is what his father knew about the case. Maybe he knew something that wasn't in any of the files.

He shrugs a shoulder. "From what I remember, he thinks that she was sneaking around on John—seeing some man. My father couldn't seem to find out who it was, though, so it wasn't something they looked into. But my father was almost certain that was the reason John snapped and killed Gigi."

I twist my lips, glancing at Zade to find him already staring at me with an unreadable expression.

He's skimmed through her diaries and knows she had a stalker. But it doesn't seem that Mark or his father knew that, which doesn't surprise me in the slightest. Gigi's diaries were in a safe behind a picture. The police would have had no reason to believe she would be hiding something like that.

I contemplate if I should divulge what I know. Maybe Mark would have some type of power to look into the diaries and see what he can find. But the second that thought enters, I boot it right back out.

Mark isn't a nice guy. And he would only lord those books over my head and lead me on. I'm positive I would never see them again if I handed them over.

Besides, I'm confident Daya has many more ways to get information than Mark ever could. Mark's father is presumably dead with the way he speaks about him in the past tense, and I'm sure the officers from the case are also dead, or close to it.

Gigi died in the '40s, making this case seventy-five years old.

"Why did Frank believe it was John and not the other man then?"

Mark settles back, his glazed eyes look off into the distance. "Sera was older than me at the time, by six years. She was a teenager, and I was still a ten-year-old kid who wanted to play. Of course, Sera was an angel and humored me. So, for months leading up to Gigi's death, I would ask to go over to Parsons Manor and see Sera. And every time, my father would say no. He said John developed a bit of a drinking problem and it was no longer safe for children over there. I whined and cried 'cause I only wanted to see my friend. And then Gigi was killed, and I still didn't get it.

"Now, of course, when my father told me Gigi was gone, I understood death, but not the severity. The last time I had ever asked to go to the manor was a few days after. And my father looked me in the eye and said, 'You want to die next?'" He laughs without humor. "I'll never forget that. My blood ran cold when he said that. Never asked again, and eventually, I let go of Sera."

I frown, shivers roll down my spine. Nana didn't talk much about John. She did mention before that he was a wonderful father up until Gigi's death. He did have a drinking problem, but I think he hid most of his anger from Nana in the beginning. But once Gigi died, all hell must've broken loose. Nana never told me how Gigi died, so I had just assumed he declined due to heartbreak.

But I would've never thought it'd be for a much darker reason. For the first time, I'm faced with the true possibility that my great-grandfather was the one to murder Gigi.

Clearing my throat, I take a different direction. Gigi had spoken of people breaking into her house in the diary entries due to John's gambling habits, and Nana had said in passing before that her father liked to gamble.

"My Nana mentioned before that he liked to gamble. Maybe he owed some people money, and when he couldn't pay up, they went after Gigi?"

Mark nods his head thoughtfully. "John was known to have really bad gambling habits. They almost lost Parsons Manor at one point because of it. The only reason they didn't was because Gigi came up with the money to pay off the mortgage and property tax," he explains.

I tighten my lips. According to her diary, Ronaldo paid off their overdue bills, but the excuse Gigi spun was that she borrowed it from one of her girlfriends. John wanted to know who, but she refused to tell and it caused a fight considering John was a typical man back then with pride and an ego.

But from what I gleaned from the entries, I can't be sure if Ronaldo ever paid off John's debts. He had mentioned he'd take care of it, but when the righthand man for the mafia says those words, that can mean a number of things.

Maybe he killed the people instead and gained Gigi enemies by doing so.

Jesus, it really is like time repeating itself if that's the case.

"Then how did he pay off the men he owed?"

Mark finishes off his drink before refilling. "You know, now that I think about it, I remember overhearing a particular conversation. My father told him that he needed to quit with the gambling, and John wasn't listening. He said one of the men he owed was Angelo Salvatore—who was a pretty notorious crime lord back in the day. But turns out Angelo's righthand man, Ronaldo, convinced Angelo to hire John instead."

It takes monumental effort to keep my eyes from blowing wide. John was working for Ronaldo's boss? There's no way Gigi knew about it. I imagine that's something she would've mentioned if she had.

"Why would he hire him? Why not just kill him?"

"He almost did," Mark counters. He then opens a drawer in his desk and pulls out a cigar. Lighting the tobacco, Mark leans back in his chair, the leather creaking beneath his weight. A woodsy scent fills the air as he puffs.

"I'll never forget the way my father ripped into him over it. Calling him names and telling him he could've gotten himself killed. John said Angelo had a gun to his head, ready to pull the trigger before Ronaldo stepped in. Said the man asked Angelo to consider hiring John to pay off his debts by working for him instead." Mark sucks in deeply and then coughs a few times as smoke puffs from his mouth. "Guess it worked."

So, Ronaldo saved John's life. I don't need to have been there to know he only did it for Gigi. But it's not like he could've told Angelo his real reasons for bartering John's life, which means John had to have been useful in some form— that would've been too risky of a move otherwise, and possibly could've gotten him killed if John wasn't valuable.

"Do you know what he did for Angelo?"

Mark's brows raise, and a small smile curls his lips. Almost as if he finds my question amusing. "John was an accountant back then. Real good with numbers. Pretty sure he helped Angelo launder his money, but that was never proven."

I blink. "If he was so good with numbers and money, why did he suck so bad with gambling? The man could've just counted cards or something."

Mark bursts out into laughter, his plump stomach shaking. "You're a funny girl, Addie. You're right, I think if John was in his right mind when he played, he might've won big. But he couldn't stop with the drinking. Angelo told John he didn't give a shit what he did in his free time, but if he showed up to work drunk and fucked with his money, he was a dead man."

I frown. I can't imagine Angelo would target Gigi if John messed up, but that doesn't mean he didn't do something else to piss off the mob boss.

The possibilities are endless on the ways John could've gotten Gigi killed.

"Wasn't this something Frank told the detectives since he believed John was guilty? They didn't look into this?"

He huffs out a dry laugh. "You ever try to pin a crime on a mob boss? Not that easy, kiddo. They got all kinds of people in their pockets. It was dropped due to a lack of evidence. If you want my opinion, I think John got a taste for the danger, and whether it's because Gigi was having an affair or because she wanted to leave John, he snapped and killed her."

Jesus Christ.

The possibility of that sounds… likely. Very likely.

"I just have one last question," I say, fiddling with my dress. I'm creasing it, but I don't care. "What made Frank turn on John? They were best friends. So why not give John the benefit of the doubt instead of trying so hard to pin the blame on him?"

He takes a moment to puff on his cigar. "My guess is that he saw John for what he was, and chose to try and bring Gigi justice, even if that meant putting away his best friend. With his drinking, temper, and then getting involved in the mafia, I think it's safe to say he was becoming a violent man. Would explain why my father was so goddamn torn up over everything after John was proven innocent."

I frown and can't help but feel sympathy for Mark's father. He got caught up in a pretty toxic vortex of cheating, lies, and crime between Gigi and John. I imagine that would've taken a toll on anyone.

"Anyway, I think that's enough of that for tonight. There's an annual charity we're hosting in a few weeks. I could always expect to see you there and speak on it more then," Mark says, his eyes sparkling.

"I'll check my schedule," Zade cuts in, relieving me of having to make any commitments. In most cases, I wouldn't appreciate the implication that he's the boss, but right now, I'm nothing but grateful for it.

"Of course," Mark concedes, his smile a tad more strained than before.

Mark drones on about boring work-related stuff for another hour, drinking his alcohol, puffing on his expensive cigar, and increasingly becoming more drunk.

I barely listen, too lost in thought about everything I just learned. And maybe a little heartbroken that Gigi might've been murdered by her own husband. Someone she did love and trust, despite her affair.

Even when you're married to someone for over a decade, it's possible to never really know them and what they're capable of.

I glance at Zade. I'm learning exactly what he's capable of, and it's fucking terrifying.

Zade is fucking terrifying.

It's impossible not to consider the possibility that if I ever were to fall in love with him, that he could turn on me too.

For the fourth time, Mark's phone rings in the middle of the conversation. Every time, his face darkens when he looks to see who's calling.

"Everything okay?" Zade asks, noting his odd behavior.

Mark glances at Zade, forcing a strained smile before attempting to pocket his phone.

Drunkenly, he drops it, and it's almost painful watching him pick it up. I can hear his bones creaking from here.

As alcohol takes control over his body, all I can focus on is how it seems to age him further.

The liver spots on his balding head and darkened hands, and the bags underneath his eyes have formed a few more wrinkles.

He's an ugly man. On the inside and out. And it's a wonder how his depravity has sunk so low when the man has everything most people could want in life. Money, power, influence, and a beautiful wife that might've loved him if he weren't so evil.

"Yeah, a few of my colleagues are freakin' out over some ssstupid leaked video," Mark slurs, finally getting the phone in his pocket.

Zade stiffens beside me, though his face stays unreadable.

"Leaked video?"

Mark flaps a hand, attempting to gloss over what he confessed. I glance at Zade, noting the subtle tic in his jaw.

"Yeah, but I keep telling them they don't have to worry 'bout it. Our So-ssocciety will take care of it, and no one will be none the wissser."

I open my mouth, ready to pry, but a quick warning glance from Zade has me snapping my mouth shut.

He must be talking about the videos from the rituals.

"I'm sure they're taking the necessary steps to make sure the video is handled, alongside whoever leaked it," Zade assures casually, swirling his drink as if there's spices resting in the bottom of the cup.

"Are they ever!" Mark bursts out, slapping his hand obnoxiously on his ornate desk. "The video is handled, it'sh finding the pershon who leaked the videos that's th-the problem. They've been interrogating an-and watching our every move for months now!"

I didn't think it was possible for Mark's face to turn any redder, but he's starting to look like the Kool-Aid Man.

"Well, whatever the case, I'm sure it'll be handled soon."

Zade is careful with his words and is deliberately refusing to pry and dig out extra information. I'm not sure if whatever Mark is saying is sufficient, or if Zade is in for the long haul.

"Yeah, sure," Mark mutters. "Guessh the bright shide is that nothing can happen to us. I-If one of us goes misshing and the Society ss-suspects foul play, guess what? They will up and relocate within hourss." Under his breath he mutters, "we all will know who to blame anyway." I can't hear the rest of what he says, but for a second, it sounds like he says Z.

A pregnant pause passes, and it seems like Zade has to collect himself. Mark is too wasted to be mindful of the word vomit spewing from his mouth.

I don't know what the fuck this Society is, but they obviously can't trust an inebriated Mark and his big mouth. He's spilling all kinds of shit, and though I can't make sense of most of it—Zade clearly can.

"Good thing, wouldn't want anything to happen to my new friend," Zade teases smoothly, his face morphing into a relaxed state as he lies to Mark's face.

Mark believes it, laughing alongside Zade and spending the next ten minutes telling my shadow how grateful he is that they met.

I nearly snort from the irony. Zade is both Mark's judge and executioner, and he's too stupid to see it.

Zade sips at the amber liquid in his cup throughout the whole mushy tirade, but by the time we're rising to leave, it looks like he barely consumed an ounce of it.

"Thank you so much for having me," I say graciously. Mark cups my hand in both of his, and a cold feeling embeds beneath my flesh, digging deep like a parasite. His hands are sweaty, but all I can feel is ice.

This man… he's evil. It feels like touching a corpse.

I slide my hand from his, resisting the urge to wipe it against my dress.

I wouldn't want to ruin such a pretty dress anyway.

Just as I'm walking out, Mark calls out, "I'll be seeing you, Adeline."

The second the door closes, Zade growls beneath his breath, "You'll be dead before that will ever happen."

I never thought I'd condone murder, but with Mark... maybe I can overlook it just this once.

Another week passes, and Zade continues to haunt my house. My dreams. My goddamn nightmares. And in this moment, with Zade's hand firmly wrapped around the column of my throat, squeezing until my vision blackens, it feels less like a nightmare and more like Hell.

For the tenth time, I freeze and can't seem to coerce my limbs to move. Heat lashes at my insides, and the raw look in his eyes—the unrelenting pleasure he takes out of draining the life from me—it does nothing but stoke the single flame burning in my core.

He lets go with a click of his tongue and a sidelong look. As if he knows precisely how twisted up my organs are.

Fuck him.

I'm sweating profusely and becoming increasingly irritated beyond belief. He keeps calling me little mouse, but mice don't look like drowned sewer rats last time I checked.

"You're ten times larger than me, you expect me to break a chokehold?" I snap, more so out of embarrassment for my continued failure.

"That's what I'm saying," Zade says patiently, a tiny smirk lifting his lips. I'm going to punch him.

"I've tried several times," I point out. "And failed."

"Because you're not listening. You're hardly even *moving*."

I scoff and argue, "I am too."

He cocks a brow, unimpressed. "Every time I choke you, you just get flustered and try to knee me in the dick. You're not doing the movements I've taught you to do."

Blood rises to my cheeks, and I just know that I look like a bright red cherry.

"That's a lie," I shoot back. He just smirks and grabs my throat in a tight grip, pushing me back against the wall behind me. My eyes round, and if I had any sense, I'd do the movements he's been walking me through for the past hour.

But all I can do is stare.

"Break the hold, Addie," he says quietly, his deep voice sending delicious shivers down my spine.

I go to clear my throat but then remember it's being crushed by Zade's rather large hand.

You can do this Addie. You're only hot because you forgot to open the window.

Lifting my arm, I twist forward and bring it over his extended arm, and jerk down with all my strength. His arm stays tight and his body twists with mine, counteracting my escape.

"You can't do that!" I shout, my fist bounding off his steel muscles when I go to land a punch on his chest.

He releases me.

"Do you really think an attacker is going to do what you *want* them to do? If you're attempting escape, they're going to do everything in their power to make sure you don't succeed."

I huff, out of breath and ready to go back to kneeing him in the balls, or attempting to, at least. Maybe I'll just drop kick them instead. Even if my toe merely grazes the hairs on his balls, I'll feel more accomplished than I do now.

"You're too slow. I can see your intent from a mile away. You need to be quicker, catch me off guard from the swiftness and strength of your attack."

He goes through the movements with me several more times, keeping his hands loose as he guides my arms.

We've been doing this all week. Now that Mark has set his eyes on me, Zade is paranoid that I will go missing in the dead of night.

I've seen his eyes crease with worry when he explains the possible threat looming over my head. A threat far more serious than Max and his cronies.

Zade's men have been lingering outside my place, and I get the feeling they've been there since the moment I walked out of Mark's house. I hadn't noticed them until a few days ago, and my lack of awareness did knock some sense into me.

The frustration of my situation mounts as I fail once more at breaking free of Zade's chokehold. I wouldn't need to know any of this shit if Zade would've just left me alone. Let me live my life in peace and blissful ignorance of the terrors of the world surrounding me.

I was happy. Bored, but happy.

And now my very own stalker is teaching me self-defense moves. Not against himself, but his enemies. The irony is not lost on me, unlike my success in not getting choked to death.

"This is all your fault, you know," I hiss, a bead of sweat dripping into my eye. The burn is minuscule compared to the fire raging in my chest.

Zade stills, and his eyes study me closely. "Is it?" he counters.

"You pretend like you care about me, or whatever you convince yourself that you feel for me, but I've been in danger because of *you*. You do know that, right? Max would've never came aft—"

He steps into me, and my mouth involuntarily snaps shut. His presence is powerful and invokes my will to bend to him. Whether I want it to or not.

"Don't pretend like fucking Archie would've been the end of it. The man would've dragged you into a life full of pain and suffering, and Max and the rest of them would've stood idly by while Archie destroyed you from the inside out. I *saved* you from that life."

I snarl. "But he wouldn't have come after me if you didn't kill Arch."

"You're right, and that was my mistake to not take out Max when I took down the rest of Archie's family. But I'm not going to apologize for what I did. Had I left you and Archie alone, you would've been hurt and traumatized, and I would've ended up killing him anyway. If I hadn't killed him for touching what's mine, I would've for hurting you instead. Archie's fate was sealed the moment he led you up those stairs."

"*You* traumatized me."

He leans down and snips, "A gun in your pussy certainly is traumatizing, little mouse, but only because I used it to make you come, not to make you bleed."

I snarl, refusing to acknowledge that. "And Mark? I would've never been on his radar."

"False," he snaps. "Mark didn't show up at Bailey's because of me, Adeline. And he wasn't seated where he could get a perfect view of you because of me. I brought no attention to you whatsoever and did my best to keep him distracted, but I can't control a man's wandering eye. Even if you're a decade older than his normal taste."

I balk, disgust curling deep at his implication.

"You knew I was at Bailey's," I guess. "And you knew he was heading there? So why not redirect him somewhere else?"

His spine straightens. "Do you think I possess magic and can influence a man to do everything I say? I regret to inform you that I can't."

I tighten my lips at the condescension in his tone. "I tried to, but Mark was insistent on going to Bailey's, and trying to force him to go elsewhere would have only aroused suspicion." He takes another step into me, crowding me against my bedroom wall. "And that's the last thing I need when Mark's trust in me means saving lives. Because you know what I *can* do, little mouse? I can protect you. And I can teach you to protect yourself. But those children and girls that are being held captive? They don't get that privilege right now."

My eyes drop to my toes, and all I can manage to feel is shame. He tips my chin up with his finger, and I'm too lost in thought to fight.

"You're allowed to be angry and frustrated with your situation. You're even allowed to be angry with my stalking you. Life strips you of power often, but what you can control is pointing the blame in the right direction. Don't misplace Max's and Mark's ill intentions onto me when I've been doing my best to keep you safe from them. What we've been doing all week is to keep you *safe*. So, you can either redirect all the effort you've been putting into acting like a brat and apply it towards something useful, or you can continue to be powerless in the situations life throws you in. You choose, baby, because I'm not going to keep making these decisions for you."

I had forgotten what it felt like to truly be scolded like a child. My mother does it often, but considering that's all she's ever done, it felt less like being scolded and more just like a normal conversation with her.

But now? I feel nothing but small and bent out of shape, like a piece of paper wadded up in Zade's fist. Pride bucks against that feeling, and I want nothing more than to snap something clever back and hold on to my dignity.

I'd only be proving him right, though. He'd look at me with superiority, and I'd only shrink further beneath him.

"Okay," I relent. "Fine. I'll just be mad at you for being a creep then." I pause, hating the words but knowing they need to be said. "I'm sorry for misplacing blame, but I'm *not* sorry for the ass beating you're about to get."

He suppresses a smile, but he can't contain the emotion in his yin-yang eyes. Pride. Amusement. Something deeper and far scarier than Zade's hand wrapping around my throat.

I don't give myself time to panic, nor do I hand myself over to the heat he invokes, I just let my body take over. I jerk to the left, bringing my elbow down on his outstretched arm before he can blink.

His grip loosens. And I seize the moment, pouring all my frustration into my limbs. I may not be able to hate him for Max's misplaced blame for Arch's death or Mark's wandering eyes, but I can use that against him in a different way. In a way that matters.

I curl my fist and swing it back into his face and then crush my elbow directly into his nose.

His head jerks back just in time, my elbow striking true but hardly enough to be gifted with a bloody nose.

He lets go and it feels like I can finally breathe. Not because he was squeezing hard enough to genuinely choke me, but because I finally succeeded.

He chuckles, deep and low, as he steps away from me. The bastard doesn't look the least bit ruffled, but I choose not to dwell on that. If I focus on everything I didn't do, then I'll only be stripping myself of power.

"There you go. That was really good, baby."

"Don't call me that," I mutter, but really, I feel a tinge of pride swelling deep in my chest cavity.

"Or what?" he challenges. I sigh, not having the mental capacity to spar with Zade right now. I need a hot shower and then a long soak in the bath. I refuse to bathe without washing the dirt and grime off first. I don't like to spend hours pruning in my own dirty bath water.

He goes through the motions with me for another hour, forcing me to perform the move over and over until I'm panting, and he has a bruise forming under his eye.

Somehow, it just makes him look sexier, and I want to punch him in the face for the tenth time all over again for it.

"That's enough for today," he announces, smiling despite the fact that I just nailed him in the face again with my elbow.

"Good, because I need to take a shower, and you need to leave because you're definitely not coming within six feet of that bathroom," I grouse, planting my hands on my hips.

A smile curls his lips, slowly and salaciously, until flames lick at my cheeks again.

Bastard of a man.

"Who said I even need to be in the same house in order to watch you bathe?"

My eyes narrow into thin slits. "There are no cameras in the bathroom."

He chuckles with the same sinful undertones. He seizes my neck in his hand once more, but my body refuses to go through the motions again. His intention is dangerous, but not directed towards my life.

But rather my vagina.

Traitorous, useless thing, you are.

"That you know of," he taunts in a low, husky whisper before placing a soft kiss on my lips and effectively silencing me. It's short and anything but sweet. His hand flexes, and my pussy pulses in tandem. "Just don't forget to scream my name when you're holding that showerhead to your pussy. You can come knowing that I'll be shouting yours, too."

He releases me, slips a rose in my hand, and strides out of the bedroom, shooting me one last heated glance before clicking the door shut behind him.

I look down at the rose, twirling it in my hand as the world around me blurs. I'm not even capable of considering where he was hiding it this entire time. My heart is firmly lodged in my throat while I try to process his words. They're currently wading through the animalistic arousal convoluting my body and struggling to make their way to my brain.

Was he just fucking with me? Or am I really about to tear apart my entire bathroom instead of taking a well-deserved bath? Because I did have plans with that showerhead, and Zade's name tends to break free of my tongue when I make myself come.

I don't want him to witness that.

I rock on my toes, deciding if I should just go kick his ass again instead.

But my bones are weary, sweat is trickling into places that only my loofah should be touching, and I'm well and truly horny now. Kicking his ass will somehow turn into him gaining entrance to mine, and I'm too tired to put myself in that situation.

Whatever. He can look just this once, but at least the dickhead can't touch me from behind his stupid screen.

February 14th, 1946

John almost got Sera and I killed today.

I can barely write even still. It's late at night. The police have been here all day. I'm tired and my nerves are shot, but I need to get this out on paper.

My husband- a stupid, stupid man, almost got us killed.

He owes money to a few people. And he hasn't been able to pay it off apparently. Explains why we almost lost our house. Thank God for Ronaldo, he paid off all of our bills.

Though John still doesn't believe I got the money from a friend of mine.

But what does that matter when John's bad habits will get my daughter and I killed anyway?

Two men broke into the house and held me at gunpoint while Sera hid in her bedroom. They demanded that I give them money. Money that I don't have.

John just so happened to show up in the middle of it, and Frank was with him. The two men ran and managed to get away.

I pray that Frank finds the culprits.

But the worst part?

John still hasn't apologized. He thinks he did nothing wrong. And I... I want to kill him.

Chapter Twenty Seven
The Manipulator

I'm just drifting off into a deep sleep when I hear the creak of a door, my body jolting from the disturbance.

When I turn to look at the door, it's firmly closed. My brow crinkles in confusion. Just when I convinced myself I was only hearing things, I see a movement out of the corner of my eye.

Sucking in a sharp breath, I turn and see Zade standing outside my balcony doors, a red cherry pulsating in the moonlight.

Wide awake, I sit up and glare. "How long have you been out there, you creep?" I snap.

Zade opens the doors the rest of the way, smoke billowing from his mouth.

"Awhile," he answers flatly.

He flicks the butt of the cigarette out over the balcony and then reaches up and pulls his hood down from his head. The moonlight shines directly on him, making him glow beneath the soft aura.

Such a contradiction that something so dark shines so brightly beneath the light.

"Stop littering."

"You're much more pleasant when you don't know I'm around," he murmurs, his voice subdued as he walks in and closes the doors behind him.

I frown, squinting my eyes in an attempt to see his face clearer. There's something off about him right now. He's not his usual smirk-y hoity-toity self at the moment.

He was here just a couple of nights ago, going through more training with me. I finally got the hang of several of the moves he's taught me.

I'm going to be a badass pretty soon.

"What's wrong with you?" I snip, though the heat is missing. It's almost like I'm feeling actual concern right now.

I raise a hand to my forehead and feel for any warmth. I must have a fever and be delirious from the sickness.

He steps from the shadows and comes closer. My body locks as he trudges to the bed and sits down on the edge. It's not unusual to see his muscles straining against his clothing. I think he purposely shops for shirts and hoodies two sizes too small. But right now, his body looks rigid, and the muscles in his neck and shoulders appear bunched up.

"Just tired today," he says quietly.

I frown harder, not liking this side of Zade. Or rather, not liking how much it bothers me seeing this side of him.

A battle renders me frozen as I try to decide what to do. Kick him out of my house, attitude be damned. Or pry into his odd behavior and show him that I just might care.

His head rolls, cracking his bones and making me cringe from the disturbingly grotesque noises.

"You uh, gotta lot of tension going on there, buddy," I say, awkwardness dripping from the words. That makes me cringe harder.

He huffs out a laugh, but the amusement is missing.

Sighing, I relent and push the covers back. With great reluctance, I crawl towards Zade and kneel behind him. His body tenses, and I never thought I'd see Zade wary of me.

That concerns me more than anything.

"Take this off," I demand softly, plucking at his hoodie. His head turns, presenting me with his side profile.

Very few people have attractive side profiles. That's something that most people just don't possess. But Zade looks beautiful, no matter what direction you look at him from.

"Why?" he asks, his tone flat.

Bristling, I open my mouth and begin to snap something at him. I'm trying to be *nice*, and he's actually being difficult when this is already hard enough as it is. What's that saying, don't bite the hand that feeds you?

But I stop myself, the harsh words dangling from the tip of my tongue before falling to their death. This isn't about me and how I feel, getting defensive isn't going to solve anything. It'll only result in making him feel worse and probably end up leaving. And oddly, that would just serve to make me feel like shit.

It shouldn't. But it would.

"Because it would make things easier for me," I say softly.

He opens his mouth, but whatever he was going to say fell to its own death alongside my defensive words.

Relenting, he grabs his hoodie from behind his shoulders and pulls it over his head, dragging up his white t-shirt. I see a glimpse of an elaborate tattoo before his shirt falls back down.

He doesn't say anything, just rests his elbows on his spread knees.

Balancing my butt on my heels, I blow out a breath and start kneading his shoulder muscles. It feels like pressing my knuckles into a boulder.

"Jesus," I mutter, pressing harder. He groans deeply, his head dropping low between his shoulders as I dig at the knots polluting his muscles.

We don't speak. Not for a little while. My hands grow tired, but I don't complain, nor do I stop. Slowly, he relaxes beneath my touch, his muscles beginning to loosen beneath my persistent fingers.

"Tell me," I whisper, attacking a particularly brutal knot that pulls a groan from deep in his chest.

He doesn't respond right away, and I can feel the internal battle from outside his flesh and bones.

"I lost a young girl today," he confesses, his voice hoarse and uneven.

I swallow, sadness spearing deep in my chest. He pauses, and I don't speak. Letting him find the words at his own pace.

"She was very traumatized and wouldn't stop screaming. I wasn't in the building yet, I was still working my way in when I heard the gunshot go off." He pauses, taking a moment to collect himself. "I heard the conversation before I killed them. She was fighting them tooth and nail. It didn't matter how much they threatened to kill her, she fought anyways."

His hands fist, and every muscle I worked hard to relax stiffens again as Zade fights against his own demons. I pinch my eyes shut, berating myself for what I'm about to do. But if I don't... it would be unforgivable. I would hate myself.

Sighing softly, I sit on my butt and wrap myself around him like a koala on a tree. Legs and arms around his torso and my head resting against his broad back.

He doesn't move, a stone pillar amongst the wreckage of his mind, just like the ruins in Greece.

"Dying isn't the worst thing that happened to her. It's just the worst thing that happened to you and her family," I whisper. I feel the shift of his head, his eyes peering over his shoulder at me. But I don't meet his gaze.

"The life she would've had to live would've been far more painful than where she is now."

"You think it's a good thing she died?" he asks, his tone flattening.

"Of course not," I placate, squeezing him tighter. "Being stolen from her life. Her family and friends. And then being put into an incredibly horrendous and fucked up situation. It's the worst thing that could've happened to her." My voice breaks on the last few words, and it takes a minute to put myself back together.

"But dying? Dying is not, Zade. She was screaming because she was fighting against the life that she was being forced to endure the only way she knew how. It wasn't his right to end her life. But he did it anyways, and I... I hope he suffers for it. But after what they did to her, I know that she is more at peace now than she would've been alive."

He stays silent, and I'm not sure if I've made him feel worse or better. But I told him what I believe to be true. Sometimes people just aren't meant to live through that trauma. A shell of who they could've been. Broken and fighting every day *not* to die.

I think if she had lived, she could've learned to be happy again. I think everyone who suffers from internal demons can find that. We're all capable. But sometimes, unseen forces take it out of everyone's hands, and maybe that just means they were meant to find their happiness in the afterlife instead.

I unwrap myself from Zade and move away. His head drops, and he looks almost disappointed. He stands, and aims for the door, but he doesn't make it two steps before I'm snatching his hand and tugging him back.

He looks back at me, silent and confused.

"I still hate you," I mumble, and the lie tastes chalky on my tongue. "But I want you to lay down with me, Zade."

I peel back the covers, indicating for him to get in. It takes tremendous effort to look away from him as he kicks off his boots and climbs in next to me. He makes it a point to stay on top of the duvet, part of me resenting him a little for that.

I'm nervous. Up until now, every encounter Zade and I have had was forced upon me. And now that I've made the decision for him to be here, I don't know what to do.

"Why were you on my balcony?" I blurt. He chuckles, facing me and urging me to do the same. Stiffly, I roll to my side and try not to faint from the intensity of this man.

"I wanted to watch you," he confesses. And then he tacks on with dry amusement, "In peace."

I snort. "So sorry for being so disruptive to your stalking. Next time I'll strike a couple poses for you."

I'll never admit how his answer gives me chills. Both ice cold and fiery hot. He smirks, and it makes me sad that it doesn't reach his eyes.

"I'd appreciate that," he murmurs distractedly. His eyes are tracing my curves like they're scripture, and he's a sinner that is searching for proof of a God that he no longer can hear.

"You need space from me while wanting to be close. Sounds like a marriage," I deadpan.

"It will be."

It's instinct to deny that. I still want to and do so in my head. But I don't give voice to it. Not tonight, I won't.

So, I swallow the words and let him dream.

We fall into silence, but it's weighed with sadness, guilt, and anger. He's swarming in the emotions like a beekeeper holding a nest. I'm getting stung by it, and it's making my skin burn.

"Kiss me," I whisper. If it could only ease the burn in both of us. He stills, and my bravery is slipping, so I lean forward and make a move instead.

I capture his lips within my own, relishing over the different type of burn that blooms from our connected lips. He doesn't hesitate to kiss me back, but it's slow. While it's no less intense, it lacks his usual ferocity.

And that's something I didn't realize how much I've missed until now.

Getting nearly desperate, I nip at his bottom lip before sucking it into my mouth. His hands grip my waist in a tight hold, and for a moment, I think he almost pushes me away.

But then he breaks, his resolve shattering, and finally—*finally*—he feasts on my lips. Tasting me like he's licking ice cream out of a cone.

My hands dive into his hair, exploring the soft strands as his own bless my body with the same honor, slipping beneath the duvet and roaming my curves. His tongue battles against mine, creating a tornado of passion and a million pent-up emotions.

The duvet feels heavy and suffocating on my body, but when I try to wriggle loose, Zade traps me further. I yank away from him, and he follows, making escape futile when his lips are impossible to deny.

"Let me out," I gasp between a nip of his teeth.

"We're not taking it past this, Addie," he declares with finality.

"Why?" I breathe, and the logical part of me rallies against the stupid question. I should be relieved.

"Because the first time I fuck you, I want you to have all of me. Not just bits and pieces." He takes a breath. "I'm not whole right now. And I can't worship you when all I see is her."

Reaching up, I trace his scar, and a breath shudders out of him in response.

"Okay," I whisper. I get it. He's suffering right now, and I'm only a temporary distraction. It doesn't bother me when I know the girl occupying his mind is a little girl that is now dead. A death he blames himself for.

"I'm sorry, you're right. But I just want you to know that it's not your fault. The *what ifs* will plague you as long as you let them, Zade. But you need to remember all the girls that you did save. Don't forget to remember them, too."

He doesn't deign me a verbal answer. Instead, he leans in and skates his lips across mine. I let him explore, our kiss much calmer. The burn is a low sizzle, bubbling beneath the surface but depleted of oxygen to allow it to grow.

Sex isn't something either of us needs right now. He's not in the right mindset, and I don't know if I ever will be. This thing with Zade—it's confusing.

And eventually, I'm going to have to put a stop to it.

Just not tonight.

My phone vibrates in my hand, and I sigh when I see it's my mother. Despite my brain screaming at me not to, I click the green button and slap the phone on my ear.

"Hey, Mom," I greet, trying to keep my voice from betraying how I actually feel.

"Hello, honey. How are you doing?" she asks, her prim voice tightening my body into stone. It's a trained reaction when passive aggressive insults are being slung my way most of the time.

"I'm good, just getting ready for the fair," I answer, glancing over at Daya.

We're in my room getting dressed, a heady sense of anticipation in the air.

Satan's Affair is tonight, and we always have the best fucking time. I know tonight won't be any different. I'll finally have a night where my headspace isn't filled with dangerous men and a murder gone cold.

Or maybe a particularly dangerous man I haven't seen in a week.

"That haunted fair you go to every year?" she asks derisively. "I don't understand why you like going to those things. I swear there's a mental condition associated with finding enjoyment out of horror." She mutters the last part, but not quiet enough for it to clearly transmit through the phone.

Pesky radio signals.

I roll my eyes. "Was there a reason you called, Mom?"

Daya snorts, and I shoot her a glare.

"Yes, I wanted to know what your plans are for Thanksgiving. I expect you and Daya will be visiting?"

I suppress the groan working its way up my throat. Daya and I are like a married couple and split holidays between our families.

She has a large family, and they've always welcomed me with open arms. Their get-togethers are loud with laughter and games, and I die of bliss every time I eat their food.

While my family is small and stiff. My mother has mean cooking skills, but she lacks the warmth and comfort, and I usually end up going to bed early and leave in the morning.

"Yep," I confirm. I roll my lips, contemplating doing something very stupid now that I have her on the phone.

"Hey, uh, Mom?"

"Hmm?" she hums, a note of impatience laced in her tone.

"Can I ask you a few questions about Gigi's murder?"

Daya's eyes widen almost comically, and she mouths, "What are you doing?"

She knows as much as I do that Mom might not take well to us investigating Gigi's murder. But I have to ask.

She might have some valuable information, and getting in an argument with her might be worth it if there's a possibility of learning something new.

She sighs. "If it'll convince you to move out of that place."

I don't deign her a response to that, letting her believe what she wants if it gets her talking.

"Did you know Grandpa John's best friend? Frank Seinburg?"

She's silent for a beat. "I haven't heard that name in a long time," she says. "I didn't know him personally, but your Nana spoke of him."

"What did she say about him?"

She sighs. "Just that he was around a lot up until Gigi was murdered, then he kind of disappeared."

I roll my lips. "Do you know about Grandpa John's gambling habits?" I push, incapable of keeping the hope out of my tone. Unfortunately, she detects it.

"Why are you asking, Addie?" she deflects with a tired sigh. She's always weary when it concerns me.

"Because I'm interested, okay? I met Frank's son," I admit. "Mark. He talked to me about Gigi. He remembered her, and he brought up some interesting things about John's gambling."

I don't admit that I'm investigating her case myself. I'd prefer she assumes that we happened to have a connection and spoke on it, nothing more.

"How did you even come into contact with a man of that social standing? God, Addie, please tell me you didn't sell yourself to him."

A fly could buzz into my mouth, and I wouldn't notice. My mouth hangs open, and all I can feel is hurt.

"Why... why would you think I'd ever do something like that?" I ask slowly, the heartbreak evident in my tone. I can't keep it hidden—not when my mother just accused me of being a prostitute.

She's silent again, and I wonder if she realized she went too far. "Well, then how did you meet him?" she finally asks, deflecting a question I'd really like to know the fucking answer to.

I sniff, deciding to let it go. It doesn't matter why she thinks it, just that she does.

"Daya has friends in high places. We met at a dinner party and he said I looked familiar, so I told him who I'm related to, and he connected it from there," I lie, working to keep my voice even. Daya quirks a brow but doesn't comment.

It feels like an arrow has been shot through my chest—the sensation tight and sharp.

"Your Nana said that John put them in a dangerous situation with his gambling, but not too long before Gigi's death, it all seemed to go away. He stayed out late and came home short-tempered just to fight with Gigi about whatever he was pissed off about that day.

"Frank was a sponge for their relationship. With their marriage failing, I think he was put in the middle of it a few times. Nana spoke of one incident sometime before Gigi died where she and Frank got in a fight. Nana didn't remember much about what happened, just that Frank had grabbed Gigi and pushed her on the ground and said something about a betrayal. That's all I know," she explains stiffly, as if reciting a verse from the Bible.

That was her apology. And though the tightness in my chest hasn't receded, I take it anyway.

I mull that over, curious as to why Frank was so upset because Gigi was cheating on John. Maybe because Frank was often put in the middle, he grew tired of it. John's behavior was steadily declining, and it seemed to start when Gigi's attitude changed towards him after she began falling in love with Ronaldo. It's possible Frank blamed Gigi for John's behavior and the fact that he was losing his friend to a dangerous addiction.

"Just one more question," I barter, sensing her need to hang up. She called to ask about Thanksgiving dinner and got roped into an honest conversation with her daughter. "Do you remember Nana going up in the attic all the time? Do you know why she did?"

"Yeah. That was where she'd go for alone time when I was a kid. I don't know the reason why, she had only ever said that's where she went to think. We were never allowed up there. Why do you ask?"

My heart plummets to my stomach as an unwanted thought intrudes.

I don't feel comfortable telling her what I found. So instead, I shrug and say, "I thought I remembered her going up there a lot, too, but couldn't be sure. Just curious."

"Okay, well, if that's all, I have to cook dinner for your father. I'll text you the details," she says.

"Bye," I grumble before hanging up the phone.

"What did she say?" Daya asks softly, but I know what she's really asking. What did my mother say to make me look so damn wounded.

I scoff. "She thought I might've prostituted myself to Mark."

Her mouth drops, but she quickly picks it back up. "That's terrible, Addie. I'm so sorry," she apologizes, her face twisting with empathy. Daya's always had a wonderful family, but she's been around long enough to understand what growing up with my mother is like.

I wave a hand. "She's said worse."

"What did she say about Frank?"

I reiterate everything Mom told me, and when I'm done, she just stares at me with wide eyes. I got the same reaction after I told her what I found out from Mark about Ronaldo and John.

"All I know is Gigi started a lot of shit by falling in love with Ronaldo," I finish on a sigh.

Daya rolls her lips. "Speaking of stalkers... are you not going to tell your mom about Zade?"

I shoot her a look. "That's like asking if I'm going to tell her about how one time, I let a guy fingerbang me in the middle of a concert."

She snorts. "Yeah, okay, you win that one." Hesitation flashes across her green eyes, and I know the question that's coming. I straighten my spine, preparing for it.

"He hasn't said anything else about what he does for a living? Or why he's involved with Mark?"

That last question right there is exactly why I can't tell her who Zade is. He had said no one else knows about Mark and what he's really involved in except the few people who assist him.

I shake my head, refusing to give voice to my lie.

Daya nods, accepting my answer without thought, and the guilt that resides within me is almost unbearable. I lied to her face, and she didn't even question it.

She pours a shot of rum and hands it to me. "Here, this will cheer you up. Pregaming before a haunted carnival is like, law."

I accept the shot and gulp it down. When I lower the glass, the smile is back on my face. Alcohol won't cure the guilt, but at least I'm not mad about my mom calling me a prostitute anymore. She snorts when she sees my face.

"What do you think the haunted houses will be like this year?" she asks, patting some shimmery brown eyeshadow on her eyelid.

She's going to look dangerous when she's finished. The eyeshadow will bring out her sage green eyes to hazardous levels and attract all the monsters.

"I don't know, it's always hard to guess. It's like trying to guess the next theme for *American Horror Story*."

The houses in Satan's Affair usually all follow the same theme. One year, most of the haunted houses were set up like prisons, and in each house, you had to figure out how to escape.

That's still one of my favorite themes thus far. That was also the same year Daya peed herself.

She brings an extra change of clothes now, and I tease her every time.

"You ready?" she asks, swiping at her eyelashes one last time with her mascara wand.

"Girl, I was born ready. Let's go pee-body."

"Bitch," she mutters, but I barely hear it over my evil cackling.

Satan's Affair is one of my favorite places in the world. At night, the fair comes alive with laughter, peals of screams from terror and excitement, and moans of joy from the fried food.

Walking into the field full of haunted houses, carnival rides, and food trucks is like walking into pure static energy.

Daya and I immediately get sucked into the crowd. It's five o'clock, pitch black already, and some of the monsters are already starting to trickle into the crowd.

My eye snags on a girl dressed up as a broken doll, sitting on the bench and happily eating a philly cheesesteak sandwich. I nearly groan, the scent of grilled meat making my mouth water.

I nudge Daya and point her out. "She's dressed as a doll."

Daya hums, and both of our eyes track over the houses. They're not lit up yet, but some of them make it obvious what the theme is.

"Our childhood," I murmur, noting the dollhouse dubbed *Annie's Playhouse* alongside a house called the *Tea Massacre*. The entrance is a massive teddy bear with a missing eye, a torn ear, and blood splattered across its fur while a bloody knife is gripped in its hand.

It gives life to a memory from my own childhood, alongside millions of other little girls, sitting at a table full of stuffed animals and empty teacups.

That house won't be a pleasant tea party, but one full of killer stuffed animals and creepy monsters.

"This is going to taint every single one of our childhood memories, isn't it?" I conclude.

"Oh yeah," Daya says, her lips twisted with both excitement and dread.

I grab Daya's hand and lead her towards the food trucks. We like to eat first before we get harassed by monsters. It makes it awkward when a corndog is shoved halfway down my throat while a creepy monster is standing over me and breathing down my neck.

"What sounds good?" I ask, my eyes roving hungrily over the endless options.

"How can you even choose?" Daya whines, sharing my dilemma.

"We have to at least get a mean hot dog and the truffle fries. Oh! And the fried veggies. Oh, and maybe—"

"You're not narrowing it down like you think you are," Daya interrupts, her tone dry.

"Okay, fine. That broken doll over there is eating a philly steak. What about that and some fries for now?" I ask.

"Lead the way," she says, throwing her hand out in an impatient gesture.

I don't even laugh—I take food just as seriously when I'm hungry.

By the time the lady in the food truck is handing me my food, I'm ravenous and shaking with the need to sink my teeth into something of substance.

Grease sizzles on our fries as we shove them into our impatient mouths, forcing us to suck in air as they singe our tongues. And by the time we find an empty bench, my fries have already been devoured, and I've taken several delicious bites of my sandwich.

Daya's even further done than I am—probably because the wench has been relying on me to find the spot to sit.

Finally, I sit down and shove the sandwich in my mouth, not caring about the juices dribbling down my chin.

In the back of my mind, I wonder if Zade is here. Watching me like he usually does. Would he be disgusted by my lack of manners?

I fucking hope so.

Then again, the prick would say something about how he likes me dirty, and then I'd want to vomit in his face.

Liar.

Just as we finish our food, the haunted houses come to life, the lights switching on and signaling that it's time for guests to get in line.

Daya and I rush over to *Annie's Playhouse* first, nabbing a spot pretty close to the front.

We're leaning against the rails when an icy feeling tingles at the base of my neck, traveling down my spine. It feels like holes are being drilled into my back.

"Addie?" a voice calls from behind me along with a soft tap on my shoulder, just as I'm getting ready to turn around.

My eyes widen, and I whip around, coming face to face with Mark.

Oh, fuck me.

"Mark!" I exclaim in surprise, forcing a smile onto my face. I've never been very good at acting, especially when I have to pretend to be glad to see a pedophile standing behind me.

Make that four *pedophiles.*

With him is Claire, and three other elderly men. I vaguely recognize them, and assume they're politicians of some caliber as well.

"What are the odds? I didn't know you came here," Mark says, his eyes consistently straying to Daya. "Who's your friend?"

Daya smiles, though she doesn't even try to make hers seem genuine. "Daya," she answers for me.

Sensing her indifference, Mark flashes a tight smile. "Well, it's very nice to meet you. Addie, these are my colleagues. Jack, Robert, and Miller."

We exchange pleasantries, all the while inching up in the line.

"So where is Zack?" Mark asks, peering around me as if a man well over six feet would be hiding behind me.

"He went to find a bathroom," I lie. I don't know why I do, there's no reason to. But I have a gut feeling that if Mark thinks Daya and I are here alone, that maybe he'll pull something shady.

"Speaking of Zack," Miller cuts in. "I heard you two are quite the lovebirds. How did you meet?"

My heart drops, and for a moment, I think maybe Mark might've found out about the movie theater incident. But then I remember Zade assured me the cameras have been wiped when he drove me home.

Miller looks like he needs to be carrying an oxygen tank around with him. Mark is well into his eighties, and I'm sure the other men aren't far off, but Miller in particular seems as if he's defying gravity by standing upright.

I spin the same made-up story that Zade did in Bailey's, hoping that the knives usually in my eyes when dealing with my shadow are replaced with hearts.

Claire asks a few questions of her own, her voice demure. Like how long we've been together, and if we're planning on getting married soon.

Sweat lines my hairline, the lies spilling from my mouth like the fantastical worlds from my fingers when I write. Luckily, it takes only a few more minutes to come up to the front of the line, and we're free of Mark and his creepy friends.

Even though we're walking into a stuffy haunted house, it feels lighter in here.

The house is adorned in pink, with white wooden floors, frills everywhere, and dead little girls giggling all around. Down the hall, I swear I spot a four-foot doll crossing the hall, her body distorted from the colorful smoke and her face bloody.

She's gone before I can tell for sure.

Daya and I huddle together, looking left and right—not quite sure which direction to go. A man with a peeling, bloodied face slips out from the shadows before us, and another girl dressed up as a demented doll comes out, a bloody knife in her grip.

It's so sudden, I jerk back. Daya's screams pierce my ears as they give chase, pushing us towards a living room with a blue couch and a mannequin giving birth to a child.

I don't get the chance to look long enough before another monster is jumping out at us.

I laugh through a scream, running away from a mechanical mannequin that resembles a Grim Reaper.

Daya's nails dig into my arm. An assortment of monsters and dolls jump out at us, getting in our faces and scaring the living daylights out of us.

One reason that Satan's Affair is so popular is that they carefully pick their actors.

They're *too* good at their job. Not only do they have the best makeup, but they know exactly what to do to scare the absolute shit out of you.

We swing around back to the foyer, but this time, we're chased up the stairs. Daya trips on one of the steps, and her curses are swallowed up by my cackling.

"Fuck off," she squeals through laughter, her eyes still wide with fright as she continues to fall up the stairs to get away from the monster.

We finally make it to the top, nearly sprawling on the floor as we're overcome with a mixture of laughter and terror.

The monster leaves us be as we right ourselves and make our way down the hallway, the flickering strobe lights creating a trippy effect. The smoke is heavier up here, making it harder to see.

At the very end of the hallway is a massive mannequin, its skin burnt so severely that it's bubbled up in boils. An unnaturally wide bloody mouth, and big yellow eyes top off his grotesque features. We veer into the closest room, avoiding that monstrosity.

We enter into what looks like a doll's bedroom. More pink and white décor, a twin bed filled with deformed, creepy dolls, and a mirror in the corner of the room that I'm almost sure is going to show something standing behind me.

It looks innocent in here, but the strobe lights flash ominously, while the blue, purple, and pink smoke swirls around us like wicked fingers, and the music in the backdrop creates a dangerous vibe.

And then, out crawls a demented looking doll from under the bed, her body twisted oddly as she comes skittering towards us.

Daya's and my screams pierce the air as we trip over each other to get out of her way. We run towards the other exit door and are led out into another room.

It takes all around ten minutes to get through the rest of the house. My adrenaline sinks lower and lower, leaking down in between my legs as monsters chase after me.

It's my favorite aphrodisiac, and something I can never assuage until I'm home alone afterwards.

On the way down the stairs leading towards the exit, I hear a faint screech. It sounds like someone yelled out the name "Jackal" but it's too loud in here to tell.

When we're out of the house, we breathe in deep, fresh air. The chill of the air is a soothing balm to our lungs. The only downside is it does get incredibly stuffy in the houses.

The next several hours are spent running around to all the rides in between haunted houses. It breaks up the constant adrenaline rush with a different kind of thrill.

I'll never get tired of the feeling of flying through the air at a breakneck speed. It's one of the few times where I feel like nothing can get me. Nothing can touch or hurt me.

Nothing can *catch* me.

It's one of the cheapest thrills I can get nowadays that doesn't cost me my morals and sanity.

February 25th, 1946

Frank confronted me about the affair. I denied it of course. But he didn't believe me.

He's been such a good friend to John, and he used to be a good friend of mine too.

But not so much anymore.. His temper is shorter and sometimes, it seems as if he can hardly look at me.

He told me to stop the affair.

Because he said I'm hurting the man that loves me most in the world.

His loyalties are to John, I get that. He doesn't owe me anything at all.

And I don't owe him anything either. Which is why I couldn't tell him that I will never stop seeing Ronaldo. But I don't think I needed to. He saw it in my face.

And for a moment, he almost looked heartbroken.

I suppose I would be too if my best friend has become what John has become.

I think I need to get divorced.

Chapter
Twenty Eight
The Shadow

Fucking imbeciles, man.

It blows my mind how sick in the head these men are. I arrived here just in time to see Mark eyeing up a doll eating a sandwich while his wife, Claire, sits right next to him and watches him eye-fuck a young girl.

She doesn't look the least bit jealous but incredibly concerned for the girl dressed up as a broken doll.

It takes all my strength not to charge up to him and smash his head into that wooden bench until nothing remains but brain matter and bone.

But I stay in the shadows, keeping one eye on Mark, and the other on the crowd, looking for my little mouse.

She's going to be a distraction tonight, and that could cost me. I roll my neck and blow out a breath. Addie running into Mark is a slim possibility but not impossible. If she stays far away from them, then she should be safe to have a fun time.

Mark and his partners came here with the intention of stealing a child or two. Though they'd never do the dirty work themselves. They're public figures and would never risk being caught.

Notably, none of the men have their kids, which proves they came here with a plan and didn't want the hindrance. They'll be here under the guise of spending time with their wives and nothing more.

But I'll bet my left nut he takes pictures, and sics a lackey on whoever he deems... appetizing.

My goal tonight is to prevent any kidnapping attempts from being successful. I have several men on standby stationed all throughout the fair, keeping an eye on each of Mark's business partners, whoever they target, and any other suspicious activity.

And it looks like Mark may have found his first target.

The broken doll is in a staring contest with Mark, exchanging smiles like an addict and their dealer. She's not a child by any means, but she's still young enough to sell into the skin trade.

"I got eyes on Mark," I inform. Jay and the other mercenaries will be able to hear me through the earpiece fitted snugly in my ear.

Keeping a safe distance, I maneuver around passing bodies to get a better view of the doll's face. The creepy-ass smile warping her lips speaks of a challenge far more than words ever could. Daring him to come after her. Based on the glimmer in her eyes, it feels deeper than just performing for her job.

Claire is still staring at the girl, too. But fear is radiating from her pores as brightly as the blush painted on her hollow cheeks. Mark doesn't notice, but it seems the doll does.

The latter hops off the bench, winks at Mark, and skips off towards a haunted dollhouse. Mark's eyes follow her the entire way, his gaze pinned to her ass and tongue swiping at his crusty lips.

And then he's sliding his phone out of his pocket and making a call. My eyes thin, splitting my attention between Mark and the doll that disappeared inside *Annie's Playhouse*.

He stays on the phone for all of a minute before he's hanging up and turning to Claire. His wife nods imperceptibly, just a single dip of her chin. What Claire has knowledge of is a mystery to me. Mark may hide most of his dealings, but I imagine she's not completely ignorant to how her husband spends his free time.

The haunted houses come to life almost immediately after. Flickering lights blare from the windows, and eerie music fills the air, mingling with the startled screams from guests. The colorful smoke that's been drifting across the open field now clouds the inside of the houses.

Hordes of people start drifting towards the creepy structures, forming lines outside the still locked doors.

Mark clenches Claire's arm and drags her up from the bench, speed walking directly towards *Annie's Playhouse*. And emerging from the bustling crowd behind Mark are his colleagues. Jack, Miller, and Robert.

Well, I'll be fucking damned.

"I got eyes on all four," I say quietly.

"Location?" Jay asks, keyboard clicking in the background. Whoever owns this park doesn't believe in safety. No cameras exist around the entire field, forcing Jay to use a small drone that hovers above the carnival. It won't be able to go into any of the houses undetected, but it will be able to capture any kidnapping attempts.

"Annie's Playhouse."

"Let us know if you need us," one of the men, Barron, says. His deep baritone voice is easy to pick apart from the others.

I open my mouth, ready to respond, but then I see a flash of cinnamon hair already in line for *Annie's Playhouse.*

Fuck me with a pogo stick.

The broken doll must be conspiring with God because only divine fucking intervention would bring all of them together like this.

The minute I see Mark tap Addie's shoulder while they stand in line, my entire stomach bottoms out. He and his colleagues happen to be standing right behind her, and it took less than five seconds for Mark's eyes to land on Addie and Daya's ass. It took more effort to drag his eyes up to their faces and recognize who was standing before him.

Addie turns, and surprise flitters across her face, followed by a forced smile and an enthusiastic display, despite finding the fucking Crypt Keeper standing behind her. Daya looks Mark up and down, an unimpressed glint in her eyes despite the polite smile curling her lips.

I watch them talk for a few minutes, Mark his usual boisterous self as he introduces her to his colleagues.

Even now, I know Addie well enough to know there's beads of sweat gathering along her hairline. I'm sure Mark has asked where I am, and I'm only curious to know what her response is.

The whole interaction makes my skin tight, and I'm gearing up to storm over there.

I was trying to give Addie space tonight, but that's no longer an option. Now that four predators are about to enter into a house with her, there's a high possibility Addie and her friend will never make it home.

If I wasn't here, of course.

Mark may like me, but he doesn't respect me. Not more than the Society, at least. And his buddies aren't going to even consider me when they're ushering two beautiful girls into a non-descript van. The only thing on their minds will be pussy and dollar signs.

I beeline towards Mark, barreling through a guy that looks like he roasts in a tanning bed like it's the Fountain of Youth. Doesn't make sense, but clearly the kid doesn't possess any if he's pointedly standing in my way and refuses to move after he sees me coming. Exactly why he ends up on his ass, curses following me as I continue on my path.

Just as I approach, Addie and Daya are ushered into the house, leaving Mark and his friends behind. The houses have an occupation limit to prevent the cramped space from becoming too congested. Especially with people running like their life depends on it.

"Mark!" I greet loudly, a smile stretched across my face. I can feel my scars tightening from how hard I'm forcing it, but the old man is too self-absorbed to notice.

Mark looks startled as he turns to me, but just like Addie, a strained smile stretches across his face.

"Zack! You made it! I just saw Addie go in with her pretty friend. She said you went off to find a bathroom."

Smart little mouse.

She left it open to the possibility that I'm around somewhere and could show up any minute. Fucking love that girl.

I flash my teeth again. "Yeah, I just found a quiet spot real quick," I say, pointing over my shoulder lazily.

"Ah, being a man is God's gift," he laughs, slapping my arm. "You've met my colleagues here."

I exchange quick pleasantries, but I shift, wearing my impatience on my sleeve. The employee opened the door and is waiting for me to enter. "Mind if I cut ahead? I want to catch up."

Mark swoops his hand forward, gesturing for me to go ahead, his lips tightened into a thin line.

Someone shouts behind me, noticing that I cut in line. Mark's placations are cut off by the slam of the door.

Walking into this house feels like stepping into another dimension that demons inhabit. My skin prickles as I look around the pink monstrosity.

"What in the actual hell?" I mutter under my breath, momentarily distracted by the eyesore this house is. If Addie and I have a daughter, I hope she has some goddamn sense and prefers black.

It feels like my eyeballs are physically cringing from all the pink. Did Barney come in here and shit everywhere? Jesus fucking Christ.

Addie's light brown hair flashes in my peripheral. Just as my eyes slide to her, she's disappearing behind a corner, getting chased by a monster. Their screams fill up the smoky atmosphere, bringing a smirk to my face.

It's a good taste of what I'm going to make her sound like later.

My feet work on autopilot, trailing after her. I hear the door open again, followed by Mark and his friends' voices. I'll be sure to keep a firm barrier between my girl and the dipshits behind me.

Addie and Daya will have fun, undisturbed by the real monsters in the house.

It's when they scramble up the stairs, a laughing heap of limbs and screams—I lose sight of them. I run up the stairs, hearing their screams from behind the first door.

I study the hallway system. There are too many doors in this hallway, making it physically impossible for this many rooms. Some of them are false doors, which means they could end up in any one of these rooms when they come out the other side. They might not even come back out in the hallway at all if the rooms connect on the inside.

Sighing, I make my way down the hallway, intent on peeking in a few rooms and finding the best place to camp. Singing erupts moments later, and I freeze from the ice-cold chills traveling down my spine, the hair on the back of my neck rising. It could be a part of the haunted house experience, but something niggles at the back of my mind. Warning me of incoming danger.

Not shit I can do about it until someone comes out swinging.

Ignoring the singing, I forge on. There should be an exit sign hanging over one of the doors in the case of a fire, so guests know where to evacuate. I suspect it'll be in one of the back rooms. I can camp out in the room opposite, which will allow me to keep an eye on the hallway and I'll know exactly when Addie leaves.

When I enter the room on the left, I sweep my eyes across the small area, looking for the exit. In tandem, I feel a presence come up behind me—one that doesn't want to invite me to their tea party anytime soon—while mechanical mannequins burst from an armoire and a closet. My heart stalls in my chest, but I stay calm as I turn towards the malicious presence at my back.

The last thing I expect to see is the broken doll from earlier—the one taunting Mark.

Her brown hair is pulled up in pigtails, with pink bows wrapped around them. Dull, brown eyes stare at me, intent shining brightly behind the makeup on her face. Up close, she's a lot creepier than I had expected.

Probably because the look in her eyes is murderous. I glance down, taking quick inventory of her. She's wearing a thin white nightgown, leaving little to the imagination. I barely notice her nipples poking through the thin fabric. No, what my eyes lock in on is the outline of a knife strapped to her thigh.

My blood chills. If this bitch tries to hurt my little mouse…

"Where are they?" I ask, keeping calm. I'm waiting to see confusion bloom on her face, followed by a question on who I'm talking about. But she doesn't give me that sense of security.

She seems to know exactly who I'm talking about.

"Safe from you," she snips. Then she turns her head to the side, staring at the wall. "Let the others know two women are being followed and make sure they get away safely. I have this handled."

I can't help the smirk that tips up the corners of my mouth. While part of me is tripped up on who she's talking to, I'm mostly amused that she thinks she can handle me.

Her eyes track something that I can't see, as if she's watching them leave.

"So, you're crazy, huh?"

She rears back, offended by my assessment. Frankly, I couldn't give a less of a shit.

Anxiousness is curdling in my stomach like spoiled milk. Addie and Daya still haven't stumbled their way to the back of the hallway yet. And this little girl must think I'm like Mark and here to hurt them and well... she's not entirely wrong. Except I'm only interested in hurting one of them, and by the time I'm done, she'll love the way I make her scream.

She snaps, "Don't call me that. You're the one preying on women."

I arch a brow, on the verge of laughing in her face. "That just makes me disturbed. Not crazy."

Her tiny hands ball into tight fists, and a snarl pulls her face taut with anger.

The doll lifts her nightgown far enough to bring out the knife and kicks the door shut behind her.

I can't tell if I should laugh or rage. She's deliberately keeping me from my little mouse, and that makes me very fucking unhappy.

"What are you going to do with that, dolly?" I ask, a mocking smirk on my face. This should be over quickly.

"I'm going to kill you, monster."

I don't have time for this shit.

The longer I'm trapped in a room with Chucky's Bride, the more opportunity handed over to Mark. If the men notice I'm nowhere to be found, and Addie is left vulnerable, nothing will stop them from seizing the moment.

She's more interested in talking, and time is ticking. I charge at her, but I'm surprised by how much fight she has in her.

I humor her, the sloppy attacks beginning with a knife and ending with her fists. The entire time, she rages like a petulant child. Throwing a fit because she can't land a strike.

I see the desperation leaking into her expression, just as antsy to take me down as I am her.

Finally, I land one good sucker punch to her nose, causing her to lose her footing and go crashing to the ground.

She screeches out some idle threat, but my focus is on the door. I storm past her, whipping out the door and charging down the hall.

"Jackal!" she screeches from behind me, but I pay her no mind. I don't know who the hell she's talking to, but I don't give a fuck.

I stop short when I look to my left and see the four men of the night packed into a room.

I breathe out a sigh of relief, a small weight lifting off my shoulders with the confirmation that they didn't get the chance to trap Addie.

Until I hear the words that come out of their fucking mouths.

"Where did she go?" Miller asks, staring at Mark. "The van is already set to go. They just need to know their location."

I snap straight, and my body stiffens like cement being injected into my spinal cord.

"We'll find them," Mark placates. "Zack wasn't with them, so he must've lost them in the chaos. It's the perfect time."

"You do realize you're going to have to handle him, right? When he finds out Addie is gone?" Robert cuts in. "With those nasty scars on his face, I have a feeling you're underestimating him."

Mark waves a hand, dismissing Robert's concerns. His very fucking *valid* concerns.

"He got those scars because he was weak, Robert."

I laugh silently, my head thrown back and shoulders shaking as I let his very ill-minded assumption wash through me. And then my laugh bleeds out, rocketing through the small space and blending with the other creepy noises pinging around this house.

The four men's heads snap towards me, and bleed dry of whatever color was left in their faces. The four of them are sweaty and look like they have watched their worst nightmares come to life. They'll soon realize that I sit on the fucking throne, and their nightmares bow to me. I'm far worse than any monster they could ever imagine.

I walk into the room, the grin on my face widening when they flinch away.

"Za—" Mark starts.

"You know how old these scars are, Mark? Very old. My opponent was a formidable one, but do you want to know who ended up on the floor with their throat slashed and holes where their eyeballs used to be? Certainly wasn't me, fucker."

Mark tries to brush off my story with a laugh, the sound choked and broken. "Zack, please, we weren't speaking of your girlfriend."

"Mark, the last thing you want to do is lie to me."

Just as Mark opens his mouth, a little door in the room springs open and out crawls the biggest fucking nuisance of the night.

"For the love of God, please leave me alone," I snap. Mark and his friends turn to find the doll straightening, a determined gleam in her eye.

Her face brightens. "God has nothing to do with this, silly."

Chapter Twenty Nine
The Manipulator

 think if I don't go sit the fuck down, I'm going to collapse. You'll have to peel me out of this mud."

I point towards a bench. "Go ahead and relax. I'm going to go through the House of Mirrors real quick."

"Fine by me, it'll take you forever to get out of that thing, and it'll be time to go."

The House of Mirrors has always been one of my favorite places. It's an elaborate maze of mirrors, and very difficult to find your way out of. It's one of the biggest buildings at the fair, and they fill every inch of it with mirrors.

The fair will close in about a half-hour. It's pushing it, but it should be just enough time to get through it if I concentrate.

The house is painted all black—no array of colors, flashing of lights, or smoke. I've always thought it was trippier like this. Sometimes it feels like being in a silent room, left with nothing but your thoughts as your own image haunts you.

It takes all of five minutes before I'm thoroughly lost. I keep my hands held out before me, preventing me from running face first into one of the mirrors.

I did that a couple of years ago and my nose was bruised for a week.

A few minutes pass by with nothing but the company of my own reflection. My heart rate is pumping erratically, my breathing uneven with excitement. Despite the pounding in my chest, this is where I feel most... normal.

Off in the distance, I hear a faint shuffling of feet. Not very many people come in here, especially this late, but there's plenty of people who like to take on the challenge.

Continuing on my wayward path, I concentrate on where I'm going, soon forgetting about anything else going on around me. The trick is to focus on the floor and not your reflection.

Just as I almost face plant a mirror, I hear a dark chuckle. My head snaps up, the tone of the laugh sounding evil. A spark of adrenaline ignites, pumping the chemical into my heart and kicking up the speed further.

Did an employee dressed as a monster sneak in here to mess with me? I wouldn't hold it past them. They're known to follow people around and terrorize them.

Swallowing the lump in my throat, I turn to find my bearings. If there is a creepy monster in here with me, I'd rather they not get close enough that I have to look at a thousand of their reflections.

Finding my way past the mirror that almost gave me a nose job, I start ahead again.

"Little mouse." The whisper seems to travel from every direction.

My limbs lock, not sure if my imagination is playing tricks on me or if Zade is actually here.

Unfreezing, I force myself to keep moving, hoping I'm just imagining things.

"Where are you, little mouse?"

I gasp, the deep voice closer. Another sinister chuckle echoes, and Jesus Christ, this man is capable of evil. No one sane sounds like that.

Squeezing my eyes shut, I take three deep, calming breaths, trying to ease my racing heart.

He's fucking with me. Trying to scare me. And it's fucking working when I'm trapped in a maze of mirrors, and he's laughing like a goddamn lunatic.

He can't just let me have my night, can he? For once, I didn't think about him and my conflicting feelings. And though Zade doesn't quite scare me as much— except for maybe right now—the feelings he brings out of me certainly *do*.

Maybe if I keep quiet, he won't find me.

Restarting my path, I quicken my pace until I'm speed walking through the labyrinth of mirrors.

I've no idea how far I am, but I don't even think I've made it halfway through.

It's right then that I see the first image of Zade reflected back at me. Dressed in all black, with his scarred face hidden deep in his hood. I gasp, whipping around just to find more of his reflection.

He's not behind me, but he's somewhere close.

"Stop it," I bite out, fear constricting my chest.

He doesn't answer, and of course, the fucker doesn't listen. I'm caught in a whirlwind, my body continuously moving in circles, desperate to pin exactly where he is.

"You all alone, baby girl?"

I swallow. "Obviously," I whisper, still searching for where he is. It feels like I shouldn't have said that.

"No one here to save you?"

A shot of anxiety hits me in the chest.

"Why the hell would I need to be saved, Zade? You going to hurt me?"

It's then he lifts his head, just enough for me to provide a view of his mouth. A wicked smirk is stretched across those lips.

I try to remember that he won't hurt me. He was just in my bed a week ago, sad and vulnerable. By the time I opened my eyes in the morning, he was gone, and I haven't heard from him since.

But my brain is having trouble connecting who he is now to who he was then.

Because now... he looks savage.

"I'm going to ruin you," he corrects. I take a step back, a lump forming in my throat. His image moves, his body walking in a different direction. Is he coming closer? I can't tell. I take another step back, the adrenaline in my system rising to dangerous levels.

He's scaring me.

"Run," he growls. My lungs constrict at the guttural command. "If I catch you, I fuck you."

Eyes widening, I listen, my body catapulting into action.

I run.

In here, I'm completely vulnerable to him. I'm well and truly trapped in the spider's web, and the son of a bitch is poisonous.

His reflection follows me everywhere I go. There were a few times I was convinced I'd truly lost him, seeing nothing but my own image. And then he'd step out from somewhere, crushing my hopes.

After a few minutes, I'm out of breath. The adrenaline and fear are getting to me. My chest is constricted too tight, my lungs reduced to strings and no longer capable of holding oxygen.

I'm lost and trapped with a very dangerous man who is going to absolutely devastate me. I don't think I'm running from him anymore, but rather from the person I'm going to be when he's finished with me.

I was ready to give myself over to him when he emerged from my balcony doors and came to me with a heavy heart. The man put some type of spell on me, because when he was hurting, all I wanted to do was make him feel better. Give myself over to him if that's what would help.

But I know that I would've woken up the next day and hated myself. Because I would've slept with a stalker, a murderer and a man who has forced himself on me on several occasions. I would've slept with a man who doesn't respect my boundaries, my personal space, or the word *no*.

And I know without a shadow of a doubt that's exactly what's about to happen. How do I accept that? How do I toss away the moral compass that's been directing my entire life?

For a man that I should loathe, but... I don't. I just don't. He's all those things, but he's also one of the most admirable men I've ever met. The devotion and passion he has for saving women and children stolen away from their homes and lives, he's doing something massive in the world and making an impact in a substantial way. I can't even begin to put into words the way he makes me feel.

He's such a fucking oxymoron. Contradicting in the most agonizing ways.

And despite his cracked moral compass, I feel safe with him. Even now, when fear is rewiring my brain.

I stop running, panting heavily.

Hopeless.

That's what running from Zade is. Fucking. Hopeless.

Chest pumping, I wait for him to find me. Obviously, I'm not going to be able to outrun him. My only chance of escaping is to somehow incapacitate him, and then try to run.

A laugh bubbles up my throat.

He's been training me to do just that, right? My shadow has been giving me the means to protect myself.

Against him.

Hot breath tickles my ear, sending chills down my spine. I close my eyes, biting my lip until I taste copper when I feel his body press into my back.

He keeps his hands to himself for now, but I know that won't last much longer. It's no secret how much he loves to touch me without my permission.

"I'll scream," I threaten in a breathless whisper.

His breath fans across my neck as I feel him lean down. Soft lips brush the shell of my ear. Shivers cascade down my spine like a raging waterfall.

"That's such a good little girl," he replies.

I whip around, ready to tell him off, but not a syllable escapes when my lips are captured between his the second I come face-to-face with him.

Instinctively, I bite down on his bottom lip. A deep groan swirls through my mouth, spurring me to bite harder. Explosions riot from our connected mouths, along with the flavor of mint and a hint of smoke.

He tastes delicious, and I want him out of my mouth.

As if hearing my thoughts, his palm reaches up to wrap around the back of my head, his fingers tangling in the depths of my hair and pulling me impossibly closer.

And then I do something really stupid.

I suck his bottom lip into my mouth, lost in the taste of him. The feel of his lips against mine.

Realizing what I'm doing, I release his lip, attempting to pull away from him. His mouth is a drug, and just like the real thing, it causes me to make incredibly stupid decisions.

He doesn't let me go and instead returns the sentiment. Sucking my lip into his mouth and delivering his own sharp nip. I gasp from the pain, granting him access and allowing him to invade my mouth.

My pussy responds in kind, throbbing from the feel of his tongue. Memories bombard me, remembering what that tongue felt like sliding against my clit.

An involuntary moan escapes, and the second he tastes my body's betrayal, his kiss turns fierce.

He completely consumes me, sucking and licking my lips and tongue in a way I've never experienced. I'm helpless to stop him, just as I am helpless to fight it.

Another growl pings through my mouth, my only warning to his next move. He grabs my waist and twirls me right up against a mirror, pinning me against the cool glass as his body molds into mine.

"Such a good fucking girl," he praises against my mouth before wrapping my swollen lips into another bruising kiss.

Breathless, I force my head away, sucking in precious oxygen. He clamps my cheeks between his large hand, growling against me.

"Give me those fucking lips," he snarls, forcing his tongue back into my mouth.

My hands wedge between our bodies, traveling up his stomach bulging with muscles to his firm chest. Roughly, I push him away, our lips separating with a loud smack.

"Wait, stop," I pant, my mind foggy and discombobulated.

"What did I say?" he demands sharply. His mismatched eyes capture my gaze in a drug-inducing hold. It's hard to look away when I feel like I'm looking into the eyes of a predator.

He *is* a predator.

"What?" I breathe, still dizzy from the kiss.

"If I catch you, I fuck you," he repeats slowly, gravel lining his throat.

My mouth opens, but the words are slow to release.

"You're not fucking me," I refuse, pushing against his chest harder.

His lips whisper across my cheek, trailing along my jawline before dropping down to my neck.

"Because you're afraid you'll like it too much," he concludes before delivering a sharp nip on my neck. My back arches, goosebumps rising on my skin from the chills. "Because you know that you'll become as addicted as I am."

"No," I deny in a whisper. "Because I don't want you to."

He lifts his head, a knowing smirk on his lips.

"So, you're going to be my bad girl tonight? Lie to my face and act like your pussy isn't aching to be filled up with my cock."

I feel the blood rush to my cheeks, a mix of anger and embarrassment.

"Not everything has to come down to physical attraction," I respond finally. "Maybe my body wants you, but up here"—I tap my temple— "doesn't."

He nods his head slowly, his eyes flitting across my face in contemplation. He

411

takes a step back, leaving me bereft and cold.

It feels like a black shroud encasing the sun on a hot summer day—just a sudden, bone-chilling cold.

He grabs my hand and pulls me away from the mirror. He spins me until I'm looking at the countless reflections that surround us, echoing our image from every angle.

I watch him through the mirror. He presses his body back into mine, his warmth soaking into my pores once more. My eyes settle on one mirror, our eyes clashing through the glass.

Slowly, he bends down until his mouth is right at my ear, his eyes never straying from mine.

"You want to know why I love the house of mirrors?" he murmurs in my ear, eliciting sparks throughout my nerve endings. His voice is full of dark promises and dangerous beginnings.

I swallow thickly. "Why?" I whisper.

"Look around you," he commands softly. Hesitantly, I pull my eyes away from his, dragging my gaze across the dozens of mirrors.

"What you're seeing now is what I see every day. No matter how far I run, how hard I try to escape you—you're everywhere I go. You're everything I see. Loving you is like being trapped in a house of mirrors, little mouse. And I've never felt so at home while being so lost inside you."

My breath hitches, my eyes snapping back to his.

My heart tripped and fell down a flight of stairs the second the word 'love' came out of his mouth. A word he tossed out so casually, I'm not sure if it's a confession or not.

"I don't think you know what love is," I whisper.

He grunts with amusement. "I don't think anyone does, baby. Love is an enigma, and it's redefined every time someone says it."

I frown. All I can feel is disappointment. Not because of what he said, but because of how fucking easy it was for him to accomplish what he set out to do.

Just like he wants, a reckless, impulsive feeling consumes me. All I ache to do is let him have me. So many nights, where he'd sneak into my bed and take advantage of my weakness—whether the weakness was in my body or brain—he used that against me time and time again. But he never took it all the way, and every morsel inside my being has been waiting for this moment. Anticipating it.

I'm dying to deny him, yet I have to fight my body from turning and pulling him into me.

Maybe just this once...

I bite my lip, rolling the bruised and abused lip between my teeth.

He watches me closely, studying every movement like he's trying to interpret a dead language hidden in the lines of my body.

"Are you only saying that because you think it'll work?" I ask, my voice husky and uneven.

His mouth is still angled towards my ear, with his eyes locked onto mine. Slowly, he shakes his head, his face severe and gaze intense.

"You're telling the truth?" I push, my voice hitching with the desperation for him to just lie and tell me no.

"Yes, Adeline," he whispers.

I close my eyes, resignation seeping from my pores. Sensing the change, his hand travels across my flat stomach. I tense beneath his touch, goosebumps rising on my skin.

His long fingers latch onto the zipper of my hoodie, slowly pulling it down, parting the material at a painful pace. The sound of the metal teeth separating disrupts the sound of my erratic breathing.

"Don't torture me," I bite out, anger flashing from his deliberately slow pace.

A wicked smile flashes, and even the mirror can't lessen the cruelty.

"Poor little mouse," he taunts. "You're sadly mistaken if you thought I was going to make this anything but painful."

Chapter Thirty
The Manipulator

e has the strangest ability to suck the air from my lungs with a simple look. And when his terrifying words accompany the deadly stare, it feels like I don't have any lungs at all.

The hoodie parts and he slowly pulls it down my arms. The material drops to the floor, where muddy shoes have trekked across a thousand times tonight.

It feels like a cruel metaphor. Along with my clothes, my flesh and soul will be stained tonight.

"Someone could come in here," I whisper, my voice barely penetrating the tension in the air.

He smiles—a wicked smile that tells me he wouldn't mind if someone did.

"What do you think they'd do?" he implores as he lifts my shirt, the pads of his fingers grazing my skin. Goosebumps rise, a physical reaction from the electricity dancing across my skin wherever he touches me.

"Do you think they'd watch?" he asks. "Do you think they'd enjoy the sight of your naked flesh on display? Maybe they would get off on seeing your dripping pussy reflected back at them everywhere they look. Or the pretty flush on your chest when you come. I think they'd even enjoy watching your eyes roll to the back of your head when my cock fills you so fully, you can't fit any more of me inside you."

A shot of fear injects straight into my heart, forcing the muscle into overdrive. But yet, my body still responds in a much darker way.

Just like his words, I feel my pussy pulsate as my panties gradually dampen until it's exactly like he said—dripping.

Would I be okay with a stranger watching? I don't think so. But something about the way he paints the picture makes me wonder if I'd let it happen anyway.

"You'd be okay with other people seeing me naked?" I challenge breathlessly, watching my shirt flutter to the black floor. His fingers drift up my spine, slow and deliberate. They burn like lava searing my flesh.

"No," he murmurs in my ear. I watch him through the mirror, his eyes drifting down until they're targeted on my chest. The band of my bra tightens, the material biting into my skin before it loosens. The black lacy cups supporting my breasts fall and bare me completely.

My nipples are painfully tight. When he catches sight of my hardened peaks, his tongue drifts across his lower lip as if he's salivating at the sight.

"You want to know what I'd do?" he questions. "I would let them watch. I would let them watch me claim you as mine and own every inch of your body.

They would watch *my* cock fill every one of your holes and then watch you cry because of how hard you came. And then I'd fucking kill them. My cock would still be wet from your cum as I'd slice their throats for even daring to look at what's mine."

The fear inside me tightens into a sharp point, threatening to pop the balloon of sanity I have left.

"You're psychotic," I gasp. This time he laughs, the dark rumble traveling straight to the apex of my thighs.

"You will learn to love it," he murmurs distractedly. His attention has been pulled away as his hands drift across my flat stomach and cup my breasts. I don't have small breasts by any means, I was blessed with good genes. But the size of his hands—they're so big that they make my breasts look small, barely overflowing his hands.

He's a monster. Inside and out.

Still, I feel my panties becoming more drenched.

It shouldn't be possible for the body to concurrently feel hate and desire, but I suppose we would all be lifeless without the complexities of human emotion.

He squeezes my breasts, nearly to the point of pain.

"I'm going to fuck these soon," he promises before releasing them and moving his hands to the button of my jeans.

With a single flick of his hands, my actions creep in no stealthier than a bank robber in a vault full of money.

What the fuck are you doing, Addie?

Fuck, I don't know. This is wrong. So, very wrong. But I don't stop him from unzipping my jeans. Nor do I stop him from hooking his thumbs on either side and pulling them down.

He helps me out of my shoes first and then slips the jeans completely free. I'm left in nothing but my black lacy thong.

I swallow, my heart racing as I take in our reflection. He's still fully clothed, his eyes ping-ponging across the mirrors to look at every angle of my undressed state. He looks as if he can't decide which mirror to settle on. I fight the urge to cover myself. I find the act of hiding more embarrassing than standing almost fully naked in front of a beautiful man.

"You have to undress, too," I insist. No way am I going to be the only one left exposed.

Finally, he comes out from behind me and stands before me. It hurts to meet his mismatched eyes. It feels more real when I'm not looking at them through a glass mirror.

For the first time, this moment with Zade feels consensual. And I'm not sure if I want that. But what fucking sense does that make? To *not* want it to be consensual.

Yet, there's some sick part of me that wants him to force this. So I can play victim later? Go on pretending that my pussy isn't weeping for him and that I'm not anticipating the feel of him inside of me?

It's easier to play the victim when you're not the mastermind behind all your bad decisions.

"If you really want that, little mouse, then you're going to have to do it," he says quietly. He looks at me as if he doesn't believe I'll willingly undress him. And I think he knows what that look does to me. The asshole knows exactly how incapable I am of backing down from a challenge.

I pay him the same respect he paid me. I undress him slowly. Gently. Deliberately brushing my fingers against his skin and earning my own shivers and growls of impatience.

I gasp when I remove his shirt. The scars on his face don't end there. Two severe knife wounds blemish his skin—one cutting across his heart and the other across his defined abs. The skin is raised and jagged, a stark pink against his tanned skin.

And they still hurt him.

When I brush my fingertips over them, he tenses beneath my touch and bares his teeth.

It's not a physical pain. These scars have long healed. But they're like icebergs. They're unmistakable and imposing on the outside, but beneath the surface is something much bigger and threatening. Something capable of sinking someone to the pits of their depravity, just like the Titanic.

They hurt him deeply on the inside, and I really want to know what caused them.

Where there aren't scars, there are intricate tattoos. A dragon coils up his side and across his chest, fire blooming from its mouth and down Zade's shoulder. A mermaid rests on the opposite side, a beautiful woman peering over her naked shoulder.

The mirrors allow me a full view of all the others covering his body—down both arms and his entire back. All beautiful and expertly done.

"You didn't tattoo over any of your scars," I observe quietly, brushing my finger over the dragon's face. In fact, it looks like the tattoos deliberately evade the raised flesh.

"I don't hide from my failures."

His failures aren't the only thing that make his body beautiful. He's packed to the brim with muscle but not too bulky. His physique makes it very clear he can kill you with his pinky without looking like he takes steroids for breakfast.

And as if that doesn't turn my knees to jelly, the thick veins roping from his neck, down to his thick corded arms, and to his massive hands are my undoing.

He's... fucking phenomenal.

Carefully, he watches me, the intensity in his eyes blazing as I study him. He's nearly vibrating beneath my slow perusal, so I move on and resume my torture. It takes a total of zero seconds before he's bristling with the need to fuck me.

I feel so much power in my fingertips, I can't imagine how much power I'd have if I loved him.

With every inch of his skin revealed, I grow shakier and wetter. It's not fair for someone to be so perfect, marred and scarred as he is. If anything, the obvious abuse his body has endured only makes him that much more edible.

I choke on air when I pull down his pants, his hard cock jutting out from the confines of his jeans. It will never get any less intimidating, no matter how many times I see it.

Not unless I suddenly accept death via dick one day.

When he's entirely naked, I take a big step back from him and look around. I stare at him from every angle the mirrors provide, just like he did with me.

Thick thighs, tight round ass, and a defined back that I want to rub myself all over, and the most beautiful cock I've ever seen.

I want to run away. Far, far away.

This man is going to ruin me after tonight. I can taste it on my tongue.

"Are you scared?" he asks in another dark whisper. He's staring at me with an unreadable expression on his face.

"Yes," I answer truthfully.

He smiles, and the sight nearly brings me to my knees.

It's not right—how beautiful he is. He's definitely the fucking Devil. I'm sure of it now more than ever.

"You should be," he says, his voice lilted with danger.

I take another step back, but he doesn't move to stop me.

"Get on your knees, little mouse," he orders darkly. I pause, unsure if I should listen or find the common sense I dropped somewhere on the way into the House of Mirrors and run.

"Don't make me ask twice," he growls, his face dropping to a severe expression. He tilts his jaw down, glaring down at me.

The danger in his face scares me, and my juices dampen my thighs in response.

"I don't want you to ask me," I say slowly. Confusion flits across his eyes for a brief second, and I show him exactly what I mean at that moment.

I turn and start to run.

But he's too fast. His hand snaps out and wraps around my hair, yanking me backwards.

A sharp gasp escapes as I go weightless. He manages to twist my body so I land painfully on my knees. Just like we both wanted.

"You like it when I force you?" he snarls, yanking my head back until I'm looking up at him. His cock brushes against my cheek, warning me of what's coming.

"You like being a bad little girl, don't you? You like to defy me because you love it when I scare you. You're a silly little girl playing with fire," he taunts, a cruel snarl on his face.

Tears prick my eyes from the force of him holding my hair. Burning, just like the inferno of ire and lust in his eyes. And if I didn't know any better, I'd think there's a blaze of fire behind me, reflecting in his mismatched eyes.

"Tell me, little mouse, have you ever been fucked by a man like me?"

"Better," I hiss, the dormant hate for him reawakening. Something very dark and dangerous shutters over his eyes. He arches that damn brow, and I immediately shrink in on myself.

It was a lie. We both know it.

That's the first thing I learned when I was put in Catholic school as a child. Good girls don't lie.

The second lesson is don't trust the Devil and his influence. But what they forgot to mention is not to piss him off once you've been influenced.

Maybe because that's common fucking sense.

My lip trembles as I berate myself for being so stupid. The bitterness and distrust are still churning beneath the surface. I don't know why I thought I could let him dominate and fuck me without fighting back.

He'll kill me before I ever fall in love with him.

"Open your fucking mouth, bad girl. Right now, before I suffocate you on my cock."

This time, I listen. The second my lips part, he's forcing the tip past my lips and straight to the back of my throat.

He hisses through his teeth, followed by another feral growl. I whimper and then gag when he forces his dick deeper. He's hardened steel wrapped in silky satin, but the smoothness does little to ease the pain.

He's too thick and too long for my small mouth.

Tears instantly flood my eyes and spill over as he keeps forcing himself deeper. Instinctively, my hands grip his thick thighs, pushing against him.

As quick as a snake, he snatches both of my hands up and grips them together in one hand, and resuming the hold on my head with the other. He holds my hands up high and against his stomach. It looks like I'm a woman praying on my knees, my hands bound together as I worship the devil himself.

"This is what you wanted, right?" he growls. "Fucking suck it. Now."

I do as he says, if it means he'll ease up. I suck hard, hollowing out my cheeks and smoothing my tongue over the thick vein on the underside of his length.

"That's it, baby," he breathes, finally allowing me to ease back. But in seconds, he's pulling me back in. Guiding my head back and forth as I continue to suck him. Muttered words of encouragement and deep groans of pleasure fall from his lips while he grows more forceful. With every syllable and moan that leaves his lips, I grow more desperate to please him. To correct my mistake.

"Let's see. Greyson Parker, he was better, huh?" My eyes widen, confused how he knows him and dreading where this is going. "I almost killed him when he ran from your house naked, so somehow I doubt he was better than me. Who else?" he emphasizes the last word by shoving himself deeper into my throat. I choke, and he lets me struggle for a few seconds before easing up.

"Brandon Havatti, Carlos Santonio, Tyler Sanders..." he continues to list off every man I've been with. Which admittedly isn't that many, but it's a lot when you've just put their life in danger.

He jerks my head back sharply, allowing me a single breath as he says, "I'll enjoy killing each and every one of them, little mouse."

Before I can muster a response, let alone another breath of precious air, he's back to choking me on his cock again.

My vision darkens around the edges from how deeply he's plunging into my throat. It doesn't matter how much I gag and fight against him, he only grows impossibly harder.

"You want me to come in your mouth, don't you? You've been thinking about sucking my cock since you worshipped me on your knees with a belt wrapped around that pretty little neck of yours."

I glare up at him, hate burning brighter than lust for just a moment. He smiles—or rather bares his teeth—when he sees the anger reflecting from my brown eyes.

"You want it, but you're not going to fucking get it. You haven't earned that privilege yet."

Without warning, he jerks my head back hard, his cock popping free.

He lifts me up by my hair until I'm on the tip of my toes.

"Zade, please," I whimper, my vision blurred from the tears and chest tight due to lack of oxygen. I'm not even sure what I'm begging for—my life or the innocent men I've just put on death row.

"That's such a good girl," he praises. "I love it when you're scared and begging."

Just when I finally think I can breathe again, he steals it right back. His lips seal over mine in an electrifying kiss. My nails claw against his chest, earning me a low growl as he consumes my mouth with his own.

The energy between us crackles and explodes as we both drink from each other. Sparks of fire and the taste of bitter wine invade my tongue.

Poison has never tasted so good.

As our tongues fight for dominance, he grips my waist and lifts me effortlessly. My legs instinctively curl around his trim waist just as I feel the cool glass press against my back.

The temperature warring in my body feels just like his yin-yang eyes. The chill from the mirror threatens to send shivers curling through my body, yet the press of his body against my own is scorching hot.

A sharp bite of my pain on either side of my hips has me gasping into his mouth. In one swift tug, he rips my thong away from my body, the shredded fabric getting trapped somewhere between our bodies.

He pulls away and positions the head of his cock at the entrance.

"Spread your pussy for me, little mouse," he orders. I open my mouth to argue, ready to tell him to just fuck me, but the look on his face renders me speechless.

Frustration mounting, I reach both hands between our bodies and do as he says. A red flush stains my chest as I spread myself apart. It's demeaning when he knows I'm not supposed to want it.

He knows I want him to force himself inside me. And as punishment for insulting him, he's going to make me show him how much I want him. By spreading my pussy and inviting him in.

God, I hate him.

His hands tighten on my hips painfully. Tomorrow, I'll wake up with handprint bruises, and a part of me dreads that. It will be impossible to forget what happened when I'm wearing the imprint of his hands on my skin.

"Don't you dare move your hands," he threatens, a second before he's pulling me down on his awaiting dick.

"Ah!" I shout, my hands seconds from flying to his chest so I can push off of him. He's too much, stretching me wider than I've ever been.

My eyes are rounded into giant saucers as I whimper from the assault. I feel his girth slide between my fingers as he works himself inside deeper. "Stop! It doesn't fit," I gasp.

"What a poor little mouse," he coos mockingly, his tone husky and tight. "Maybe one day you'll let me treat this cunt like glass and show it all my love, but you've been a bad girl, haven't you?"

When I don't answer, he jerks me down on him harder, earning another pained whimper. "Haven't you?" he barks.

"Yes!" I shout breathlessly, squeezing my eyes shut against the invasion.

"Are you going to be a good little girl now?"

"Yes," I mewl desperately. The pain is morphing into something far more intense and breathtaking. He slides out and pushes back in, gentler this time, but no less angry.

It feels like my body is on the cusp of bursting. This isn't natural to be so goddamn *full*.

He pulls out to the tip, and then he slams his entire length inside of me, so deep, I swear I feel him coming up my throat. I cry out, my voice breaking from the swell of emotion building inside my chest.

Not fucking natural.

"God*damn*, Addie, I can barely fucking fit."

Must be why it feels like he's tearing me in half.

He starts out slow and forceful. Harsh thrusts, then dragging himself out at a torturous pace, before slamming inside me again. I feel my body beginning to relax, sucking him in greedily as he damns my soul with every stroke.

Widening his stance, he braces himself against the mirror, and my stomach tightens, sensing the oncoming damage he's about to inflict on my organs.

Shockwaves scatter throughout my nerve endings as he quickens his pace, roughly fucking me against the mirror while loud noises I've never made in my life fall from my lips. The pleasure is blinding, and the feel of him sliding in and out between my fingers only heightens the potent lust stirring in the pit of my stomach.

"Look at us in the mirrors," he demands roughly. It takes immense effort, but I pry my eyes open and sweep them over the dozens of mirrors. Every angle imaginable is staring back at me.

It's too much—watching him drive himself inside me. His ass is clenched from the force of his thrusts, while a red flush is spread up to my rosy cheeks. My eyes are at half-mast, and my face is twisted into undeniable bliss.

He turns his head and our eyes clash in one of the mirrors. My heart drops as I tear my eyes away to look around and see his eyes pinned on me from several directions, it's the most intense feeling I've ever experienced.

Like that gut feeling when you know someone is watching you but multiplied by a dozen.

My eyes lock back onto his, and a slow smile takes over his face. He leans in close, his lips skating across mine as he watches me slowly come apart at the seams, all the while grinning at me.

"Tell me, little mouse, have you ever been fucked by a man like me?"

I bite my lip and shake my head, fighting the urge to roll my eyes to the back of my head. He readjusts our position, sliding each arm under my knees and hiking them up high. An embarrassing scream escapes as he changes the angle of his hips and hits a spot that instantly makes my legs violently shake.

"Oh my God," I moan. And this time, I can't stop my head from dropping back to the mirror behind me and my eyes from rolling backwards.

"That's right, baby. I am your fucking God," he growls before I feel his teeth sink into my neck.

My stomach is tightening and I can feel an orgasm building dangerously fast. It feels like an angry Poseidon is in my stomach, forming a devastating tsunami that will surely kill me.

The mirror begins to violently shudder from how hard he's fucking me. It feels like it's going to shatter any second now, but I can't bring myself to care.

Just as I reach that peak, he pulls completely out. I whimper, the sudden emptiness almost painful.

"What—" he drops me to my feet and steps back, pointing to the floor. My knees wobble, my balance screwed from the sharp pleasure pulsating between my thighs.

"Get on your hands and knees."

I don't argue, mainly because the loss of the orgasm is painful and my legs are incapable of supporting my weight much longer.

Angry tears line the edges of my eyelids, but I bite back my snarky comment. He'll only make my punishment worse.

I expect him to slide back inside of me from behind, but his hands dart between my legs and grab me from the underside of my hips, lifting me up until my knees are no longer on the ground and forcing me to catch myself from face planting. I feel his hot breath fan across my pussy a second before his teeth latch onto my clit.

I yelp, jerking from the bite of pain. But he doesn't torture me like last time. Immediately he suctions my clit in his mouth and laps at my dripping cunt.

He hums, sending delicious vibrations radiating throughout my core. "You taste so fucking good," he murmurs, before flicking his tongue against my clit.

I look up and shamelessly watch him feast on me from behind. I turn my head until I get the best view of him on his knees behind me, eating my pussy like a starved man.

The impending orgasm is renewed and more looming than before. I'm incapable of grinding back into his face like I want, so I'm helpless against his lashing tongue.

"Zade, please," I beg, my eyes crossing from the pleasure.

"Does my little mouse want to come?" he asks, his own voice breathless and uneven.

I would call him a liar if he ever tried to deny his desire for me, but that's the thing about Zade—he's never tried to hide how much he wants me. He's never sugarcoated or denied the fact that he desperately craves me.

"Yes," I plead on a groan.

He pulls away, and I scream at him in frustration, pounding my fist against the floor. Fury from being denied a second time overwhelms me, and I thrash against his hold.

He laughs at my attempt.

"You motherfucking ass—"

He interrupts my tirade by seating himself inside me, his balls slapping against the sensitive nub. I choke on my words, this angle allowing him in far deeper than before.

I arch my back and dig my nails into the floor, clawing at the dirty tile as he relentlessly pounds into me.

He grabs my hair and snaps my head back roughly, forcing me to look in the mirrors directly in front of me and watch him fuck me.

"You want to come all over my cock, baby?"

I nod my head frantically. He smiles in response. "Have you been my good little girl?" Another wobbly nod. "Then fucking say it, Adeline."

I clench around him when I hear my full name spoken in his gravelly tenor. "I'm your good little girl," I breathe, too far gone to feel anything but blinding lust.

He molds his front to my back, spearing through my tightening pussy. The hand in my hair travels down around my throat and squeezes tight while his other palm splays across my flat stomach. "Tonight is just practice but I promise you, little mouse, this body *will* be carrying all my babies one day," he snarls, teeth gnashing.

His image blurs as my eyes roll and the tsunami wave finally crashes through me. I scream so loud, the noise nearly rattles the mirrors. Zade's name spills from my lips on a neurotic chant as my entire world combusts into tiny pieces.

"Fuck! That's it, baby. Your pussy is so fucking tight, milk my fucking cock," Zade grinds out. He ends his sentence on a roar, his hips shuddering as he slams into me one last time, filling me with his seed until I can no longer fit anymore inside of me.

I feel our combined juices pour down my thighs, as I'm left panting and breathless on the floor. My body convulses from the aftershocks, even after I come down from the biggest orgasm I've ever had.

I can't fucking breathe, let alone move or think coherent thoughts.

None of that was natural. Absolutely none of it.

"I hope you know," I pant. "I'm on birth control."

He chuckles breathlessly. "For now."

Before I can respond, a loud buzz disturbs the heavy atmosphere. My eyes snap towards the direction, locating the source immediately. My phone is lit up in my discarded jeans, buzzing wildly.

Fuck. Daya.

I scramble up and towards the phone, clenching my teeth from the feel of him sliding out of me. My thumb trembles violently as I click the green button on my screen.

"Hello?" I answer, wincing when I hear how shaky and hoarse my voice is.

"Where the *fuck* are you?" she shouts through her receiver, her own voice trembling and full of anger.

430

"I got lost, and my cell reception has been spotty," I lie sheepishly, not willing to admit what really happened. Ignoring Zade's presence, I scramble to pull my clothes on. Cringing both from the yelling in my ear and the slickness trailing down my thighs.

"The park is closed, Addie! I got kicked out already, and they said that the House of Mirrors had already been cleared out.The stupid asshole security guard didn't believe me when I said you didn't come out. I've been worried fucking sick."

Just as I slip on my shoes, a muttered, "shit," sounds from behind me, drawing my attention.

Zade is staring at his phone, his face is cast in a severe expression.

He's wearing nothing but his black boots and undone jeans slung low, giving a mouthwatering view of the defined V disappearing beneath the fabric.

Daya's ranting fades to the background as my attention snags.

The light from his phone accentuates the muscles straining against his smooth flesh, the scars and the black, intricate tattoos only adding to his savagery.

The veins threading throughout his hands and arms are bulging and *goddamn*, if I wasn't already leaning against a mirror, I'd collapse from how devastating he looks right now.

That masterpiece of jagged scars and rough edges fucked me into oblivion and vowed that I'd have his babies one day. I can't breathe.

"*Addie*, I swear to fu—"

"I... I'll be right out, Daya. I'm so sorry," I respond, forcing my gaze away back to my surroundings, trying to gather my bearings.

Which is really hard to do in a house of a million mirrors.

She takes a deep, calming breath. "Okay, I'm sorry. I've just been really scared, Addie."

I flinch as a different kind of tsunami overwhelms me. This one is filled with every negative emotion imaginable. Guilt. Shame. Regret.

"I'm really sorry, Daya. I'll see you in a few."

I hang up the phone and immediately start walking off in the direction I think I'm supposed to be going in.

"Wrong way, little mouse. Follow me," Zade says, his deep tenor causing me to tense, my shoulders rocketing to my ears. He's finished dressing and is heading in the opposite direction.

Stiffly, I turn and follow after him. Not asking or caring how he knows where to go, as long as he gets me out of here.

After fifteen tense minutes, we find the exit door and I rush out, the cold air a balm to my heated face.

The fair is a stark difference to when I came in. The field is completely devoid of life. Not a single soul on the grounds nor any lights.

How long were we in there for? I check the time, and my eyes bug when I note that it's twelve-thirty in the morning.

Two hours! I've been in there for two fucking hours. Sure, half of that was getting through the mirrors but *still*. Normal people don't fuck for that long, do they?

Zade is somewhere behind me, so I glance over my shoulder and say, "Don't follow me out. Daya is waiting for me, and I don't want her to see you." Even I can detect the coldness in my voice.

The entire fifteen minutes it took to find our way out, all I could think about is how I want to fuck him again.

And that scares the absolute shit out of me.

It was the reality check I needed—a very stark reminder that I just had sex

432

with my stalker. I shouldn't have let any of that happen.

I feel his hand clamp around my wrist a second before he whips me around. I stumble into him, but he catches me quickly, wrapping a hand tightly around the back of my neck.

"I'm late for a date with a psycho girl anyways," he says easily. My eyes round and he smiles when he detects the anger in my eyes. "Don't be jealous, little mouse. It's not a real date. She's not my type of crazy. Despite the fact that she's not *you*."

I scoff. "I'm not jealous. Let me go," I snap, attempting to pull away from him.

He pulls me in close, his lips brushing across mine as he stares deeply into my eyes.

"That will never happen, Adeline. I will never let you go." I stiffen, thrown off by the severity in his tone. He's actually serious.

He crushes his lips to mine before I can respond. And because this will be the last time I will ever allow this man to touch me, I respond in kind. I claw at him, tugging at the collar of his hoodie roughly, and clenching his bottom lip between my teeth, biting down hard until I taste his blood on my tongue.

He growls and devours me whole, his mouth still tasting of my pussy. And then he rips away from me, breathing hard.

"Go," he demands roughly.

I don't hesitate. I stumble out of the field and to my waiting car, the only one left in the parking lot. A fidgeting Daya sits behind the wheel, her stare boring into me.

I sigh, readying myself for a tough conversation I don't know how to have. I'll stick to my story. I got lost. That's it.

I open the car door and nearly collapse in. When I meet her stare, she's glaring at me with the heat of a thousand suns.

"Why the *fuck* do you look and smell like you just got fucked?"

March 2nd, 1946

I told Ronaldo I might ask John for a divorce. He became so excited that for a moment, I felt like he and I might finally have a future together.

But then I told him that I want him to quit his job. He deflated. Like a popped balloon. He said that might not be possible. That he was tied to his boss, and he doesn't think he'll ever be able to leave.

It escalated into a fight. I understand his position. But I told him I don't know if we can truly be together while he's involved with something so dangerous.

He made a smart comment that my husband is just as involved with danger as he is.

I wasn't sure what that even meant. His gambling habits? We stopped having trouble with that soon after the break in, so I assumed that John had cleaned up his act.

Whatever the case, I stood firm on my decision. Sera and I will figure things out together. If that means becoming a single mother, then that's what I'll do.

Chapter Thirty One
The Shadow

"What took you so long?" the psycho girl snaps, her dull brown eyes alight with fire. The same inferno in her eyes is what's still residing in my chest.

My heart hasn't stopped pounding, and I'm plagued with the unbending need to fuck her again. My brain feels like it's been tossed into a skillet and pan-seared to a crisp. I need to focus, but it's nearly impossible when the taste of Addie lingers on my tongue, and I'm still gripped by the feel of her tightly wrapped around me.

I don't know how I'm supposed to concentrate when I just found God. Or rather, I think I just became one.

But how can I feel like a god, yet be completely stripped of power when it comes to her?

I don't know.

All I know is I fucking love haunted fairs now.

"I got caught up with something," I murmur, sweeping the room for lingering employees. Or any deadly surprises if the murderous look in the psycho girl's eyes is anything to go by. She's still planning on killing me, and the notion is laughable.

If it were so fucking easy to kill me, I would've been dead long ago. These scars are proof of that.

After our confrontation, the broken doll and I decided to team up for the time being. Since Mark decided to take matters into his own hands and try to kidnap and enslave my girl, I decided he was no longer worth keeping alive. The two seconds it took for him to conspire against Addie was the equivalent to writing his name in a Death Note.

There's no chance of his survival.

So, we knocked out the four of them. The doll said she'd take them somewhere where the guests wouldn't find them and meet up at midnight to get my answers and finish them off for good.

Claire, of course, witnessed the entire thing, and the doll sent her running. I couldn't do anything at the moment when I had four men to handle, but the second I walked out of that haunted house, I had one of my men find her and take her somewhere safe.

Plain and simple, Claire is an abused woman who deserves to live a life in peace. But she also bore witness to a crime, and I can't allow her the opportunity to tell someone.

Afterwards, I immediately went and found Addie and tracked her the entire time. I let her have her fun, visiting all the haunted houses and creepy carnival tents, and ride the thrill rides, all while I stayed quietly behind her, just out of sight. Making sure no one even looked at her funny without consequences.

"Where are they?" I ask, pinning my eyes back on the strange girl. Blood is already splattered across her white nightgown. I arch a brow but don't say anything.

She nods towards the stairs. "Up in my playroom."

She begins to lead me up the stairs but stops short and looks off into the foyer, seemingly staring at something. But I see nothing.

"Stay down here until I call you guys up," she says, still staring off into space. My brow lowers as I try to figure out who the hell she's talking to. She pauses for a moment before she says, "I can handle myself," and continues up the stairs.

Well, this is fucking awkward. I've gotten myself into a lot of interesting situations over the years. *Real* interesting situations. But this one hits the top of the list.

Clearing my throat, I ask, "So, uh, what's your deal?"

"What do you mean, *my deal?*" she snaps.

"Those people you were talking to—do they not like me?" I ask, amusement prominent in my tone. I'm still not entirely sure what's going on with her. Maybe she's high off drugs, maybe she's mentally ill, or maybe she can see spirits or some shit.

"My henchmen? No. Nor do they trust you."

Her *henchmen?* The fuck is this girl actually seeing? And are they supposed to be her helpers or something?

"You uh, told them to stay down there and that you can handle yourself?" I ask. "They're not coming up too?"

She pauses on the steps, whips towards me, and throws her arm out to point behind me. "Do you see them walking behind you?"

I don't even turn to look. No one will be there. Aside from the two of us and the four men upstairs, no one else is inside this house.

I smirk. "No."

"Then there's your answer! I don't need my henchmen to protect me from *you*. And since you're here, I figured they could sit this one out," she explains impatiently.

So, she's mentally ill. Got it.

"Ah."

"*Ah?*" she repeats, aghast. "What does that mean?"

"It means you're fucking insane, little girl. Where are these demons again, or whatever you call them?" I ask, my own tone becoming clipped.

It took five seconds to no longer give a fuck about what she's seeing. It doesn't impact me at the end of the day, so I couldn't give less of a shit at this point. If she wants to pretend there's gigantic talking bananas following me around with pitchforks, then I'll indulge her as long as I get my time with the four men waiting for me upstairs.

When she brings me into the room, they immediately start screaming. Wriggling about like worms caught on a hook. I can't tell if Mark is screaming because he thinks I'm going to help him or kill him, but I suppose I'm going to do both. Help him atone for his sins and then kill him for it.

"Do they know you?" the doll asks, and I hum in confirmation, taking in their appearances and broken bones.

The other three men look at me like I'm the boogeyman. And that's as Zack, the self-made millionaire. Wait until I tell them who I really am—I'm sure their faces will look like Casper's.

I only need to learn about two things. Find out where the rituals are being held and how to get into the place, and find out if the Society is after Addie. Whatever else they have to say is no longer a concern.

"You sure no one can hear them?"

"I do this all the time," she answers simply. I inspect her from the corner of my eye, looking her up and down.

"You kill people often?"

She's a small thing, but the girl can fight. And by the near-constant murderous gleam in her eye, it truly doesn't surprise me.

She shrugs. "Only the demons."

I can't help the small grin. "Do you call yourself the demon-slayer too?"

She snarls and stomps her foot like the child she's dressed up to be. "You're not funny!"

I disagree.

But instead of arguing, I turn my attention back to the matter at hand.

Just as expected, the second I rip the tape from his mouth, he starts pleading for his life. And the minute I tell Mark who I really am, his reddened face instantly drains of all blood until his skin is an ashen, grey pallor. The other three men's faces follow suit, looking at me as if I'm the grim reaper.

I smile.

I *am* the fucking grim reaper.

I ignore Mark's reminders that we were friends and his pathetic attempt to point the blame on his business partners while citing his own innocence.

It doesn't surprise me that he'd pass off the blame so easily to others. He's selfish, narcissistic, and a complete imbecile. And by the look on the distressed men's face sitting next to him, they don't think highly of him right now, either.

In the short time that I've known Mark, I've discovered not very many of his colleagues do.

He's loud, boisterous, and outspoken. Always trying to be the cool guy and fit in with the crowd. I've also heard through the grapevine that Mark tends to disagree with a lot of his colleague's political views. Always voting opposite on bills within his own party.

Don't give two fucks about politics either, at least not the kind that deals with laws and regulations. I break those on a daily basis. The fuck would I care about what laws are getting passed when I've never applied them to my life anyway?

I also manage to piss off the demon-slayer when she starts whining about not getting to kill them yet.

"By all means, start the killing," I say, gesturing towards Miller, Jack, and Robert. "Don't let me stop your demon-slaying."

The air whistles, my only indication that some type of weapon is on its way to plowing into my head like the asteroids that killed off the dinosaurs. I jerk to the side, watching the blade sluice right past my head and into Mark's gut.

That looks like it fucking hurts.

And then she goes off the deep end, tackling Robert and stabbing him until he's literally mush. Despite the fact that he's no longer a solid mass, she keeps going. It's when Mark starts puking that I've had enough.

Sighing, I get up and walk over to her, grabbing her hand and stopping her from her inane stabbing. She's got strength and energy, that's for sure. It takes a lot to stab someone repeatedly. It's more exhausting than people give it credit for. Stabbing someone even up to a hundred times with the force she's using would have a grown man panting for breath.

And while a thin layer of sweat coats her made-up face, she looks like she's ready for more.

"Now you're going to stop me from demon-slaying?!" she shrieks, her voice pitched so high, it nearly makes me cringe. *God.* Fucking women and their screeching.

"Little girl, there're quite a few things you need to get serious help for, but I'd say anger management is top of the list."

She stares at me, her face starting to get twitchy. She looks like a malfunctioning robot, and I'd say that this experience now takes the number one spot of the interesting situations I've gotten myself into.

She looks on the verge of exploding, so I reign in my temper and demand, "Look at me."

Her big ass brown eyes stare up at me, and if it wasn't for the crazed glimmer in her eye and the fact that she's covered head to toe in blood, she'd look innocent and sweet.

What a fucking lie that would be.

"Drop the knife." Her hand instantly seizes, letting the knife clang to the blood-soaked floor. "What's your name?" I ask.

"Sibel." She pauses. "My friends call me Sibby."

A pang of pity stabs at me. Something tells me the only friends this girl has are the people in her head. This girl is alone—completely alone. Judging by her niche for lurking in the walls, I would bet money that no one that works at this fair is even aware of her presence.

Sighing internally, I decide to throw the girl a bone. Don't know if it's because I feel fucking bad for her or what, but fuck, I guess I do.

"You're an interesting person, Sibby. But I'm going to need you to calm the fuck down. I can't interrogate in peace when you're over there stabbing someone like a cracked-out banshee, you feel me?"

She physically relaxes at the use of her nickname. At me declaring her as my friend. And fuck if that doesn't make me feel a little worse for her.

Reluctantly, she nods her head, and after reassurance that I'm not making fun when I call her a demon-slayer and wiping an eyeball off of the tip of the knife, I hand it back to her as a peace offering. And then I go back to interrogating Mark.

This time in fucking peace.

"Mark, are you going to give me the information I need? I want to know where you do the rituals," I ask, my voice as emotionless as my expression.

"Z, I *swear*, I don't know anything!" Mark lies. There's vomit stuck on his lip from when he puked while watching Sibby completely obliterate his dear old friend.

Shit was brutal, even I can admit that.

I reach down, pick up Mark's hand, dig the tip of my knife under his nail and pluck it right off. Mark screams bloody murder, but the sorry piece of shit hasn't even felt real pain yet.

"Try again," I say evenly. He protests again, lying through his veneers, so I rip off another nail with the tip of my blade. When I position my knife under the third nail and lift, he finally gives.

I almost laugh. The children he kidnaps last longer with torture than he does, which shows that Mark was always weak.

"Okay, wait, wait!" I pause, lifting a brow and waiting for him to continue. His breathing is erratic as tears and snot track down his face. Licking his lips nervously, he confesses, "S-some of the kids we take, we take them to an underground club."

Sibby comes closer, her face enraptured as Mark confesses his dirty sins. I shoot her a warning glare to back off before I turn my attention back to Mark.

"Where is this place?" I ask calmly, though a burning heat simmers beneath the surface. It takes practiced control to keep my voice even.

"You can only access it through a private gentlemen's club—*Savior's*. You need special access to even get in the club, let alone gain access to the..." he trails off, and it seems as if he's struggling with his words. Finally, he forces out his next words. "To gain access to the dungeon."

A growl builds in my chest, but I wrestle it back down. My hand nearly shakes with the need to plunge this knife deep into his throat, but I refrain.

"Yeah? And what do you do in this dungeon?"

His eyes shift nervously, and his mouth flops soundlessly.

In one quick motion, I flick off the nail my knife was poised under. The answering scream does little to abate the fury crawling throughout my body.

I will thoroughly enjoy killing this man. His tortured cries as his body slowly dies will be my lullaby as I fall asleep tonight.

It's not until I position the knife under another nail before he finally says anything of value. Crimson rivulets are spilling from Mark's hand, but I've barely begun truly making Mark bleed.

"Wait! I said, *wait*, goddammit!" I cock a brow at him again, urging him to continue. "We uh—we perform rituals on them." He tightens his lips, a pained expression on his red face. "That's how we're sworn in to the secret society. We must perform a ritual and drink the blood of a virgin."

He confirms what they do to the children, the government's involvement, and I make sure to have him clarify the two men left breathing next to him are a part of these fucked up rituals. It takes stabbing Jack in the thigh before he admits to his sins, but Miller admits it immediately, not wanting to suffer like Jack and Mark.

"Can I play now, Zade?" Sibby asks impatiently from beside me. She's vibrating with the need to kill, and in this moment, I can relate to the little demon slayer. We have the same mission, and that is to murder some fucked up individuals.

"Go ahead and have fun with those two. I have a couple more things to get out of dear old Mark first," I concede, nodding towards Jack and Miller.

"If you don't let me go, I won't tell you anything else! Nothing!" Mark shouts, desperate as death draws nearer.

"You're a weak man, Mark. You'll tell me anything I want to know once the pain becomes too much. You either die slow, or quick."

Sibby happily prances towards them and goes for Jack first. She slashes up his face, and it takes monumental effort to ignore her. Especially when her cheeks flush so brightly, I can see it through the makeup.

I swear to God, if she gets off right in front of me, I'm leaving.

I bend down, getting eye level with Mark and hold the knife to his dick. The tool he uses to torture young children will definitely be getting a knife plunged through it tonight while he's still breathing.

"Who did you speak to about Addie?" I ask.

Mark stutters, his eyes continuously glancing over to his friend's torture. A bone cracks, followed by Jack's loud wail of pain.

I dig the knife down further. Mark's eyes snap back to mine at the clear threat.

"Focus on me, Mark," I say darkly. "Who did you speak to about Addie?"

Licking his lips, he asks, "In what regard?"

"In any regard that has to do with you kidnapping my girl and selling her, like you were planning to do before I walked in. Did you speak about her to anyone in a position of power involved with these rituals or Savior's?"

I know the answer before he opens his fucking mouth and says it. The dimming of his eyes as he accepts that he's about to suffer a great deal more pain.

"Yes," he whispers.

I lose my composure for just a second, enough to snarl and slice my knife across his chest.

He screams, his face beat red from the agony coursing through him, but I'm not done. Not by a fucking long shot.

"Who?" I bark, losing my control over the beast threatening to rip out of my chest.

When Mark continues to moan in pain, I poise the knife right back over his dick and dig it in sharply. Enough to break skin, but not enough to cause any real damage.

Yet.

"Okay, okay!" Mark yelps, his eyes widening at the pain.

"Who?!" I boom. "I want fucking names, Mark."

He sniffles but gives me the names I need to know. The names of the people operating the rituals. Names that are more than likely aliases. But it's a start.

He admits he's never seen their faces before, and all communication has been through a video feed where they're shadowed in darkness.

They're some type of secret underground government, and based on Mark's ramblings, they have far more control over our government than I thought.

The President is just a puppet, and these people who refer to themselves as the Society—they hold the real power.

"Tell me why you did this, Mark. Why did you insist on going after Addie when you knew she was mine?"

His chin trembles, the waste of flesh the epitome of a pathetic old man.

"She was already marked."

My heart drops, thudding down my spine like a deflated basketball rolling down a staircase.

"I took a picture of her because she looked familiar. And when she told me her name, I realized that she was a target of the Society's. It worked out perfectly that they happened to call me, and I told them everything. She... she's worth a lot of money, man. And the Society wants her. It doesn't matter to them who you are—it doesn't even matter who *I* am. When the Society wants someone, they get them. And if I was the one to bring her in... I would've been highly rewarded."

He sniffles, though it doesn't prevent the snot from leaking out of his nose.

"Why did they target her?"

Mark sputters out a wet, humorless laugh. "Why do they target anyone? If they're young and beautiful and happen to be noticed, they're on the Society's radar. She brought attention to herself in one way or another. It could've been from her books, or you know how women are these days. With the way they dre—" I snatch his hand again and flick off another nail before he can finish such a stupid fucking sentence.

As if showing any amount of skin is a goddamn invitation to be raped and kidnapped.

His answering scream does little to lessen the fury.

"I-I'm sorry, okay? I'm sorry. Look, you just don't ignore the Society's demands. And they're going to come after you, Z," Mark warns, his voice tight with pain but also grave.

I hope they do.

They'll be saving me the trouble of coming to them.

Knowing that Addie was marked doesn't only spark anger, it sparks genuine fear for my little mouse.

It never mattered if I came into her life or not—Addie was destined for human trafficking, and the fact that she happens to be the girl I'm absolutely crazy about feels like kismet.

It feels like fucking destiny that the man who haunts her is the same man who dedicated his life to destroying the people set out to take her life.

"I know you don't care," Mark forges on, noting the look on my face. "But the second they find out I'm dead, they'll up and move."

I've accepted this.

I look over at Sibby, the girl now having moved onto Miller. She could be a scapegoat.

If the Society gets word of a deranged girl killing these four men—a girl who's killed before—they would chalk it up to the partial truth. Wrong place, wrong time. An unhinged girl who swears she can sense evil sniffed these men out and decided to murder them in cold blood.

She's the perfect scapegoat, actually.

But the thought of using her—it doesn't sit right with me.

She's a lonely, fucked up girl who helped me carry out these murders. Doesn't matter that she would've done it anyways had I not been there. Without her, I wouldn't have gotten the information I did tonight. And I can't let that go unrewarded.

So, I resign myself to protect Sibby. I'll clean up the evidence, dispose of the bodies and do everything I can to infiltrate Savior's before they relocate.

"Will they demolish?"

"Yes," Mark answers quickly. I let out a slow breath and nod. By saving Sibby, I'm giving up the first lead I've truly had.

"I-If you let me go, I can get you in," Mark barters desperately. "I'll help you and you can do whatever you want. Just as long as you let me live."

"The other three are already dead," I say. "They're going to relocate anyways."

"Not if you pin everything on this girl. That's what you planned, right? To let her take the fall for it?"

Sibby is still too blind with bloodlust to hear what Mark is saying, but I would've been honest about it anyway. Sibby and I never promised each other anything, and I'm pretty sure the girl still plans on killing me.

But she won't succeed because despite what she thinks, it's only her against me. And I've fought far too many bad guys to allow a little girl to take me out. Even if she is a little badass.

I refocus on Mark. "Do you know where they'd relocate?" I ask. Mark hesitates, sensing that he will no longer hold any leverage if he confesses. I dig the knife deeper into his dick to drive home my point.

I'll know if he's lying.

"No," he admits, his lip trembling. "They wouldn't tell us until afterwards."

I nod my head, lift my hand, and plunge the blade deep into his pelvis. His screams do little to abate the pit of dread and anger churning in my stomach.

Chapter Thirty Two
The Shadow

Sibby took the fall for the murders.

After chopping the bodies into pieces and loading them in the trunk, we sat on the hood of my Mustang, where I was once again reminded just how broken this doll actually is. Sounds like her father was a piece of shit.

Can't help but muse over the fact that she has a reason to end up the way she did and I... don't.

Just as I was getting into my car, the cops pulled up. Sibby refused to get in, insisting that she needed to stay with her henchmen. Men who don't actually fucking exist.

And I didn't have time to stay and argue. I had chopped up pieces of body parts in my trunk and needed to not only get away from the police but dispose of the evidence without getting caught.

So, I left. The police chased me for five miles before I lost them. I have backup license plates on hand, so once I got to a safe area, I changed my plates and clothing, burnt the evidence, and drove home.

There are one hundred and sixty-two people in Seattle with the same make and model, but they'll never be able to pin anything on me even if they magically narrowed it down to me.

In the end, the police pinned the murders on a mentally unstable girl and an unknown accomplice. I figured the Society would look into the crime and find an unknown accomplice suspicious. Enough to up and move.

But after looking into Sibby myself, I found that she was born into a fucked-up cult and wanted for the murder of her father.

Her father rivaled Jim Jones, spouting about being God's disciple and tricking hundreds of people into believing in his word.

He was a rich man who came from old money. He spent his riches on building a compound for his followers, confining them to a stretch of land for the rest of their lives. That's where Sibby was born and raised, up until she committed a heinous crime and fled.

There are reports of Sibby's mother committing suicide via poison, and it seems that's what led to the broken doll finally snapping. She snuck into her father's bedroom at night with a knife and stabbed him to death.

One hundred and fifty-three times to be precise. Rage was a factor. Sibby made it clear that she is perfectly capable of stabbing a man past her body's physical limits if angry enough. Robert was proof of that.

It took three days for them to connect Sibby to murders across the country. All cities that Satan's Affair has rooted the haunted carnival in have numerous cases of missing person reports in each location for the past five years.

If all the people reported missing from Satan's Affair had connections to her, Sibby has killed around fifty people.

I was genuinely surprised that the haunted fair didn't come under fire sooner with so many reports connected to them, but then I had learned that most of the victims were lowlifes, with very few people that cared enough to look for them.

Whether Sibby was correct in thinking they were demons is subjective. But what I can say is that even though none of them have records, save for a few petty crimes, it doesn't seem like they were good people either.

So, in the end, an unknown accomplice will be looked into, but with Sibby's past coupled with her claims of having henchmen, there's a good chance the murders of the four men will be chalked up to what I had hoped.

Wrong place, wrong time.

She really was the perfect scapegoat. I just wish I didn't fucking care.

That was three nights ago, and with the threat of the Society relocating, Jay has been monitoring Savior's closely. We've hacked into their camera feed on the main floor, and by the looks of it, they're staying still.

Obviously, no cameras reside in the dungeon. That'd be too easy.

"Any word on the building being demolished?" I ask Jay, my phone to my ear.

"Nope," he replies, popping the P dramatically. I want to pop him in the face for it. "You going in tonight?" he asks.

"Yes," I say, rolling my head and cracking my neck. The tension has already started seeping into my shoulders. I have a sinking feeling I'm going to see some shit that will threaten to send me into a tailspin.

But I have to maintain control. If I don't, I will die before I save those kids, and that's just not an option.

"Still keeping an eye on Addie?"

Jay sighs. "Yes..." he trails off, and I can feel the question hanging from the tip of his tongue. I want to reach through the receiver, snatch it, and crush it before he can speak, but he's too quick. "So, uh, this is like the love of your life or some shit?" he asks awkwardly.

The sigh I try to keep internal bleeds out and through the phone. "The one and only," I clip, my tone signaling that I don't want to speak about Addie right now, but the fucker doesn't ever listen when it comes to my personal life.

"She feel the same?"

I can't help the slight smirk from forming on my face. "She's getting there," I reply cryptically.

Jay finally takes the hint and drops it. "Well, you will be happy to know that no one has gone in and out of her house except her friend for the past three days."

Mark's threat still rings around in my head. Like a stray bullet ricocheting in a constant loop inside my brain.

The Society knows about Addie, making her a target. They may love children, but they absolutely do not pass up beautiful young women to sell and ship off to other countries. There's no shortage of demand when it comes to the skin trade. Evil people have their tastes, and some prefer their victims to be fully grown women just as much as some prefer them adolescent.

The tension in my shoulders grows as my thoughts run away from me. A single moment—that's all it takes for her to go missing. Vanish out of thin air within a short trek from her car to the grocery store entrance.

She doesn't know the danger she's in, but that will change soon. I refuse to hide the truth from her. And I'm sure she's not going to like hearing that our self-defense lessons are going to be ramping up.

Now I just have to figure out how to keep my dick out of her during those lessons.

Fuck it. Won't happen.

I smile, knowing she will try to use those moves on me, but the thought only makes my cock thicken in my slacks.

I haven't seen her since the House of Mirrors, and I know deep down that makes her angry. She probably feels like I fucked her and got bored, but that's the furthest thing from the truth.

I'm a fucking fiend for her now. It's been the most challenging three days of my life staying away, but I need to infiltrate Savior's and save these kids. I haven't had a minute to myself, and as much as I ache for my little mouse, these kids need me more.

This time when more tension rolls in, it's because of my visceral need to be inside Addie, fucking her into oblivion and making her delirious with how hard I'm going to make her come.

"Be ready, I'll be at Savior's in an hour," I warn Jay before hanging up the phone.

For now, I need to push Addie out of my head. But later tonight, I'll be pushing myself inside her so deeply, I'll be ingrained in every crevice inside her body.

"There's some pretty high-profile people there," Jay announces through the small chip in my ear. I'll be taking it out before I get out of the car. Currently, I'm in a line, waiting for valet parking.

"Including the president," Jay tacks on at the end.

I inwardly sigh, rolling my neck from the stress spearing into my muscles. This job is hard on my body, even when I'm not shooting people in the face and actively avoiding flying bullets. Maybe I can entice Addie to give me another massage later. I'd love nothing more than to return the favor.

"Anyone I should be concerned about?"

I hear Jay typing a mile a second in the background, the keys clacking obnoxiously. I have asked the fucker to get a less noisy keyboard, but he insists the loud clicking brings him peace.

And as much as it annoys me, we get so little of peace in our daily lives. So if a fucking obnoxious ass keyboard brings him some sort of semblance of it, then I won't give him shit.

Well, not too much, at least.

"Several senators and governors, along with a few A-list celebrit—ah shit, is that Timothy Banks? Come *on*, don't tell me he's a part of this shit too?!"

I roll my eyes, shaking my head at Jay's theatrics.

"Jay," I snap. "Focus."

There are only a few cars ahead of me, so I don't have much time to talk until I can get in and put the chip back in without anyone noticing.

I'm not walking past their security systems with it in my ear. I'd be shot and killed right then and there.

"Sorry," Jay mutters, his voice now somber from finding out his favorite actor is a pedophile.

"Really, Jay. We know a lot of celebrities are involved."

"But, *Tim Banks,* man? Fuck. Anyways. There's no one I can see at the moment that is of high concern. Not any more than they already are, considering you're walking into a pit of pedos. Let me know when the chip is back in, I'll keep you updated."

Just as it's my turn, I pluck the earpiece from my ear and slip it deep into an inner pocket with lead lining. Handing over my keys to the stone-faced valet guy, I round the car and pause in front of Savior's.

Snapping my jacket closed, I refrain from cracking my neck again. Tonight is about making an impression. Others will know that I was friends with Mark, and after his unfortunate death, they will be looking at me.

Mark has spread my name around to plenty of his colleagues at this point.

I may be new to Savior's, but they've been expecting me.

Savior's looks like the type of club I'd expect to run an elite sex dungeon and perform rituals.

The main room is massive. The stage is right in the middle of the room, a large pole front and center with a girl swinging around it—completely naked. Her tits bounce as she lifts herself up, wrapping her long legs around the pole and bending backwards, her breasts on full display as she gyrates her hips.

I don't bother looking at her body. What I look at are her eyes. And it takes control to keep my jaw from clenching when I see the telltale glazed film in them. Black circles decorate the flesh beneath her dead gaze, and I want nothing more than to carry her out of here and get her somewhere safe.

Biting back the anger, I chant to myself in my head that all these girls will be saved. Just like the other clubs, I'm going to get them all out. There will be nothing left of these fucking gentlemen's clubs when I'm done.

And then I'll move on to the next city, the next state, the next country if I have to.

I refocus on the rest of the club as I work to keep my face blank and my breathing even.

Evidently, I've walked into a place where people enjoy the taste and look of blood.

The ambiance is dark and moody and shows clear signs of sadism. The lighting is dim, the shadows swallowed by the black walls and furniture.

A deep red, the color of blood, is accented across the entire area. Red frames around old age paintings that indicate devil worship and sacrifice. Red shades around the mini lamps adorned on each wall. Red glasses, ashtrays, and drinks… And red heels and outfits that are covered in real diamonds and crystals.

Though I wouldn't exactly consider their clothes as outfits. More like strings of fabric and jewels.

Yet, they managed to make the place drip with elegance and money.

"Zack! So nice to see you here," a voice booms from behind me. Arranging a calm, but pleasant look onto my face, I turn and see a man I recognize very well. Daniel Boveri.

He's a lawyer for the president, and someone Mark mingled with often. He's a charming man—the tall, dark, and handsome type. With his thick black eyebrows set low over dark eyes that give him a menacing look, black hair, and a snake-like smile. He's pushing his fifties, but the man isn't hurting for women.

Dan exudes confidence and from the few times we've spoken, I understand why he's a lawyer for the president. He's incredibly manipulative.

"Dan, nice to see you," I respond, shaking his hand firmly when he holds his out to me.

"I was wondering when I'd see you here. Mark spoke about bringing you a few times."

"I'm sure he did," I murmur. That's news to me.

"Very unfortunate what happened to him. Can't believe some psycho little girl managed to do all that to those four. Still never found their bodies, did they?"

I shake my head empathetically, appearing to be just as shocked by Mark's death.

"Not that I'm aware of, man. Doesn't she keep talking about henchmen or some shit?" I ask with a mocking smirk on my face. I hate to use Sibby's mental illness to my advantage, but in this case, if it means saving hundreds of children and women, I'll weaponize whatever I need to in order to see that I complete my mission.

God, I even sound a little like her. Sibby believes killing evil people is her mission in life, something she was born to do.

And I can't entirely disagree with the thought when you're constantly risking your life to do something you feel is right. Even if other people will see it as wrong.

Dan laughs, the tone cruel and judgmental. "Yeah, thought I heard someone mention that."

I scoff in disgust. "Girl says she had five henchmen. If they only saw one getting away, can't imagine if there's more out there on the loose."

That little remark will circulate and taint the minds of the Society. If they believe that Sibby's henchmen are real, then it'll keep suspicions low. At least until the therapists get to Sibby and realize that her henchmen are all in her imagination.

By then, these fuckers will all have bullets in their heads, and the children they exploit will be long gone.

Dan and I mingle for the next several hours. The women here are abused, all blitzed out of their minds and accepting of the punishments for doing nothing wrong.

A metal chalice out of the corner of my eye catches my attention. It's sitting atop a table, an older man drinking from it steadily. Subtly glancing around, I notice a few more. They look exactly like the goblets that were used in the leaked videos.

My heart sinks, but so far, I can't see any signs that blood is in them.

"Are you looking to be initiated into the club?" Dan asks casually, pulling my attention to him sipping his Scotch and eyeing me over the rim of his glass.

His gaze is probing and studious, but I give him nothing in return. The muscles in my face stay firmly in place as I respond, "Aren't I already in?"

A smirk crosses Dan's face, and with the dim lighting and the dancing shadows, it makes him appear sinister. I don't even blink at the sight.

I'm much fucking scarier.

"Not even close, brother."

I quirk a brow, sipping at my own whiskey. When I give him an expectant look, he chuckles.

"If you truly want it, you need to have an acquired taste."

"I have many acquired tastes," I say, adding a bit of darkness to my tone. Not hard to do when I'm not lying. Their tastes are spilling the blood of the innocent, and mine just happen to be killing everyone who does so.

"Pray tell, what do those tastes entail?" Dan inquires, his tone whimsical and almost amused.

I shrug a shoulder nonchalantly and take a sip of whiskey while pulling my phone out with the other hand. I pull up a picture of Daniella, a girl I saved five years ago.

She's deep in a safehouse, as she was an orphan with no home to return to when I rescued her. It's an innocent picture of her dressed in Barbie pajamas. What sells the illusion is the haunted look in her eyes and the bruises marring her skin. The picture was taken after we first rescued her. She was ten at the time, and I made sure to ask her permission before showing this to anyone.

This is the first time I've had to befriend pedophiles before I killed them, but I knew that if I was ever going to convince them I was just like them, I'd need to show proof.

And I'll be damned if I show a random girl off the internet and risk their safety. At least with Daniella, it's an old picture and I can ensure nothing will ever happen to her.

Handing the phone to him, I say lowly, "My latest toy."

The words taste like fucking tar on my tongue, but I force them out anyways.

Dan's brows skyrocket to his forehead, but an evil, happy little smile forms on his face.

"You share?"

I nearly break his hand when he hands me the phone back, his gaze lingering on the picture. Instead, I tuck the phone back in my pocket and bare my teeth.

"I get jealous."

His head tips back, and a booming laugh echoes across the space. The noise of the room swallows the sound, but it feels like dynamite in my ears.

"Understood, my friend. And when they grow too old?"

I smile salaciously. "Organs are a hit in the black market."

He grins. "I think you'd be perfect for initiation then. Next one is a week from now. You interested?"

"What's this initiation entail?"

"The expectations will be asked of you when the time comes. But when it's over, you get lots of that," he enlightens, nodding towards my tucked away phone. He flashes a feral smile. "Lots of that, in whatever shape, size and gender."

"And this is safe?"

Dan shrugs a shoulder. "We had a spy, leaking videos, but the Society is confident they've found the traitor. And those videos haven't been seen. They were immediately taken down once they were uploaded."

False. The particular place they're uploaded on the dark web, I had a signal put in place. The second that video was posted, Jay or I would immediately get a notification. We had forty-five seconds to download it before it was removed.

That quick.

But it was plenty of time for *Z*.

Interesting that they believe they caught the mole. I've no way to verify that, but it doesn't matter anymore.

Where there was once a mole, is now a wolf.

I finish off the last of my whiskey in one swallow, relishing in the burn as it travels down my throat. I smile at him once more—a feral smile of my own. I feel the scars on my face crinkle and the demonic feeling swirling in my gut slipping through, glinting in my mismatched eyes. He takes it for what he wants to see it as.

"I'm in."

Chapter Thirty Three
The Manipulator

The light from the T.V. blares across the dark room as the news reporter's voice rings out.

"...The murders of the four government officials are still under investigation. The autopsy reports have been released to the public, revealing extreme torture before the men had died."

A mugshot of a girl is pictured on the screen. She's a pretty girl, with plain brown hair and brown eyes. The unsettling part is the look in her eyes. A single glance is all it takes to know that she's clearly unstable.

She was the broken doll I saw eating at the fair.

And she was in Annie's Playhouse that night. Hiding in the walls and watching every guest that came through. At one point, she looked at me and probably made a decision on whether she was going to kill me or not.

I shudder, knowing how close I could've come to death that night.

Snatching up the remote, I click off the T.V., shaking as I throw the remote back on the couch.

The asshole fucked me and then went and murdered a bunch of men with a psychotic chick.

Mark fucking Seinburg is one of the men, along with three other government officials I had met while standing in line for Annie's Playhouse. He had said he had business to take care of with a psycho chick, and for some reason, him going off to murder people was the last thing I had expected.

Stupid. That's what he does, *Addie. Murder people.*

The fear and anxiety are overwhelming. I knew he killed people. Arch's hands showing up on my doorstep was proof of that. His entire family being wiped out...

I *knew* he was a murderer. He admitted it. But somehow, seeing his heinous crimes broadcasted on live television is eye-opening. He murdered four government *politicians.*

This isn't just a boy playing dress-up with a mob boss's suit and handgun. Arch was insignificant in the grand scheme of things. But this... this is *big.*

Did Mark deserve it? Absolutely. But I was at his house. I was someone on his radar. And now that he's dead, what if they come for *me?*

Shit. You really are an idiot, Addie.

I rest my elbows on my knees and slump my head into my hands. My thoughts are spiraling out of control.

Who cares if it happened to be the most mind-blowing sex I've ever had in my life? And probably will ever have. The dude is just as crazy as the girl on screen.

He's killed before, and he's obviously going to do it again, and what if he tries to take out the goddamn President next? Or someone else with connections to some very unhinged people?

I just don't think I'm okay with that. I look up at the screen again, a news reporter standing in front of flashing siren lights at Satan's Affair.

I'm just not okay with *this*. With the fear that some terrifying people are going to come after me because Zade keeps killing off high-profile people. He's a goddamn serial killer.

I need to end things with him. For good.

It doesn't matter what he makes me feel. He's going to put my life in danger, over and over. And how does someone just... be okay with that?

I'm rocking in Gigi's old chair when a flash of movement outside my window catches my eye. My heart skips several beats when I find my shadow standing on the other side, several feet away with that damn red cherry blaring in the night.

Fuck. He's here.

He's not going to listen to reason when I tell him to leave me alone. He never did before, it won't be any different now. I need to figure out how the hell to get him away from me permanently. Maybe I'll look into that bodyguard Daya spoke about before.

But right now, the only thing I can do is call the police. They'll be here quick if I lie and say I'm in serious danger, and in the meantime, I'll try to convince him to leave.

Adrenaline and a heady mix of fear trickles into my bloodstream as I scramble up and away from the window and look for my phone.

Looking around frantically, I tear apart the living room in search of my phone. My heart is pounding, the sound resonating in my ears as my breath draws short and choppy.

It takes several minutes before I finally find my phone lodged beneath a couch cushion. When I straighten and glance out the window, I finally do freeze.

He's gone.

Oh my fuck, where did he go?

Hands trembling, I dial in the numbers. 9-1-. I feel his presence press into my back a moment before he plucks the phone from my hand. My breath hitches as he clears the numbers, and the phone disappears from view.

His breath tickles my ear as he leans in. "Were you about to call the police on me?" he tsks. "And here I thought we were past this."

My breath stutters. "I don't want to do this anymore, Zade. I-I don't want *you.*"

His quiet breathing is swallowed by the news reporter droning on in the background.

Finally, he says, "When did you become such a liar?"

Closing my eyes, I take a steadying breath. And then I lift my leg and stomp on his foot as hard as I can. He grunts, but before I can make a run for it, his arms encircle my waist and trap me against him.

"That's very naughty, little mouse. And you know what happens when you're naughty?" A heartbeat passes before he finally growls into my ear, "You get fucking eaten."

Fire licks at my insides, igniting my entire being from the inside out. His words cause an elicit hunger to claw its way down from my throat, through my stomach, and straight to the sensitive spot between my legs.

But I will not give in so easily. I will not let this man continue to get inside my head—my body.

"I'm not your fucking prey."

"Then why do you let me consume you?" he whispers before encircling his hand around my throat and squeezing tight. Stubble pierces my skin as his cheek rubs down the side of my own before his mouth descends on my neck. A sharp nip pulls a gasp from my lips.

His hand tightens further while my breath shortens. Words rise to my tongue, but they fail to release when a low growl vibrates from his chest, and throughout my body.

"You know how much I love it when you run," he rasps. His other hand travels across my stomach roughly before sliding up to my heaving breasts.

He cups one in his hand and squeezes. I feel the blood rise, rushing to my face as another whimper is wrung from my throat. My nipples are hardened into twin peaks, rubbing almost painfully against the fabric of my bra. Once he bares me completely, he'll see the evidence that I'm enjoying this far more than I should.

Somehow, that always seems to be the case with him.

"Stop it," I choke out, attempting to get away, but his grip holds firm, tightening around my throat until black pinpricks dot my vision.

"You don't want this, baby? You don't want to be full of my cock and discover a new religion each time I make you come?"

"You have a lot of faith in your abilities," I croak.

He chuckles, as deep and dark as the ocean. "You need faith to be a believer." He cups me between my legs. "And this pussy deserves to be worshipped."

My eyes shutter as his hot breath fans down the expanse of my chest. Goosebumps rise and a shiver crawls down my spine.

His fingers pinch my nipple through the fabric of my shirt and bra, tugging hard and wringing a pained cry from my throat.

Yet, my body reacts without permission. I grind back into him, feeling the hard expanse of him pressing into my back.

The hand around my throat pulses, tightening almost to unbearable levels. I rise on the tips of my toes to decrease the pressure, but he doesn't let up.

"Does it scare you?" he whispers, his breath tickling my ear. "Or does it make your pussy wet knowing that I hold your life in my hands, and I allow you to breathe?"

Blood rushes to my head, and fear begins to pump through my veins. Just when I think he's not going to stop, his hand loosens, and I greedily suck in precious air.

But he doesn't let me breathe for much longer. He twists my body around and backs me towards the wall beside the T.V., smiling viciously as I stumble away from him and towards exactly where he wants me to be. When I'm a foot away, he grabs me and slams me into the wall, pressing the entire length of his body against mine. Before I can take another breath, his hand is once more encircling my throat, and his mouth is on mine.

Just like he said, I let him consume me. Tears burn the back of my eyes as his mouth tears my lips apart, feasting on my tongue without permission.

I can't do this.

I can't fucking let him do this to me.

Ripping my mouth away, I push him back, but he doesn't move a fucking inch.

"Stop!" I snap, struggling against him. "I'm not letting you do this. You just murdered dangerous people, Zade—which means they have dangerous friends. It's like Max all over again. You're a *monster.*"

The hand still wrapped around my throat tightens before he thumps my head against the wall, ceasing my struggles.

"And you're the sweet little angel that I'm going to drag down to hell with me," he rasps, his voice deep and husky as he whispers his omen into my ear.

"I hate you," I spit, glaring with all the disgust I can muster in my body. He just won't fucking listen.

He only smiles, the gesture mocking. "And I will never let you fuck me again, Zade." I'm not ashamed by the way my voice wobbles. Let him hear how serious I am. It's not fear making my tone erratic, it's the animosity bleeding out from my soul.

He presses deeper into me, a snarl forming on his face. He looks vicious and enticing all in the same breath, like the handsome devil sitting on a throne of bones.

"Are you willing to bet your life?" he asks, his smooth voice a stark contrast to mine. He grinds his pelvis against me, the hard, thick length of him digging into my stomach.

When I don't answer, he smiles. "I think my little mouse is a *liar*," he growls the last word into my ear, sending violent tremors throughout my body.

His mouth caresses my cheek, the soft flesh of his lips skating lightly towards my lips. His mouth skims against mine, eliciting electric shivers from every spot that our skin clashes.

I suck in a sharp breath, the ever-present fear and adrenaline still steadily pumping into my bloodstream, nearly drugging me with the potency and making me delirious.

"Yes," I whisper, answering his question before I snap my leg up and knee him right between the legs. He manages to dodge the brunt of the hit, but it gives me enough room to slip from his grasp and run.

A loud, cruel laugh rings out as I nearly rip the door off its hinges before taking off into the night air.

Cold, wet droplets of rain splash onto my skin, soaking me immediately, but I don't let the downpour deter me.

Terror pushes me forward, my legs kicking as I bolt off into the woods. My feet slip from the slickness on the porch, and it's then that I remember I'm fucking barefoot.

Too late now. I forge on, gritting my teeth against the bite of rocks in my feet as I bolt across the driveway.

As a child, I had always wanted to explore these woods. They're deep and incredibly easy to get lost in. My mother and Nana never let me step foot inside them as a kid. Somehow, that restriction carried into my adult life.

The warnings I received as a child subconsciously kept me from ever going into the woods and exploring. And now, I wish I had.

It doesn't even take a minute before I'm completely turned around. The only light offered is from the moon, and even that is weak due to the canopies of trees clouding the sky.

I keep pumping my legs, harder and faster. Too scared to stop. Too frightened of the devil nipping at my heels.

Until I trip over a root, my body pitching forward and then crashing noisily into the ground. I land awkwardly on my hands, pain flaring in both wrists as they give beneath my weight. My toe throbs from where it caught on the root, my feet bloodied and abused from running barefoot in the goddamn woods.

I'm breathing heavily, heaving out panicked puffs as I roll onto my back. I have to shut my eyes from the onslaught of rain, blurring my vision and leaking into my nose and mouth.

Raising a hand to cover my face, I open my eyes and look around.

I can't see him, but that doesn't mean he isn't close.

My chest is tight, and I work to calm my erratic heartbeat and take deep, long breaths so I can chill the fuck out long enough to hear if he's coming.

The wind rustles the leaves on the ground, stirring up dirt and debris and drawing out goosebumps across my skin. The sound is ominous. Threatening. Like any moment, the wind will part the trees, and I will see my shadow standing there, watching and waiting.

My soaked t-shirt and leggings provide no protection from the unrelenting rain. The clothing molds to my body, trapping the cold beneath the fabric and allowing it to seep beneath my skin. My bones rattle from the violent shivers that wrack my body.

Sitting up, I suck in a deep breath and hold it, training my ears to listen for footsteps. It takes several seconds before I hear a snap of a twig. The sound comes from directly behind me.

I whip my head around, my eyes frantically searching the woods and my breath once more speeding up. Slowly, I rise to my feet, ignoring the pain pulsing in my battered hands and feet.

I need to hide.

Just as I take a silent step, I hear another snap of a twig. My heart jumps wildly as a foot appears in my field of vision. Like a demon rising from a fire pit, I watch him emerge from between two trees. My eyes widen, my mouth drying from the sight of a massive man stepping out from the shadows, a hood drawn over his face as he stalks towards me.

With that, I turn and I run.

I run with everything I have, pumping my legs and arms as fast as they will go. But in the end, it's for nothing. I only make it ten feet before a hand is wrapping around my arm and jerking me backward. My body goes flying into his, crashing into his hard chest and knocking the breath out of my lungs.

I struggle against him, fighting like hell to get away, but he's too big—too strong. He easily overpowers me, circling an arm around my waist and trapping me against his heated body.

Hot breath whispers against my ear a moment before his deep voice penetrates the haze of panic and terror circulating in my brain.

"You can't escape me, little mouse. I will always find you." He grabs my face, clenching my cheeks tightly between his large hand. The pinch of the soft flesh digging into my teeth produces a pained moan from my throat. An answering, low growl rumbles from his chest right before he asks, "Are you ready to be eaten?"

Using the hand gripping my face to turn me around, he pulls my body tightly against his. But I won't go down without fighting.

I thrash my arms and kick my legs, twisting my body to get loose from his unforgiving hold. My violent struggles cause my foot to slip and my body to go teetering backwards.

We both fall, but the impact of my body against the unforgiving ground is saved by his hand catching both of us, keeping him suspended while his arm holds me tight against his body.

Of course, this still doesn't deter me.

"Let me go, you fucking maniac! I will fuckin—"

"Do what?" he hisses, cutting me off with an angry growl. He traps my body between his and the cold ground, the freezing temperatures invading my body.

Grabbing both of my wrists, he pins them above my head in one hand, while the other wraps around the back of my neck.

"Tell me, Addie. Do you think killing pedophiles is wrong?" he asks sharply, his one light eye shining bright in the darkness.

"I think killing people is wrong," I shout in his face, breathing heavily and allowing my body a moment's rest. I'm scared, but my body is exhausted.

"Why?" he volleys back. "Because society told you it was? Because humans fabricated morals so they can control and manipulate people into law and order? Do you think other mammals follow the same morals and rules? We're all fucking animals, baby. The only difference is I don't suppress mine."

Panting and angry, I buck against him, trying to rear him off me, but it accomplishes nothing. It's like an elephant sitting on a hamster.

He presses my wrists tighter against the ground as he rearranges himself, using his knees to spread my legs and settle between them.

Even in the cold rain, he's as hard as a fucking rock.

"You're going to get me killed!" I argue. "Because you had to be sick and torture them so badly, it made national news!"

"You want to know what's fucking sick, Addie? Those men you're so upset about dying are the same men that hurt, rape, and torture innocent fucking children and get off on it. They thrive off of it. Do you think any amount of punishment in this world will ever make up for even one child they tortured and killed?"

I snap my mouth shut, tears burning my retinas.

"And what's worse is that despite claiming you as my own, the Society had already marked you before I even came into the picture. Which means you are in danger, whether he's dead or not. Did you know he tried to have you kidnapped at Satan's Affair? While you were running through Annie's Playhouse, he was in the middle of siccing his dogs to kidnap you. And I made sure that didn't fucking happen, Addie.

"If you thought you had any fucking chance of getting rid of me, get it out of your head. You need my protection more than you need my cock, but I fully intend on giving you both."

My eyes widen and my heart drops. The Society has been targeting me? Jesus Christ, what the fuck did I do in my past life to deserve this shit?

I was in so much danger and never realized it. Never even felt it looming nearby.

Because the man pinning me to the ground kept me safe and protected so I could enjoy my night.

My lip trembles as he continues. "He was an evil man, Addie. And one of the worst things he ever did was put you in danger. The worst thing I ever did was make it so easy for him to find you."

The tables have turned. Where I once accused Zade of failing to keep me hidden from Mark, I am now confessing the harsh truth. He never really stood a chance against fate.

"You couldn't have stopped him from noticing me," I admit on a soft whisper.

"Maybe not, but I brought you further into his sight. I had hoped claiming you would save you, but Mark was always going to turn you in. And every motherfucker who even comes within a mile of your house is going to have my knife in their throats.

"I have never pretended to be a good person. But what I did do was create my own fucking morals to live by. I will keep killing every deranged individual who resides on this goddamn planet if it means children don't have to die, and you don't have to live in danger."

My lip wobbles, and all of the fight I had burning inside of me bleeds out in one breath.

I have nothing to say. No argument.

I've been holding so tightly onto the notion that all murder is wrong, but I need to let that go. Because Zade is right, whether he came into my life or not, I would always end up in danger. And I can't get upset every time he kills someone who meant me harm.

If that makes me selfish, then I don't care anymore.

Whether I like it or not... Zade isn't going anywhere. And it's far more exhausting holding onto morals that do nothing but fight against the one thing keeping me safe.

I study his face, needing to ask one last question.

"Have you killed an innocent person?"

"What's your definition of innocent?" he questions, leaning in close until his minty breath skates over my cold, wet face. "People like Archie? Who have hurt others, but there was always a chance of redemption, right?"

I swallow, opening my mouth to respond, but he leans closer, his lips mere centimeters away from mine. The words die on my tongue while his flicks out, licking a droplet off my lip. The small touch should be insignificant, like a butterfly landing on your finger. But instead, it felt like a lightning bolt traveling down my spine and straight to my core.

"Do you think there's redemption for me?" he whispers, the tenor of his voice dark and sinful.

I lick my lips, searching for the words before I ask, "Do you want there to be?"

The rest of his body molds into mine, creating a dangerous cyclone of fire and ice inside of me. The frozen ground and the raging heat of his body war with each other, while I try to fight past the delirium his close proximity is causing.

He grinds his pelvis into mine, eliciting a sharp pleasure from between my legs. Without conscious thought, my back arches and a moan slips free.

"If my redemption resides somewhere within you, then I will spend the rest of my life searching for it inside of you." He flexes his hips again, wringing another breathless moan from my lips. "I will fill every inch of you, Adeline. And in time, my redemption will become your salvation."

His words create a visceral reaction deep inside of me. There's no stopping the flood of arousal between my legs, no more than I can control the intense need to hand over every bit of my soul to him on a silver platter.

He's still a stalker, Addie.

The small voice inside my head is becoming weightless. So small and insignificant that its words are no longer holding power. I'm becoming annoyed with the voice of reason because nothing I feel for Zade is reasonable. He stirs up emotions too powerful for reason and logic. Too strong to be eclipsed by a little voice in my head.

"What if I don't want you to?" I croak, though my words are in direct contrast to my actions. One leg hikes over his hip, bringing him closer while my mouth still attempts to push him away.

"What if the last thing I want is you inside me?" His lips skim over mine, traveling down my cheek and to my jawline. He nips harshly, his teeth pulling out another moan as pain and pleasure stab at my nerves.

This time when he grinds into me, I meet his thrust, desperate for him to be closer. Still, I can't give up, even though my body already has.

"What if I come to hate the feeling of you inside me?"

Finally, he releases my pinned wrists, grabs the collar of my shirt, and tears it in half. I gasp from the brutal onslaught of cold rain pelting my skin. My back arches as his hands sweep up harshly across my stomach, sending waves of electricity dancing across my flesh. His touch alone is making me feel crazed. Nothing has ever felt so fucking good.

And then he's clawing at my bra, exposing my breasts, before that too is torn away from my body.

"You would hate the feeling of coming so hard that your body gives out?"

Before I can answer, he nips at my jaw again, softer this time, before moving down to my neck. His mouth pauses over the sensitive spot right below my ear. He releases a single breath, and that action is the only warning I have before his teeth clamp down.

The only response I'm capable of is a garbled scream. My eyes roll, his tongue lapping at the sting and drawing out the intense pleasure.

Sharp bites descend down past my collarbone until one of my nipples is being sucked into his hot mouth. A strangled cry releases, and I shudder beneath his lashing tongue.

My back arches while I claw at his hair, tugging on the strands just as brutally as he sucks on my nipple.

Finally, his teeth release me, and I take a brief moment to shoot fire out of my lungs. "I can make myself come harder than you ever could."

I feel his smile, and I don't need to see it to know how cruel it is. He lifts his head, just enough to peer down into my eyes.

My heart sinks, and my instincts sense the doom long before his words confirm it.

"Are you prepared to prove that to me, little mouse? Because if not, I'm going to make you eat your fucking words."

Chapter
Thirty Four
The Manipulator

I've never been religious, despite my berating a phantom in the sky for constantly testing my sanity. But in this moment, I seriously hope that something is looking out for me. Because I have a feeling when Zade is finished with me, my soul will be decimated, and nothing will be able to save me from his damnation.

Swallowing thickly, I ask, "How do you plan on doing that?"

I try to insert an ounce of confidence, but the calculating look on Zade's face completely shreds that notion. I shiver, but not from the relentless rain soaking my skin.

Instead of answering verbally, he reaches down and grips the waistband of my leggings. In one sharp tug, he's ripping the fabric down my legs and flinging it somewhere out in the forest.

Definitely won't be getting those back.

My eyes round when he harshly jerks my yellow thong, the lace easily tearing beneath his strength.

"Zade..." I gasp, attempting to close my legs to block the freezing rain from my exposed core. He deflects my attempts, prying my knees apart until the rain batters against my center. I squeal from the sensation, sucking in a sharp breath.

Zade may resemble a God, but he's never been the forgiving type.

Adjusting his grip to the underside of my thighs, he pushes my legs back until my knees are hiked up to my ears, and my pussy is completely bared to the unforgiving elements.

"Zade!" I shout, my hands shooting out to cover myself.

"Touch yourself, little mouse. Let me see how hard you can make yourself come," he orders, his voice thick with desire.

"I'm not—" He bars his left arm across both thighs and uses his now free hand to swipe my hands away. Before I can ask what the hell he's doing, he delivers a sharp slap straight on my pussy.

I yelp loudly, pain lancing through my clit and up my spine. The only reprieve is with his body now leaning over me, the rain is no longer pounding against my sensitive core.

"What the fu—"

"What did I just tell you to do, Adeline? Don't make me ask you again."

My mouth flops, the words having escaped me. He stares up at me, his face cast in a severe expression that brokers no room for argument.

Biting my lip, I contemplate arguing with him. But it takes all of two seconds to come to a single conclusion.

I don't want to.

Keeping my gaze locked on his, I slowly slide my hand back to the apex of my thighs, the gathering slickness having nothing to do with the rain.

Reluctantly, as if he can't decide if he wants to watch my face or my hand, he pulls his gaze away and settles those yin-yang eyes on my pussy. Right as I'm dipping a finger inside me.

His nostrils flare, and his hand on my thigh becomes bruising.

"Fuck," he mouths silently, his eyes flaring with heat. Heat that extends to me, spreading like wildfire until the pattering rain against my flesh is a balm to the incessant burn.

Dragging my finger out of my pussy, I circle my finger across my clit, my mouth falling open and a husky moan slipping past my lips.

Pleasure exudes from where my digit continues to circle, and I can't help but rock my hips against my own hand, seeking a touch past my own. A touch that would be rougher, firmer—better.

Ignoring my body's silent plea, I focus on my ministrations, my head kicking back as my orgasm builds.

Zade lifts up, removing his arm from across my thighs and taking up his former position of kneeling before me with his hands firmly holding my knees to the ground on either side of me.

This way, his body is no longer providing protection against the rain, the cold drops of water like ice between my legs.

I lift my head, my heart thundering as Zade's eyes sear through me. The knowledge that he is watching everything I'm doing to myself only heightens the pleasure. I've never been so turned on in my life, and the unfiltered moans are impossible to control.

I'm too lost in the moment to care about how loud I am. Too high on the euphoria coursing through my system as I reach that cliff.

Sensing my stiffening limbs, Zade looks up at me and whispers, "Show me how deeply I've ruined you."

My brows contort, and my mouth falls open as I topple over that edge. I cry out, my hips rocking relentlessly, searching for something more.

The orgasm that washes over me is sharp and quick. Before, I would've been satisfied with that. But now, with the cruel man kneeling before me, I feel fucking robbed.

I keep my mouth closed, the downpour and wind seeming silent now that my moans have ceased.

A wicked smirk forms on his lips, emphasizing the scars on his face.

"Was it better?" he asks, but it sounds like he already knows the answer.

I nod, not brave enough to speak my lie but too prideful to say no. For a brief moment, it feels like the world around me stills. The rain, the wind, the leaves on the trees. And then everything is speeding up, too fast for me to stop him from moving my hand and delivering another sharp slap to my pussy.

Instinctively, I try to close my legs to abate the pain, but he pins my knees back, leaning over me menacingly.

The dormant fear flares back up again as he stares down at me.

"Lie to me again," he threatens. "My patience only stretches so far."

I swallow the lump in my throat, my wide eyes locked on his.

"Was it better?"

It's at this moment, my brain decides to remind me that I'm in the middle of the woods, alone, with a very dangerous man. A man who had tortured and murdered four men only three nights ago.

"No," I whisper, eyeing him carefully. I'm tense, waiting to see what his next move will be. Zade has always been unpredictable. That feeling is nothing new.

He won't hurt you, Addie.

No, but maybe I want him to.

He releases me and stands. "Get up," he clips.

Shock renders me frozen, but my brain catches up after a few seconds and I'm scrambling to my feet.

I'm readying to ask... I don't even know, but before I can figure it out, he's bending down and grabbing the back of my thighs. He lifts me up, my legs instinctively curling around his waist. My sensitive center clashes with his hard cock straining in his jeans, nestling firmly between the folds of my pussy.

A soft whimper escapes, and I'm still too shocked to move or say anything as he begins to carry me, assumingly back towards my house.

"What's happening?" I finally manage, shuddering as every step rubs his jeans against my overstimulated clit.

"I'm going to remind you how good it feels to be mine."

Zade's steps are purposeful as he carries me, the silence between us strained with terrifying promises. The rain hasn't relented, seeming only to grow heavier as time passes.

I've no idea how he knows where to go, and I'm both impressed and suspicious. The only reason he knows these woods so well is because he's spent a lot of time in them. Stalking me.

Is he hiding the dead bodies in there? The question is lingering on the end of my tongue, but I let it die. I don't want to upset the small, albeit shaky, truce we've seemed to reach.

His large palms cup my bare asscheeks, the tips of his fingers a mere inch from my entrance. He doesn't explore, the teasing touch setting me aflame and flooding me with anticipation.

He's driving me mad with desire, and it's only fair I return the favor. If he takes me on the cold, wet ground, I'd be glad for it.

The smile that graces my lips is nothing short of evil.

My lips trace the column of his throat, brushing so softly that the touch merely feels like a whisper. His grip tightens, and my smile grows. Parting my mouth, my tongue darts out and licks a path from the base of his throat to the spot behind his ear.

A growl vibrates against my tongue, spurring me into action.

He marked me relentlessly so many months ago. Isn't it fair I mark him, too?

I bite down on that spot, lapping and sucking at the flesh trapped between my teeth until I'm sure the skin is bruised. And then I retreat and find a new spot to mark, over and over as he gnashes his teeth, hands gripping me with bruising force.

"Addie," he growls, his voice guttural and so deep, it sounds demonic.

I trail my lips up to his ear and bite down, sucking the lobe into my mouth. And then I withdraw, gliding my teeth sharply against the flesh as it pops free.

"What's wrong?" I whisper into his ear. "Can't handle what you dish out?"

I nip at his neck again, delighting in the sound of his control slipping and a moan slipping free. It's the sexiest sound I've ever heard, and I'm nearly feral with the need to bring it out of him again.

The light from my front porch is just piercing through the trees when he gives in, slamming me against a tree trunk, my bare back scraping against the rough bark. His jeans are undone in record time, his cock bursting free from the confines and driving up inside me before I can process it.

I scream from the intrusion, his cock stretching me so suddenly that all I can feel is fire. But he doesn't relent, fucking me against the tree until I'm clamping down on him, an orgasm tearing through me that nearly causes permanent eye damage from how hard they roll.

He spills inside of me on a hoarse shout, ramming me so deeply into the tree, I swear there will be an imprint of my ass.

I'm sure the squirrels will find that fascinating.

Pulling out of me, he harshly tears me away from the tree and speed walks the rest of the way back. A visceral energy radiates off him, and I can't tell if it's full of anger or desire.

My back is on fire, accompanied by the dull throb radiating between my legs. It's the sweetest agony I've ever felt.

In the duration of the trek back to my house, my brain has come back to Earth, and yet nothing has changed.

That unsettles me more than anything.

The fact that I'm no longer delirious from fear or bliss, and still, my desire and need for this man hasn't lessened in the slightest. If anything, it's only grown with the weight of anticipation hanging over my head.

The small light hanging over my door is like a beacon. As if the house will make me feel any safer from the man holding me in his arms.

Instead of beelining towards the door as I expected, he heads for my car. Despite the back of my SUV being spacey, Zade is no small man, and being cramped in a small space with him suddenly feels intimidating.

If I change my mind, it'll be impossible to get away from him.

"Why not the house?"

"I'm not waiting any longer," he answers tightly.

His tone is serious, and if it wasn't for his still-hard dick currently trying to play tag with my stomach, I'd think he was mad at me.

Opening the back door, the barbarian nearly tosses me in, barely giving me enough time to scoot away before he's following in after me, slamming the door behind him.

The rain patters loudly against the car. It's a sound many sleep apps have tried to replicate, but nothing can ever come close to imitating the sound of Seattle rain.

I back myself into the opposite side of the car, but the second he realizes what I'm doing, he grabs both of my legs and drags me right back to him.

He hovers over me, my back pressing into the leather seat and instantly sticking to it like hot glue on paper.

It's now that my brain focuses on all the insignificant details. Like that I'm completely naked and he's fully dressed, and somehow, that makes me feel a little embarrassed.

Or that the scent of rain and dirt clings to both of us, yet somehow leather and smoke linger on his clothes. I notice how small this car feels with him in it and how incredibly tiny I feel with him crowding me.

Those things shadow over the details I'm too chicken to acknowledge. Like the fact that he's staring down at me so intently, it feels as if his retinas are electromagnetic, and he can see everything I'm hiding inside. I'm not brave enough to meet his stare.

Or that his hands are settled back on my waist, the coarseness of his skin sending delicious static shocks throughout my nerve endings.

He leans down close, until his lips are a mere inch from mine. My eyes snap to his, like two opposite magnets. I can't stop the force and once our gazes clash, all thoughts—all those details—are forgotten. I can't think of anything else but how much I want him to kiss me, touch me, and claim me as his, over and over until I'm too delirious to fight any longer.

"You like to pretend," he observes, a touch of amusement in his tone.

"Maybe I'm not," I retort.

"Maybe you're in denial."

I tighten my lips, refusing to answer.

He smiles knowingly, and the sight is devastating. While I'm busy having a mini heart attack, he pulls me in close, wrapping one arm around my waist while his other hand cups the back of my neck. His minty breath fans across my face, caressing my lips like a light breeze in the spring.

"What are you feeling right now?" he asks softly.

My breathing escalates. "Confined."

"Trapped?" he volleys back. My mouth tightens because while a part of me wants to say yes, the truth is that I don't.

I feel... safe.

Protected.

Treasured.

"One day, you will realize that you are not trapped in a prison," he murmurs roughly. "You are in my church where I am your God, and you are my equal. I'm not a jail, little mouse, I am your sanctuary."

My mouth dries. The tip of my tongue darts out, wetting my bottom lip and swiping across his lips. Just a brush, but enough to light a spark. An answering growl arises as I ask, "Does that make me a goddess?"

He pulls me impossibly closer, his lips now pressed against mine lightly. "Baby, you rule the fucking kingdom, and I will gladly bow to you."

I let him ensnare my lips between his in a vicious kiss before pulling away, my breath left behind. He goes to recapture them and growls when I evade him once more. Keeping my mouth dangerously close, I whisper against his tongue, "Prove it."

"Mmm," he hums, the sound of a beast growling from the depths of darkness. "I do love getting on my knees for you," he murmurs, nipping at my lips playfully. This time, he's the one to evade me, instead biting and licking until I'm bristling with need.

He only teases for a few moments before his mouth is crashing on to mine. The inferno in my body escapes from my throat and ignites our connected lips. Without thought, I arch into him, desperate to feel more of him against me.

His lips move over mine with raw hunger. He doesn't just kiss me. He fucks my mouth with his tongue. Traps my lips between his teeth and bites. Explores every inch of my mouth as he devours me.

And I let him. I let him consume me because I'm beginning to forget what it feels like to be whole without Zade. He's in every part of me.

I plunge my hands beneath his hoodie, clawing at his stomach and allowing myself to explore a body I've explored far too much.

A body I haven't explored *nearly* enough.

My fingers drift over his abs, familiarizing myself with the hard divots while he takes over my mouth once more. My nipples scrape against his chest, and I can't stop the moan that releases from my throat. The sound swirls in our mouths, and he rewards me with a harsh nip to my bottom lip, dragging the sensitive flesh between his teeth before letting it go with a *pop*.

He rears back and looks down at me, his eyes slowly taking in my naked form. The wet strands of my hair, now darkened to a mocha brown, are snaked all across my chest and the seat beneath me. Tendrils curl across my breasts and around my nipples, a sight his eyes snag on and can't seem to look away from.

"Your turn," I whisper. His eyes drift back to mine and hold. He doesn't look away, even as he lifts up and slides the hoodie over his head, exposing his bare torso.

I suck in a sharp breath, the tattoos covering his corded muscles and the various scars are a sight to fucking behold.

I want to know the story behind those scars. And wanting to know anything past how hard he's going to make me come is terrifying.

But I've always loved that feeling. I've always craved more of it.

After some maneuvering, he kicks off his boots and socks and manages to wrangle his wet jeans down his legs. It's a moment that would usually feel awkward, but with Zade, it only dries my mouth as he exposes his glorious body to me, inch by inch.

Chests pumping in tandem, we look each other over, our eyes thirsty as he settles back between my legs—this time, with nothing between us.

His mismatched eyes pin me against the seat. I couldn't move if I wanted to.

And that's the problem. I *don't* want to.

I love the way his fiery orbs trace over my body, like a paintbrush tracing the curves of a woman on a canvas. The wetness pooled between my legs is becoming too much—too heavy.

Too painful.

The quick fuck against the tree only took the edge off while simultaneously ramping up our need to toxic levels.

"I'm waiting for you to bow," I taunt in a husky whisper.

His eyes dilate and his nostrils flare. My words hang in the air like the oxygen has been sucked out of the room. A tense pause, and he snaps.

He grabs my biceps and yanks me up. Turning me towards the gap between the driver and passenger seat, he directs, "Bend over between the seats."

I do as he says, keeping my knees on the backseat bench while I fit my body in the small gap between the two seats, planting my hands on either side for balance.

Zade leans forward, grabbing the seatbelt on the passenger side and looping it around my body before clicking it in the driver's side buckle.

"What are you…" He shushes me, repeating the process with the driver's side seatbelt. When he's finished, I'm completely strapped in place, unable to move. It does allow me enough leeway to turn my head and look back at Zade.

Like a king on a throne, he sits on the bench behind me, arranging himself between my legs so my ass is directly in his face. Butterflies hatch in my stomach at the sight of Zade sitting behind me, his legs splayed wide and his hard cock jutting up past his belly button. From this angle, I have no idea how it ever fit inside me.

He grins at me. "I'm too big for this car, baby, so this is the closest I can get to bowing right now. But I'll be sure to get on my knees for you later."

And just like in the House of Mirrors, he lifts my ass up until my knees are no longer grounded, the seatbelts digging into my sensitive flesh, and feasts on my pussy like a starved man.

Like I'm his last meal, just as he asked me to be not too long ago.

My eyes roll as his tongue laps up my cunt, circling my clit and spearing into my opening. It's too much—too good. I force myself to find something to focus on, to draw out the pleasure. My gaze locks on the fogged windows, the trails of rain marring the clouds. I try to concentrate on the millions of splashes against the glass. Or how the rain is falling so hard, it rivals the husky moans falling from my lips.

But I lose focus, and it all fades to black as his teeth join in, sucking and biting before easing the sting with his tongue.

"Fucking nirvana," he murmurs before suctioning my clit into his mouth. I cry out, pleasure consuming me whole. And he's right. The way Zade eats pussy *is* nirvana.

It doesn't take long before his tongue lashes at my clit in just the right way that an orgasm explodes out of me before I can process it.

My screams echo in the confined space as he swallows everything I have to give him. And then he's unbuckling both seatbelts and jerking me backward until I'm on my back, and he's crowding over me again.

Our bodies clash, and with fluidity, he lifts my body against his. My legs encircle his waist while my hands seek balance from his broad shoulders.

Our eyes stay locked, even as my pulsing core presses against the rigid length jutting between my legs. He snarls, his lip curling ferociously at the feel of my heat enveloping him.

My eyelids droop, and with an ease I never knew I possessed, I grind my hips against him, spreading my juices across his cock.

His hand shoots up, curling into my wet hair and pulling tightly. My head cranes backwards from the pressure, but my eyes don't leave his near-feral face. His teeth are bared, and the blackness starts to consume his one white eye. Darkness bleeding into purity—tainting it.

Just like he's done to me.

Without warning, he pulls his hips back and pushes all the way inside, nearly tearing me apart from the force. My mouth drops from the stretch. Fucking me against the tree and then making me come again just now still couldn't loosen me enough to fit him inside of me comfortably.

"Remember this moment," he growls deeply, withdrawing to the tip before pushing deeper inside of me. "Because the next time I fuck you, you will be deeply in love with me, Adeline. I'm your stalker and a murderer, and you will love me anyways."

And then he pulls back once more before he sinks himself to the hilt, hitting the spot inside me that has my eyes threatening to cross.

"That's not true," I pant. When his eyes flare, I continue, "Did you think this was the only time you would fuck me tonight?"

He growls, his lips pausing a hair's breadth away.

"What did I say, little mouse? The next time I fuck you, you *will* be in love with me."

The car rocks from the force of his next thrust, and the scream that rings out from my mouth is both embarrassingly loud and a sound I have never made before. I thought porn stars only made those noises—completely fabricated and practiced screams. But when he continues to drive into me with the force of a bull, those screams continue to fall from my throat, growing louder and hoarser each time.

The rain falls mercilessly, the loud pings from the raindrops only accentuating the sound of skin slapping and the wet noises Zade is drawing from my pussy.

My nails score across his chest, and if he's so sure that I will fall in love with him by the time this is over, then I can be sure that I've added new scars to his collection.

The answering growl is feral and vicious. And all it does is heighten the pleasure radiating from where our bodies connect.

His arm circles around my waist, and in one swift motion, he lifts me up and twists us, so he is sitting on the seat again while I straddle his lap.

When he grabs my waist and yanks me down on his cock, my eyes pop open wide. This new angle has him far deeper than before—a lot deeper than I thought my body was capable of taking.

"Zade!" I gasp, my nails now digging into his shoulders.

"Ride me, baby. I want to feel your pussy grip every inch of my cock."

"Fuck, I can't," I groan, my body still working to adjust to the sheer size of this man.

"You have five seconds before I rearrange your organs," he threatens. It does the job, kicking my ass into high gear and immediately rising up and sliding back down slowly.

After a few different readjustments, I finally find an angle that allows me to completely seat myself on Zade without feeling him come up my throat. With this new angle, he hits that perfect spot he was abusing moments before.

My teeth chatter, my nails digging deeper as my movements quicken.

Zade draws me in, bringing my body flush with his. One arm curls around my waist while the other hand tears through my wet hair, yanking my head to the side and giving him access to devour my neck.

I cry out, my hips moving frantically and erratically as his teeth bite the sensitive skin below my ear. My nipples scrape against his chest, sending delicious shivers straight to my pussy.

"That's it, baby," he croons into my ear. "Your sweet little pussy is gripping my cock so fucking tight."

The arm that was curled around my waist is now wedging between our bodies until his thumb reaches my clit. My head kicks back as I let out a feral cry of my own. My eyes are rolling, and I can hardly breathe past the orgasm curling in my stomach.

It's too much. Too powerful. My movements grow choppy and uneven as my core tightens unbearably.

"Zade," I grind out through clenched teeth, sweat forming on my forehead. I don't know what I'm asking for, but I think I know what I need.

The salvation he so steadily promised me.

The hand in my hair grips tighter until strands are ripping from my scalp. His fiery eyes catch mine, holding me hostage as I climb higher and higher—to a cliff far beyond Parsons Manor's. The one and only cliff I wouldn't mind jumping off of, even if I never get back up again.

"Let me feel you fall in love," he whispers.

I can no longer hold on. My vision goes dark, the pleasure blinding and dynamic as the orgasm rips through me, tearing everything in my body to shreds. My fight, my willpower, and my goddamn heart.

I scream so loudly, my throat grows hoarse.

"Fuck, Addie!" Zade shouts, and my vision clears enough to watch his own head kick back, the veins in his arms bulging and traveling all the way up to his neck. He bares his teeth, a roar that can only come from the depths of Hell vibrating throughout the car.

His cock becomes impossibly thicker before he grabs ahold of me with both arms, forcing me to still as he spills inside of me.

"Fuck, Addie, fuck," he grinds out through clenched teeth, each word punctuated by a thrust of his hips. My pussy milks him dry, wringing out every last drop until I'm impossibly full of him. His seed nearly bursts from me when he pulls out, the thick semen streaming down my legs like the raindrops on the windows.

Our heavy breathing and the pounding of my heart is the only thing left to listen to.

The rain has subsided to a light trickle, as if to mock me. Because when it was pouring, I was calm and sure of my resolve while the world around me was howling and raging. I wanted him—craved him—but I was certain I would never love him. And now that the rain has calmed, my resolve has shattered, and I'm left with a screaming heart and a silenced world.

April 3rd, 1946

I'm scared.

I don't know how it's gotten this way, but after that night, he's lost his mind.

When I told him I'm going to get a divorce, he completely lost it on me.

He's gotten so angry. So aggressive. He says that he owns me. No one else can have me but him.

I don't know what to do.

I'm just scared.

So very scared.

Chapter Thirty Five

The Shadow

he's nervous. Fidgety. Whereas before, she could hardly look at me out of fear and hatred, and now it's because she remembers how many different positions I fucked her in last night.

My dick legitimately hurts. I don't think I've ever fucked so much in one night, but I'd keep going if it wouldn't literally send me to my knees if I got hard right now.

I bowed for Addie several times last night, worshipping her pussy just like I promised. But this time, I'd be bowing from pain and praying for my dick not to fall off.

Addie and I are leaning against the railing on her balcony. It's an unusually warm day as we near winter, so we both decided to enjoy it.

She sips her coffee, her hair tangled and frizzy from last night and blowing gently in the breeze. I think my hands were in her hair so often, the strands had dried while wrapped around my fingers.

We stayed up until dawn with either my cock, fingers, or tongue filling up one of her holes at all times. We only managed a couple of hours of sleep before my phone started ringing.

Another video was leaked last night, and my headspace is too fucked up to work the tension out of Addie's muscles.

Dan had said they believed they apprehended the person leaking the videos, but they were obviously wrong. Whoever they are, they're incredibly fucking brave, and I'm very curious how the hell they're doing it with the Society watching.

I was at Savior's yesterday, which means the video could've been from the same night I attended. The very same goblets used in the videos were used that night... and now I'm sure they were filled with an innocent child's blood.

While I was drinking overpriced whiskey, shooting the shit with a man I have grown to loathe, a kid was dying, his blood draining into chalices for deranged men to drink.

Buzzing energy forms beneath the surface and it takes effort to keep my bones from jumping out of my skin.

I need to get away from Addie.

Because if she gives me attitude or her usual hatred, I don't think my response will be what she deserves.

Sensing my growing anger, she sets the coffee cup down on a little table with a dead plant on it.

I point at it. "Baby, if you can't keep a plant alive, how are you going to keep our babies alive?"

She smacks my chest. "Calm down, Zade. No baby talk, I don't even like you like that."

I grin, but her expression turns contemplative, a tiny frown tipping the corners of her lips down as a crease forms between her brow.

"Do you ever wonder about Gigi and her stalker and find it strange? Maybe even far-fetched?"

When I tilt my head, signaling my confusion, she licks her lips and starts fiddling with the belt on her purple robe.

"You already know my great-grandmother had a stalker. One that she fell in love with. And now so do I. Living in the same house and…"

"Falling in love?" I finish for her, keeping my face blank so she's sure I'm not teasing.

She glances at me and gives a slight lift of her shoulders, but she doesn't deny it. Cop out, but I let it go.

"It just seems crazy and… I don't know, impossible, I guess."

I lean down on the railing and tilt my head up until I catch her eyes. Once they snag onto mine, they're anchored. The breeze ruffles her hair again, the cinnamon strands dancing in the wind.

"Do you think you're a reincarnation of Gigi, Addie? And that I'm a reincarnation of Ronaldo? We'll never really know, will we? It's highly unlikely but not impossible. But I can't say I don't like the idea of it."

A little snarl takes over her face. "You just like the idea of stalking me for several lifetimes."

This time I do smile, and the dilation of her eyes has my cock growing stiff.

Fuck, stop it. It hurts.

But when her tongue darts out, wetting her lips, I no longer give a fuck about the pain.

My hand snaps out, grabbing the back of her head and bringing her in close. She gasps, her pink lips parting, and in this moment, all I want to do is slip my cock past them and watch them wrap around me. I'd walk on glass if it meant getting to fuck Addie's mouth again.

She struggles, but I hold her steady, her hands planted on the railing to support her weight. Her purple robe is draped open, but not enough to expose the bite marks I left last night on her tits.

"You're right. I do love the sound of watching you for lifetimes." I drop my voice low, as deep as I want to shove my cock inside her. "I also love the possibility that I have fallen in love with you in each life. Fucked that sweet pussy of yours and made you fall in love with me as much as I am with you. What did I tell you, little mouse? That you couldn't escape me. If it's real, then I've chased you across time and space, and you've never been able to get away."

She gapes at me, seemingly speechless for several moments before she gains her wits. "You don't even know if that's true," she whispers. "Or how many lifetimes you've stalked me for."

I grip her hair and twist until her ass is flush with the metal rail. Her hand grips mine, nails scoring my flesh as she fights against me, but it doesn't deter me from bending her backward over the railing, the tips of her toes scarcely touching the floor.

"What the hell, Zade?!" she screeches, her smoky voice breaking from fear. But my little mouse stills, her chest heaving. And it's then that I nearly break.

She trusts me.

"Hush, baby," I murmur. I keep one hand firmly lodged in her hair while my other hand glides across her stomach. I hover over her and inspect every curve and detail that makes up the face of the woman I'm madly fucking in love with.

Even with her eyes rounded in panic, she's the most enthralling creature I've ever laid eyes on.

My fingers trail across her freckled cheekbone, down her jaw, and to her neck. Her breath catches, and her pulse thunders. I can't help but smile, pleased by the reaction I draw out of her every fucking time I touch her.

I trail my fingers down to her parted robe, those bite marks on her tits now on full display. A low hum gathers in my chest, building to a growl when I pull apart her robe further until it falls completely to the sides, baring her creamy flesh and those rosebud nipples.

They tighten in the cool wind, and my mouth waters with the need to bite down on them.

"My little unsuspecting mouse, living each life without any knowledge of what's to come. Not knowing that I'm yearning for you, watching in the distance until I make myself known." I drag my lips across her collarbone, trailing up the column of her throat towards her ear. "For centuries. Both of us wearing different faces, inhabiting different bodies. But the same souls, colliding over and over, until this planet decides to crumble and our souls have nowhere else to go." I hum in amusement, enjoying the quickening of her breath.

"Can you imagine it?" I ask softly.

I pluck a nipple between my fingers, another low groan vibrating my chest. She shivers beneath my touch, her little pants desperate and breathy.

"Can you imagine what it would feel like to have my love for that long?"

She swallows, her eyes pinned on the water beyond the cliff as a shaky breath loosens past her lips. "Do you know what it sounds like to drown? That's what it would feel like," she says, her voice husky and uneven.

"Tell me, baby. What does drowning sound like?"

"Like the first breath of air after being trapped underwater. It's a sound of both pain and relief. Of desperation and desire. When you've gone so long without oxygen, that first breath is the only thing that makes sense, and your body takes it in without permission."

"Isn't it the most exquisitely painful thing you've ever felt?" I jerk her head closer, wringing another gasp that skitters across my lips. "You're mine, Adeline," I growl. "I don't care if we're reincarnated or not. Here and now, this is fucking real. And in *this* lifetime, you are mine."

I let her go, and she doesn't waste time scrambling up and plastering herself against the house, her hands gripping the siding as if I had shaken her world, and she's grasping for something to ground her.

I can feel the intensity radiating off of me. The buzzing has grown louder, and I'm not sure whether I need to fuck Addie or go shoot someone in the face.

"Are you okay?" she asks quietly, sensing the turmoil raging inside of me.

I look over to her, and it seems as if she shrinks beneath my gaze. It's not until I notice the tremor in her hands that I realize I'm glaring.

"Fuck," I say, swiping a hand roughly down my face. The raised scars only serve as a reminder. "I'm sorry, mouse. I got shitty news this morning. I *keep* getting shitty news."

She frowns, a crease forming between her brows.

She clears her throat, draws the robe closed, and cautiously steps back towards me, fidgeting with the belt again.

Brave girl.

Her awkwardness almost makes me smile, but I feel a little too empty to do anything other than stare.

"Do you want to talk about it?" she finally asks, glancing up at me before she reaches for her coffee.

"Do you want to hear about it?" I counter, cocking a brow. A red flush rises to her cheeks, but she lifts her eyes and holds them steady.

"Yes."

This time, it's me who looks away.

"That involves hearing about what I do for a living. Which is kill people."

She releases a shaky breath, but instead of retreating as I had expected, she nods her head. "Okay."

That single word only made up for four letters, meant more to me than she could ever imagine.

"You're not going to like what you hear," I argue, and for the first time, I think I'm searching for an excuse not to tell her. I've always been honest with her, but right now, I don't think I can handle her vicious rejection.

"Maybe not," she concedes. "But you said before you save women and children. Was that not true?"

I pin her with my stare, conveying just how serious I am. "That *is* what I do. All of what I told you is one hundred percent the truth. I just didn't go into detail about what I do once I catch them."

"Torture them," she easily guesses. Those four politicians exposed that truth.

She pauses, her caramel eyes boring into me. She's absently chewing her lip, contemplating something, it seems. Whatever she decides, she nods her head slightly to herself.

I'm very curious to know what's going on in that head of hers.

"Tell me," she says, her tone firm and unyielding. "I want to know everything… about you." She ends her sentence with a wrinkle of her nose as if she thought she'd never say those words. It brings a small grin to my face.

"You mean besides what it feels like to have my cock in every hole of your body?"

She scoffs, a pretty blush staining her cheeks.

"You have not," she snaps.

"Yet," I promise. I haven't taken her ass yet, but I fully intend to. Soon.

"Zade, focus," she hisses. But her clenched thighs and blown eyes don't go unnoticed.

I look off to the side and stare out at the Bay, focusing on something mundane, despite how beautiful it is with the water sparkling beneath the sunlight.

Everything is mundane when Addie is present.

There's a small thicket of trees leading up towards the cliff, the crooked branches deprived of leaves and reaching towards the sky as if begging for life again. They're dying, and it imitates what I feel on the inside right now.

"I target specific people. Politicians. Celebrities. Businessmen. People in positions of power or who have money. And even people who are the lowest of the totem pole and will do anything to get by. At the end of the day, it doesn't really matter what their job is or how much money they have because they're all the same. They're human sex traffickers.

"For years, I've been targeting pedophile rings and dismantling them. Rescue the girls and children and either send them back to their family or send them to a safe, undisclosed location where they can live the rest of their lives in comfort.

"But about nine months ago, a video leaked of a sadistic ritual taking place. They were sacrificing a child and drinking his blood. Since then, a few more videos have leaked, including one last night." I pause, clenching my jaw and trying to regain the composure that is beginning to slip through my fingers.

Blowing out a deep breath, I continue. "I've told you already that Mark was in the first video, which is why I targeted him and the three other men I killed. All four of them were performing the ritual. The night I killed Mark, he disclosed the location to me, so I went there yesterday to insert myself, gain trust, and be invited into the dungeon. They were drinking out of the same goblets that they use in the ritual."

I pause, nearly blind from rage as I admit, "I think this recent video was from last night, and those goblets were full of blood from a sacrifice they performed while I was there."

The coffee cup clatters against the metal table, nearly toppling over as Addie attempts to set it down. Her hand is badly shaking and it looks like a piece of the ceramic breaks off.

"What the fuck," she breathes, her eyes wide with shock and repulsion. Though, they don't stray from me as she says, "Zade you couldn't have known that's what was happening. You can't blame yourself for that."

I clench my teeth against the snarl threatening to take over my face, the muscle in my jaw threatening to burst. "The fuck I can't," I snap.

She flinches, her face softening.

"I didn't build Z and become who I am today to allow for a child to be sacrificed right fucking below me. And watch sick fucks drink their blood like its goddamn water."

Tears form in her eyes, but she stays silent while I work to calm myself down.

"I've dedicated almost six years to eradicating human trafficking. Seattle happens to be a prime location for pedophile rings, but in reality, they're everywhere. And I plan to take them all down. Or as many as I can until this life takes me down first."

Addie doesn't speak. She stares into her nearly depleted coffee as if it's an 8 Ball that will give her whatever answer she's looking for. The sound of the furnace kicks on, filling the otherwise static silence.

After a few moments, she looks up at me, an unreadable expression on her freckled face.

"Why?" she whispers. "Why did you choose to put your life in danger and hunt down these people and kill them? What made you decide to do this?"

Her tone isn't laced with judgment, but the need to understand. But I'm not sure my answer will offer her the understanding she's asking for.

"Because I want to, baby."

Her brows jump in surprise, not expecting my answer. "You're expecting me to give you a legitimate reason for why I took this path in life. Maybe I had a sister or mother who was kidnapped and sold. Maybe I was myself. But none of those things are the case. When I learned about human trafficking and the depths of its depravity, I was sickened. And I have the skill to do something about it, so I am. I'm saving innocent people because I want to. And I'm torturing and murdering the bad because I want to."

Her eyes widen in surprise when I prowl towards her. She doesn't back away from me, but I see the tension roll into her shoulders like thunderclouds swollen with rain.

I grab the back of her neck and pull her into me. She stumbles, steadying herself with her hands on my chest. Her breathing has escalated, the short little breaths escaping through her puffy, bruised lips.

I lean in close, making sure her eyes are locked onto mine as I say, "And the reason I stalk you, little mouse, is because *I want to.* Everything I do in life is my choice. I choose my morals. I choose the ones that are worth saving and the ones

503

that are worth killing. And I choose you.

"If you're expecting a tragic story, you're not going to get one. My parents were incredible people who loved me and supported me. They died in a car crash when I was seventeen. The roads were terrible, and they hydroplaned off a cliff. I lived with my father's best friend—my godfather—for a year before going to college for computer science and started my career as a hacker.

"My parents' death was heartbreaking but an accident. Aside from losing them, nothing bad has ever really happened to me that would lead me to slaughter evil people for a living. I make my own choices in life, Addie. That's all there is to it."

She swallows, her eyes darting between mine. Slowly, she raises her hand and traces a finger lightly over the scar running down my eye. I clench my jaw, relishing in the fire that her fingers leave in their wake.

Despite the severity of the conversation, my cock hardens to steel in my jeans. I'm tempted to unzip, bend her over the railing, and take her right here.

But I know we're both incredibly sore by now, and I would crash right back into the dark headspace the second I slip out of her.

Addie doesn't deserve that. She doesn't deserve to have her body used so I can escape my demons.

"And your scars?"

"The first time I infiltrated a ring. One of the ring leaders was a brute and knew his way around a knife fight. He cut me up good. And it was the lesson I needed in order for me to learn how to defend myself and fight properly. No man has ever come close since. I wear these scars proudly because in the end, I won and every innocent in that building went home safe."

"But they still haunt you."

I nod once. "They do."

It was the first time I was confronted with the possibility of failure. And that feeling has never quite let me go from its clutches. It's the feeling that imprints on me like a bad tattoo each and every time I invade a ring.

Her hand drops to the side, dangling loosely as she stares at me. I stare back, each of us trying to read the other. Figure out what the other is thinking. Feeling.

"One last question," she barters.

"Ask me as many as you want."

"The roses. Why the roses?"

I smile. I was waiting for her to ask me about those.

"My mother. Her favorite flowers were roses. She always had them all over the house with the thorns clipped so I wouldn't hurt myself. One year, I told her that I would be sad when she died because all the roses would die with her. So, she gave me a plastic rose and said that as long as I have that rose, she would never be truly gone."

I shrug. "I guess I wanted to see roses all over your house, too. Maybe because you feel like home."

She inhales sharply, seemingly taken aback by my words. Those beautiful eyes are fixated on mine, both shock and raw hunger reflecting in her caramel pools.

Licking her lips, she admits softly, "It's going to take me some time to fully accept some things, Zade. I can't tell you how long it'll take me, but I can tell you that I will try. But what I can definitely accept is you saving the children and girls."

Her lip wobbles. Before I can reach down and snatch it between my teeth, she sucks it between her own.

After a few seconds, she continues. "I admire you more than I can say for being one of far too few people willing actually to do something to save them. The world needs more people like you, Zade."

"Maybe," I murmur, giving in and placing a soft kiss on the corner of her lips. "But all I need is you."

Her eyes close, and she nods to herself. I don't know what conclusion she comes to in that pretty little head of hers, but when she opens her eyes and gazes up at me, it looks a little like she needs me, too.

My hand slides into her hair, and just as I'm closing the distance, a voice filters in through Addie's bedroom door.

"Who's ready for a murder inves—" the loud voice trails off, replaced by a loud gasp.

Mine and Addie's heads both turn at the same time. Standing in her bedroom staring at us with a mixture of disbelief and anger is Addie's best friend.

"Hello, Daya," I greet, my mask falling into place as I smirk and step away from Addie.

My little mouse is embarrassed. I note the hint of shame, but it was expected. It's going to take time for Addie to truly accept within herself that she has given in to her stalker.

"What the hell? Is this him?"

My smirk widens, and I turn to look at Addie. "Have you been gossiping about me, little mouse? Did you tell her how big my cock is?"

Addie's eyes pop comically. Her hand curls and swings it right into my chest. It feels like she just threw a slice of bread at me.

"Asshole! No!"

If it wasn't for the small figure charging towards me, the loud stomping would be a clear indicator to the storm coming my way. I turn and swoop out of the way of another flying fist. This one packing a lot more punch.

That one might have felt like a whole loaf of bread.

I can tell the girl can hit, but fists don't affect me these days. I've grown too accustomed to the bite of a bullet instead.

I laugh, catching Daya by her arm before she flies ass over teacup over the balcony.

She wouldn't look so pretty with her face bashed in and her skull cracked open.

"Damn, you both woke up and chose violence today, huh?"

Daya rips her arm from my hand and glares at me, her pretty green eyes full of ire. And then she turns to Addie. "I thought we hated him."

I cock a brow, also staring at Addie and waiting for her answer. At this point, she can lie and say she still does. I know the truth, and that's what matters. I have a single feeling in my body, and it's attached to the freckled-face girl who looks like she's having a stroke. It's going to take a lot more than her lying to her best friend to hurt it.

Addie's face is red and her mouth flops, but no words come out. She might even be going into cardiac arrest.

Daya trains her glare on me and opens her mouth, but I cut in, "I'd be very careful about your words and any swinging limbs. I do sign your paychecks."

Her eyes widen, taken aback. "So it *is* you. You are Z?" she demands.

"What, does my face not meet your expectations?"

The look that comes over Daya's face is pure entertainment. I swear you can't find this shit on T.V. anymore.

She flounders for an answer but comes up short. All she really can do is just stare.

"I hope you understand that Addie never really stood a chance. Don't blame her."

Addie crosses her arms, huffing at me and finally finding her voice. All I had to do was piss her off. "I make my own decisions, Zade. Quit acting like I didn't have a choice."

I just smile, letting her think what she wants. Whatever gets her pussy willingly wrapped back around my cock, I guess.

"You knew I already had suspicions, Addie. Why wouldn't you just tell me?" This time, Daya's voice softens, full of hurt and sadness. Addie's face drops, and that's my cue to leave.

"I'm really sorry. I haven't been sure how to even explain what's happening with him."

I take a step back, attracting both of their eyes. "I have to deal with the video. I have men stationed outside the property already."

"What the hell? Why? I didn't see any men," Daya asks, her eyes widened with alarm.

"They're not meant to be seen, Daya. You know that already, don't you?" When her teeth click, I continue. "You two kiss and make up. I trust your judgment so whatever you decide to divulge, you have my permission."

Addie bites her bottom lip, glancing at her best friend with guilt.

"I'll see you later, little mouse." I wink at her suggestively, and her eyes narrow in response.

Daya sputters, but I'm out the door before she can relearn how to speak again. I've got far more pressing matters to deal with than Daya's newly developed speech impediment.

Chapter
Thirty Six
The Manipulator

I look down at my hands like a scolded child. After Satan's Affair, I had admitted Zade and I had sex, but I still didn't confirm his identity to her, and she hadn't asked. I think she was too concerned with my mental health to think about it. Rightfully so.

Regardless, if I had just been upfront and told Daya that I couldn't share details about Zade and Mark, I think she would've learned to accept it. It was lying to her that hurt her most.

She followed me down to the kitchen, her anger a heavy gaze burning into the back of my head the entire way. And now, she glares at me from across the island.

"How long have you known? And why are there men stationed outside the house? And he trusts you to tell me *what*?"

I bite my lip. "For a little while," I confess. "Look, I didn't say anything because his involvement with Mark is top secret. I didn't want you to keep asking questions that I wasn't sure I could answer. It wasn't my story to tell and what he's doing is incredibly sensitive."

"Did you know who he was when I asked you about him before Satan's Affair?"

I cringe and nod my head, confirming what she already knew. Hurt flashes in her eyes, and all I want to do is cry—the guilt I've been carrying for lying to her bleeds from my pores.

She blows out a breath and nods, accepting my answer for what it is. "Okay, fine. Can you tell me now?"

I go on to explain Zade's current mission, outside of bringing down pedophile rings. About the sick rituals being performed on little children and how hard Zade has been working to find the location and bring it down. Daya listens attentively, face souring as I explain the horrific things being done to innocent children, aside from being tortured and trafficked.

As if that wasn't fucking bad enough.

"I'd like to say I'm surprised, but I'm not," Daya mutters, fidgeting with the hoop in her nose. "So Zade killed Mark because of these rituals?"

"Not exactly, though it definitely played a part in it. Remember how we saw him at Satan's Affair?" When she nods, I continue. "Apparently, Mark targeted us that night and had made a call for someone to come… extract us."

I explain Zade's role that night, and how he had made sure that Daya and I never ended up in the back of a van. Even worse, how the Society has put a target on my head, and that Mark was trying to fulfill that.

As I continue telling her everything I know, Daya stares at me with a somber expression on her face.

When I finish, she stays quiet. Halfway through the story, I poured us both a shot of vodka. We both needed the liquid courage to hear about just how fucked up this world can be.

"I'll be keeping an eye on you as well," Daya says after a few moments. Silence had settled in, and as it stretched on, I grew more and more anxious that she was going to walk out.

I hurt her.

"You don't have to do that," I say, my voice small.

"It seems I do," she sighs, a frown pulling her lips down.

"I'm sorry," I apologize again. "Ever since he came into my life, shit has been insane, and I've barely had time to come to terms with it all. Not to mention that I still don't know how to process... him. And I think I wanted just to pretend that I was handling a stalker how I should be. Not by going off and... well—"

"Fucking him?" Daya finishes, her voice stern.

I cringe, biting my lip against the sting of her words. I deserved that.

"Yeah," I whisper.

Daya's shoulders drop. "I'm sorry, you didn't deserve that," she says, as if reading my mind. "I'm not mad at you for your relationship with Z, Addie. I mean, I don't understand it... I don't understand how anyone could accept that their lover is a stalker. I also don't think it's the makings of a healthy relationship. The dude obviously has issues."

I nod, agreeing with her assessment. What she's saying are the same things that I have thought myself.

"But knowing that Z is your stalker oddly reassures me. I never knew him personally, *obviously*. I didn't even know what he looked like, but what he does... it's incredibly admirable. He puts his life on the line every day, walks into the lion's den himself and saves a lot of innocent souls. He's helped countless people and taken down so many rings already. And I don't have to see what's in the videos to know that Z takes them to heart."

She sighs, and a sardonic smile flashes on her face. "He stalks people for a living, so I suppose it's no surprise that tendency has bled into his love life."

I make a face, showing her how unimpressed I am with him not keeping his work habits where they belong.

"And I get why you didn't tell me," she admits softly. "Mark put you in a pretty shitty situation to begin with, and I understand more than most how delicately that situation needs to be handled. I would've understood if you had said so from the beginning." She shoots me a look. "But I get it. You're not used to this dark corner of the world, so I can't expect you to know how to deal with it all."

My body relaxes with her acceptance, relieving me of some of the weight resting on my shoulders.

I can't stand when Daya's mad at me. I'd take Zade pointing a gun in my face over my best friend's anger any day.

"Daya, I just want you to know it wasn't because I didn't trust you. And I'm so sorry I lied. Getting involved with Zade really tests my morals, and I still don't know what to think of everything. I mean, falling in lo—" I cut myself off, my teeth clicking from the force. I feel the blood drain from my face as I swallow the words back down.

"Do you—"

"No," I cut in, the response too rushed and snappy to ring true.

Daya blinks, an array of emotions in her sage eyes, but she takes pity on me and doesn't push.

"Well, whatever the case, I guess I can't blame you for not being able to resist

him." She flashes a toothy smile. "He is *really* hot, and you *really* needed to get laid."
I find a random envelope sitting on the island and whip it at her in response.

She cackles, dodging the envelope.

"Dick," I mutter, increasing her laughing. What I'm not going to tell her is
that sex with Zade is far beyond getting laid. It's not just incredibly intense, it's
metamorphosing. I walked out of that House of Mirrors a completely different
person. And after last night, I don't think I will ever be able to go back to the
Adeline Reilly before Zade.

"Have you heard anything from Max?" I ask, the simple question erasing the
light hearted tone.

Daya shrugs a shoulder. "No, actually. Ever since he visited us at that
restaurant, I haven't heard from him. Or the twins."

I nod and say, "Zade implied several times that they've been handled, but I'm
not sure what exactly that means. I haven't even thought to ask, my mind has been
so wrapped around everything else. Do you think they're dead?"

She chews her lip and shrugs, appearing a tad uncomfortable. Her best friend
has a serial killer for a… I don't know what he is. Boyfriend? Lover? Gross, no.
God can smite me before I refer to a man as my lover.

Whatever he is, he's crazy.

But I think she might even know that better than I do, with him being her
boss. I'm sure she's aware of the minute details on Zade's operations when he
extracts girls.

"I don't think they are, but I'll look into it. Regardless, they've left us alone
and I'm glad for it."

I nod in agreement. Can't say I have any complaints either.

Daya makes a move towards the coffee pot when she steps on the envelope I threw at her.

Pausing, she picks it up off the floor and sets it down on the island. That's when I notice that it's an odd envelope. It's thick as hell, as if it's packed to the brim with papers or something.

Brows dipping in confusion, I reach over and snatch up the thick paper. Noting the look on my face, Daya turns her attention back to me.

"What is it?"

My address is handwritten, but there's no return address.

"I don't know," I mutter, eyeing the envelope like it's a bomb. I can't explain the exact feeling, but anxiety pools in the pit of my stomach.

Carefully, I peel open the flap, grab the thick stack of papers and slide them out. Except it's not all just papers. Dozens of photographs fall out, along with a weathered note.

Daya and I glance at each other, our eyes connecting with mutual confusion and trepidation.

I pick up the pictures first, immediately recognizing a younger version of Gigi in them. Most of them, her smiling red lips stare back at me, the same man predominant in all the photos.

"Who is that?" I mutter, not expecting any real answer at the moment. I don't recognize the man. He's not pictured in any of the photographs that were hanging on the wall when I moved in.

Once I renovated the house, I decided to take them all down. I had decided that they'd judged me enough after the Greyson debacle.

Zade fucked me in that hallway last night—that's as far as we made it before he pinned me up against the wall and took me from behind. When Zade and I had left the bedroom this morning, we had both discovered I had gouged nail marks into the paint. It was my only anchor with his hand firmly gripping my hair, bowing my body back, and using it as a rope as he fucked me into oblivion. I had collapsed after that orgasm, and he was forced to fuck me on the rug, right smack in the middle of the hallway.

I'll never look at that spot on the rug or the wall the same.

So, I can only imagine how judgy their frozen eyes would be after not only seeing their descendent actually get railed this time, but by her stalker no less.

Thank *god* I took those down.

"Is there anything written on the back?" Daya asks, flipping over a few photos herself to look. I flip over mine and see a date written.

January 8th, 1944.

Several months before Gigi had started writing about her stalker.

In the picture is Gigi, smiling brightly up at the camera, her hair pinned into the type of curls you only saw in the 40s. Next to her, the unfamiliar man has an arm wrapped loosely around her, a slight smirk on his face. Something about him seems familiar, but I can't put my finger on it.

"No names on this one," I observe, flipping over a few more pictures. All with dates but none that reveal the identity of the man.

We spread the photos out and arrange them in chronological order. The last picture is two weeks before her death.

Gigi seems to be curled in on herself, hunched and small as she holds a glass of wine. Her smile is strained, while the mystery man stands next to her, looking down at her with a pinched brow and a frown. At this point, she was already in fear for her life.

But from the man in the pictures, or someone else?

Next, I pick up the weathered letter. It's addressed to Gigi.

My Genevieve,

It pains me to write this letter. I sit here and I mourn. For what could have been. For what could still be but yet you refuse to see.

I've loved you since the moment I saw you, Genevieve. I've loved you though you have married another. And now that I know you have given yourself to a different man—a man that's not me, my love still persists.

I've waited so long for you already, and now yet another has come between us. Has stopped me from taking you as mine.

Why do you insist on doing this to me? To us?

It plagues me. Keeps me from sleeping at night. The only thing I can think of doing is cutting you from my life to end this misery. For good.

Sincerely,

Your true love

"What the fuck did I just read?" I ask in a strained whisper. Daya reads over my shoulder, and when I look back at her, her wide eyes are on me, alight with confusion and concern.

"That sounded ominous. Threatening," she says, her green eyes glancing at the letter like it's a curse written on paper.

I nod distractedly, setting down the note and sorting through the pictures again. Looking for clues on who this man might be.

But there are none.

"He looks so familiar," I murmur, studying another picture. They look to be at a party of some sort. The image is in black and white, so I can't tell the color of the dress, only that it's a dark shade. Jewels decorate the ends of her sleeves and around the collar of the dress. And of course, I don't need the picture to be in color to know she's wearing her red lipstick.

The man has his hand resting high up on her thigh. With the way he's clutching her, it almost seems possessive. Domineering.

I've never met this man in my life and yet I know he's a damn bastard, that I can bet money on.

And by the strained smile on Gigi's face, and the tightening around her eyes, my great-grandmother clearly thought so, too.

"Hold on, let me take pictures and upload them onto my computer. I can do a reverse image search."

I watch her do her thing, her brow pinched with concentration. Within minutes, she's turning the laptop towards me, staring at me carefully.

"Mark's father. That's who's in all these pictures."

My eyes snap to hers while my heart rate picks up speed.

"Are you thinking the same thing as me?" I ask.

"What, that your great-grandfather's best friend could have been in love with Gigi and killed her when he found out she was having an affair with a man that wasn't him?" she summarizes, plucking the exact thoughts out of my head.

She sighs and stares down at the photos. "I don't know. It's a big conclusion to come to just based off of some creepy photos and a note. While the note does have a threatening tone to it, it certainly isn't enough to convict him of murder."

I nod, having thought the same thing. Something about these pictures puts me on edge and gives me a creeping chill down my spine. As much as I revolted against Gigi's diary and how she fawned over her stalker, it never gave me a bad feeling the way the note and pictures do. Still, I can't solve a murder case purely based on feeling. I need evidence.

"Logically, Gigi's stalker is still more likely, but that doesn't mean Mark's father being the murderer is out of the question," she goes on, absently picking up one of the pictures and observing it.

"I see motive in this note. So, even if it's a small chance, I think we should still look into it."

"Have you found any more information on Ronaldo?"

She sighs. "Yes. He died in 1947 of a cardiogenic shock." My brows plunge.

"A heart attack?"

She shifts. "A broken heart. He died of broken heart syndrome." My mouth dries. "I found some family history on him, but not much else. His life was kept pretty tightly under wraps, and I assume his boss had something to do with that."

"So, a dead end," I conclude, nodding my head. I bite my lip, rolling it between my teeth as I contemplate my next move. "I think I need to go up into the attic," I say with resignation. I may love ghosts, but fuck, that doesn't mean I still have the desire to be possessed by a demon or whatever is up there.

Daya's sage eyes whip to mine. I told her about the last note I found and how I felt there was something very negative up there.

"You're a masochist. You're gonna get possessed if you go up there."

I snort. "I think it would've done so by now if it really wanted to. There could be more up there."

Daya sighs. "I'm going to die today," she mutters.

"You won't die, just maybe a little possession," I chirp as I round the island and make way towards the staircase.

"Yeah, and guess who I'm terrorizing first?"

518

That cold, heavy weight instantly drops on my shoulders the second I enter the attic. It's like in those cartoons when a piano drops out of the sky and lands on top of an unsuspecting person.

"Okay, hurry the fuck up, I don't like it up here," Daya says, her voice tight with fear. It's crawling across my bones too, sending my heart racing. Yet, heat slithers through my muscles, settling low in the pit of my stomach.

I use the flashlight on my phone to search through the walls. I start with where I found the last note, but all that's left are cobwebs and spiders.

I make my way over each wall, pressing on the wood paneling in hopes of finding one of them loose. It's not until I get close to the mirror that I find one. The wood rattles beneath my palms, and with the heavy feeling surrounding us, I waste no time ripping the wood from the wall.

I bounce the beam of light around in several different directions, finding nothing but more bugs and webs. I almost give up, until I see a flash of something shiny.

"I think I found something," I announce excitedly.

"Thank fuck," Daya mutters from behind me. I barely hear the words. Plunging my arm into the hole before I can consider the bugs, I grab at the piece, my hand closing around something plastic. I go to pull that out, but my hand grazes what feels like paper, so I make a grab for that too.

I swipe at my arm, cringing at the feel of cobwebs sticking to me. I don't even look at my arm, I just keep brushing it off all while beelining for the steps.

"Let's go," I breathe, right before I'm nearly knocked on my ass from Daya pushing past me and running down the stairs.

Whatever is in my hand, it's something big. I'm as sure of it as I am of the eyes on my back, watching me leave.

Slamming the attic door behind me, I lean against it and heave, shaking out the bone-chilling cold that seems to cling to me like glue.

"I'm never going up there again," Daya says, panting.

"I don't think I want to, either," I say. Finally, I look down at my hand and see a Ziploc bag with a gold diamond encrusted Rolex in it and blood streaked across the plastic. And the note in my hand is a quick scrawl that says, *"hide this, no one can know I did it. Remember that."*

"Holy shit," I breathe.

"Let me see it. We can't touch it or we'll get fingerprints on it, but those have serial numbers. I can probably trace that back to its owner."

We rush down into the kitchen, the demon residing in my attic forgotten. I find a pair of spare rubber gloves that Daya and I used when we were cleaning out the house. She snaps the gloves on and carefully pulls out the bloodied watch.

"I don't want the blood to flake off, but I need to remove the bracelet in order to see the serial number," she murmurs, handling the watch piece with care. "Do you have a thumbtack?"

I whip around and open up the junk drawer in my kitchen, confident I have one somewhere. After rummaging for a minute, I let loose a celebratory *ah-ha* and hand Daya a blue thumbtack.

It takes her a minute, but she finally gets the bracelet unhooked between the lugs of the watch.

"Motherfucker," she curses.

"What?"

"Someone scratched at the serial number. It's barely legible."

Daya looks up at me, disappointment radiating from her green eyes. I deflate, a frown tugging my lips down in defeat.

"I'm not gonna give up. We're getting this blood tested and I'm going to figure something out with this watch. Let me handle it?"

I nod, trusting Daya to figure it out. She's incredibly intelligent, and her resources on finding out information are astronomical.

And then a light bulb goes off in my head. "In those pictures with Gigi, Frank was wearing that watch."

I pick through all the papers scattered across the island until I find the small stack of photos.

"Same watch," I reiterate, handing the pictures over. Daya peers down at the photos, a grin pulling her lips up.

"Now we just have to prove it."

May 8th, 1946

I'm going to die. He's coming for me, I can feel it in my bones.

And all I can think of is Sera. My sweet, sweet Sera. She's only just turned sixteen, and she's so bright. So full of life.

How do I tell her that I may not be around much longer. And I only have myself to blame. I've made so many mistakes these past two years. I should've done things differently.

But it's too late.

And my daughter will be the one to suffer the most.

Oh, Sera. What do I do when I'm going up against a man that feels he's been scorned?

I'm just so tired. I think I'm going to lay down for a nap.

Chapter Thirty Seven
The Shadow

T*here's nothing you could've done.*

You can't change what has already happened, man.

You can't save them all.

I'm grateful for Jay. I really am. I don't trust many men in this field, especially to do a part of the job I have a very hard time relinquishing—but I can't be on the floor and have my face in a computer at the same time.

And Jay has been more than efficient at helping with that side of the job.

But what the fucker is *not* skilled in is making me feel better.

He's trying. I get it.

But I have a hard time appreciating his effort when it's taking all of mine not to go into Savior's and blow the entire place up.

If it wasn't for the fact that there are innocent people who work there—or rather are being kept hostage there—I'd fucking do it.

I was there.

I watched them drink the blood of a little boy. An eight-year-old kid sacrificed on some stone altar to welcome the new members of a devil-worshipping, blood-drinking, pedophile club.

I'll never understand why. I'll never understand the desire to hurt someone so young, so pure, so innocent. But those qualities are what attract them. That's what draws the devil to the angel.

They want to corrupt. To hurt. To taint. To cause harm and suffering upon those that never asked for it. That's the sick thrill of it.

"He was eight years old, Jay," I grind out through gritted teeth. "He had a family. Two mothers, three brothers and a sister. He was loved. He was brought up in a good home by parents who loved him. And they stole him in a fucking grocery store and sold him to the skin trade and used him as a fucking sacrifice."

Jay stays quiet, seeming to realize his standard feel-better responses are moot.

I was there.

And I did nothing to stop it.

I open my mouth, ready to go on another tangent when another call comes through. I glance at the phone and a feral snarl takes over my face.

"I have to go," I snap, hanging up the phone on Jay and immediately answering the call.

"Daniel. So nice to hear from you," I greet. Like a blanket being thrown over a fire, my tone is cool and collected.

"Zack, sorry to call so unexpectedly. I wanted to ask something of you."

I lean back in my chair, rolling my neck, the muscles cracking loudly. My eyes never stray from the computer screen displaying the picture of the little boy who was killed in the last video.

I'll never forget him, but gluing my eyes to his face reminds me that there's more out there in the same situation. And right now, that reminder is the only thing keeping me from going ballistic.

I need my wits. If I lose it now, I'll ruin what I've been working so hard for.

"What can I do for you?"

"Consider it a preliminary initiation. We have our hearts set on what we'll be having for dinner this Saturday, and it's really special. We want to make sure this goes off without a hitch, so Friday, we decided to have ourselves an appetizer, if you will."

My brows crease, and a pit of dread forms in my stomach, like the sky opening up and releasing a torrential downpour on a drowning city.

"Without a hitch?" I repeat, my tone dropping.

"Don't take it personally. Most men who are initiated have been around for years. We're all taking a gamble here, so my superiors thought it best we have dinner beforehand."

The Society is testing me. My mind is already racing with how I'm going to prevent a child from dying in front of my face without killing them all.

"Is that so?" I say, my tone intrigued.

"All I ask is Friday night, you meet me at a dinner party I'm hosting."

Friday is two days from now.

My head spins as I try to figure out what Dan is planning. It's something evil, I know that much.

"What's the purpose of this appetizer?"

If Dan has a problem with my questioning, he doesn't make it known. And frankly, I don't give a fuck.

Feeling the urge come over me, I switch my screen to a live feed of security cameras I have set up around Addie's property. She's home, and Daya's car is still parked outside of her house.

Later, I'll have to go over more training with her. I've gone over several things she should do if ever kidnapped but I want to make sure Addie is fully prepared. Not because I plan on ever letting her be taken, but because I'm a realistic and logical person and understand that I can't control everything.

I've been in this business far too long to know better. Getting taken can happen in a single second, when you're doing the most mundane thing that every single person does every day. Walking to their car. Walking in or out of a store. Putting gas in your car. Going on a walk in a park. And some even force bait to knock on your door and ask for help.

"Well, to get our fill before the main event, of course. We have the perfect appetizer picked out just for you. One that resembles your own meals at home. It's safe to say you'll join me, yeah?"

My fists tighten until I hear the bones crack. The appetizer is a little girl. One that apparently looks similar to the girl who was in the picture I showed him at Savior's. He went out and handpicked a girl based on what he thinks I like.

I'm past the sickening feeling that stirs in the gut and makes you want to vomit—I'm seeing red now. The red of his blood, leaking from his throat as I slice into it. The red flowing from his mouth as he slowly suffocates. I see so much red.

"Of course," I say breezily. "Wouldn't miss it for the world."

"Make sure the men are watching over Addie while I'm gone," I remind Jay, tightening the tie around my neck.

It feels like a goddamn noose, and playing nice with these men tonight is the proverbial bucket being kicked out from beneath my feet.

Socializing with some of the most depraved men to ever live certainly feels like hanging myself from the ceiling rafters. They deserve to die, and instead I'll be drinking expensive whiskey with them and imagining all the ways I'm going to slaughter each and every one of them.

"Her house is being watched around the clock. Discreetly, of course," Jay assures from behind me.

Doesn't feel good enough. Something I learned from when she was just a girl getting undressed in her room, while I watched from afar through her window. I knew her skin was as soft as silk and that her pussy would feel like fucking paradise. But being so far away and only just watching—it wasn't good enough.

And now, her safety feels precarious. I have the best men in the world watching out for her, but if the Society were to send someone after her—they wouldn't hire some low-life off the streets.

They'd hire someone just as trained to hunt and kill as the men circling the perimeter of her house.

I spare a glance at Jay through the mirror, his shaggy black hair curled around his pale face as he fiddles with the plastic red rose on my nightstand. I don't feel particularly comfortable having him in my personal space, but Jay decided he didn't care and walked into my bedroom and sat on the bed anyway.

Addie hasn't even gotten the chance to come here yet. I'll have to rectify that soon.

I walk over to him and snatch the rose from his hand, his fingernails painted

527

black today. Every time I see them, they're a different color.

Never one to shy away, Jay prods. "Is that personal? Where did you get it?"

I cock a brow at him, but he just stares up at me with faux innocence in his hazel eyes, patiently waiting.

Whatever.

"My mother gave it to me a long time ago. She loved roses and had them all over the house. She gave this to me to always remember her by." My tone suggests that Jay keep his mouth shut.

So, he does.

I twirl the rose, getting lost in the memory of my mother. She was beautiful. Long, black hair with eyes as dark as my right eye—nearly black. But she carried a shroud of sunlight around her. Dad always joked that she kept herself in the shadows so everyone else could shine. She was selfless and kind, always giving but never taking.

Deep down, I know my mother would be incredibly proud of what I'm doing. She may not approve of my methods, but I think she would've found a place with the girls I save. Helping them and taking care of them.

She would've been happy.

Setting the rose down, I turn and glance one last time at the mirror. I make sure my three-piece suit doesn't have a wrinkle in sight. The Armani suit has been tailored to mold perfectly to my body and drips with capitalism.

Good thing I steal from the rich.

"You look beautiful," Jay says wispily, wiping a fake tear from the corner of his eye. I give him a droll look and slap his forehead as I walk by.

I ignore the muttered *ow* and grab my keys and wallet before slipping on the earpiece and loading myself with two guns. I grab my white gold Rolex, fastening it around my wrist. It's no ordinary overpriced watch though. Right by the clasp on my inner wrist is a tiny button I installed. The moment I press it, a diversion will ensue and hopefully allow me to get the poor child out safely.

I've already hacked the cameras inside and out of Daniel's place, and while he has hired security detail, the few guests I saw enter didn't get patted down nor were required to walk through a body scanner.

This tells me this is more of an intimate affair with few people who are trusted enough not to shoot the place up.

I roll my neck, my muscles brimming with tension. Something about this night feels off. It feels like being shot at in a metal room, just waiting for the bullet to ricochet and hit me somewhere vital.

There's absolutely no way I'm letting a young child get sacrificed or abused tonight. This will be a matter of how to get the girl out safely while maintaining innocence. If I'm to be brought into the underground dungeon tomorrow, then I need to stay on Daniel's good side.

"I want your eyes on Addie tonight as well. If something happens, you tell me immediately."

He chuckles. "Do you think she'll like it when I stalk her, too?"

I pin him with a glare. "You watch her for any purpose other than ensuring her safety, I'll cut your dick off and feed it to you."

His face scrunches up in disgust, but I don't miss the flash of terror in his eyes. "Just kidding, dude," he assures, his hands raised in surrender. "I like my women willing."

A wicked smile forms, though the heat in my eyes remains. "Sounds to me like you don't understand a woman's body well enough to know when it sings for you, even when her mouth tries to resist."

Jay's sputtering follows me out, and I can't help but laugh when I hear him on the phone immediately after, getting reassurance from one of his booty calls.

"So glad you could make it, Zack," Daniel greets, gripping one hand in a handshake and slapping me on the back with the other.

Dan's house is just as ostentatious as any other person with a bank account sitting in the millions. His house is rustic, with an accent wall made of wood to imitate a cabin, exposed beams, wooden floors that he paid big money to look weathered, and a lot of tan and brown accents.

Abstract paintings decorate the walls, each painting with an earthy tone of reds, browns and yellows. I pause at one in particular, the drone of Daniel greeting other guests behind me turning into a low buzz.

The painting looks like two big brown eyes, with streaks of bright red trailing from them. Soft yellows and reds make up the round, short curves of the girl's face. My eyes roam, taking in every detail until the full picture comes together.

It's a little girl crying tears of blood.

"Beautiful, isn't it?"

I drag my eyes away to find Daniel standing next to me, his eyes roving over the painting with a wicked gleam in his eyes.

He stares at the painting with pride as if he painted it himself.

"Yes," I murmur, before turning away. I'm not going to stand there and interpret art as if I'm not standing in a museum of depraved paintings. One glance around shows the other paintings are carved in subtle morbidity.

I shake hands with a few people I recognize from Savior's and Pearl. Minutes later, Daniel has us all join him in the dining room, the twenty-foot-long table set for at least twenty people.

It's not a normal set up. There are crystal glasses, white plates and a fork and knife set on a thick plastic covering. The entire middle of the table is completely empty. Normally, flowers and decorations will take up space in the middle to add a taste of class to dinners.

I keep my face blank, despite my heart thudding heavily beneath my ribcage.

"Take a seat next to me, Zack, please," Daniel insists, pointing towards the chair to the right of him. Of course, he sits at the head of the table, smiling at his guests like a king.

He leans over and mutters to me, "I'm very excited for you to see tonight's entrée."

I smile, and even I can feel how ice cold it is. "What would that be?" I ask.

"Well, we wouldn't want to ruin the surprise, now would we?" Dan deflects before turning his attention to the guest on his left side.

I stay silent, instead observing the guests seated around me. Everyone looks to be at complete ease, talking amongst each other, laughing, and smiling.

As if it's just another day, sitting at a dinner table and waiting for a young child to be served.

There are three exit points in the dining room. One leads into the kitchen, where there's a back sliding door. The second leads down a hallway towards the game room and deeper into the house. The third leads back towards the front door.

I imagine the girl is in the kitchen. I don't know if she's already dead or if this will be like their rituals in the dungeon.

My question is answered five minutes later when the kitchen door opens, and an older man walks in, hand in hand with a little girl no older than six.

Her brown eyes are wide with terror, looking upon the table like every boogieman in her nightmares has come to life.

The monsters inside her dreams were only there to show her what they look like on the inside.

"Ladies and gentlemen. Dinner is served."

Chapter Thirty Eight
The Manipulator

ll the information Daya and I have gathered so far is splayed out on the island before us. I twist my lips as I mull over what we know for the millionth time, while Daya twists the ring in her nose 'round and 'round. She's waiting on a call back to get the DNA results for the blood on the watch.

"You know, we still never found out who sent me the envelope with all those pictures and the note," I mumble.

"I know," Daya says, dropping her hand and pursing her lips. "That's so odd. I have no idea who it could've been."

Just as I open my mouth, Daya's phone rings. She picks it up so fast, you'd think it was sitting on a burning stove.

"Hello?" she answers, clicking the button to put it on speaker.

"Yes, Daya Pierson?" a woman's voice asks.

"This is her," she responds, anxiety making her eyes pinball around the room. She chews her bottom lip, the tiny gap between her front teeth on display, while I abuse mine just the same.

"Yeah, I got the results back pertaining to the sample you sent in." She pauses, and it feels like when a rollercoaster crests the top of the hill. And just for a single second, you're suspended in time before you go crashing back to the ground. "We did get a match. Genevieve Parsons."

Brown eyes clash with green in a symphony of shock and excitement. Daya clears her throat.

"Perfect, thank you, Gloria. I appreciate it."

"No problem," she chirps before the line disconnects. Mutual silence descends as Daya and I both process the new information.

"Holy fuck."

Before I can fully process the information, Daya reaches over to her bag and pulls out a thick manilla envelope.

"I had some testing and research of my own done. I went ahead and found a sample of Frank's handwriting in a police report and the note we found and sent it in to an analyst. Now just to make you aware, graphology isn't always taken seriously in the name of science, but there have been cases where it held up in court. Regardless, I think it'll be good evidence to have."

My eyes widen with excitement. "Really? Let me see."

She holds up a finger, signaling for me to wait. "Also, remember how the serial number was illegible on the watch?" When I nod, she continues. "I have a friend that's pretty good at deciphering shit like that, and he thinks he got a match.

534

This, Addie, is where the real evidence is. If we confirm it's Frank's watch that had Gigi's blood all over it, and if the handwriting is a match, that's sufficient evidence to prove that Frank was the murderer."

"And?"

She bites her lip. "I wanted to wait to open the email with you. So, you ready?"

I nod my head eagerly, impatience ballooning in my chest.

She opens the envelope first and slides out the results. Laying them flat on the island, we both nearly bonk heads in our pursuit to read them.

...concerning the two samples provided, it has been determined that the handwriting...

"Oh my God. It's a match!" I squeal, almost breathless from excitement.

Daya grins, giddy with her own excitement.

"Okay, now for the real test." She slides her laptop closer, her email already pulled up. She clicks on an unopened message.

Daya,

I checked into the serial number like you asked. It was pretty fucking difficult, whoever scratched that number did it pretty good. But not well enough to get past me. The serial number was tracked down to a buyer by the name of Frank Seinburg. Hope this helps.

James

"Oh my god!" I shout, nearly jumping out of the seat with excitement.

"Holy shit," Daya breathes, her expression full of shock and awe. "He did it. It was fucking Frank."

"He was in love with her, and he must've found out about Ronaldo and killed her in a fit of anger," I conclude, nearly stumbling over my words.

Daya whips around, grabbing the bottle of Grey Goose sitting on the counter. "This calls for a celebratory shot. We can finally bring justice to Gigi. Even if Frank is dead, at least the world will know that he was a piece of shit."

I grin, a weird mix of emotion clogging my throat. I'm thrilled that we solved her case. But I'm also sad. And I'm struggling to pin down why exactly. This murder investigation consumed a large part of my life for the past several months. And letting it go almost feels like losing a small piece of myself.

"We still don't know who hid the watch," I muse before taking the shot. My face screws up from the taste. I don't care what anyone says. Alcohol tastes like shit when it's not mixed with something. I will die on that hill.

But I do relish in the burn as it slides down my throat and settles in my stomach, fire blooming and warming me from the inside out.

I scoot the shot glass back to her, signaling another.

Daya glances at me, and what looks like shame is clouded in her sage eyes.

"What?" I ask flatly.

She points towards my refilled shot glass before shooting hers back. I follow suit. This time it feels like this shot is to gain courage. For what, apparently only Daya knows.

"So, I uh, Frank's note wasn't the only one I sent in," Daya starts, hesitation prominent in her expression. Her hand lifts to fiddle with her nose ring, but she catches herself and twists her fingers together instead.

"Okay," I say, narrowing my eyes in suspicion. She's being weird. And not the kind of weird that involves us taking our pants off and dancing to *I'm a Barbie Girl* at three o'clock in the morning while drinking boxed wine.

That's only happened once, but we both woke up the next morning with regrets.

She sucks in a deep breath, and I'm tempted to tell her that we're sharing the same oxygen—she's not going to find any particles in there that will give her superpowers and make her brave. I'd know, because I want to run and hide from whatever she's about to say.

She picks up the manilla envelope and slides out two more pieces of paper. Shooting one last glance my way, she sets down the documents and we both read them over.

One says it's a match, and another says no match.

"What am I looking at?"

"The handwriting in the confession note matches your Nana's handwriting," she rushes out so quickly, it takes several beats before I comprehend what she said.

"What?"

That's all I'm capable of uttering. She groans and pours another shot.

"This is for the confession note and a sample of your Nana's and John's handwriting."

"Okay, wait," I say, splaying my hands out. "You had suspicions about my Nana being the one to cover up the murder?"

Her lips tighten into a hard line. "Yes."

I shake my head, at a loss for words. "Why?"

She throws her hands up. "Because it would've had to be someone that lived in this house, Addie. It was either John or your Nana. And your grandmother was attached to the attic, was she not?"

"Where did you even get a hold of things with their handwriting on it?"

"You put aside some old documents she had written on. I took pictures. And well, John was a bit more complicated, but I managed to scrounge up a will he had written on."

"Why didn't you just tell me you were doing this?"

She sighs. "Because I knew you'd have a bad reaction to it. I wanted to be sure of my suspicions before I ruined your day."

Blowing out a breath, I nod.

"You're right," I concede. "It makes sense." It sounds like I'm trying to convince myself. Probably because I am.

She stays quiet, giving me space to process the fact that my Nana helped cover up her mother's murder.

"She was forced to," I say finally, glancing over Nana's confession lying on the island, the note I had found in the attic after seeing what I think was Gigi's apparition. I don't move to pick it up, but I remember the words well. The quick scrawl on a piece of paper containing words of a young girl forced to cover up her own mother's murder.

"Your Nana was what, sixteen when Gigi was murdered? Frank obviously threatened her, and she felt she had no choice. He was a detective, for God's sake, of course, she would've believed him."

I nod, a frown marring my features. The fear Nana must've felt. And the absolute sickening feeling knowing she was helping Gigi's murderer.

Jesus.

I can't even begin to imagine how she must've felt.

"That's probably why she spent so much time up there—why she stayed in this house. She was probably punishing herself. Forcing herself to stay in a house with such terrible memories as penance for helping cover it up, even if it wasn't her choice. I mean, who knows what was going through her head. God, Daya, she was always so damn bright and happy. But on the inside... she must've felt such dark things."

Sympathy etches into the lines around Daya's frown. "She lived a long, happy life. I'm sure of that. Especially because she had you."

The alcohol has started to kick in, creating a pleasant buzz in my head. It makes the revelation a little bit more bearable. But not enough to deter the stabbing pain in my chest.

I'm heartbroken for Nana. She lived until she was ninety-one years old. Seventy-five years carrying that weight on her shoulders.

I wonder if Grandpa ever knew. He was a quiet man that loved Nana fiercely. I'd like to think he did and shouldered some of the weight for her.

A memory sparks of about two years ago, a year before she had passed. Nana sitting in Gigi's chair, staring out the window at the rain.

I was in town visiting her, and she looked so sad.

"What's wrong, Nana? You feeling okay?"

"Yeah, baby, I'm fine. Nana's just tired."

"Why don't you lay down and rest?"

A small, sad smile graced her lips. "Not that kind of tired, my love. But you're right. I'll go lay down for a bit."

Another memory replaces that one of when I was about twelve years old. I was coloring at the kitchen island when I had asked her a seemingly innocent and random question.

"Nana, if you won a million dollars, what would you buy?"

"No money in the world could buy me what I truly want," Nana says, a teasing grin on her face.

"Well, what do you want?"

Her smile drops, just for a second, too quick for my twelve-year-old brain to think much of it.

"Peace, baby. All I want is peace."

539

I go to bed that night just a little drunk and even sadder.

I miss Zade.

He's off doing something dangerous tonight—some dinner party. I know he's there to save a little girl, but there's still that selfish part of me that wishes he were here.

My instinct is to hate myself for it. Part of me still does. I don't know how long it's going to take before I fully accept the fact that I've started to fall for him. That I'm accepting him into my life.

How long has he been stalking me for? Three months? Not very long at all. In fact, that's such an insignificant amount of time, it almost makes me sick. There's still so much I don't know about him. What's his favorite color? Does he have allergies? I hope he's allergic to all my favorite foods so I don't have to share. Or, at least I hope he doesn't like them. More for me.

And I hope I don't like his favorite foods because if I do, I'll probably eat off his plate, too.

He probably wouldn't mind. And that softens my heart into a pile of mush. Because somehow a man that wouldn't care if I ate his food fell in love with me. That's so fucking cute.

I flop onto my bed and groan. Daya left an hour ago. We spent the rest of the day working on our respective work. She let me be for the most part while I stewed over the revelations. And after she left, I kept drinking until I stopped thinking about it.

Tomorrow, I'll regret it. I'm not even halfway through the next installment in my series, and I have a lot of readers pushing for it. The pressure always starts getting heavy when several months pass between releases.

Whatever. Maybe Zade will stop by and magically cure my hangover since he's good at making me feel things that should be physically impossible. Especially when he arches his brow and that wicked grin graces his lips.

I clench my thighs, a flood of arousal stirring between my thighs. My breathing escalates, just with the memory of one look, and I'm melting. How is that possible?

I kick off my leggings, a burning sensation in my stomach spreading until it feels like I'm drowning in a pit of flames. A flush is already forming on my chest, and I know pretty soon it'll start creeping up my neck.

Next, I rip my t-shirt over my head, leaving me in only my matching bra and panty set. It's white and silky, and that insane part of me wishes Zade was here to see it. He'd probably think I look so innocent. An angel and a demon. Forbidden but drawn to each other anyways.

That could be a book... based on the attraction between two opposite souls.

Biting my lip, I snake my hand down the front of my underwear, the tip of my finger scarcely brushing across my clit. The contact is so light but yet has electricity zipping through my veins. I close my eyes, releasing a shaky breath. And I pretend that Zade is kneeling before me. Ordering me to touch myself for him. To show him what I do when he's not here.

My heart pounds heavily in my chest, like a basketball on a court. I slip my fingers further down, dipping the tip into the pool of wetness that has gathered. I'm embarrassingly wet.

Licking my lips, I plunge my two fingers inside, a moan falling from my lips as my body seizes with pleasure.

Zade's deep, bottomless voice whispers in my mind of all the dirty things he's growled in my ear. All the words that have stopped my heart in my chest.

My redemption will become your salvation.

I was convinced he would be my damnation. But at this moment, it feels like I've walked into paradise.

Nirvana.

Just like he said when his tongue was plunged deep inside of me, like my fingers are now.

I moan louder, the crescendo building as the image flickers to Zade sitting behind me in my car, feasting on me—no, *drinking* from me like a dying man deprived of water.

The pleasure builds as I swirl my sopping fingers up to my clit and rub the sensitive bud in tight circles. My head kicks back as my spine curves. Panting out breathless moans, I circle my clit faster and harder until I'm nearly chasing the orgasm.

And finally, I tip over the edge. I yelp loudly, calling out Zade's name as the orgasm crashes through me quickly and without remorse. It's over before I'm able to regain my breath.

Slumping, I heave out a sigh, the corners of my lips pulling into a frown. My body is languid and boneless, but my chest—it's tight still. That orgasm was only a temporary reprieve. And I realize that the weight isn't going to go anywhere.

Tonight, I'm just... sad.

May 18th, 1946

The face of death is petrifying. But it's the only thing I see these days.

He won't leave me alone. I've pleaded with him. Begged for my life. I'm a mother. He can't take me away from my child. She needs me for god's sake.

I don't know what to do. If I tell the police, will they believe me. Or will they believe him?

Someone that is obviously dangerous, and has incredible connections.

I have no chance.

How did my life turn out this way?

And how could he do this to me?

I trusted him.

Chapter
Thirty Nine
The Shadow

You eat meat raw?" I question, the deep note of my tone traveling across the table. Everyone quietens.

"Well, of course not!" Daniel booms, laughing at what he probably considers a stupid question.

"A sacrifice must be made first. Then we drink the blood and take her—"

"We don't get to have fun with her first?" I interrupt, my voice deepening with disappointment. "That's half the fun, brother."

Eyes shift, glancing at each other, waiting for Daniel's response to my demands. He stares at me, a slight smile on his face. I cock a brow, waiting for my answer.

When I do, Daniel laughs, a pleasant surprise radiating from his face. My own is serious, eyes never straying from Daniel's.

He breaks eye contact first, looking over to where the servant is holding the scared little girl.

"Bring her here."

I rest back in my chair, my movements languid and relaxed. On the inside, there's a war raging—the battlefield in my gut bloody and vicious. I want to tear this entire house down, shredding every sick individual in here with only my hands and teeth.

I'll show them what it feels like to be eaten by a monster.

The servant hurdles the girl forward, consistently shoving the girl forward due to her digging her little heels in. She knows something bad is coming.

But what she doesn't know is I will do everything in my power to stop that from happening.

When the girl reaches us, my hand snaps out, gripping the girl's tiny wrist in my hand. Her wide eyes jerk to mine, and what I see in them nearly breaks my heart. Her eyes are swirling with sorrow and fear. It's an expression no child should ever wear on their face.

"What's your name?"

Dan scoffs, but I ignore him. "S-Sarah," she says quietly, her voice mousy. I want to hurl her into my chest and run out of here, but I think we both know that's not possible.

"Sit on my lap, Sarah," I order firmly.

Reluctantly, she listens. Her eyes drop as she climbs on my lap, but I don't miss the tears welling in her eyes beforehand.

The sick feeling grows more potent as I help her up, keeping her body at my knees with one hand high on her back and my other on her knee. Areas that are not sexual but will be perceived as dominating to the others. I'd prefer not to touch her at all—she's viewing this as something predatory—but I feel safest with her close when there's a bunch of adults eyeing her like she's their next meal.

Literally.

I force a predatory smile on my face and lean in, my lips at her ear, and whisper so only she can hear, "You're safe with me. Keep quiet."

Dan observes the interaction closely, a hint of displeasure in his eyes. From his vantage point, he wouldn't have been able to read my lips. And he's not the type of man that appreciates secrets being told in front of his face.

Sarah is smart. She doesn't react. Doesn't nod or speak. She just continues to look at her clasped hands, tremors wracking her petite body as if she's in the middle of a snowstorm.

I look up at Daniel. "Am I expected to have an audience, or can I enjoy her elsewhere?" I ask, looking at the girl with anticipation.

He will think I'm anticipating all the ways I'm going to hurt her, but in reality, I'm picturing little Sarah being carried away by Ruby while I poise his head over a knife.

Dan's mouth quirks at the look on my face, his expression softening back into ease once more.

I'm a damn good actor. I'd never survive in this field of work otherwise.

"We would love to watch," Dan says smoothly, leaning back in his own chair, while one hand snakes under the table. I can't see what he's doing from my angle, but I don't need to in order to know that he's squeezing himself.

I'm going to enjoy killing him.

"P-please take me home," Sarah cries, the dam bursting as tears spill over her lashes and down her cherub cheeks.

I wipe the tears from her cheeks, silently praising her for flinching away from my touch, even though it makes me feel like my insides are in a dumpster fire.

"Don't cry, sweetie," I coo aloud. She cries harder, and my heart blisters from the fury.

Dan licks his lips with unrestrained hunger, reaching over to do what—I don't know. My hand that's wrapped around her neck whips out, grabbing his hand with a firmness that has him instantly freezing.

"I don't share," I growl, letting some of the pent-up anger loose. Dan jerks his hand away, raising them in the air in surrender.

"Possessive," he chuckles, glancing at the guests. Embarrassment flashes in his eyes, but it's gone before it can truly settle. That just might come back to bite me in the ass—Dan also isn't the type of man that takes well to public humiliation.

Not that I'm truly concerned with the backlash. He'll be dead soon anyways.

While Dan's eyes cast over the dinner table, I slyly press the button on my watch, keeping my hands under the table. By the time his eyes are drifting back to me, my hands return to their previous position.

"Please, proceed... brother," he tacks on at the end, the word said with an inflection of challenge.

I flash a feral grin, not holding back in the slightest. His eyes heat at the sight, likely assuming that he's about to get a show of a lifetime.

Before either of us can move, a loud banging on the front door startles us both. A muffled, indiscernible shout follows. Dan's eyes look towards the front of the house, brow furrowing in confusion.

"Who the hell would dare...?" he mutters under his breath, aghast that someone is nearly breaking down his front door.

Panicked, hushed whispers rise from the group, the guests turning to each other with fearful gazes.

"Daniel," I snap, catching his attention. "I don't want to wait much longer."

"Of course, I'll be sure to hurry," he placates, appearing more flustered as others from the table continue to speak their concern and discomfort. Another loud crash startles the group, and then seconds later, a booming crash sounds, causing the guests to jump. Some even rise from their seats, ready to bolt.

And then, "FBI! GET DOWN ON THE GROUND NOW!"

The rest of the guests jump up now, myself included. Gently, I set Sarah down beside me but hold onto her arm firmly as the room breaks out into chaos. The dinner guests scatter like ants, screams and shouts bouncing around the room.

The door to the dining room crashes open, eliciting more screams. Several FBI agents storm the room, shouting out demands for everybody to get down.

"Let's go," I whisper to the girl, attempting to guide her towards the kitchen door.

She struggles and screams for one of the agents, that dormant fire in her finally erupting.

I'm so fucking proud of her.

I pick her up and whisper in her ear. "Those FBI agents are with me. I'm going to take you back home, but I need you to work with me."

The second the word *home* leaves my mouth, her struggling ceases. She looks at me, her brown eyes full of tears.

"You could be lying," she sniffles, distrust in her eyes. Another surge of pride overtakes me as I stuff my hand in my pocket and pull out a fake FBI badge, flashing it to her discreetly—the first lie I've truly told her. She reluctantly concedes, nodding her head. I bolt towards the kitchen door, not wasting another second.

In the chaos, no one will notice me slipping out. But if they do, it won't hurt my case with Dan. I plan on telling him I did exactly that.

No one is in the lavish kitchen. If anyone were in here before, they probably ran when they heard the FBI break-in.

I slip out of the back sliding door, making my way across the massive porch, and towards the stairs.

The cool air is a balm to my heated skin. This suit is confining. I much prefer my jeans and hoodie to this shit.

"Are you going to take me back to my mommy and daddy?" Sarah asks quietly. Her soft, sweet voice is almost a shock to my system.

Adrenaline has been coursing through my veins steadily since the moment she was brought into that room. The chemical won't dissipate from my body until she's off this property.

"I am," I promise gently.

Her hand lifts, her tiny finger tracing one of the scars on my face.

"Does this hurt?"

"Not anymore," I say quietly, suppressing the urge to lean away from her touch. I'm not used to anyone touching my scars. When Addie did, it felt like fire lacing across the dead skin. Now, with Sarah, it feels a tad uncomfortable. But not unbearable.

"Did the bad guys that took me do this to you?"

"Not the same bad guys, but bad guys all the same."

She seems to think that over, digesting my words slowly. She blinks at me and wipes away some snot leaking from her nose.

"Do you know if mommy and daddy are alive?"

I nearly trip over my feet when she asks the question.

Considering I didn't know the girl's identity beforehand, I haven't had a chance to look into her background. I've no idea who her parents are, or what kind of home she comes from.

"Is there a reason you think they wouldn't be?" I ask. I make it to the meet up spot, outside of view of any cameras and the front of the house where Dan is.

Her eyes drop, long lashes fan across her chubby cheeks, still damp from her tears.

"I don't know where they are," she says simply.

"When's the last time you saw them?"

She shrugs her little shoulders and says, "I dunno."

I sigh, giving in to the urge and rolling my neck to ease some tension. Ruby should be here soon to take care of Sarah while I finish up business.

Soon, the agents will lug Dan and anyone else out to be taken down to the station on false charges.

They're false agents to begin with, hired by myself. Luckily, I have a few high-ranking FBI agents in my pocket, which is the only thing that made this night possible.

They'll bring Dan down to the station on suspicion of smuggling drugs. They will release him by tomorrow morning when they don't find anything.

Dan will insist the FBI agents responsible be fired, and considering no real agents were involved, the fake ones will be easily let go of. False paperwork will be filed, and Dan will be satisfied. Or as satisfied as you can be when your dinner party is interrupted by your front door getting kicked in.

"How old are you, shortcake?"

"Five," she chirps.

"I'll try to find your mommy and daddy, okay? If I can't, I'll make sure you're safe."

She nods her little head, her brown eyes now latched back onto me.

"Then will you be my daddy?"

Fuck. Can't say I've ever been asked that one before. I force a smile. Adoption isn't out of the question, but that's something I'll have to consult with Addie first. She'd be her mommy, after all.

Before I can answer, Ruby is sneaking up to take Sarah off to a safe place. Ruby stays silent, understanding how dire the situation is. When she approaches the small child gripping onto my hand, she whispers to her quietly, urging her to come with her so she can make sure she's safe. Sarah hesitates.

"You can trust her," I say softly. Sarah looks up at me with massive brown eyes and fuck, I'm a puddle of ice cream.

"Will I see you again?"

Swallowing, I nod, incapable of giving a verbal answer. Sarah is satisfied though and allows Ruby to lead her off into the night.

Before they completely disappear around another house, Sarah turns her head and gives me one last look.

I'm a goner.

Just as they round the corner, an FBI agent comes up behind me and grabs my arm roughly.

"Thought you could sneak away?"

I laugh quietly, even as he jerks both my arms behind my back and slaps handcuffs on them.

Roughly, he leads me up back towards the front of the mansion, where Dan is still loud-mouthing the agents and demanding his lawyer.

"Got a runner," the agent attached to me calls out. Dan pauses mid-tirade to look over at us. I can't be sure from this distance, but it almost appears as if Dan's face goes lax with relief for just a moment.

"He has nothing to do with anything," Dan says, his face tightening once more with anger.

"Yeah, okay, buddy," the agent snorts from behind me. I'm actually surprised by the fact that Dan is trying to defend me.

"Why am I even being arrested?" I snarl, feigning anger.

"You tried sneaking off during an FBI raid. That's grounds for suspicion."

"I'm terribly sorry about this, Zack," Dan cuts in. "This doesn't involve you."

I shrug a shoulder, the movement awkward against the cuffs. "S'kay. These assholes will be fired by morning," I say with a shit-eating grin.

Dan scoffs and corrects me, "By the end of the night."

"Yeah whatever, fuckers. Get in the car before I accidentally smash your head off the car on the way in."

I twist in my binds. "What's your name?"

The agent grins. "Michael."

"Well, Michael, I hope you don't mind shitting out teeth because you're about to eat them."

Michael laughs, a glimmer in his eyes. Dan starts up again when another agent leads him into the back of a cop car. His rant is cut off by the slam of the door.

"Get in the goddamn car, Z. I am hungry, but it's not for my teeth."

Chuckling, I comply.

Chapter Forty
The Shadow

I don't remember ever being a needy child. Growing up, I had a great relationship with my parents. My mother was incredibly loving, and my father was supportive and very involved in my life.

But I was always a naturally independent person. Determined to do things on my own without help. And because my parents showered me with love and attention, it wasn't something I sought out.

I can't say that anymore.

Addie's mouth is wide open, drool steadily leaking from her mouth. She's snoring softly, and I don't think I've gotten the chance to tease her about that yet. She's going to get angry, and I smile just thinking about it.

Despite her disheveled state, my cock is incredibly hard. The witch went to bed in nothing but a white, silky set, and the second I slowly drew back the covers, I nearly went to my knees.

Did my little mouse wear that just for me?

Reaching out, I trace a finger up her thigh, enjoying the sight of her skin puckering. She shifts, moaning softly at the disturbance in her sleep.

How would she feel waking up with my cock inside her?

She shifts again when I finger the strap of her underwear. Normally, she wakes up fairly easily. And despite Addie giving in to me, I'm not foolish enough to believe I don't set her on edge still.

Which means she had a few drinks.

Grinning, I toe off my shoes and slide out of the suffocating suit I've been wearing all night.

After we got to the station, they hauled Dan off to a separate room and let me go. I came straight here, my body strung tight with the need to bury myself inside my little mouse.

Completely naked, I slide into the bed next to Addie, curling her body into mine.

Her eyes flutter, and I watch as she regains consciousness. When her eyes slide up to my face, they widen ever so slightly.

I could've tried to fuck her while asleep, but I decide to hold off on that until Addie admits her love for me and freely accepts mine. Until I can fuck her without a fight, though I think some part of Addie will always fight me.

Although I've taken advantage of Addie on several occasions, at least her being awake and coherent allowed me to watch her body's reactions. Doesn't make it right. But her body has always wept for me.

And if it ever didn't, I wouldn't have touched her until it did.

"Why are you in my bed staring at me like a creep?" she asks, her voice groggy with sleep.

I chuckle. "I thought it'd been established that I'm a creep already?"

"It has, and yet you still keep doing it."

"Would you like me to stop?" I query, sliding my hands down her backside. She sucks in a sharp breath, appearing much more awake and alert as I grip her plump ass in my palms.

"No," she admits quietly. She looks so tiny and vulnerable admitting it, so I stay quiet.

She trails her finger across the tattoos on my chest, her eyes averted firmly away from mine.

"Do these mean anything?" she murmurs, seeming as if she's concentrating hard on the design.

"No," I answer. "I have them because I like them. I prefer to keep anything of significance as a possession."

Frowning, she peers up at me through long lashes. "Why? I would think your body would be the one place you would have anything meaningful. You carry it around everywhere you go."

I lift a shoulder. "My body is just a vessel that my soul inhabits, attached to a shell that it'll one day leave. And when that day comes, I won't care to let that shell go. I carry my body around because I have to, not because it's a choice. But when I possess something meaningful, I'm choosing to hold on to it. Carrying something meaningful in my skin is effortless but holding onto something that I could lose—that takes devotion."

She drops her eyes back down, seeming to contemplate my words. I curl my finger under her chin, wanting—no needing, her eyes back. They suck the oxygen from my lungs, and I've always loved to toe the line between life and death.

Those pretty brown eyes fasten on mine, big and round, and all I want to do is consume her.

"I will always possess you, little mouse. So, know that you have all of my devotion to keeping you."

"Why does it always sound like a threat?" she wonders aloud, though a small smile tips the corner of her lips.

I grin. "Because it is."

I roll to my back, bringing her with me so she's sprawled out on my chest.

"Zade," she warns, but her words contrast against her actions. She shifts her legs, so she's straddling me, her center lined up on my cock. I can feel how hot and wet she is through the silk of her underwear.

Gritting my teeth, I ball my hands into fists, fighting the instinct to rip the sorry excuse for panties to shreds so that I can feel how ready she is to take me inside her.

"Adeline," I echo.

Her light brown eyes are shaded, but I can feel the effect all the same. She's leaning just above me, her soft body molded to mine. I swear I can feel the tension lining her hips as she resists the need to grind her pussy on me.

"What?" she whispers, feigning ignorance.

"Sit on my cock. Now."

Her breathing hitches, and with her breasts pressed tightly against mine, I can't tell if the rapid pulsing in my chest is from her heart or mine.

The internal struggle in her head is loud, and indecision radiates from her.

Eventually, she sits up, her body cutting through the strands of moonlight shining through the balcony doors.

And I crumble.

Her curvy body is cascaded in both shadows and light, the two forbidden lovers clashing on her skin and creating a fucking masterpiece.

Her beauty is blinding, turning my body into ash beneath her light.

She drags her hand down her flat stomach until her fingertips tease the edges of her underwear.

"Addie," I snarl through clenched teeth. My hands slide up her thighs, pausing at the juncture where they meet her hips. I'm a weak man, and I don't possess the strength to deny the need to touch her.

"Yes, Zade?" she asks, her husky voice low and breathy. My hips jerk impatiently in response. She smiles, the act wicked and cruel.

Finally, she lifts up and slides her underwear to the side, baring her pussy. I lift my hips again, desperate for contact, but she evades me, hovering just out of reach.

"You have five fucking sec—"

"Shh, baby." I'm so thrown by her calling me 'baby' that my threat vanishes, as if my voice were a ghost teasing the corner of your eye.

Her smile widens at my incredulous look, but I'm only confused why she thought calling me baby would calm me down.

Now all I want to do is flip her on her knees, pin that pretty face into the sheets, and fuck her until her head is coming out the underside of the bed.

Before I can make good on it, she finally drops her hips. I groan at the feeling of my cock being enveloped by slick heat as she glides up and down my length. My head kicks back, and my hands tighten on her hips. Bruises will mar her skin and the thought only enrages the beast more.

"Fuck, Add—"

I have no time to even finish my prayer before the tip of my cock is slipping inside, and I'm completely incapable of formulating words.

Slowly—tortuously, she works my cock inside her, balancing her weight on my stomach. Little, breathless pants puff from her mouth while I tremble beneath her.

So fucking tight.

"God, I'm too full," she whimpers, her own body trembling as she works to take me in.

"Baby, I'm not going to be able to control myself much longer. Sit. Down."

Sucking her bottom lip between her teeth, she lifts up one last time before seating herself completely on my cock.

A yelp bursts from her lips, her eyes round discs. My body hums from the euphoria of her pussy wrapped so fucking tightly around me.

Goddamn nirvana. There's nothing like it.

"Now move," I rasp out, my control slipping as I pump my hips up once. It's enough to send electric shocks down my spine.

Her chin tips up, eyes rolling as she swivels her hips.

"Oh," she moans, continuing the movement until we're both delirious. She moves slow and languid, sliding up and down and twisting her hips in a way that makes me see entire constellations.

Her eyes are pinched shut, her little mouth parted as she gets pleasure from my cock. It feels incredible, enough to make me come if I allowed it, but I need more. I need her fast, and hard.

"Little mouse," I call, my voice hoarse with need. Her hips still, and her eyes creak open. "Run."

Her eyes pop open, and her breath stalls. A moment passes where we're both frozen in time, and then she springs into action. I hiss from the sensation of sliding out of her, and then she's catapulting towards the end of the bed.

She bolts out of the room and guns for the stairs. I stay right at her heels, enjoying the startled screams that slip from her throat every time she sees me so close.

Purposely, I let her run, my cock hardening further from the chase.

My little mouse loves to be scared. And I get off on making her so.

Barreling down the stairs, she aims for the back of the house. I grin when I realize exactly where she's going.

I let her get to the hallway before I snatch her up, relishing in the bite of her nails in my arm.

"Trying to relive a favorite memory, naughty girl?"

She growls in response, kicking her legs at air. I nearly bust into the sunroom, the beauty of it lost on me when I hold the most precious gift in my arms.

I drop to my knees and twist her around, laughing as she struggles. "Feel familiar?"

"Zade!" she cries with indignation, but I don't give her a moment to get her bearings. She's on her back in a matter of seconds, staring up at me with wide eyes.

"Let me know which stars you prefer. The ones above you, or the ones I make you see."

And then I'm driving into her tight heat, not giving either of us a moment to prepare for it. She cries out, her back arching and her claws sharpened as she scores them down my arms.

"Jesus fuckin—" her words are cut off from another sharp thrust, a moan replacing her sinful words.

I shudder, my control completely in tatters as I drive into her, fucking her so hard that I'm forced to keep dragging her back down towards me.

Sharp screams fill the air and there's a moment where the pitch is so high, I fear I broke something inside of her.

But then her pussy clamps tight, making it almost impossible to move before she comes around my cock, her body nearly convulsing from the power.

My name falls from her lips, but I can't stop. The sound of our skin slapping and her garbled words bounce off the windows surrounding us as I continue to slam into her.

Her tiny throat is in my hand, squeezing until she can no longer utter a word. A hand wraps around my arm, branding bloody crescent moons into my skin as she fights for oxygen. I'll gladly sacrifice my name on her tongue if it means climbing up to heaven with her.

I bare my teeth, intense pleasure racing down my spine and building at the base.

Fuck, I feel the explosion right at the precipice. Parsons Manor will always be destined to be the house that burns and takes lives.

"Give me another, baby," I urge, my other hand reaching down until my thumb circles her clit.

Her face pinkens, nearing red when she falls back over. I release her throat, the dizzying rush from lack of oxygen coupled with her orgasm has her back coming entirely off the floor. Like a woman possessed, she clings to me, as more scratches are torn into my skin.

Gnashing my teeth, I sit back, bringing her squirming body with me until I'm kneeling with her legs wrapped tightly around my waist.

She gyrates down onto me relentlessly, riding out her orgasm and pulling me down over the edge with her. I come with a roar, clutching her to my chest so tightly that we're both only capable of small, jerky movements as we grind into each other.

I lose myself. My name. My identity. My soul. It's been hurdled away into the vortex our bodies have created. Like being sucked into a wormhole and kicked out into a new universe.

And when we come down, the stars surrounding us suddenly look so dull and lifeless compared to the ones shining in her eyes.

"I have an extraction tomorrow. It's what I've been building up to for months now," I say, my fingers tracing across her bare back. "It's going to be pretty dangerous. I just want you to be aware of that."

Addie's head lifts, her face much more visible now that we're in a room housed in windows. I can see the barest hint of the freckles dusting her nose and cheeks, and I want to kiss each and every one of them.

We collapsed after I fucked us both stupid, and neither of us has felt inclined to get up since.

"Is it the rituals?"

I nod and tell her all about the night I had. She was aware of the fucked-up dinner party, and when I tell her it was successful, her face softens with relief.

"I can't wrap my head around people actually doing that. People just came over and sat at that table as if they were going to eat fucking lobster tail?"

"Yeah," I murmur. I bite my lip, a shit-eating grin already forming on my face for what I'm about to tell her. Her head just settled back on my chest when I say,

"The little girl I saved, Sarah? She asked if I'd be her daddy."

Addie's head snaps up so quickly, she comes close to breaking it.

"Careful, this world would be in trouble if you died."

Her mouth flops. "What did you say?"

I shrug. "I didn't really get to say anything. She had to leave so I could go get fake arrested. If I didn't, Dan and the Society might've found the raid too convenient. Luckily, I was able to play it on a charge that Dan has gotten in the past."

She blinks. "Would you? Adopt her, I mean?"

I lift my hand, gently swiping a lock of her hair from her face and curling it behind her ear. She tries to hide the shiver, but her body is pressed too closely into mine for it to be successful.

"I wouldn't do anything without your say-so. But yes, I would."

She swallows. "Why do you need my permission?"

"You think I stalked you just because I wanted a quick thrill? No, baby. It's you and me forever. Which means if I become a daddy, then you become a mommy."

Her eyes widen, and what looks like panic flashes in her irises. I curl a finger beneath her chin and land a quick peck to her lips.

"Don't worry 'bout that right now. Sarah is safe, and at the moment, we're more worried about her trauma and getting her mental health taken care of."

She nods, though I don't miss the lingering look before she settles back on my chest.

Chapter Forty One
The Shadow

"**Y**ou ready for tonight?" Jay asks in my ear.

"I've been ready," I answer easily as I pull up to the gentlemen's club, Savior's. The Society choosing this club as the front for an underground dungeon must be their version of a sick sense of humor.

I slip the earpiece out of my ear, stuff it in my inner suit jacket, and then make my way up to the entrance.

The outside of the building is like any other high-priced strip club—a marble black monstrosity that drips money and power. The security guard standing outside of the doors gives me a once-over, before putting me through the customary *what's your name* and *let me check your asshole. Cough once.*

Unlike Detective Fingers, this one actually manages to keep his hands in the safe zone and lets me through without a hitch.

For obvious reasons, I'm not permitted to carry firearms on me. But that won't be an issue.

After Mark confessed the location, several of my men were able to infiltrate the security detail hired for this club.

Powerful men and women certainly wouldn't be showing up to kill children if they didn't feel protected while doing so.

Security is required to carry firearms, and I have it on good authority that some of them might let me borrow a gun or two when the time comes.

Just like when I was here last time, when I walk into the club, it feels like walking through a portal to hell. It's stifling in here, the air so full of depravity and sickness that it's a physical weight on my shoulders.

Jesus fucking Christ.

I feel like I need a goddamn gas mask.

I walk directly into the main area, the massive layout an open concept. It's dimly lit and ominous—the perfect place to hide in the shadows without being noticed.

The floors are black marble, and unlike the seedy strip clubs downtown, these floors shine as brightly as my freshly polished shoes. The blood red walls are bare of creepy art, but plenty of creeps occupy the booths and tables surrounding the stage. A woman swings around the pole, shaking her ass to the beat while money is thrown on the stage.

Low music pumps through the speakers, though not so loud that I can hardly hear myself think. Loud moans ring out from somewhere down a hallway, and I make sure to stay far away for now. If I go back and see some fucked up shit happening, I'm going to blow the entire thing.

"For a second, I thought you weren't going to show up," a voice says from behind me.

I turn to see Dan standing there, peering at me with a satisfied grin on his face.

"A man can't enjoy some strippers after getting arrested?" I retort, my tone laced with dry amusement. Dan laughs and shakes his head, stuffing his hands in his pockets.

"I still can't believe that happened. I am so sorry. Every man on my lawn got fired that night, I assure you."

I flash my teeth. "I expected nothing less. What charges did they try to pin on you?"

"Fucking drug smuggling," he scoffs in that *can you believe that shit* way. "I haven't had a line of coke up my nose in months, and it sure as shit wasn't my product."

I quirk a brow. "What happened to the girl?"

His face darkens, and for the first time, I see true evilness reflecting back at me. I knew it was there, residing just below the surface. But this is the first time Dan truly let that hateful demon out.

"I believe one of my guests took advantage of the chaos and stole her for themselves."

"The cameras?" I push.

He shakes his head and spits, "Fucking ruined. The FBI must've done something to mess with the signal when they came. Probably because they weren't authorized to kick down my goddamn door. Regardless, the little girl is gone, and ninety-thousand dollars went down the drain."

My displeasure is prominent as I say, "Do you have any idea who it was? I would love to talk to them about stealing from me."

A smirk forms on his face. "As soon as I have confirmation, I will let you know. Otherwise, keep the beast contained." He pats my chest and motions towards an empty booth. "Let's have a drink. The ceremony won't start for a few hours."

"Lead the way."

"So, my wife said that she's going to leave, right? I told her there isn't a goddamn inch that exists in this world where she could hide, and I couldn't find her." He finishes his statement with a huff and shake of his head, boggled that his wife would even try to find a happy life somewhere else.

Somewhere that doesn't involve eating children for dinner. And whatever else sick shit they do to them in the meantime.

"Women like to run, but they like to be caught even more," I murmur.

He looks at me, a wicked grin curling his lips. "Exactly, man. Too bad the bitch isn't worth chasing. So by the time I catch her, she's going to wish she did find that inch. You know how exhausting it is to be married to someone who doesn't share the same tastes as you? I've tried to initiate her several times, but she refuses. Can you believe that?"

How does someone with a shred of decency even answer that?

You don't.

I shake my head casually, taking a sip of my whiskey. Addie's grandfather has better taste than these old dicklickers.

Glancing at his Rolex, he motions for me to follow as he stands. "It's time.

Let's head on down," Dan says, swallowing the last of his whiskey before setting the empty crystal glass on the table. He turns and checks out a passing stripper, his eyes leering on her exposed backside.

"And when we're done, I'm going to take a bite out of that one next. These initiations always get me in the mood."

The whiskey in my stomach sours.

Swallowing down what I *really* want to say, I motion for him to lead. He saunters towards the hallway where the moans are emanating from. Steeling my spine, I follow after him.

We enter through a hallway riddled with doors on either side. The moans escalate, but now that I'm closer, I hear the notes of fear and pain laced in them. Cracks of whips, flesh hitting flesh, and the loud grunts of men accompany the moans.

Fuck. *Think of the child lying on a stone altar somewhere. They need me more.*

At the end of the hallway is a black marble door. Dan wraps his fist around the knob and pauses before peering back at me, his lips curled with excitement.

"You ready?"

"Considering I was teased last night, I'm more than ready."

Dan flashes a malicious smirk before opening the door. I'm met with a dark hallway, scarcely lit by dim LED lighting on either side of the floor.

The hallway is long and almost feels never-ending. And it seems the further we walk, the narrower it grows. But it's just my mind playing tricks on me.

At the end is another marble door. I glance back and notice we were going down a subtle incline, where I see a small group of men coming down the hallway in the distance.

Dan opens the door, and we're greeted by a room full of people. The black marble extends into the room, but the walls are rock. On either side are long rows of familiar black robes I've seen in the last few videos. The people gathered in here are speaking in low tones, slipping on the oversized robes.

My heart pounds, almost in disbelief that I'm finally here. The moment I've been working towards for so long.

It's surreal.

"Grab one," Dan orders, his tone serious. Without a word, I unhook a robe and slip it on. The material is silky smooth, but it feels like I'm wrapping myself in wool. Despite my large stature, the material still hangs past my feet and hands.

"This another newcomer?" a nasally voice asks from my left. I turn to see a weasel of a man standing next to me. He's at least a good three feet shorter than I am, with a receding hairline, a hooked nose, and round glasses.

"I am," I answer cryptically. "And you are?"

The man smiles nervously. "Also a newcomer. My name is Larry Verenich."

"Zack," I offer.

Several robed figures start pouring out of the room through another black door straight ahead.

"Let's go," Dan says, nodding his head towards the group.

As I approach the door, a low hum gathers at the base of my neck, causing the hairs to rise. The room is just like I've seen in the videos. It's like walking into an underground cave, only instead of moisture in the air, it's dry and heavy. The dark space is lit by hundreds of candles lining the rock walls. But the small flames are no match for the oppressing shadows.

We're on a rounded platform, a simple black rail as a barrier to about a forty-foot drop. In the center of the room is a stone altar, a wriggling little girl on top of it. Black straps circle her tiny wrists and ankles, keeping her in place.

She can't be more than six or seven years old.

The hum grows louder until it sounds like it's coming from inside my own head. My hands clench beneath the fabric, and I'm only thankful that the sleeves are long enough to hide my reaction.

"To your left are the stairs," Dan says, pointing in the direction. "Go ahead and stand by the altar. One of you will be offered the knife to bleed out the sacrifice. Drink the blood, and you will be initiated into the Society."

I nod my head and take off in the direction. The rocky, uneven stairs are just around the bend, where Larry is already heading.

I lift the hood over my head, glancing around the areas until I spot the security guards—three of them on the bottom floor where the altar is, hidden off in the shadows. From my vantage point, I'm unable to see their faces. But I know Michael is one of them.

Two other men follow behind me as I make my way down the steps. The minute my foot hits the ground, a low chant begins, gaining in pitch as I approach the altar.

I stare at the little girl on the stone slab, tears tracking down her dirty cheeks. She's sobbing, her little lip curled in a frown as her wide blue eyes stare at us in absolute terror.

My heart constricts so tightly it's debilitating. By sheer willpower, I force myself to stand still.

"Fuck, I'm already getting hard," a guy whispers from my left. My teeth nearly crack from how hard I clench my jaw in that moment. Slowly, I turn to see a guy that looks like he's in his early twenties, his hood down. His brown, bottomless eyes glance up at me, and all I can see is pure excitement radiating from them.

He's going to be the first one to die.

He's close enough that he can see my face, and I work to keep it neutral. He grins at me, but I give him no reaction. And though his smile falters just a little, the sick fuck has no idea that I just did him a huge favor. Because had I reacted, I would've reached down his throat and ripped out his windpipe with my bare hands.

"P-p-please, I want my mommy," the little girl begs from below me. Her red and puffy eyes are full of tears and she's staring up at me with terror and desperation. Her little lip trembles, and I have to physically restrain myself from reaching out and grabbing her tiny hand in my own.

"Pleeaasssee," she cries, her blues full of tears, despite the rivers streaming down her cheeks. "I wanna go ho-oome."

Snarling, I force my mouth to stay shut. More than anything, I want to reassure her. Comfort her. Promise her that she *will* get to see her mother again. But I can't allow any of those words to escape.

Not yet.

The chant around us grows louder, building until it feels like the cave vibrates from the sound. But it's muted, like I'm under water. All I can concentrate on is the small girl pleading for my help.

I'm staring at her so hard, trying to convey the assurances in my eyes, that I don't even notice the black figure that approached until they're right before me, standing on the other side of the little girl.

Their face is hidden in the depths of their hood, and black gloves cover their hands. I've no idea if this person is a man or a woman, or how significant they are.

They could be from the Society.

In fact, my intuition tells me they are.

In each hand are two goblets twined between their fingers. The figure holds out their arms, and the four of us each grab one. And then, the figure reaches down by their leg and pulls out a curved black blade.

They don't speak. They just balance the blade in the palm of their hand and hold it out straight, an offer for any one of us to take.

I swipe the blade, already sensing the frat boy next to me gearing up to snatch it. I can feel his disappointment, assumingly because he wanted to be the one to plunge the blade into a child's chest. And for that, I'm going to make sure his death is slow. He won't get the honors of getting his jugular sliced open so he can bleed out in seconds.

No, no. He won't be that fortunate.

The chanting escalates until the haunting noise radiates off the cave walls. I feel the figure's eyes boring into me. And though they can't see my face either, I return the stare.

Finally, they turn and walk away, disappearing back into the shadows.

My heart thumping heavily in my chest trumps the noise around me. I can't hear anything beyond the racing organ beneath my rib cage until the little girl's screams pierce the air. I've lifted the blade over her, the sharp point hovering right above her chest.

The handle is fisted in my grip. I stick out two fingers, pausing for a few seconds to make sure the signal is seen before tucking them back in.

And then I look down at the girl.

"Close your eyes," I whisper. "And don't open them until I tell you to." Her lip wobbles, but she listens, closing her eyes to the horror that will happen around her.

Gripping the blade tightly, I lift it up and swipe my arm to the left. Directly into the frat boy's throat.

The chanting stutters before stopping completely, gasps ringing out as the boy beside me suffocates on his blood. I jerk the blade out, the suctioning noise swallowed by his choked gasps.

He's staring at me, eyes wide with disbelief. And then he collapses, no longer capable of holding himself up.

Gunshots ring out. A security guard stationed behind me falls to the ground, his brain matter splattered into the shadows.

That was the trigger. The entire room bursts into action. Panicked screams and running bodies aim for the exit. I don't let Larry make it a step before the curved blade is plundering through his eye. Glasses and everything.

His body convulses, and then collapses when I rip it out of his head, the suctioning noise lost in the chaos.

I look down at frat boy, and watch him take his last breath, the life snuffed out from his eyes. And I smile.

Michael erupts from the shadows, running towards me. When he's close enough, he flings a gun at me. I snatch the weapon in the air and face the direction the black figure disappeared off into.

Urgency flooding my veins, I glance down at the little girl, her eyes still faithfully closed. Blood is splattered across her body, and I hate that evil still managed to touch her.

Slipping the hood off my face, I lean down over the girl. "Open your eyes, pretty girl. But I want you to look only at me, okay?"

Slowly, she cracks them open. The tears have dried, but her face is still twisted with panic.

"My friend here is going to take care of you. He's going to make sure you get back to your mommy, okay?"

Immediately, she bursts into tears again. I swipe her blonde hair from her face.

"It's okay, pretty girl. What I want you to do is keep your eyes on him and only him. Close them if you have to. He'll let you know when it's safe."

"Okay," she whispers, her little voice cracked.

She nods, and I gently sweep a tear from her face before straightening my spine.

"Take care of the girl," I order, looking up at Michael. "Ruby should be here, she'll take care of her and then you come back and help finish this shit off."

Michael nods while I start towards the area I last saw the black figure disappear. If they really were a part of the Society, then I want them for information.

Screams erupt from the entrance I came in through, followed by more gunshots. One of my men must've let my team in.

Absolute carnage is consuming that cave, but I don't worry about that, trusting that no one that participated in this ceremony will make it out alive. That was a very clear order I made.

This world will be better off without them.

I only make it about ten feet before an explosion blasts through the cave, sending me flying. Time slows as my body hurtles through air, sound becoming inconceivable.

And then it speeds again, and my body is colliding into the stone altar. The oxygen is knocked from my lungs as my back hits the corner of the altar before I collapse to the ground.

Loud ringing reverberates throughout my head, but it's no louder than a whisper when the pain is deafening.

For seconds, minutes, hours—all I can manage is to lay there as confusion and pain swirl around me.

Groaning, I crack open my eyes, squinting through the dust clouding the area. I can't hear a goddamn thing, but as the dust settles, the body parts strewn across the place tells me how loud it is.

Bodies are running around chaotically. There's a man dragging himself towards the steps, one leg completely missing while part of the railing protrudes from his side. He must've been on the top floor and gotten blasted through it.

Along with several other people, some of them missing limbs, others just covered in blood and seriously injured. Cradling some part of their body as they process the utter shock of the explosion.

The ringing recedes, and an onslaught of screams filter in.

I groan again, forcing my body into an upright position as I try to figure out what the fuck just happened.

My head is fuzzy and my vision swims, the pain flaring brighter with every movement.

Jesus fucking Christ. What the hell *happened*?

A person is charging towards me, their tall, lanky body emerging from dust clouds and bloody limbs. Their mouth is open in a shout, and it's not until they're nearly a foot in front of me that my eyes process what I'm seeing.

It's Jay. Why the fuck is Jay here?

He should be behind a computer desk somewhere.

"Zade, dude, are you okay?" Panic etched into every line on his face, and his hazel eyes are rounded with fear as he kneels before me, his hands sweeping over my body to check for injuries.

"The fuck happened?" My head is fucking throbbing, and my back feels damn near broken. "Why are you here?"

"I came as soon as I figured it out. It was a setup. This last video... they knew we were coming... I don't know how, man. But they purposely leaked the fucking video. It was a *fucking setup.*"

I'm so focused on Jay's mouth, slowly trying to process the words coming out of them that the sound of a gun being cocked and the cold press of metal in the back of my head registers too late.

"Glad you could figure that out, Jason Scott. Now let's see those hands, otherwise this single bullet will find its way in both of your fucking heads."

Jay looks up at the person standing behind me, his eyes growing impossibly larger.

"You?"

Chapter
Forty Two
The Manipulator

"Are you surprised?" I ask through the phone, twirling the red rose between my fingers. I woke up to Zade gone, and a rose in his place.

My mother sighs. "No, I'm not. It explains a lot about your Nana and her strange attachment to the house."

I'm curled up on the couch watching the news channel, a sense of pride filling my veins as the words *Breaking News* and *Seventy-Five-Year-Old Cold Case Solved*.

Daya and I reported our findings to the police early this morning. They spent hours and hours going over our evidence. Still, after verifying the serial number and DNA test results were authentic, they declared Frank Seinburg the man that murdered Genevieve Parsons in cold blood. His motive—unrequited love.

They confiscated the diaries for now, but I made them pinky swear they would give it back. The police officer looked at me like I was unhinged when I physically made him pinky swear. But it made me feel better about parting with the diaries, even if it is temporary.

The news reporter on the screen speaks of the victim's great-granddaughter stumbling across hidden diaries in the wall and how it led to the discovery of her murder and who did it. I glance over at the window, an array of flashing lights blaring through the glass.

The news reporters are standing outside my house. They wanted to get Parsons Manor in the background. What would a creepy story be without an old Victorian house looming behind a pretty blonde woman with red lipstick on her teeth?

"She must've felt so much guilt all her life," I say quietly, the spike of sadness lingering since the realization that Nana helped cover up the murder.

Surprisingly, Mom doesn't have a snarky reply. "I imagine so, Adeline. That's a heavy weight to carry, especially because she was only sixteen years old when it happened. She was probably very traumatized."

I frown harder. "It amazes me that she was always so happy."

"Sometimes the happiest people are the saddest," she says, reciting a common quote.

"Then what are the miserable people in the world?"

"Tired."

"Sounds miserable."

She huffs out a dry laugh. "I have a showing soon. I have to go. I'll see you in a couple of weeks for Thanksgiving."

"Hey, Mom? I have one last question," I rush out, the words bursting out of me. Something has been bothering me about this case, and the pressing need to ask is unbearable.

She sighs but stays on the line, silently urging me on.

"Did you happen to send me a black envelope full of pictures and a note?"

She's silent, and my heart thumps in my chest. "Mom?" I prompt.

She clears her throat. "I guess your Nana and I are more alike than you thought."

My eyes widen as realization dawns, hitting me directly in the chest. She *did* send me the envelope. Which means she knew all along about Gigi's murder and Nana's role in it.

Un-fucking-believable.

"You kept her secret," I whisper.

"I have to go now, Addie. I have a house showing in five minutes."

"Okay," I murmur, but the line has already gone dead.

There's no way of knowing when exactly Mom found out about Nana covering up the murder—I doubt she'll ever tell me—but I imagine it was sometime before I was born, considering I have no memories of those two ever getting along.

Mom's bitterness and dislike for Nana suddenly make more sense.

Nana covered up her mother's murder, and in return, her daughter covered up her involvement.

My brain gets clogged with all that information, and the utter shock that my mother also played a hand in covering up Gigi's murder. It's too much.

I turn and stare out at the window as my thoughts turn to Zade. Really, they never left. He's been sitting in the back of my brain all day, weighing down on my shoulders.

Is he safe? Alive?

When did I start worrying about his safety?

I need my head checked. But I will never make the initiative to do so. In a roundabout way, I'm starting to accept my new reality.

I'm falling in love with my stalker. The shadow that haunts me in the night. The man that hunts me down and completely wrecks my entire world.

And not only do I have to come to terms with that, but the fact that my life will now be consumed with worry. He's dangerous, but the situations he puts himself in are just as terrifying. One day, he could go out and never come back home.

How do I deal with that?

Standing, I make my way into the kitchen to make myself a mixed drink. I flip on the light but pause immediately.

Resting on the counter is a red rose, with the thorns clipped. For the life of me, I can't figure out why tears spring to my eyes. Maybe because now that I care about the stupid asshole, I don't know if this is the last time I'll get a rose or not.

Sniffing, I walk over to the rose and pick it up, twirling the stem in my fingers.

"Goddammit, Zade," I mutter aloud. "I'll never forgive you if you die."

A loud buzzing from my phone wakes me out of a dead sleep. Drool leaks down my cheek, and I absently swipe at it with one hand while I grab my phone with the other.

The bright light draws out an immediate headache as I squint at the screen. It's only eleven o'clock at night. I couldn't have been asleep for more than an hour.

My phone buzzes again, alerting me to a text message. Opening the app, I see that Daya has texted me several times.

DAYA: Are you awake?

DAYA: I'm really upset right now and could use a friend.

DAYA: Will you come over?

DAYA: I'd really appreciate it.

I frown, both confused and worried. We haven't spoken since we parted ways earlier, after the police collected all of our evidence. She had to go to her niece's birthday party, and I haven't spoken with her since.

Tapping the Call button, I bring the phone to my ear and sit up. The phone just rings before the automated message comes up.

My heart starts to pound as I swing my legs over the bed and pad over to my dresser, rummaging through the drawers until I find sweatpants and a hoodie.

I call Daya's phone two more times, and by the time the automated message kicks on, I'm panicking.

Swiping my keys from by the front door, I rush out of the house and into my car. It's sprinkling outside, the rain pattering lightly against the windows as I race down my long driveway and towards Daya's house.

During the drive, I call her phone several more times. But she never answers.

When I'm a few miles away, I notice headlights behind me closing in. Glancing in my rearview mirror, I step on the gas further, a sinking feeling in my chest.

Something about this isn't right.

Daya would never text me to come over and then ignore me.

And the car behind me is becoming dangerously close, nearly disappearing behind the back of my car.

"What the…"

I'm violently jerked forward, my head nearly smacking off the steering wheel. A startled scream slips free as my car starts to spin.

I regain control of the car, stepping on the gas harder and attempting to gain some space between us. I scramble for my phone but realize it's on the floor of the passenger seat.

It must've flown from my hand when the van crashed into me.

Shit. Shit. Shit.

Who the fuck is after me? It could be Max, finally getting his revenge for a murder I had nothing to do with. Or it could be the men Mark sicced on me. Finally coming to collect me.

The rev of their engine is my only warning. This time, I'm prepared for the hit, despite the force of it still taking my breath away.

Before I can wrangle control over the vehicle, they're crashing into me again. My car whips side-to-side as I fight for control. My chest pumps with adrenaline and panic, and dread has started to form in the pit of my stomach. I have a sinking feeling that I'm not going to be able to get out of this.

My gas pedal can't go down any further, and the higher the speed, the more I lose control.

It takes one more hit before I go careening off the side of the road and into a ditch. My world spins as the bumper of my car hits the ditch at an angle before my car upends, flipping over on itself twice before landing harshly on the roof.

The impact is deafening as the windows explode. Glass shards blast against me from all directions, slicing my skin to shreds.

When everything settles, I realize I'm still screaming.

I suck in a sharp breath, the sound nearly animalistic as panic takes over. I'm upside down, still strapped into my seat. The seatbelt is digging painfully into my chest, constricting my already tight lungs further.

"You hit her too hard," a voice calls from somewhere outside my car. "Shit, check to make sure she's not dying, you fucking idiot."

Just as the voice filters through, so does the pain.

I squeeze my eyes shut, my body pulsating with sharp agony. I moan as the feeling worsens until I can't think past my broken body.

A head appears in my window. I meet the gaze of a man with darker skin and bottomless black eyes.

"She's alive," he announces, a relieved smile curling one side of his lips.

"Get her out," an answering voice demands sharply.

"What do you want from me?" I groan, swatting weakly at his hands that are messing with the buckle on my seatbelt. He doesn't answer, so I keep asking.

"Shut the fuck up before I knock you out!" he bellows. The click of the seatbelt is my only warning before my body drops down headfirst. I scream, pain lancing down my neck and shoulders.

The man grabs my arm and works my body out of the driver's side window, dragging my body across glass and sharp metal.

"Stop it," I moan, sobbing as he finally gets me out. "Why are you doing this?"

Panting, the man leans over me and looks me over.

"Once you're healed up, you're going to be worth a pretty penny," he says, a crooked grin on his face.

"Just get her in the van, Rio. Max's already going to be pissed we fucked up his van, so quit fucking around. The police will be here soon."

Another flash of a grin, "Time to go to sleep, princess."

And then darkness.

He came for me

The second and final installment to the duet is here! Scan below to buy!

Want sneak peaks, exclusive offers, and giveaways?
Join my Facebook group <u>H. D. Carlton's Warriors</u>!

MORE BOOKS BY
H.D. CARLTON

Acknowledgments

I feel like I have so many people to thank for this book, and I have no idea where to start. But what I do know, is this is going to be long, but I think we can tell by the size of my books I don't do short.

So, I'll start where I always do. The readers. I can't thank all of you enough. Like all authors, we can only hope that you love our books. These stories—we write them for ourselves. We write what makes us happy. Because if we don't, we'll never survive in this career. Most know, writing books is really fucking hard, so it feels impossible when you don't love it. And if *we* don't love it, how could we expect someone else to? And then, what's the point in writing if no one loves it?

At the end of the day, we want our readers to love them *with* us. To enjoy something we poured our souls into, and come out of it feeling like you experienced this story right along with us. There's honestly no greater joy than that. And I appreciate all of you for taking this journey with me.

There's no one else I can begin with other than the two people who played a major role in this book and in my life. Cue the sappiness.

I met them both in the same exact way—I reached out and asked them to take a chance on me and read my book, and they both became two of the most important people in my life. They listened to me talk endlessly about this book and these characters, brainstorm, asking questions and offering advice, and reading snippets and yelling at me for splattering (aka doubting myself.)

First, Amanda. You're my best friend, plain and simple. You're my other half, my soulmate, and everything else in between. If it wasn't for you, I'm not sure

I'd still be in this community. You've helped me through some pretty dark times and showed me love when I felt completely alone. We have a connection unlike anything else and sometimes, I'm still in awe that I got so lucky to find you. I just hope you know you're stuck with me—forever.

May, what the hell would I do without you? I can't fathom it and I don't want to. When I first met you, I felt a connection to you that I couldn't quite explain. So much so that even when I barely knew you, I asked you to be my alpha reader. I just knew you were someone special and I wanted you to be more than just a reader, but a friend. Yet, you've become so much more than that. Thank you for being my constant. You're always there, checking in on me and Zade and selflessly offering up your help whenever I need it. And you've shown me endless support and love, and I seriously can't express enough how much that means to me.

I love you both, even more than Z could ever say. I don't deserve either of you, but I'm selfish enough to accept it. Haunting Adeline would not be what it is without either of you. *I* would not be who I am with you two.

And I haven't forgotten you, Abby. I could never. You came into my life exactly when I needed you most, and I've never looked back. I knew from the beginning that you were exactly who I needed. You're more than a PA, you're an incredible friend, a shoulder to lean on and someone that I can rely on. I've been hit hard and blindsided by untrustworthy people in this community, and you've gotten the shit end of the stick by dealing with my doubts, assumptions and wariness. Yet, you handle it like a boss and remind me every day that I'm safe with you, and I sleep better at night knowing that you're someone I can trust. Thank you for everything you do and helping Haunting Adeline become the best it can be. I love you.

To my betas, Rita, Keri, Autumn, Taylor, Caitlyn, RS and Mandy, thank you all so much for your incredible feedback and support. You all offer up your free time and energy to do something you don't have to do, and each and every one of you are appreciated and loved. I can't thank any of you enough for walking alongside me and helping me become a better author.

Lastly, to my editors. The two beautiful ladies that have polished this book and made it so pretty. Angie and Sarah, I seriously can't thank you both enough. You've both shown me so much support and love, and I will forever be indebted to both of you.

Just... thank you. To all of you. Thank you.

About The Author

H. D. Carlton is an International and USA Today Bestselling author. She lives in Ohio with her partner, two dogs, and cat. When she's not bathing in the tears of her readers, she's watching paranormal shows and wishing she was a mermaid. Her favorite characters are of the morally gray variety and believes that everyone should check their sanity at the door before diving into her stories.

Learn more about H. D. Carlton on hdcarlton.com. Join her newsletter to receive updates, teasers, giveaways, and special deals.

9 781957 635002